Tarr

by

P. Wyndham Lewis

Double 9 BOOKS

Tarr

by P. Wyndham Lewis

ISBN: 978-93-68099-56-7

Published by

DOUBLE 9 BOOKS
2/13-B, Ansari Road
Daryaganj, New Delhi – 110002
info@double9books.com
www.double9books.com
Tel. 011-40042856

ABOUT THE AUTHOR

P. Wyndham Lewis was a British writer, painter, and influential figure in the modernist movement. He is best known for his novel "Tarr," which critiques social pretensions and explores the lives of artists in pre-World War I Europe. Lewis was a prominent member of the Vorticist movement, which he founded, emphasizing dynamic forms and bold colors in art and literature. During World War I, Lewis served at the front as an artillery officer. Later, he was commissioned as a war artist, one example is "A Battery Shelled" which combines representational elements with the angular style characteristic of Vorticism.

His work often addressed themes of identity, nationalism, and the human experience amid societal upheaval. Throughout his career, Lewis produced novels, essays, and art, making significant contributions to both literature and visual culture. His sharp satirical style and avant-garde approach established him as a key figure in the early 20th-century artistic landscape, influencing generations of writers and artists.

CONTENTS

PART VII

SWAGGER SEX

PROLOGUE

This book was begun eight years ago; so I have not produced this disagreeable German for the gratification of primitive partisanship aroused by the war. On the other hand, having had him up my sleeve for so long, I let him out at this moment in the undisguised belief that he is very apposite. I am incidentally glad to get rid of him. He has been on my conscience (my conscience as an artist, it is true) for a long time.

The myriads of Prussian germs, gases, and gangrenes released into the air and for the past year obsessing everything, revived my quiescent creation. I was moved to vomit Kreisler forth. It is one big germ more. May the flames of Louvain help to illuminate (and illustrate) my hapless protagonist! His misdemeanours too, which might appear too harshly real at ordinary times, have, just now, too obvious confirmations to be questioned.

Germany's large leaden brain booms away in the centre of Europe. Her brain-waves and titanic orchestrations have broken round us for too long not to have had their effect. As we never think ourselves, except a stray Irishman or American, we should long ago have been swamped had it not been for the sea. The habits and vitality of the seaman's life and this vigorous element have protected us intellectually as the blue water has politically.

In Europe Nietzsche's gospel of desperation, the beyond-law-man, etc., has deeply influenced the Paris apache, the Italian Futurist *littérateur*, the Russian revolutionary. Nietzsche's books are full of seductions and sugar-plums. They have made "aristocrats" of people who would otherwise have been only mild snobs or meddlesome prigs; as much as, if not more than, other writings, they have made "expropriators" of what would otherwise merely have been Arsène Lupins: and they have made an Over-man of every vulgarly energetic grocer in Europe. The commercial and military success of Prussia has deeply influenced the French, as it is gradually winning the imagination of the English. The fascination of material power is, for the irreligious modern man, almost impossible to resist.

There is much to be said for this eruption of greedy, fleshy, frantic strength in the midst of discouraged delicacies. Germany has its mission and its beauty. We will hope that the English may benefit by this power and passion, without being unnecessarily grateful for a gift that has been *bought* with best English blood, and which is not as important or unique as the great English gift bestowed centuries ago.

As to the Prophet of War, the tone of Nietzsche's books should have discredited his philosophy. The modern Prussian advocate of the Aristocratic and Tyrannic took *everybody* into his confidence. Then he would coquet: he gave special prizes. *Everybody* couldn't be a follower of his! No: only the *minority*: that is the minority who read his books, which has steadily grown till it comprises certainly (or would were it collected together) the ungainliest and strangest aristocratic caste any world could hope to see!

Kreisler in this book is a German and nothing else. Tarr is the individual in the book, and is at the same time one of the showmen of the author. His private life, however, I am in no way responsible for. The long drawn-out struggle in which we find this young man engaged is illuminated from start to finish by the hero of it. His theory, put in another way, is that an artist requires more energy than civilization provides, or than the civilized mode of life implies: more *naïveté*, freshness, and unconsciousness. So Nature agrees to force his sensibility and intelligence, on the one hand, to the utmost pitch, leaving him, on the other, an uncultivated and ungregarious tract where he can run wild and renew his forces and remain unspoilt.

Tarr, in his analysis of the anomalies of taste, gives the key to a crowd of other variants and twists to which most of the misunderstandings and stupidities in the deciphering of men are due. He exaggerates his own departure from perfect sense and taste into an unnecessary image of Shame and Disgust, before which he publicly castigates himself. He is a primitive figure, coupled with a modern type of flabby sophistication: that is Bertha Lunkin. The Münich German Madonna stands nude, too, in the market-place, with a pained distortion of the face.

Tarr's message, as a character in a book, is this. Under the camouflage of a monotonous intrigue he points a permanent opposition, of life outstripped, and art become lonely. He incidentally is intended to bring some comfort of analysis amongst less sifted and more ominous perplexities of our time. His message, as he discourses, laughs, and picks his way through the heavily obstructed land of this story, is the message of a figure of health. His introspection is not melancholy; for the strange and, as with his pedagogic wand he points out, hideously unsatisfactory figures that are given ingress to his innermost apartments become assimilated at once to a life in which he has the profoundest confidence. He exalts Life into a Comedy, when otherwise it is, to his mind, a tawdry zone of half-art, or a silly Tragedy. Art is the only thing worth the tragic impulse, for him; and, as he says, it is his drama. Should art, that is some finely-adjusted creative will, suddenly become the drama of the youth infatuated with his maiden, what different dispositions would have to be made; what contradictory tremors would invade his amorous frame; what portions of that frame would still smoulder amorously? These questions Tarr disposes of to his satisfaction.

So much by way of warning before the curtain rises. Even if the necessary tragic thrill of misgiving is caused thereby (or are we going to be "shocked" in the right way once again, not in Shaw's "bloody," schoolgirl way?), it may extenuate the at times seemingly needless nucleus of blood and tears.

P. Wyndham Lewis

1915

PART I
BERTHA

CHAPTER I

Paris hints of sacrifice.—But here we deal with that large dusty facet known to indulgent and congruous kind. It is in its capacity of delicious inn and majestic Baedeker, where western Venuses twang its responsive streets and hush to soft growl before its statues, that it is seen. It is not across its Thébaïde that the unscrupulous heroes chase each other's shadows. They are largely ignorant of all but their restless personal lives.

Inconceivably generous and naïve faces haunt the Knackfus Quarter.—We are not, however, in a Selim or Vitagraph camp (though "guns" tap rhythmically the buttocks).—Art is being studied.—Art is the smell of oil paint, Henri Murger's *Vie de Bohème*, corduroy trousers, the operatic Italian model. But the poetry, above all, of linseed oil and turpentine.

The Knackfus Quarter is given up to Art.—Letters and other things are round the corner.—Its rent is half paid by America. Germany occupies a sensible apartment on the second floor. A hundred square yards at its centre is a convenient space, where the Boulevard du Paradis and Boulevard Pfeifer cross with their electric trams.—In the middle is a pavement island, like vestige of submerged masonry.—Italian models festoon it in symmetrical human groups; it is also their club.—The Café Berne, at one side, is the club of the "Grands messieurs Du Berne." So you have the clap-trap and amorphous Campagnia tribe outside, in the café twenty sluggish common-sense Germans, a Vitagraph group or two, drinking and playing billiards. These are the most permanent tableaux of this place, disheartening and admonitory as a Tussaud's of The Flood.

Hobson and Tarr met in the Boulevard du Paradis.—They met in a gingerly, shuffling fashion. They had so many good reasons for not slowing down when they met: crowds of little antecedent meetings all revivifying like the bacilli of a harmless fever at the sight of each other: pointing to *why* they *should* crush their hats over their eyes and hurry on, so that it was a defeat and insanitary to have their bodies shuffling and gesticulating there. "Why cannot most people, having talked and annoyed each other once or twice, rebecome strangers simply? Oh, for multitudes of divorces in our *mœurs*, more than the old vexed sex ones! Ah, yes: ah, yes—!" had not Tarr once put forward, and Hobson agreed?

"Have you been back long?" Tarr asked with despondent slowness.

"No. I got back yesterday," said Hobson, with pleasantly twisted scowl.

("Heavens: One day here only, and lo! I meet him.")

"How is London looking, then?"

"Very much as usual.—I wasn't there the whole time.—I was in Cambridge last week."

("I wish you'd go to perdition from time to time, instead of Cambridge, as it always is, you grim, grim dog!" Tarr wished behind the veil.)

They went to the Berne to have a drink.

They sat for some minutes with what appeared a stately discomfort of self-consciousness, staring in front of them.—It was really only a dreary, boiling anger with themselves, with the contradictions of civilized life, the immense and intricate camouflage over the hatred that personal diversities engender. "Phew, phew!" A tenuous howl, like a subterranean wind, rose from the borderland of their consciousness. They were there on the point of opening with tired, ashamed fingers, well-worn pages of their souls, soon to be muttering between their teeth the hackneyed pages to each other: resentful in different degrees and disproportionate ways.

And so they sat with this absurd travesty of a Quaker's meeting: shyness appearing to emanate masterfully from Tarr. And in another case, with almost any one but Hobson, it might have been shyness. For Tarr had a gauche, Puritanical ritual of self, the result of solitary habits. Certain observances were demanded of those approaching, and quite gratuitously observed in return. The fetish within—soul-dweller that is strikingly like wood-dweller, and who was not often enough disturbed to have had sylvan shyness mitigated—would still cling to these forms. Sometimes Tarr's cunning idol, aghast at its nakedness, would manage to borrow or purloin some shape of covering from elegantly draped visitor.

But for Hobson's outfit he had the greatest contempt.

This was Alan Hobson's outfit.—A Cambridge cut disfigured his originally manly and melodramatic form. His father was a wealthy merchant somewhere in Egypt. He was very athletic, and his dark and cavernous features had been constructed by Nature as a lurking-place for villainies and passions. He was untrue to his rascally, sinuous body. He slouched and ambled along, neglecting his muscles: and his dastardly face attempted to portray delicacies of common sense, and gossamer-like backslidings into the Inane that would have puzzled a bile-specialist. He would occasionally exploit his blackguardly appearance and blacksmith's muscles for a short time, however. And his strong, piercing laugh threw A B C waitresses into confusion.

The Art-touch, the Bloomsbury stain, was very observable. Hobson's Harris tweeds were shabby. A hat suggesting that his ancestors had been Plainsmen or some rough sunny folk, shaded unnecessarily his countenance, already far from open.

The material for conversation afforded by a short sea voyage, an absence, a panama hat on his companion's head, had been exhausted.—Tarr possessed no deft hand or economy of force. His muscles rose unnecessarily on his arm to lift a wine-glass to his lips. He had no social machinery, but the cumbrous one of the intellect. He danced about with this, it is true. But it was full of sinister piston-rods, organ-like shapes, heavy drills.—When he tried to be amiable, he usually only succeeded in being ominous.

It was an effort to talk to Hobson. For this effort a great bulk of nervous force was awoken. It got to work and wove its large anomalous patterns. It took the subject that was foremost in his existence and imposed it on their talk.

Tarr turned to Hobson, and seized him, conversationally, by the hair.

"Well, Walt Whitman, when are you going to get your hair cut?"

"Why do you call me Walt Whitman?"

"Would you prefer Buffalo Bill? Or is it Shakespeare?"

"It is not Shakespeare—"

"'Roi je ne suis: prince je ne daigne.'—That's Hobson's choice.—But why so much hair? I don't wear my hair long. If you had as many reasons for wearing it long as I have, we should see it flowing round your ankles!"

"I might ask you under those circumstances why you wear it short. But I expect you have good reasons for that, too. I can't see why you should resent my innocent device. However long I wore it I should not damage you by my competition—"

Tarr rattled the cement match-stand on the table, and the *garçon* sang "Toute suite, toute suite!"

"Hobson, you were telling me about a studio to let before you left.—I forget the details—"

"Was it one behind the Panthéon?"

"That's it.—Was there electric light?"

"No, I don't think there was electric light. But I can find out for you."

"How did you come to hear of it?"

"Through a German I know—Salle, Salla, or something."

"What was the street?"

"The Rue Lhomond. I forget the number."

"I'll go and have a look at it after lunch.—What on earth possesses you to know so many Germans?" Tarr asked, sighing.

"Don't you like Germans?—You've just been too intimate with one; that's what it is."

"Perhaps I have."

"A female German."

"The sex weakens the 'German,' surely."

"Does it in Fräulein Lunken's case?"

"Oh, you know her, do you?—Of course, you would know her, as she's a German."

Alan Hobson cackled morosely, like a very sad top-dog trying to imitate a rooster.

Tarr's unwieldy playfulness, might in the chequered northern shade, in conjunction with nut-brown ale, gazed at by some Rowlandson—he on the ultimate borders of the epoch—have pleased by its à propos. But when the last Rowlandson dies, the life, too, that he saw should vanish. Anything that survives the artist's death is not life, but play-acting. This homely, thick-waisted affectation!—Hobson yawned and yawned as though he wished to swallow Tarr and have done with him. Tarr yawned more noisily, rattled his chair, sat up, haggard and stiff, as though he wished to frighten this crow away. "Carrion-Crow" was Tarr's name for Hobson: "The olde Crow of Cairo," rather longer.

Why was he talking to this man? However, he shortly began to lay bare the secrets of his soul. Hobson opened:

"It seems to me, Tarr, that you know more Germans than I do. But *you're ashamed of it*. Hence your attack. I met a Fräulein Fierspitz the other day, a German, who claimed to know you. I am always meeting Germans who know you. She also referred to you as the 'official fiancé' of Fräulein Lunken.—Are you an 'official fiancé'? And if so, what is that, may I ask?"

Tarr was taken aback, it was evident. Hobson laughed stridently. The real man emerging, he came over quickly on another wave.

"You not only get to know Germans, crowds of them, on the sly; you make your bosom friend of them, engage yourself to them in marriage and make Heaven knows how many more solemn pacts, covenants, and agreements.—It's bound all to come out some day. What will you do then?"

Tarr was recovering gracefully from his relapse into discomfort. If ever taken off his guard, he made a clever use immediately afterwards of his *naïveté.* He beamed on his slip. He would swallow it tranquilly, assimilating it, with ostentation, to himself. When some personal weakness slipped out he would pick it up unabashed, look at it smilingly, and put it back in his pocket.

"As you know," he soon replied, "'engagement' is an euphemism. And, as a matter of fact, my girl publicly announced the breaking off of our engagement yesterday."

He looked a complete child, head thrown up as though proclaiming something he had reason to be particularly proud of.—Hobson laughed convulsively, cracking his yellow fingers.

"Yes, it is funny, if you look at it in that way.—I let her announce our engagement or the reverse just as she likes. That has been our arrangement from the start. I never know at any given time whether I am engaged or not. I leave all that sort of thing entirely in her hands. After a severe quarrel I am pretty certain that I am temporarily unattached, the link publicly severed somewhere or other."

"Possibly that is what is meant by 'official fiancé'?"

"Very likely."

He had been hustled—through his vanity, the Cairo Cantabian thought—somewhere where the time could be passed. He did not hesitate to handle Tarr's curiosities.—It is a graceful compliment to offer the nectar of some ulcer to your neighbour. The modern man understands his udders and taps.—With an obscene heroism Tarr displayed his. His companion wrenched at it with malice. Tarr pulled a wry face once or twice at the other's *sans gêne.* But he was proud of what he could stand. He had a hazy image of a shrewd old countryman in contact with the sharpness of the town. He would not shrink. He would roughly outstrip his visitor.—"Ay,

I have this the matter with me—a funny complaint?—and that, and that, too.—What then?—Do you want me to race you to that hill?"

He obtruded complacently all he had most to be ashamed of, conscious of the power of an obsessing weakness.

"Will you go so far in this clandestine life of yours as to *marry* anybody?" Hobson proceeded.

"No."

Hobson stared with bright meditative sweetness down the boulevard.

"I think there must be a great difference between your way of approaching Germans and mine," he said.

"Ay: it is different things that takes us respectively amongst them."

"You like the national flavour, all the same."

"I like the national flavour!"—Tarr had a way of beginning a reply with a parrot-like echo of the words of the other party to the dialogue; also of repeating *sotto voce* one of his own sentences, a mechanical rattle following on without stop. "Sex is nationalized more than any other essential of life. In this it is just the opposite to art.—There is much pork and philosophy in German sex.—But then if it is the sex you are after, it does not say you want to identify your being with your appetite. Quite the opposite. The condition of continued enjoyment is to resist assimilation.—A man is the opposite of his appetite."

"Surely, a man *is* his appetite."

"No, a man is always his *last* appetite, or his appetite before last; and that is no longer an appetite.—But nobody *is* anything, or life would be intolerable, the human race collapse.—You are me, I am you.—The Present is the furthest projection of our steady appetite. Imagination, like a general, keeps behind. Imagination is the man."

"*What* is the Present?" Hobson asked politely, with much aspirating, sitting up a little and slightly offering his ear.

But Tarr only repeated things arbitrarily. He proceeded:

"Sex is a monstrosity. It is the arch abortion of this filthy universe.—How 'old-fashioned!'—eh, my fashionable friend?—We are all optimists to-day, aren't we? God's in his Heaven, all's well with the world! I am a pessimist, Hobson. But I'm a new sort of pessimist.—I think I am the sort that will please!—I am the Panurgic-Pessimist, drunken with the laughing-gas of the Abyss. I gaze on squalor and idiocy, and the more I see it, the more I like it.—Flaubert built up his *Bouvard et Pécuchet* with maniacal and tireless hands. It took him ten years. That was a long draught of stodgy laughter from the gases that rise from the dung-heap? He had an appetite like an elephant for this form of mirth. But he grumbled and sighed over his food.—I take it in my arms and bury my face in it!"

As Tarr's temperament spread its wings, whirling him menacingly and mockingly above Hobson's head, the Cantab philosopher did not think it necessary to reply.—He was not winged himself.—He watched Tarr looping the loop above him. He was a drole bird! He wondered, as he watched him, if he was a *sound* bird, or *homme-oiseau*. People believed in him. His Exhibition flights attracted attention. What sort of prizes could he expect to win by his professional talents? Would this notable *ambitieux* be satisfied?

The childish sport proceeded, with serious intervals.

"I bury my face in it!"—(He buried his face in it!!)—"I laugh hoarsely through its thickness, choking and spitting; coughing, sneezing, blowing.—People will begin to think I am an alligator if they see me always swimming in their daily ooze. As far as sex is concerned, I am that. Sex, Hobson, is a German study. A German study." He shook his head in a dejected, drunken way, protruding his lips. He seemed to find analogies for his *repeating* habits, with the digestion.—"All the same, you must take my word for much in that connexion.—The choice of a wife is not practical in the way that the securing of a good bicycle, hygiene, or advertisement is. You must think more of the dishes of the table. Rembrandt paints decrepit old Jews, the most decayed specimens of the lowest race on earth, that is. Shakespeare deals in human tubs of grease—Falstaff; Christ in sinners. Now as to sex; Socrates married a shrew; most of the wisest men marry fools, picture post cards, cows, or strumpets."

"I don't think that is quite true." Hobson resurrected himself dutifully. "The more sensible people I can think of off-hand have more sensible, and on the whole prettier, wives than other people."

"Prettier wives?—You are describing a meaningless average.—The most suspicious fact about a distinguished man is the possession of a distinguished wife. But you might just as well say in answer to my Art statement that Sir Edward Leighton did not paint the decayed meat of humanity."

Hobson surged up a little in his chair and collapsed.—He had to appeal to his body to sustain the argument.

"Neither did Raphael—I don't see why you should drag Rembrandt in—Rembrandt—"

"You're going to sniff at Rembrandt!—You accuse me of following the fashions in my liking for Cubism. You are much more fashionable yourself. Would you mind my 'dragging in' cheese, high game—?"

Hobson allowed cheeses with a rather drawn expression. But he did not see what that had to do with it, either.

"It is not *purely* a question of appetite," he said.

"Sex, sir, is *purely* a question of appetite!" Tarr replied.

Hobson inclined himself mincingly, with a sweet chuckle.

"If it is *pure* sex, that is," Tarr added.

"Oh, if it is *pure* sex—that, naturally—" Hobson convulsed himself and crowed thrice.

"Listen, Hobson!—You mustn't make that noise. It's very clever of you to be able to. But you will not succeed in rattling me by making me feel I am addressing a rooster—"

Hobson let himself go in whoops and caws, as though Tarr had been pressing him to perform.

When he had finished, Tarr said:

"Are you willing to *consider sex seriously, or not*?"

"Yes, I don't mind."—Hobson settled down, his face flushed from his late display.—"But I shall begin to believe before very long that your intentions are honourable as regards the fair Fräulein.—What exactly is your discourse intended to prove?"

"*Not* the desirability of the marriage tie, any more than a propaganda for representation and anecdote in art. But *if* a man marries, or a great painter represents (and the claims and seductions of life are very urgent), he will not be governed in his choice by the same laws that regulate the life of an efficient citizen, a successful merchant, or the ideals of a health expert."

"I should have said that the considerations that precede a proposition of marriage had many analogies with the health expert's outlook, the good citizen's—"

"Was Napoleon successful in life, or did he ruin himself and end his days in miserable captivity?—*Passion* precludes the idea of success. Failure is its condition.—Art and Sex when they are deep enough make tragedies, and *not* advertisements for Health experts, or happy endings for the Public, or social panaceas."

"Alas, that is true."

"Well, then, well, then, Alan Hobson, you scarecrow of an advanced fool-farm, deplorable pedant of a sophistic voice-culture—"

"I? My voice—? But that's absurd!—If my speech—"

Hobson was up in arms about his voice: although it was not his.

Tarr needed a grimacing, tumultuous mask for the face he had to cover.—The clown was the only rôle that was ample enough. He had compared his clowning with Hobson's Pierrotesque and French variety.

But Hobson, he considered, was a crowd.—You could not say he was an individual.—He was a set. He sat there, a cultivated audience.—He had the aplomb and absence of self-consciousness of numbers, of the herd—of those who know they are not alone.—Tarr was shy and the reverse by turns. He was alone. The individual is rustic.

For distinguishing feature Hobson possessed a distinguished absence of personality.

Tarr gazed on this impersonality, of crowd origin, with autocratic scorn.

Alan Hobson was a humble investor.

"But we're talking at cross purposes, Hobson.—You think I am contending that affection for a dolt, like my fiancée, is in some way a merit. I do not mean that. Also, I do not mean that sex is my tragedy, but art.—I will explain why I am associated sexually with this pumpkin. First, I am an artist.—With most people, not describable as artists, all the finer part of their vitality goes into sex. They become third-rate poets during their courtship. All their instincts of drama come out freshly with their wives. The artist is he in whom this emotionality normally absorbed by sex is so strong that it claims a newer and more exclusive field of deployment.—Its first creation is *the Artist* himself, a new sort of person; the creative man. But for the first-rate poet, nothing short of a Queen or a Chimera is adequate for the powers of his praise.—And so on all through the bunch of his gifts. One by one his powers and *moyens* are turned away from the usual object of a man's poetry, and turned away from the immediate world. One solitary thing is left facing a woman.—That is his sex, a lonely phallus.—Things are not quite so simple in actual fact as this. Some artists are less complete than others. More or less remains to the man.—Then the character of the artist's creation comes in. What tendency has my work as an artist, a ready instance? You may have noticed that it has that of an invariable severity. Apart from its being good or bad, its character is ascetic rather than sensuous, and divorced from immediate life. There is no slop of sex in *that*. But there is no severity left over for the work of the cruder senses either. Very often with an artist whose work is very sensuous or human, his sex instinct, if it is active, will be more discriminating than with a man more fastidious and discriminating than he in his work. To sum up this part of my disclosure.—No one could have a coarser, more foolish, slovenly taste than I have in women. It is not even sluttish and abject, of the J. W. M. Turner type, with his washerwoman at Gravesend.—It is bourgeois, banal, pretty-pretty, a cross between the Musical Comedy stage and the ideal of the Eighteenth-Century gallant. All the delicate psychology another man naturally seeks in a woman, the curiosity of form, windows on other lives, love and passion, I seek in my work and not elsewhere.—Form would perhaps be thickened by child-bearing; it would perhaps be damaged by harlotry.—Why should sex still be active? That is a matter of heredity that has nothing to do with the general energies of the mind. I see I am boring you.—The matter is too remote!—But you have trespassed here, and you must listen.—I cannot let you off before you have heard, and shown that you understand.—If you do not sit and listen, I will write it all to you. You will be made to hear it!—And *after* I have told you this, I will tell you why I am talking to a fool like you!"

"You ask me to be polite—"

"I don't mind how impolite you are so long as you listen."

"Well, I am listening—with interest."

Tarr was tearing, as he saw it, at the blankets that swaddled this spirit in its inner snobberies.—A bitter feast was steaming hot, and a mouth must be found to eat it. This beggar's had to serve. It was, above all, an ear, all the nerves complete. He *must* get his words into it. They must not be swallowed at a gulp. They must *taste,* sting, and benefit by the meaning of an appetite.—He had something to *say*. It must be said while it was living. Once it was said, it could look after itself.—Hobson had shocked something that was ready to burst out. He must help it out. Hobson must pay as well for the intimacy. *He must pay Bertha Lunken afterwards.*

He felt like insisting that he should come round and apologize to her.

"A man only goes and confesses his faults to the world when his self will not acknowledge or listen to them. The function of a friend is to be a substitute for this defective self, to be the World and the Real without the disastrous consequences of reality.—Yet punishment is one of his chief offices.—The friend enlarges also substantially the boundaries of our solitude."

This was written in Tarr's diary. He was now chastising this self he wrote of for not listening, by telling the first stranger met.—Had a friend been there he could have interceded for his ego.

"You have followed so far?" Tarr looked with slow disdainful suspicion at Hobson's face staring at the ground. "You have understood the nature of my secret?—Half of myself I have to hide. I am bitterly ashamed of a slovenly, common portion of my life that has been isolated and repudiated by the energies I am so proud of. 'I am *ashamed* of the number of Germans I know,' as you put it.—I have in that rôle to cower and slink away even from an old fruit-tin like you. It is useless heroically to protect that section of my life. It's no good sticking up for it. It is not worth protecting. It is not even up to *your* standards. I have, therefore, to deliver it over to your eyes, and eyes of the likes of you, in the end—if you will deign to use them!—I even have to beg you to use your eyes; to hold you by the sleeve and crave a glance for an object belonging to me!

"In this compartment of my life *I have not a vestige of passion.*—That is the root reason for its meanness and absurdity.—The best friend of my Dr. Jekyll would not know my Mr. Hyde, and vice versa. This rudimentary self is more starved and stupid than any other man's. Or to put it less or more humbly, I am of that company who are reduced to looking to Socrates for a consoling lead.

"Think of all the *collages*, marriages, and *liaisons* that you know, in which some frowsy or foolish or doll-like or log-like bitch accompanies the form of an otherwise sensible man: a dumbfounding, disgusting, and septic ghost!

"How foul and wrong this haunting of women is!—They are everywhere!—Confusing, blurring, libelling, with their half-baked, gushing, tawdry presences! It is like a slop of children and the bawling machinery of the inside of life, always and all over our palaces. Their silly food of cheap illusion comes in between friendships, stagnates complacently around a softened mind.

"I might almost take some credit to myself for at least having the grace to keep this bear-garden in the background."

Hobson had brightened up while this was proceeding.—He now said:

"You might almost.—Why don't you? I admire what you tell me. But you appear to take your German foibles too much to heart."

"Just at present I am engaged in a gala of the heart. You may have noticed that.—I am not a strict landlord with the various personalities gathered beneath my roof.—In the present case I am really blessed. But you should see the sluts that get in sometimes! They all become steadily my fiancée too.—Fiancée! Observe how one apes the forms of conventional life. It does not mean anything, so one lets it stop. Its the same with the café fools I have for friends—there's a Greek fool, a German fool, a Russian fool,—an English fool!—There are no 'friends' in this life any more than there are 'fiancées.' So it doesn't matter. You drift on side by side with this live stock—friends, fiancées, 'colleagues,' and what not."

Hobson sat staring with a bemused seriousness at the ground.

"Why should I not speak plainly and cruelly of my poor, ridiculous fiancée to you or any one?—After all, it is chiefly myself I am castigating.—But you, too, must be of the party! The right to *see* implies the right to be *seen*. As an offset for your prying, scurvy way of peeping into my affairs you must offer your own guts, such as they are—!"

"How have I pried into your affairs?" Hobson asked with a circumspect surprise.

"Any one who *stands outside*, who hides himself in a deliquescent aloofness, is a sneak and a spy—"

"That seems to me to be a case of smut calling the kettle black. I should not have said that you were conspicuous—"

"No.—You know you have joined yourself to those who hush their voices to hear what other people are saying!—Every one who does not *fight* openly and bear his share of the common burden of ignominy in life, is a sneak, unless it is for a solid motive.—The quiet you claim is not to *work* in.—What have you exchanged your temper, your freedom, and your fine voice against? You have exchanged them for an old hat that does not belong to you, and a shabbiness you have not merited by suffering neediness.—Your pseudo-neediness is a sentimental indulgence.—Every man should be forced to dress up to his income, and make a smart, *fresh* appearance.—Patching the seat of your trousers, instead—!"

"Wait a minute," Hobson said, with a laugh. "You accuse me of sentimentality in my choice of costume. I wonder if you are as free from sentimentality."

"I don't care a tinker's blue curse about that.—I am talking about *you*.—Let me proceed.—With your training, you are decked in the plumes of very fine birds indeed. But your plumes are not meant to fly with, but merely to slouch and skip along the surface of the earth.—You wear the livery of a ridiculous set, you are a cunning and sleek domestic. No thought can come out of your head before it has slipped on its uniform. All your instincts are drugged with a malicious languor, an arm, a respectability, invented by a set of old women and mean, cadaverous little boys."

Hobson opened his mouth, had a movement of the body to speak. But he relapsed.

"You reply, 'What is all this fuss about? I have done the best for myself.—I was not suited for any heroic station, like yours. I live sensibly and quietly, cultivating my vegetable ideas, and also my roses and Victorian lilies.—I do no harm to anybody.'"

"That is not quite the case. That is a little inexact. Your proceedings possess a herdesque astuteness; in the scale against the individual weighing less than the Yellow Press, yet being a closer and meaner attack. Also you are essentially *spies*, in a scurvy, safe and well-paid service, as I told you before. You are disguised to look like the thing it is your function to betray—What is your position?—You have bought for eight hundred pounds at an aristocratic educational establishment a complete mental outfit, a programme of manners. For four years you trained with other recruits. You are now a perfectly disciplined social unit, with a profound *esprit de corps*. The Cambridge set that you represent is as observed in an average specimen, a cross between a Quaker, a Pederast, and a Chelsea artist.—Your Oxford brothers, dating from the Wilde decade, are a stronger body. The Chelsea artists are much less flimsy. The Quakers are powerful rascals. You represent, my Hobson, the *dregs* of Anglo-Saxon civilization!—There is nothing softer on earth.—Your flabby potion is a mixture of the lees of Liberalism, the poor froth blown off the decadent nineties, the wardrobe—leavings of a vulgar Bohemianism with its head-quarters in Chelsea!

"You are concentrated, systematic slop.—There is nothing in the universe to be said for you.—Any efficient State would confiscate your property, burn your wardrobe, that old hat, and the rest, as *infecte* and insanitary, and prohibit you from propagating."

Tarr's white collar shone dazzlingly in the sun.—His bowler hat bobbed and out clean lines as he spoke.

"A breed of mild pervasive cabbages has set up a wide and creeping rot in the West of Europe.—They make it indirectly a peril and tribulation for live things to remain in the neighbourhood. You are systematizing and vulgarizing the individual.—You are not an individual. You have, I repeat, no right to that hair and that hat. You are trying to have the apple and eat it too.—You should be in uniform, and at work, *not* uniformly *out of uniform*, and libelling the Artist by your idleness. Are you idle?"

Tarr had drawn up short, turned squarely on Hobson; in an abrupt and disconnected voice he asked his question.

Hobson stirred resentfully in his chair. He yawned a little. He replied:

"Am I idle, did you say? Yes, I suppose I am not particularly industrious. But how does that affect you? You know you don't mean all that nonsense. Vous vous moquez de moi! Where are you coming to?"

"I have explained already where I come in. It is stupid to be idle. You go to seed.—The only justification for your slovenly appearance, it is true, is that it is ideally emblematic."

"My dear Tarr, you're a strange fellow. I *can't* see why these things should occupy you.—You have just told me a lot of things that may be true or may not. But at the end of them all—? Et alors?—alors?—*quoi?* one asks. You contradict yourself. You know you don't *think* what you talk. You deafen me with your upside-downness."

He gesticulated, got the French guttural r with satisfaction, and said the *quoi* rather briskly.

"In any case my hat is my business!" he concluded quickly, after a moment, getting up with a curling, luscious laugh.

The *garçon* hurried up and they paid.

"No, I am responsible for you.—I am one of the only people who *see*. That is a responsibility."—Tarr walked down the boulevard with him, speaking in his ear almost, and treading on his toes.

"You know Baudelaire's fable of the obsequious vagabond, cringing for alms? For all reply, the poet seizes a heavy stick and belabours the beggar with it. The beggar then, when he is almost beaten to a pulp, suddenly straightens out beneath the blows; *expands, stretches*; his eyes dart fire! He rises up and falls on the poet tooth and nail. In a few seconds he has laid him out flat, and is just going to finish him off, when an *agent* arrives.—The poet is enchanted. He has accomplished something!

"Would it be possible to achieve a work of that description with you? No. You are meaner-spirited than the most abject tramp. I would seize you by the throat at once if I thought you would black my eye. But I feel it my duty at least to do this for your hat. Your hat, at least, will have had its little drama to-day."

Tarr knocked his hat off into the road.—Without troubling to wait for the results of this action, he hurried away down the Boulevard du Paradis.

CHAPTER II

A great many of Frederick Tarr's resolutions came from his conversation. It was a tribunal to which he brought his hesitations. An active and hustling spirit presided over this section of his life.

Civilized men have for conversation something of the superstitious feeling that ignorant men have for the written or the printed word.

Hobson had attracted a great deal of steam to himself. Tarr was unsatisfied.—He rushed away from the Café Berne still strong and with much more to say. He rushed towards Bertha to say it.

A third of the way he came on a friend who should have been met before Hobson. Then Bertha and he could have been spared.

Butcher was a bloody wastrel enamoured of gold and liberty.—He was a romantic, educating his schoolboyish sense of adventure up to the pitch of drama. He had been induced by Tarr to develop an interest in commerce. He had started a motor business in Paris, and through circularizing the Americans resident there and using his English connexions, he was succeeding on the lines suggested.

Tarr had argued that an interest of this sort would prevent him from becoming arty and silly.—Tarr would have driven his entire circle of acquaintances into commerce if he could. He had at first cherished the ambition of getting Hobson into a bank in South Africa.

As he rushed along then a gaunt car met him, rushing in the opposite direction. Butcher's large red nose stood under a check cap phenomenally peaked. A sweater and Yankee jacket exaggerated his breadth. He was sunk in horizontal massiveness in the car—almost in the road. A quizzing, heavy smile broke his face open in an indifferent businesslike way. It was a sour smile, as though half his face were frozen with cocaine.—He pulled up with the air of an Iron-Age mechanic, born among beds of embryonic machinery.

"Ah, I thought I might see you."—He rolled over the edge and stood grinning and stretching in front of his friend.

"Where are you off to?" Tarr asked.

"I heard there were some gypsies encamped over by Charenton."—He smiled and waited, his entire face breaking up expectantly into cunning pits and traps.—Mention of "gypsies" usually drew Tarr. They were a survival of Butcher's pre-motor days.

"Neglecting business?" was all Tarr said however. "Have you time for a drink?"

"Yes!" Butcher turned with an airy jerk to his car. "Shall we go to the Panthéon?"

"How about the Univers? Would that take long?"

"The Univers? Four or five minutes.—Jump in."

When they had got to the Univers and ordered their drink, Tarr said:

"I've just been talking to Alan Hobson. I've been telling him off."

"That's right.—How had he deserved it?"

"Oh, he happened to drop on me when I was thinking about my girl. He began congratulating me on my engagement. So I gave him my views on marriage, and then wound up with a little improvisation about himself."

Butcher maintained a decorous silence, drinking his beer.

"You're not engaged to be married, are you?" he asked.

"Well, that's a difficult question."—Tarr laughed with circumspection and softness. "I don't know whether I am or whether I'm not."

"Would it be the German girl, if you were?"

"Yes, she'd be the one."

There was a careful absence of comment in Butcher's face.

"Ought I to marry the Lunken?"

"No," Butcher said with measure.

"In that case I ought to tell her at once."

"That is so."

Tarr had a dark morning coat, whose tails flowed behind him as he walked strongly and quickly along, and curled on either side of his hips as he sat. It was buttoned half-way down the body.—He was taller than Butcher, wore glasses, had a dark skin, and a steady, unamiable, impatient expression. He was clean-shaven, with a shallow, square jaw and straight, thick mouth.—His hands were square and usually hot.

He impressed you as having inherited himself last week, and as under a great press of business to grasp the details and resources of the concern. Not very much satisfaction at his inheritance, and no swank. Great capacity was printed all over him.—He did not appear to have been modified as yet by any sedentary, sentimental, or other discipline or habit. He was at his first push in an ardent and exotic world, with a good fund of passion from a frigid climate of his own.—His mistakes he talked over without embarrassment. He felt them deeply. He was experimental and modest.

A rude and hard infancy, according to Balzac, is best for development of character. A child learns duplicity, and hardens in defence.—An enervating childhood of molly-coddling, on the other hand, such as Tarr's, has its advantages.—He was an only child of a selfish, vigorous mother. The long foundation of delicate trustfulness and childishness makes for a store of illusion to prolong youth and health beyond the usual term. Tarr, with the Balzac upbringing, would have had a little too much character, like a rather too muscular man. As it was, he was a shade too nervous. But his confidence in the backing of character was unparalleled. You would have thought he had an iron-field behind him.

When he solicited advice, it was transparently a matter of form. But he appeared to need his own advice to come from himself in public.—Did he feel himself of more importance in public?—His relation to the world was definite and complementary. He preferred his own word to come out of the air; when, that is, issuing from his mouth, it entered either ear as an independent vibration. He was the kind of man who, if he ever should wish to influence the world, would do it so that he might touch himself more plastically through others. He would paint his picture for himself. He was capable of respect for his self-projection. It had the authority of a stranger for him.

Butcher knew that his advice was not really solicited.—This he found rather annoying, as he wanted to meddle. But his opportunity would come.—Tarr's affairs with Bertha Lunken were very exasperating. Of all the drab, dull, and disproportionately long *liaisons*, that one was unique! He had accepted it as an incomprehensible and silly joke.

"She's a very good sort. You know, she is phenomenally kind. It's not quite so absurd as you think, my question as to whether I should marry her. Her love is quite beyond question."

Butcher listened with a slight rolling of the eyes, which was a soft equivalent for grinding his teeth.

Tarr proceeded:

"She has a nice healthy penchant for self-immolation; not, unfortunately, directed by any considerable tact or discretion. She is apt to lie down on the altar at the wrong moment—even to mistake all sorts of unrelated things for altars. She once lay down on the pavement of the Boulevard Sebastopol, and continued to lie there heroically till, with the help of an *agent*, I bundled her into a cab. She is genial and fond of a gross pleasantry, very near to 'the people'—*le peuple*, as she says, purringly and pityingly. All individuals who have class marked on them strongly resemble each other. A typical duchess is much more like a typical nurserymaid than she is like anybody not standardized to the same extent. So is Bertha, a bourgeoise, or rather bourgeois-Bohemian, reminiscent of the popular maiden."

Tarr relighted his cigarette.

"She is full of good sense.—She is a high standard Aryan female, in good condition, superbly made; of the succulent, obedient, clear, peasant type. It is natural that in my healthy youth, living in these Bohemian wastes, I should catch fire. But that is not the whole of the picture. She is unfortunately not a peasant. She has German culture, and a florid philosophy of love.—She is an art-student.—She is absurd."

Tarr struck a match for his cigarette.

"You would ask then how it is that I am still there? The peasant-girl—if such it were—would not hold you for ever; even less so the *spoiled* peasant.—But that's where the mischief lies.—That bourgeois, spoiled, ridiculous element was the trap. I was innocently depraved enough to find it irresistible. It had the charm of a vulgar wall-paper, a gimcrack ornament. A cosy banality set in the midst of a rough life. Youthful exoticism has done it, the something different from oneself."

Butcher did not roll his eyes any more. They looked rather moist. He was thinking of love and absurdities that had checkered his own past, and was regretting a downy doll. He was won over besides by Tarr's *plaidoirie*, as he always was. His friend could have convinced him of anything on earth within ten minutes.

Tarr, noticing the effect of his words, laughed. Butcher was like a dog, with his rheumy eyes.

"My romance, you see, is exactly inverse to yours," Tarr proceeded. "But pure unadulterated romanticism with me is in about the same rudimentary state as sex. So they had perhaps better keep together? I only allow myself to philander with *little* things. I have succeeded in shunting our noxious illusionism away from the great spaces and ambitions. I have billeted it with a bourgeoise in a villa. These things are all arranged above our heads. They are no doubt self-protective. The whole of a man's ninety-nine per cent. of obscurer mechanism is daily engaged in organizing his life in accordance with his deepest necessity. Each person boasts some notable invention of personal application only.

"So there I am fixed with my bourgeoise in my skin, *dans ma peau*. What is the next step?—The body is the main thing.—But I think I have made a discovery. In sex I am romantic and *arriéré*. It would be healthier for all sex to be so. But that is another matter. Well, I cannot see myself attracted by an exceptional woman—'spiritual' woman—'noble soul,' or even a particularly refined and witty animal.—I do not understand attraction for such beings.—Their existence appears to me quite natural and proper, but, not being as fine as men; not being as fine as pictures or poems; not being as fine as housewives or classical Mothers of Men; they appear to me to occupy an unfortunate position on this earth. No man properly demarcated as I am will have much to do with them. They are very beautiful to look at. But they are unfortunately alive, and usually cats. If you married one of them, out of pity, you would have to support the eternal grin of a Gioconda fixed complacently on you at all hours of the day, the pretensions of a piece of canvas that had sold for thirty thousand pounds. You could not put your foot through the canvas without being hanged. You would not be able to sell it yourself for that figure, and so get some little compensation. *Tout au plus*, if the sentimental grin would not otherwise come off, you could break its jaw, perhaps."

Butcher flung his head up, and laughed affectedly.

"Ha ha!"—he went again.

"Very good!—Very good!—I know who you're thinking of," he said.

"Do you? Oh, the 'Gioconda smile,' you mean?—Yes.—In that instance, the man had only his silly sentimental self to blame. He has paid the biggest price given in our time for a *living* masterpiece. Sentimentalizing about masterpieces and *sentimental prices* will soon have seen their day, I expect. New masterpieces in painting will then appear again, perhaps, where the live ones leagued with the old dead ones disappear.—Really, the more one considers it, the more creditable and excellent my self-organization appears. I have a great deal to congratulate myself upon."

Butcher blinked and pulled himself together with a grave dissatisfied expression.

"But will you carry it into effect to the extent?—Will you?—Would marriage be the ideal termination?"—Butcher had a way of tearing up and beginning all over again on a new breath.

"That is what Hobson asked.—No, I don't think marriage has anything to do with it. That is another question altogether."

"I thought your remarks about the housewife suggested—"

"No.—My relation to the idea of the housewife is platonic. I am attracted to the housewife as I might be attracted to the milliner. But just as I should not necessarily employ the latter to make hats—I should have some other use for her—so my connexion with the other need not imply a *ménage*. But my present difficulty centres round that question:

"What am I to do with Fräulein Lunken?"

Butcher drew himself up, and hiccuped solemnly and slowly.

He did not reply.

"Once again, is marriage out of the question?" Tarr asked.

"You know yourself best. I don't think you ought to marry."

"Why, am I—?"

"No. You wouldn't stop with her. So why marry?"

He hiccuped again, and blinked.

Tarr gazed at his oracle with curiosity.—With eyes glassily bloodshot, it discharged its wisdom on gusts of air. Butcher was always surly about women, or rather men's tenderness for them. He was a vindictive enemy of the sex. He stood, a patient constable, forbidding Tarr respectfully a certain road. He spoke with authority and shortness, and hiccuped to convey the absolute and assured quality of his refusal.

"Well, in that case," Tarr said, "I must make a move. I have treated Bertha very badly."

Butcher smothered a hiccup.—He ordered another drink.

"Yes, I owe my girl anything I can give her. It is hardly my fault. With the training you get in England, how can you be expected to realize anything? The University of Humour that prevails everywhere in England as the national institution for developing youth, provides you with nothing but a first-rate means of evading reality. The whole of English training—the great fundamental spirit of the country—is a system of *deadening feeling*, a prescription for Stoicism. Many of the results are excellent. It saves us from gush in many cases; it is an excellent armour in times of crisis or misfortune. The English soldier gets his special *cachet* from it. But for the sake of this wonderful panacea English humour—we sacrifice much. It would be better *to face* our Imagination and our nerves without this soporific. Once this armature breaks down, the man underneath is found in many cases to have become softened by it. He is subject to shock, *over*sensitiveness, and many ailments not met with in the more frank and direct races. Their superficial sensitiveness allows of a harder core.—To set against this, of course, you have the immense reserves of delicacy, touchiness, sympathy, that this envelope of cynicism has accumulated. It has served English art marvellously. But it is probably more useful for art than for practical affairs. And the artist could always look after himself. Anyhow, the time seems to have arrived in my life, as I consider it has arrived in the life of the country, to discard this husk and armour. Life must be met on other terms than those of fun and sport."

Butcher guffawed provocatively. Tarr joined him. They both quaffed their beer.

"You're a terrible fellow," said Butcher. "If you had your way, you'd leave us stark naked. We should all be standing on our little island in the savage state of the Ancient Britons—figuratively." He hiccuped.

"Yes, figuratively. But in reality the country would be armed better than it ever had been before. And by the sacrifice of these famous 'national characteristics' we cling to sentimentally, and which are merely the accident of a time, we should lay a soil and foundation of unspecific force, on which new and realler 'national flavours' would very soon sprout."

"I quite agree," Butcher jerked out energetically.

He ordered another lager.

"I agree with what you say. If we don't give up dreaming, we shall get spanked. I have given up my gypsies. That was very public-spirited of me?" He looked coaxingly.

"If every one would give up their gypsies, their jokes, and their gentlemen—'Gentlemen' are worse than gypsies. It would do perhaps if they reduced them considerably, as you have your Gitanos.—I'm going to swear off humour for a year. I am going to gaze on even you inhumanly. All my mock matrimonial difficulties come from humour. I am going to gaze on Bertha inhumanly, and not humorously. Humour paralyses the sense for reality and wraps people in a phlegmatic and hysterical dream-world, full of the delicious swirls of the switchback, the drunkenness of the merry-go-round—screaming leaps from idea to idea. My little weapon for bringing my man to earth—shot-gun or what not—gave me good sport, too, and was of the best workmanship. I carried it slung jauntily for some time at my side—you may have noticed it. But I am in the tedious position of the man who hits the bull's-eye every time. Had I not been disproportionately occupied with her absurdities, I should not have allowed this charming girl to engage herself to me.

"My first practical step now will be to take this question of 'engaging' myself or not into my own hands. I shall *disengage* myself on the spot."

"So long as you don't engage yourself again next minute, and so on. If I felt that the time was not quite ripe, I'd leave it in Fräulein Lunken's hands a little longer. I expect she does it better than you would."

Butcher filled his pipe, then he began laughing. He laughed theatrically until Tarr stopped him.

"What are you laughing at?"

"You are a nut! Ha! ha! ha!"

"How am I a *nut*? You must be thinking about your old machine out there."

Butcher composed himself—theatrically.

"I was laughing at you. You repent of your thoughtlessness, and all that. Your next step is to put it right. I was laughing at the way you go about it. You now proceed kindly but firmly to break off your engagement and discard the girl. That is very neat."

"Do you think so? Well, perhaps it is a trifle over-tidy. I hadn't looked at it in that way."

"You can't be too tidy," Butcher said dogmatically. He talked to Tarr, when a little worked up, as Tarr talked to him. He didn't notice that he did. It was partly *câlinerie* and flattery.

Tarr pulled out a very heavy and determined-looking watch. He would have suffered had he been compelled to use a small watch. For the time to be microscopic and noiseless would be unbearable. The time *must* be human. That he insisted on. And it must not be pretty or neat.

"It is late. I must go. Must you get back to Passy or can you stop?"

"Do you know, I'm afraid I must get back. I have to lunch with a fellow at one, who is putting me on to a good thing. But can I take you anywhere? Or are you lunching here?"

"No.—Take me as far as the Samaritaine, will you?"

Butcher took him along two sides of the Louvre, to the river.

"Good-bye, then. Don't forget Saturday, six o'clock."

Butcher nodded in bright, clever silence. He shuffled into his car again, working his shoulders like a verminous tramp. He rushed away, piercing blasts from his horn rapidly softening as he became smaller. Tarr was glad he had brought the car and Butcher together. They were opposites with some grave essential in common.

His usual lunch time an hour away, his so far unrevised programme was to go to the Rue Lhomond and search for Hobson's studio. For the length of a street it was equally the road to the studio and to Bertha's rooms. He knew to which he was going.

But a sensation of peculiar freedom and leisure possessed him. There was no hurry. Was there any hurry to go where he was going? With a smile in his mind, his face irresponsible and solemn, he turned sharply into a narrow street, rendered dangerous by motor-buses, and asked at a *loge* if Monsieur Lowndes were in.

"Monsieur Lounes? Je pense que oui. Je ne l'ai pas vu sortir."

He ascended to the fourth floor and rang a bell.

Lowndes was in. He heard him coming on tiptoe to the door, and felt him gazing at him through an invisible crack. He placed himself in a favourable position.

CHAPTER III

Tarr's idea of leisure recognized no departure from the tragic theme of existence. Pleasure could take no form that did not include Death and corruption—at present Bertha and humour. Only he wished to play a little longer. It was the last chance he might have. *Work* was in front of him with Bertha.

He was giving up *play*. But the giving up of play, even, had to take the form of play. He had seen in terms of sport so long that he had no other machinery to work with. *Sport might perhaps, for the fun of the thing, be induced to cast out sport.*

As Lowndes crept towards the door, Tarr said to himself, with ironic self-restraint, "*Bloody* fool, *bloody* fool!"

Lowndes was a brother artist, who was not very active, but had just enough money to be a Cubist. He was extremely proud of being interrupted in his work. His "work" was a serious matter. He found "great difficulty" in working. He always implied that *you* did not. He had a form of persecution mania as regards his "mornings." From his discourse you gathered that he was, first of all, very much sought after. People, seemingly, were *always* attempting to get into his room. You imagined an immense queue of unwelcome visitors (how or why he had gathered or originally, it was to be supposed, encouraged, such, you did not inquire). You never saw this queue. The only person you definitely knew had been guilty of interrupting his "work" was Thornton. This man, because of his admiration for Lowndes' intelligence and moth-like attraction for his Cubism, and respect for his small income, had to suffer much humiliation. He was to be found (even in the morning, strange to say) in Lowndes' studio, rapidly sucking a pipe, blinking, flushing, stammering with second-rate Public School mannerisms, retailing scandal and sensational news, which he had acquired from a woman who had sat next him at the invariable dinner-party of the night before.

When you entered, he looked timidly and quickly at the inexorable Lowndes, and began gathering up his hat and books. Lowndes' manner became withering. You felt that before your arrival, his master had been less severe; that life might have been almost bearable for Thornton. When he at last had taken himself off, Lowndes would hasten to exculpate himself. "Thornton was a fool, but he could not always keep Thornton out," etc. Lowndes, with his Thornton, displayed the characteristics of the self-made man. He had risen ambitiously in the sphere of the Intelligence. Thornton sat like an inhabitant of the nether world of gossip, pettiness, and squalor from which his friend had lately issued. He entertained an immense respect for that friend. This one of his own kind in a position of respect and security was what he could best understand, and would have most desired to be.

"Oh! Come in, Tarr," Lowndes said, looking at the floor of the passage, "I didn't know who it was." The atmosphere became thick with ghostlike intruders. The wretched Thornton seemed to hover timidly in the background.

"Am I interrupting you?" Tarr asked politely.

"No-o-o!" a long, reassuring, musical negative.

His face was very dark and slick, bald on top, pettily bearded, rather unnecessarily handsome. Tarr always felt a tinge of indecency in his good looks. His Celtic head was allied to a stocky commercial figure. Behind his spectacles his black eyes had a way of scouring and scurrying over the floor. They were often dreamy and burning. He waddled slightly, or rather confided himself first to one muscular little calf, then to the other.

Tarr had come to talk to him about Bertha.

"I'm afraid I must have interrupted your work?" Tarr said with mock ceremony.

"No, it's all right. I was just going to have a rest. I'm rather off colour."

Tarr misunderstood him.

"Off colour? What is the matter with colour now?"

"No, I mean I'm seedy."

"Oh, ah. Yes."

His eyes still fixed on the ground, Lowndes pottered about, like a dog.

As with most educated people who "do" anything, and foresee analysis and fame, he was biographically minded. A poor man, he did his Boswelling himself. His self-characterization, proceeding whenever he was not alone, was as follows: "A fussy and exacting man, slightly avuncular, strangely, despite the fineness and amplitude of his character, minute, precious, and tidy." (In this way he made a virtue of his fuss.) To show how the general illusion worked in a particular case: "He had been disturbed in his 'work' by Tarr, or had just emerged from that state of wonderful concentration he called 'work.' He could not at once bend himself to more general things. His nerves drove him from object to object. But he would soon be quiet."

Tarr looked on with an ugly patience.

"Lowndes, I have come to ask you for a little piece of advice."

Lowndes was flattered and relished the mystery.

"Ye-es," he said, smiling, in a slow, 'sober,' professional sing-song.

"Or rather, for an opinion. What is your opinion of German women?"

Lowndes had spent two years in Berlin and Münich. Many of his friends were Austrian.

"German women? But I must know first why you ask me that question. You see, it's a wide subject."

"A wide subject—wide. Yes, very good! Ha ha!—Well, it is like this. I think that they are superior to Englishwomen. That is a very dangerous opinion to hold, as there are so many German women knocking about just now.—I want to rid myself of it.—Can you help me?"

Lowndes mused on the ground. Then he looked up brightly.

"No, I can't. Because I share it!"

"Lowndes, I'm surprised at you. I never thought you were that sort of man!"

"How do you mean?"

"Perhaps you can help me nevertheless. Our ideas on females may not be the same."

Tarr always embarrassed him. Lowndes huddled himself tensely together, worked at his pipe, and met Tarr's jokes painfully. He hesitated to sally forth and drive the joke away.

"What are your ideas on females?" he asked in a moment.

"Oh, I think they ought to be convex if you are concave—stupid if you are intelligent, hot if you are cold, frigid if you are volcanic. Always white all over, clothes, underclothes, skin and all.—My ideas do not extend much beyond that."

Lowndes organized Tarr's statement, with a view to an adequate and light reply. He gnawed at his pipe.

"Well, German women are usually convex. There are also concave ones. There are cold ones and hot ones." He looked up. "It all seems to depend what *you* are like!"

"I am cold; inclined to be fat; *forte tête*; and swarthy, as you see."

"In that case, if you took plenty of exercise," Lowndes undulated himself as though for the passage of the large bubbles of chuckle, "I should think that German women would suit you very well!"

Tarr rose.

"I wish I hadn't come to see you, Lowndes. Your answer is disappointing."

Lowndes got up, disturbed at Tarr's sign of departure.

"I'm sorry. But I'm not an authority." He leant against the fireplace to arrest Tarr's withdrawal for a minute or two. "Are you doing much work?"

"I? No."

"Are you ever in in the afternoons? I should like to come round some day—"

"I'm just moving into a new studio."

Lowndes looked suddenly at his watch, with calculated, ape-like impulsiveness.

"Where are you having lunch? I thought of going down to Lejeune's to see if I could come across a beggar of the name of Kreisler. He could tell you much more about German women than I can. He's a German. Come along, won't you? Are you doing anything?"

"No, I know quite enough Germans. Besides, I must go somewhere—I can't have lunch just yet. Good-bye. Thank you for your opinion."

"Don't mention it," Lowndes said softly, his head turned obliquely to his shoulder, as though he had a stiff neck, and balancing on his calves.

He was rather wounded, or brusque, by the brevity of Tarr's visit. His "morning" had not received enough respect. It had been treated, in fact, cavalierly. His "work" had not been directly mentioned.

When Tarr got outside, he stood on the narrow pavement, looking into a shop window. It was a florist's and contained a great variety of flowers. He was surprised to find that he did not know a single flower by name. He hung on in front of this shop before pushing off, as a swimmer does to a rock, waving his legs. Then he got back into the street from which his visit to Lowndes had deflected him. He let himself drift down it. He still had some way to go before he need decide between the Rue Martine (where Bertha lived) and the Rue Lhomond.

He had not found resolution in his talks. That already existed, the fruit of various other conversations on his matrimonial position—held with the victim, Fräulein Lunken, herself.

Not to go near Bertha was the negative programme for that particular day. To keep away was seldom easy. But ever since his conversation at the Berne he had been conscious of the absurd easiness of doing so, if he wished. He had not the least inclination to go to the Rue Martine!—This sensation was so grateful that its object shared in its effect. He determined to go and see her. He wanted to enjoy his present feeling of indifference. Where best to enjoy it was no doubt where she was.

As to the studio, he hesitated. A new situation was created by this new feeling of indifference. Its duration could not be gauged.—He wished to stay in Paris just then to finish some paintings begun some months before. He substituted for the Impressionist's necessity to remain in front of the object being represented, a sensation of the desirability of finishing a canvas in the place where it was begun. He had an Impressionist's horror of change.

So Tarr had evolved a plan. At first sight it was wicked. It was no blacker than most of his ingenuities. Bertha, as he had suggested to Butcher, he had in some lymphatic way, *dans la peau*. It appeared a matter of physical discomfort to leave her altogether. It must be done gradually. So he had thought that, instead of going away to England, where the separation might cause him restlessness, he had perhaps better settle down in her neighbourhood. Through a series of specially tended ennuis, he would soon find himself in a position to depart. So the extreme nearness of the studio to Bertha's flat was only another inducement for him to take it. "If it were next door, so much the better!" he thought.

Now for this famous feeling of indifference. Was there anything in it?—The studio for the moment should be put aside. He would go to see Bertha. Let this visit solve this question.

CHAPTER IV

The new summer heat drew heavy pleasant ghosts out of the ground, like plants disappeared in winter; spectres of energy, bulking the hot air with vigorous dreams. Or they had entered into the trees, in imitation of Pagan gods, and nodded their delicate distant intoxication to him. Visions were released in the sap, with scented explosion, the spring one bustling and tremendous reminiscence.

Tarr felt the street was a pleasant current, setting from some immense and tropic gulf, neighboured by Floridas of remote invasions. He ambled down it puissantly, shoulders shaped like these waves; a heavy-sided drunken fish. The houses, with winks of the shocked clockwork, were grazed, holding along their surface thick soft warmth. It poured weakly into his veins. A big dog wandering on its easily transposable business, inviting some delightful accident to deflect it from maudlin and massive promenade. In his mind, too, as in the dog's, his business was doubtful—a small black spot ahead in his brain, half puzzling but peremptory.

The mat heavy light grey of putty-coloured houses, like thickening merely of hot summer atmosphere without sun, gave a spirituality to this deluge of animal well-being, in weighty pale sense-solidarity. Through the opaquer atmosphere sounds came lazily or tinglingly. People had become a Balzacian species, boldly tragic and comic: like a cast of "Comédie Humaine" humanity off for the day, Balzac sleeping immensely in the cemetery.

Tarr stopped at a dairy. He bought saladed potatoes, a *petit suisse*. The coolness, as he entered, felt eerie. The dairyman, in blue-striped smock and black cap, peaked and cylindrical, came out of an inner room. Through its glasses several women were visible, busy at a meal. This man's isolation from the heat and mood of the world outside, impressed his customer as he came forward with a truculent "Monsieur!" Tarr, while his things were done up, watched the women. The discreet voices, severe reserve of keen business preoccupations, showed the usual Paris *commerçante*. The white, black, and slate-grey of dresses, extreme neatness, silent felt over-slippers, make their commercial devotions rather conventual. With this purchase—followed by one of strawberries at a fruiterer's opposite—his destination was no longer doubtful.

He was going to Bertha's to eat his lunch. Hence the double quantity of saladed potatoes. He skirted the railings of the Luxembourg Gardens for fifteen yards. Crossing the road, he entered the Rue Martine, a bald expanse of uniformly coloured rosy-grey pavement, plaster, and shutter. A large iron gate led into a short avenue of trees. At its end Bertha lived in a three-story house.

The leaden brilliant green of spring foliage hung above him, ticketing innumerably the trees, sultry smoke volumes from factories in Fairyland. Its novelty, fresh yet dead, had the effectiveness of an unnecessary mirage. The charm of habit and monotony he had come to affront seemed to have coloured, chemically, these approaches to its home.

He found Bertha's eye fixed on him with a sort of humorous indifferent query from the window. He smiled, thinking what would be the veritable answer! On finding himself in the presence of the object of his erudite discussion, he felt he had got the focus wrong. This familiar life, with its ironical eye, mocked at him too. It was aware of the subject of his late conversation. The twin of the shrewd feeling embodied in the observation, "One can never escape from oneself," appeared.

This ironical unsurprised eye at the window, so vaguely apropos, offended him. It seemed to be making fun of the swaggering indifference he was bringing to bask in the presence of its object. He became slightly truculent.

"Have you had lunch yet, my dear?" he asked, as she opened the door to him. "I've brought you some strawberries."

"I didn't expect *you*, Sorbet. No, I've not had lunch. I was just going to get it." (Sorbet, or in English, Sherbert, was his *nom d'amour*, a perversion of his name, Sorbert).

Bertha's was the intellectually fostered Greek type of German handsomeness. It is that beauty that makes you wonder, when you meet it, if German mothers have replicas and photographs of the Venus of Milo in their rooms during the first three months of their pregnancy. It is also found in the pages of Prussian art periodicals, the arid, empty intellectualism of Münich. She had been a heavy baby. Her body now, a self-indulgent athlete's, was strung to heavy motherhood.

A great believer in tepid "air-baths," she would remain, for hours together, in a state of nudity about her rooms. She was wearing a pale green striped affair, tight at the waist. It looked as though meant for a smaller woman. It may have belonged to her sister. As a result, her ample form had left the fullness of a score of attitudes all over it, in flat creasings and pencillings—like the sanguine of an Italian master in which the leg is drawn in several positions, one on top of the other.

"What have you come for, Sorbet?"

"To see you. What did you suppose?"

"Oh, you *have* come to see me?"

"I brought these things. I thought you might be hungry."

"Yes, I am rather." She stopped in the passage, Dryad-like on one foot, and stared into the kitchen. Tarr did not kiss her. He put his hand on her hip—a way out of it—and led her into the room. His hand remarked that she was underneath in her favourite state of nakedness.

Bertha went into the kitchen with the provisions. She lived in two rooms on one side of the front door. Her friend, Fräulein Goenthner, to whom she sub-let, lived on the other side of it, the kitchen promiscuously existing between, and immediately facing the entrance.

Tarr was in the studio or salon. It was a complete bourgeois-bohemian interior. Green silk cloth and cushions of various vegetable and mineral shades covered everything, in mildewy blight. The cold, repulsive shades of Islands of the Dead, gigantic cypresses, grottos of Teutonic nymphs, had invaded this dwelling. Purple metal and leather steadily dispensed with expensive objects. There was the plaster east of Beethoven (some people who have frequented artistic circles get to dislike this face extremely), brass jars from Normandy, a photograph of Mona Lisa (Tarr hated the Mona Lisa).

A table just by the window, laid with a white cloth, square embroidered holes at its edges, was where Tarr at once took up his position. Truculence was denoted by his thus going straight to his eating-place.

Installed in the midst of this ridiculous life, he gave a hasty glance at his "indifference" to see whether it were safe and sound. Seen through it, on opening the door, Bertha had appeared *unusual*. This impressed him disagreeably. Had his rich and calm feeling of bounty towards her survived the encounter, his "indifference" might also have remained intact.

He engrossed himself in his sense of physical well-being. From his pocket he produced a tin box containing tobacco, papers, and a little steel machine for rolling cigarettes given him by Bertha. A long slim hinged shell, it nipped in a little cartridge of tobacco, which it then slipped with inside a paper tube, and slipping out again empty, the cigarette was made.

Tarr began manufacturing cigarettes. Reflections from the shining metal in his hand scurried about amongst the bilious bric-à-brac. Like a layer of water lying on one of oil, the light heated stretch by the windows appeared distinct from the shadowed part of the room.

This place was cheap and dead, but rich with the same lifelessness as the trees without. These looked extremely near and familiar at the opened windows, breathing the same air continually as Bertha. But they were dusty, rough, and real.

Bertha came in from the kitchen. She went on with a trivial rearrangement of her writing-table. This had been her occupation as he appeared at the gate beneath, drawing her ironical and musing eye from his image to himself. A new photograph of Tarr was being placed on her writing-table flush with the window. Ten days previously it had been taken in that room. It had ousted a Klinger and generally created a restlessness, to her eye, in the other objects.

"Ah, you've got the photographs, have you?—Is that me?"

She handed it to him.

"Yes, they came yesterday!"

"Yesterday" he had not been there! Whatever he asked at the present moment would draw a softly thudding answer, heavy German reproach concealed in it with tireless ingenuity. These photographs would under other circumstances have been produced on his arrival with considerable noise.

Tarr had looked rather askance at this portrait and Bertha's occupation. There was his photograph, calmly, with an air of permanence, taking up its position on her writing-table, just as he was preparing to vanish for good.

"Let's see yours," he said, still holding the photograph.

What strange effects all this complicated activity inside had on the surface, his face. A set sulky stagnation, every violence dropping an imperceptible shade on to it, the features overgrown with this strange stuff—that twist of the head that was him, and that could only be got rid of by breaking.

"They're no good," she said, closing the drawer, handing her photographs, sandwiched with tissue-paper, to Sorbert. "That one"—a sitting pose, face yearning from photograph, lighted, not with a smile, but a sort of sentimental illumination, the drapery arranged like a poster—"I don't think that's so bad," she said slangily, meant to be curt and "cheeky."

"What an idiot!" he thought; "what a face!"

A consciously pathetic ghost of a smile, a clumsy sweetness, the energetic sentimental claim of a rather rough but frank self.

There was a photograph of her in riding habit. This was the best of them. He softened.

Then came a photograph of them together.

How strangely that twist of his, or set angle of the head, fitted in with the corresponding peculiarities of the woman's head and bust. What abysms of idiocy! Rubbishy hours and months formed the atmosphere around these two futile dolls!

He put the photographs down and looked up. She was sitting on the edge of the table. The dressing-gown was open, and one large thigh, with ugly whiteness, slid half out of it. It looked dead, and connected with her like a ventriloquist's dummy with its master. It was natural to wonder where his senses had gone in looking at these decorous photographs. This exhibition appeared to be her explanation of the matter. The face was not very original. But a thigh cannot be stupid to the same degree.

He gazed surlily. Her musing expression at this moment was supremely absurd. He smiled and turned his face to the window. She pretended to become conscious suddenly of something amiss. She drew the dressing-gown round her.

"Have you paid the man yet? What did he charge? I expect—"

Tarr took up the packet again.

"Oh, these are six francs. I forget what the big ones are. I haven't paid him yet. He's coming to photograph Miss Goenthner to-morrow."

They sat without saying anything.

He examined the room as you do a doctor's waiting-room.

He had just come there to see if he could turn his back on it. That appeared at first sight a very easy matter. That is why he so far had not succeeded in doing so. Never put on his mettle, his standing army of will was not sufficient to cope with it. But would this little room ever appear worth turning his back on? It was the purest distillation of the commonplace. He had become bewitched by its strangeness. It was the height of the unreal. Bertha was like a fairy that he visited, and "became engaged" to in another world, not the real one. It was so much the real ordinary world that for him with his out-of-the-way experience it was a phantasmagoria. Then what he had described as his disease of sport was perpetually fed. Sex even with him, according to his analysis, being a sort of ghost, was at home in this gross and buffonic illusion. Something had filled up a blank and become saturated with the blankness.

How much would Bertha mind a separation? Tarr saw in her one of those clear, humorous, superficial natures, a Venetian or a Viennese, the easy product of a cynical and abundant life. He under-rated the potency of his fascination. Secondly, he miscalculated the depths of obedient attachment he had wakened.

They sat impatiently waiting. A certain formality had to be observed. Then the business of the day could be proceeded with. They were both bored with the part imposed by the punctilious and ridiculous god of love. Bertha, into the bargain, wanted to get on with her cooking. She would have cut considerably the reconciliation scene. All her side of the programme had been conscientiously done.

"Berthe, tu es une brave fille!"

"Tu trouves?"

"Oui."

More inaction followed on Tarr's part. She sometimes thought he enjoyed these ceremonies.

Through girlhood her strong senses had churned away at her, and claimed an image from her gentle and dreamy mind. In its turn the mind had accumulated its impressions of men, fancies from books and conversations, and made its hive. So her senses were presented with the image that was to satisfy and rule them. They flung themselves upon it as she had flung herself upon Tarr.

This image left considerable latitude. Tarr had been the first to fit—rather paradoxically, but all the faster for that.

This "high standard Aryan female," as Tarr described her, had arrived, with him, at the full and headlong condition we agree to name "love." The image, or type, was thrown away. The individual took its place.

Bertha had had several sweethearts before Tarr. They had all left the type-image intact. At most it had been a little blurred by them. It had almost been smashed for one man, physically resembling Tarr. But he had never got quite near enough to do that. Tarr had characteristically supposed this image to have little sharpness of outline left. He thought it would not be a very difficult matter for any one to extort its recognitions.

"Vous êtes à mon goût, Sorbet. Du bist mein gesmack," she would say.

Tarr was not demonstrative when she said this. He could not reciprocate. And he could not help reflecting whether to be "her taste" was very flattering. There *must* be something the matter with him.

All her hope centred in his laziness. She watched his weaknesses with a loving eye. He had much to say about his under-nature. She listened attentively.

"It is the most dangerous quality of all to possess," and he would sententiously add—"only the best people possess it, in common with the obscure and humble. It is like a great caravanserai in which scores of people congregate. It is a disguise in which such a one, otherwise Pasha, circulates among unembarrassed men. He brings away stores of wisdom, with much diversion by the way." He saw, however, the danger of these facilities. The Pasha had been given a magic mask of humbleness. But the inner nature seemed flowing equally to the mask and the unmasked magnificence. He was as yet unformed, but wished to form wholly Pasha. This under-nature's chief use was as a precious *villégiature* for his energy. Bertha was the country wench the more exalted incarnation had met while on its holidays, or, wandering idle Khalife, in some concourse of his surreptitious life.

His three days' unannounced and uncommented "leave" had made Bertha very nervous. She suffered from the incomplete, unsymmetrical appearance her life now presented. Everything spread out palpably before her, that she could arrange like a roomful of furniture, was how she liked it. Even in her present shakedown of a life, Tarr had noticed the way he was treated as material for "arrangement." But she had never been able to indulge this idiosyncrasy much in the past. This was not the first time that she had found herself in a similar position. Hence her certain air of being at home in these casual quarters, which belied her.

The detested temporary dwelling in the last few days had been given a new coat of sombre thought. Found in accidental quarters, had she not been over-delicate in not suggesting an immediate move into something more homelike and permanent. People would leave her there for the rest of her natural life unless she were a little brutal and got *herself* out somehow. No shadow of un-nice feeling ever tainted her abject genuineness. Cunning efforts to retain him abounded. But she never blamed or turned on him. She had given herself long ago, at once, without ceremony. She awaited his thanks or no thanks simply.

But the itch of action was on her.

Tarr's absences were like light. His presence was a shadow. They were both stormy. The last absence had illuminated the undiscipline of her life.

During the revealing luridness, she got to work. Reconstruction was begun. She had trusted too much in Fate and obedient waiting Hymen.

So Bertha had a similar ferment to Tarr's.

Anger with herself, dreary appetite for action, would help her over farewells. She was familiar enough with them, too, in thought. She would not stir a hand to change things. He must do that. She would only facilitate things in all directions for him. The new energy delivered attack after attack upon her hope. She saw nothing beyond Tarr but measures of utility. The "heart" had always been her most cherished ornament. *That* Tarr would take with him, as she would keep his ring and the books he had given her. She could not now get it back for the asking. She did not want it! She must indulge her mania for tasteful arrangement in future without this. Or rather what heart she had left would be rather like one of those salmon-coloured, corrugated gas office-stoves, compared to a hearth with a fire of pine.

Tarr had not brought his indifference there to make it play tricks, perform little feats. Nor did he wish to press it into inhuman actions. It was a humane "indifference," essentially. So with reluctance he got up, and went over to her.

"You haven't kissed me yet," he said, in imitation of her.

"Why kiss you, Sorbet?" she managed to say before her lips were closed. He drew her ungraciously and roughly into his arms, and started kissing her on the mouth. She covered him, docilely, with her inertia. He was supposed to be performing a miracle of bringing the dead to life. Gone about too crudely, the willing mountebank, Death, had been offended. It is not thus that great spirits are prevailed upon to flee. Her "indifference"—the great, simulated, and traditional—would not be ousted by an upstart and younger relative. By Tarr himself, grown repentant, yes. But not by another "indifference." Then his brutality stung her offended spirit, that had been pursing itself up for so many hours. Tears began rolling tranquilly out of her eyes in large dignified drops. They had not been very far back in the wings. He received them frigidly. She was sure, thought he, to detect something unusual during this scene.

Then with the woman's bustling, desperate, possessive fury, she suddenly woke up. She disengaged her arms wildly and threw them round his neck, tears becoming torrential. Underneath the poor comedian that played such antics with such phlegmatic and exasperating persistence, this distressed being thrust up its trembling mask, like a drowning rat. Its finer head pierced her blunter wedge.

"Oh! dis, Sorbet! Est-ce que tu m'aime? M'aime-tu? Dis!"

"Yes, you know. Don't cry."

A wail, like the buzzing on a comb covered with paper followed.

"Oh, dis; m'aimes-tu? Dis que tu m'aime!"

A blurting, hurrying personality rushed right up into his face. It was like the sightless clammy charging of a bat. More eloquent regions had ambushed him. Humbug had mysteriously departed. It was a blast of knifelike air in the middle of their hot-house. He stared at her face groping up as though it scented troubles in his face. It pushed to right and then to left and rocked itself. Intelligent and aware, it lost this intensity.

A complicated image developed in his mind as he stood with her. He was remembering Schopenhauer. It was of a Chinese puzzle of boxes within boxes, or of insects' discarded envelopes. A woman had in the middle of her a kernel, a sort of very substantial astral baby. This baby was apt to swell. She then became *all* baby. The husk he held was a painted mummy-case. He was a mummy-case too. Only he contained nothing but innumerable other painted cases inside, smaller and smaller ones. The smallest was not a substantial astral baby, however, or live core, but a painting like the rest. His kernel was a painting. That was as it should be!

He was half sitting on the table. He found himself patting her back. He stopped doing this. His face looked heavy and fatigued. A dull, intense infection of her despair had filled it.

He held her head gently against his neck. Or he held her skull against his neck. She shook and sniffed softly.

"Bertha, stop crying. I know I'm a brute. But it's fortunate for you that I am. I'm only a brute. There's nothing to cry for."

He over-estimated deafness in weepers. And when women flooded their country he always sat down and waited. Often as this had happened to him, he had never attempted to circumvent it. He felt like a person who is taking a little dog for a walk at the end of a string. His voice appeared husky and artificial near her ear.

Turned towards the window, he looked at the green stain of the foliage outside. Something was explained. Nature was not friendly to him; its metallic tints jarred. Or anyhow, it was the same for all men. The sunlight seen like an adventurous stranger in the streets was intimate with Bertha. The scrap of crude forest had made him want to be away unaccompanied. But it was tainted with her. If he went away now he would only be *playing* at liberty. He had been right in not accepting the invitations of the spring. The settlement of this question stood between him and pleasure. A momentary well-being had been accepted. The larger spiritual invitation he had rejected. He would only take that when he was free. In its annual expansion Nature sent its large unstinting invitations. But Nature loved the genius and liberty in him. Tarr felt the invitation would not have been so cordial had he proposed taking a wife and family!

He led her passively protesting to the sofa. Like a sick person, she was half indignant at being moved. He should have remained, a perpendicular bed for her, till the fever had passed. Revolted at the hypocrisy required, he left her standing at the edge of the sofa. She stood crouching a little, her face buried in her hands, in indignant absurdity. The only moderately clean thing to do would be to walk out of the door at once and never come back. With his background of months of different behaviour this could not be done.

She sank down on the sofa, head buried in the bilious cushions. She lay there like an animal, he thought, or some one mad, a lump of half-humanity. On one side of him Bertha lay quite motionless and silent, and on the other the little avenue was equally still. The false stillness within, however, now gave back to the scene without its habitual character. It still seemed strange to him. But all its strangeness now lay in its everyday and natural appearance. The quiet inside, in the room, was what did not seem strange to him. He had become imbued with that. Bertha's numb silence and abandon was a stupid *tableau vivant* of his own mood. In this impasse of arrested life he stood sick and useless. They progressed from stage to stage of this weary farce. Confusion increased. It resembled a combat between two wrestlers of mathematically equal strength. Neither could win. One or other of them was usually wallowing warily or lifelessly on his stomach, the other tugging at him or examining and prodding his carcass. His liking, contempt, realization of her love for him, his confused but exigent conscience, dogged preparation to say farewell, all dovetailed with precision. There she lay a deadweight. He could take his hat and go. But once gone in this manner he could not stay.

He turned round, and sitting on the window-sill began again staring at Bertha.

Women's stormy weakness, psychic discharges, always affected him as the sight of a person being seasick. It was the result of a weak spirit, as the other was the result of a weak stomach. They could only live on the retching seas of their troubles on the condition of being quite empty. The lack of art or illusion in actual life enables the sensitive man to exist. Likewise the phenomenal lack of nature in the average man's existence is lucky and necessary for him.

Tarr in some way gathered strength from contemplation of Bertha. His contradictory and dislocated feelings were brought into a new synthesis.

Launching himself off the window-sill, he stood still as though suspended in thought. He then sat down provisionally at the writing-table, within a few feet of the sofa. He took up a book of Goethe's poems that she had given him. In cumbrous field-day dress of Gothic characters, squad after squad, these poems paraded their message. He had left it there on a former visit. He came to the ode named "Ganymed,"

Wie im Morgenglanze

Du rings much anglühst

Frühling, Geliebter!

Mit tausendfacher Liebeswonne

Sich an mein Herz drängt

Deiner ewigen Wärme

Heilig, Gefühl,

Unendliche Schöne!

He put it in his breast-pocket. As soldiers go into battle sometimes with the Bible in their pocket, he prepared himself for a final combat, with Goethe upon his person. Men's lives have been known to have been saved through a lesser devoutness.

He was engaging battle again with the most chivalrous sentiments. The reserves had been called up, his nature mobilized. As his will gathered force and volume (in its determination to "fling" her) he unhypocritically keyed up its attitude. It resembled extreme cunning. He had felt, while he had been holding her, at a disadvantage because of his listless emotion. With emotion equal to hers, he could accomplish anything. Leaving her would be child's play. He appeared to be projecting the manufacture of a more adequate sentiment.

Any indirectness was out of the question. A "letting her down softly," kissing and leaving in an hour or two, as though things had not changed, that must now be eschewed—oh, yes. The genuine section of her, of which he had a troubled glimpse, mattered, nothing else. He must appeal obstinately to that. Their coming together had been prosecuted on his side with a stupid levity. He would retrieve this in the parting. He wished to do everything most opposite to his previous lazy conduct. He frowned on Humour.

The first skirmish of his comic Armageddon had opened with the advance of his mysterious and *goguenard* "indifference." This dwindled away at the first onset. A new and more powerful thing had taken its place. This was, in Bertha's eyes, a *difference* in Tarr.

"Something has happened; he is *different*," she said to herself. "He has met somebody else," had been her rapid provisional conclusion.

She suddenly got up without speaking. Rather spectrally, she went over to the writing-table for her handkerchief. She had not moved an inch or a muscle until quite herself again, dropping steadily down all the scale of feeling to normal. With matter-of-factness she got up, easily and quietly, making Sorbert a little dizzy.

Her face had all the drama wrung out of it. It was hard, clear, and garishly white, like her body.

If he were to have a chance of talking he must clear the air of electricity completely. Else at his first few words storm might return.

Once lunch had swept through the room, things would be better. He would send the strawberries ahead to prepare his way. It was like fattening a lamb for the slaughter. This idea pleased him. Now that he had accepted the existence of a possible higher plane of feeling as between Bertha and himself, he was anxious to avoid display. So he ran the risk of outdoing his former callousness. Tarr was saturated with morbid English shyness, that cannot tolerate passion and its nakedness. This shyness, as he contended, in its need to show its heart, discovers subtleties and refinements of expression, opposites and between shades, unknown to less gauche and delicate people. But if he were hustled out of his shell the anger that co-existed with his modesty was the most spontaneous thing he possessed. Bertha had always left him alone.

He got up, obsequiously reproducing in his own movements and expression her new normality.

"Well, how about lunch? I'll come and help you with it."

"There's nothing to do. I'll get it."

Bertha had wiped her eyes with the attentiveness a man bestows on his chin after a shave, in little brusque hard strokes. She did not look at Tarr. She arranged her hair in the mirror, then went to the kitchen. For her to be so *perfectly natural* offended him.

The intensity of her past feeling carried her on for about five minutes into ordinary life. Her seriousness was tactful for so long. Then her nature began to give way. It broke up again into fits and starts of self-consciousness.

The mind was called in, did its work clumsily as usual. She became her usual self. Sitting on the stool by the window, in the act of eating, Tarr there in front of her, it was more than ever impossible to be natural. She resented the immediate introduction of lunch in this way. The resentment increased her artificiality.

To counterbalance the acceptance of food, she had to throw more pathos into her face. With haggard resignation she was going on again; doing what was asked of her, partaking of this lunch. She did so with unnecessary conscientiousness. Her strange wave of dignity had let her in for this? Almost she must make up for that dignity! Life was confusing her again; it was useless to struggle.

"Aren't these strawberries good? These little hard ones are better than the bigger strawberries. Have some more cream?"

"Thank you." She should have said no. But being greedy in this matter she accepted it, with heavy air of some subtle advantage gained.

"How did the riding lesson go off?" She went to a riding school in the mornings.

"Oh, quite well, thank you. How did *your* lesson go off?" This referred to his exchange of languages with a Russian girl.

"Admirably, thank you."

The Russian girl was a useful feint for her.

"What is the time?" The time? What cheek! He was almost startled.

He took his heavy watch out and presented its face to her ironically.

"Are you in a hurry?" he asked.

"No, I just wondered what the time was. I live so vaguely."

"You are sure you are not in a hurry?"

"Oh, no!"

"I have a confession to make, my dear Bertha." He had not put his watch back in his pocket. She had asked for the watch; he would use it. "I came here just now to test a funny mood—a quite *new* mood. My visit is a sort of trial trip of this mood. It was connected with you. I wanted to find out what it meant, and how it would be affected by your presence."

Bertha looked up with mocking sulky face, a shade of hopeful curiosity.

"It was a feeling of complete indifference as regards yourself!"

He said this solemnly, with the pomp with which a weighty piece of news might be delivered by a solicitor in conversation with his client.

"Oh, is *that* all?" The new barbaric effort was met by Bertha scornfully.

"No, that is not all."

Catching at the professional figure his manner had conjured up, he ran his further remarks into that mould. The presence of his watch in his hand had brought some image of the family physician or gouty attorney. It all centred round the watch, and her interest in the time of day.

"I have found that this was only another fraud on my too credulous sensibility." He smiled with professional courtesy. "At sight of you, my mood evaporated. But what I want to talk about is what is left. It would be well to bring our accounts up to date. I'm afraid the reckoning is enormously against me. You have been a criminally indulgent partner—"

He had now got the image down to the more precise form of two partners, perhaps comfortable wine merchants, going through their books.

"My dear boy, I know that. You needn't trouble to go any further. But why are you going into these calculations, and sums of profit and loss?"

"Because my sentimental finances, if I may use that term, are in a bad state."

"Then they only match your worldly ones."

"In my worldly ones I have no partner," he reminded her.

She cast her eyes about in swoops, full of self-possessed wildness.

"I exonerate you, Sorbet," she said, "you needn't go into details. What is *yours* and what is *mine*. My God! What does it matter? Not much!"

"I know you to be generous—"

"Leave that then! Leave these calculations! All that means so *little* to me! I feel at the end of my strength—*au bout de force*!" She always heaved this out with much energy. "If you've made up your mind to go—do so, Sorbet. I release you! You owe me nothing. It was all my fault. But spare me a reckoning. I can't stand any more—"

"No, I insist on being responsible. We can't leave things upside down—our books in an endless muddle, our desks open, and just walk away for ever—and perhaps set up shop somewhere else?"

"I do not feel in any mood to 'set up shop somewhere else,' I can assure you!"

The unbusinesslike element in the situation she had allowed to develop for obvious reasons. She now resisted his dishonest attempt to set this right, and benefit first, as he had done, by disorder, and lastly by order.

"We can't, in any case, improve matters by talking. I—I, you needn't fear for me, Sorbet. I can look after myself, only don't let us wrangle," with appealing gesture and saintlily smiling face, "let us part friends. Let us be worthy of each other."

Bertha always opposed to Tarr's images her Teutonic lyricism, usually repeating the same phrases several times.

This was degenerating into their routine of wrangle. Always confronted by this imperturbable, deaf and blind "generosity," the day would end in the usual senseless "draw." His words still remained unsaid.

"Bertha, listen. Let us, just for fun, throw all this overboard. I mean the cargo of inflated soul-stuff that makes us go statelily, no doubt, but—Haven't we quarrelled enough, and said these things often enough? Our quarrels have been our undoing. A long chain of little quarrels has bound us down. We should neither of us be here if it hadn't been for them."

Bertha gazed at Tarr half wonderingly. She realized that something out of the ordinary was on foot.

Tarr proceeded.

"I have accepted from you a queer sentimental dialect of life, I should have insisted on your expressing yourself in a more logical and metropolitan speech. Let us drop it. There is no need to talk negro, baby-talk, or hybrid drivel from no-man's-land. I don't think we should lead a very pleasant married life—naturally. In the second place, you are not a girl who wants an intrigue, but to marry. I have been playing at fiancé with a certain pleasure in the novelty, but I experience a genuine horror at the possible consequences. I have been playing with you!"

He said this eagerly, as though it were a point in his argument—as it was. He paused, for effect apparently.

"You, for your part, Bertha, don't do yourself justice when you are acting. I am in the same position. I feel this. My ill-humour occasionally falls in your direction—yours, for its part, falling in mine when I criticize *your* acting. We don't act well together, and that's a fact; though I'm sure we should be smooth enough allies off the boards of love. Your heart, Bertha, is in the right place; ah, ça—"

"You are too kind!"

"But—but I will go further! At the risk of appearing outrageously paradoxical. This heart in question is so much part of your intelligence, too—"

"Thanks! Thanks!"

"—despite your execrable fatuity as an actress! Your shrewdness and goodness give each other the hand.—But to return to my point. I had always till I met you regarded marriage as a thing beyond all argument *not* for me. I was unusually isolated from this idea, anyway; I had never even reflected what marriage was. You introduced me to marriage! In so doing you are responsible for all our troubles. The approach of this horrible thing, so *surprisingly* pleasant and friendly at nearer sight, caused revulsion of feeling beyond my control, resulting in sudden *fiançailles*. Like a woman luxuriously fingering some merchant's goods, too dear for her, or not wanted enough for the big price, so I philandered with the idea of marriage."

This simplification put things, merely, in a new callous light. Tarr felt that she must naturally be enjoying, too, his points. He forgot to direct his exposition in such a way as to hurt her least. This trivial and tortured landscape had a beauty for him he could have explained, where her less developed sense saw nothing but a harrowing reality.

The lunch had had the same effect on him that it was intended to have on his victim; not enough to overthrow his resolution, but enough to relax its form.

As to Bertha, this seemed, in the main, "Sorbet all over." There was nothing new. There was the "difference." But it was the familiar process; he was attempting to convince himself, heartlessly, on her. Whether he would ever manage it was problematic. There was no sign of his being likely to do so more to-day than any other day. She listened; sententiously released him from time to time.

Just as she had seemed strange to him in some way when he came in, seen through his "indifference," so he had appeared a little odd to her. This had wiped off the dullness of habit for a moment. This husband she obstinately wanted had been recognized. She had seized him round the shoulders and clung to him, as though he had been her child that some senseless force were about to snatch.

As to his superstition about marriage—was it not merely restlessness of youth, propaganda of Liberty, that a year or so would see in Limbo? For was he not a "marrying man"? She was sure of it! She had tried not to frighten him, and to keep "Marriage" in the background.

So Tarr's disquisition had no effect except for one thing. When he spoke of *pleasure he derived from idea of marriage,* she wearily pricked up her ears. The conviction that Tarr was a domesticated animal was confirmed from his own lips. The only result of his sortie was to stimulate her always vigilant hope and irony, both, just a little. He had intended to prepare the couch for her despair!

His last words, affirming Marriage to be a game not worth the candle, brought a faint and "weary" smile to her face. She was once more, obviously, *au bout de force.*

"Sorbert; I understand you. Do realize that. There is no necessity for all this rigmarole With me. If you think you shouldn't marry—why, it's quite simple! Don't think that I would force you to marry! Oh, no!" (The training guttural unctuous accent she had in speaking English filled her discourse with natural emphasis.) "I always said that you were too young. You need a wife. You've just said yourself about your feeling for marriage. But you are *so* young!" She gazed at him with compassionate, half-smiling moistened look, as though there were something deformed about being *so* young. A way she had was to treat anything that obviously pointed to her as the object of pity, as though it manifestly indicated, on the contrary, *him.* "Yes, Sorbet, you are right," she finished briskly. "I think it would be *madness* for us to marry!"

A suggestion that their leisurely journey towards marriage was perhaps a mistake was at once seriously, and with conviction far surpassing that he had ventured on, taken up by her. She would immediately call a halt, pitch tents preliminary to turning back. A pause was necessary before beginning the return journey. Next day they would be jogging on again in the same disputed direction.

Tarr now saw at once what had happened. His good words had been lost, all except his confession to a weakness for the matronly blandishments of Matrimony. He had an access of stupid, brief, and blatant laughter.

As people have wondered what was at the core of the world, basing their speculations on what deepest things occasionally emerge, with violence, at its holes, so Bertha often conjectured what might be at the heart of Tarr. Laughter was the most apparently central substance that, to her knowledge, had incontrollably appeared. She had often heard *grondements,* grumblings, quite literally, and seen unpleasant lights, belonging, she knew, to other categories of matter. But they never broke cover.

At present this gaiety was interpreted as proof that she had been right. There was nothing in what he had said. It had been only one of his bad fits of rebellion.

But laughter Tarr felt was retrogression. Laughter must be given up. He must in some way, for both their sakes, lay at once the foundations of an ending.

For a few minutes he played with the idea of affecting her weapons. Perhaps it was not only impossible to overcome, but even to approach, or to be said to be on the same field with, this peculiar amazon, without such uniformity of engines of attack or defence. Should not he get himself a mask like hers at once, and follow suit with some emphatic sentence? He stared uncertainly at her. Then he sprang to his feet. He intended, as far as he could see beyond this passionate movement (for he must give himself up to the mood, of course) to pace the room. But his violence jerked out of him a shout of laughter. He went stamping about the floor roaring with reluctant mirth. It would not come out properly, too, except the first outburst.

"Ay. That's right! Go on! Go on!" Bertha's patient irony seemed to gibe.

This laughter left him vexed with himself, like a fit of tears. "Humour and pathos are such near twins, that Humour may be exactly described as the most feminine attribute of man, and the only one of which women show hardly any trace! Jokes are like snuff, a slatternly habit," said Tarr to Butcher once, "whereas tragedy (and tears) is like tobacco, much drier and cleaner. Comedy being always the embryo of Tragedy, the directer nature weeps. Women are of course directer than men. But they have not the same resources."

Butcher blinked. He thought of his resources, and remembered his inclination to tears.

Tarr's disgust at this electric rush of sound made him turn it on her. He was now put at a fresh disadvantage. How could he ever succeed in making Bertha believe that a person who laughed immoderately meant what he said? Under the shadow of this laugh all his ensuing acts or words must toil, discredited in advance.

Desperately ignoring accidents, he went back beyond his first explosion, and attacked its cause—indicting Bertha, more or less, as responsible for the disturbance.

He sat down squarely in front of her, hardly breathed from his paroxysm, getting launched without transition. He hoped, by rapid plunging from one state to another, to take the wind out of the laugh's sails. It should be left towering, spectral, but becalmed, behind.

"I don't know from which side to approach you, Bertha. You frequently complain of my being thoughtless and spoilt. But your uncorked solemnity is far more frivolous than anything I can manage.—Excuse me, of course, for speaking in this way!—Won't you come down from your pedestal just for a few minutes?" And he "sketched," in French idiom, a gesture, as though offering her his hand.

"My dear Sorbert, I feel far from being on any pedestal! There's too little of the pedestal, if anything, about me. Really, Sorbet," (she leant towards him with an abortive movement as though to take his hand) "I *am* your friend; *believe me*!" (Last words very quick, with nod of head and blink of eyes.) "You worry yourself far too much. Don't do so. You are in no way bound to me. If you think we should part—*let us part*!"

The "let us part!" was precipitate, strenuous Prussian, almost truculent.

Tarr thought: "Is it cunning, stupidity, disease or what?"

She continued of a sudden, shunting on to another track of generosity:

"But I agree. Let us be franker. We waste too much time talking, talking. You are different to-day, Sorbet. What is it? If you have met somebody else—"

"If I had I'd tell you. There is besides *nobody else* to meet. You are unique!"

"Some one's been saying something to you—"

"No. I've been saying something to somebody else. But it's the same thing."

With half-incredulous, musing, glimmering stare she drew in her horns.

Tarr meditated. "I should have known that. I am asking her for something that she sees no reason to give up. Next her *goût* for me, it is the most valuable thing she possesses. It is indissolubly mixed up with the *goût*. The poor heightened self she laces herself into is the only consolation for *me* and all the troubles I spring on her. And I ask her brutally to 'come down from her pedestal.' I owe even a good deal to that pedestal, I expect, as regards her *goût*. This blessed protection Nature has given her, I, a minute or two before leaving her, make a last inept attempt to capture or destroy. Her good sense is contemptuous and indignant. It is only in defence of this ridiculous sentimentality that she has ever shown her teeth. This illusion has enabled her to bear things so long. It now stands ready with Indian impassibility to manœuvre her over the falls or rapids of Parting. The scientific thing to do, I suppose, my intention being generous, would be to flatter and increase in some way this idea of herself. I should give her some final and extraordinary opportunity of being 'noble.'"

He looked at her a moment, in search of inspiration.

"I must not be too vain. I exaggerate the gravity of the hit. As to my attempted rape—see how I square up when she shows signs of annexing *my* illusion. We are really the whole time playing a game of grabs and dashes at each other's fairy vestment of Imagination. Only hers makes her very fond of me, whereas mine makes me see any one but her. Perhaps this is why I have not been more energetic in my prosecution of the game, and have allowed her to remain in her savage semi-naked state of pristine balderdash. Why has she never tried to modify herself in direction of my 'taste'? From not daring to leave this protective fanciful self, while I still kept all *my* weapons? Then her initiative. She does nothing it is the man's place to do. She remains 'woman' as she would say. Only she is so intensely alive in her passivity, so maelstromlike in her surrender, so cataclysmic in her sacrifice, that very little remains to be done. The man's position is a mere sinecure. Her charm for me."

To cover reflection, he set himself to finish lunch. The strawberries were devoured mechanically, with unhungry itch to clear the plate. He had become just a devouring-machine, restless if any of the little red balls still remained in front of it.

Bertha's eyes sought to carry her out of this Present. But they had broken down, depositing her, so to speak, somewhere half-way down the avenue.

Tarr got up, a released automaton, and walked to the cloth-covered box where he had left his hat and stick. Then he returned in some way dutifully and obediently to the same seat, sat there for a minute, hat on knee. He had gone over and taken it up without thinking. He only realized, once back, what it meant. Nothing was settled, he had so far done more harm than good. The presence of the hat and stick on his knees, however, was like the holding open of the front door already. Anything said with them there could only be like words said as an afterthought, on the threshold. It was as though, hat on head, he were standing with his hand on the door-knob, about to add some trifle to a thing already fixed. He got up, walked back to where he had picked up the hat and stick, placed them as they were before, then returned to the window.

What should be done now? He seemed to have played all his fifty-two cards. Everything to "be done" looked behind him, not awaiting him at all. That passive pose of Bertha's was not encouraging. It had lately withstood stoically a good deal, was quite ready to absorb still more. There was something almost pugnacious in so much resignation.

But when she looked up at him there was no sign of combat. She appeared stilled to something simple again, by some fluke of a word. For the second time that day she had jumped out of her skin.

Her heart beat in a delicate, exhausted way, her eyelids became moistened underneath, as she turned to her unusual fiancé. They had wandered, she felt, into a drift of silence that hid a distant and unpleasant prospect at the end of it. It seemed suddenly charged with some alarming fancy that she could not grasp. There was something more unusual than her fiancé. The circular storm, in her case, was returning.

"Well, Sorbet?"

"Well. What is it?"

"Why don't you go? I thought you'd gone. It seems so funny to see you standing there. What are you staring at me for?"

"Don't be silly."

She looked down with a wild demureness, her head on one side.

Her mouth felt some distance from her brain. Her voice stood on tiptoe like a dwarf to speak. She became very much impressed by her voice, and was rather afraid to say anything more. Had she fainted? Sorbert was a stranger. The black stubble on his chin and brown neck appeared like the symptoms of a disease that repelled her. She noticed something criminal and quick in his eyes. She became nervous, as though she had admitted somebody too trustingly to her rooms. This fancy played on her hysteria, and she really wanted him to go.

"Why don't you go?" she repeated, in a pleasant voice.

Tarr remained silent, seemingly determined not to answer.

Meantime he looked at her with a doubtful dislike.

What is *love*? he began reasoning. It is either *possession* or a possessive madness. In the case of men and women, it is the obsession of a personality. He had presumably been endowed with the power of awaking love in her. He had something to accuse himself of. He had been *afraid of giving up* or repudiating this particular madness. To give up another person's love is a mild suicide; like a very bad inoculation as compared to the full disease. His tenderness for Bertha was due to her having purloined some part of himself, and covered herself superficially with it as a shield. Her skin at least was Tarr. She had captured a bit of him, and held it as a hostage. She was rapidly transforming herself, too, into a slavish dependency. She worked with all the hypocrisy of a great instinct.

People can wound by loving; the sympathy of this affection is interpenetrative. Love performs its natural miracle, and they become part of us; it is a dismemberment to cast them off. Our own blood flows out after them when they go.

Or love was a malady; it was dangerous to live with those consumed by it. He felt an uneasiness. Might not a wasting and restlessness ensue? It would not, if he caught it, be recognizable as love. Perhaps he had already got it slightly. That might account for his hanging about her. He evidently was suffering from something that came from Bertha.

Everybody, however, all personality, was catching. We all are sicknesses for each other. Such contact as he had with Bertha was particularly risky. Their photographs he had just been looking at displayed an unpleasant solidarity. Was it necessary to allege "love" at all? The word was superfluous in his case. The fact was before him.

He felt suddenly despondent and afraid of the Future. He had fallen beneath a more immediate infection.

He looked attentively round the room. His memory already ached. She had loved him with all this. She had loved him with the plaster cast of Beethoven, attacked him with the Klingers, ambushed him from the Breton jars, in a funny, superficial, absorbing way. Her madness had muddled everything with his ideal existence. It wasn't like leaving an ordinary room you had spent pleasant hours in and would regret. You would owe nothing to that, and it could not pursue you with images of wrong. This room he was wronging, and left it in a different way. She seemed, too, so humble in it, or through it. The appeal of the *little* again. If he could only escape from *scale*. The price of preoccupation with the large was this perpetual danger from the *little*. He wished he could look coldly on mere littleness, and not want to caress and protect it when it was human. Brutality was no doubt necessary for people like him. Love was too new to him. He was not inoculated enough with love.

He had callously been signing his name to a series of brutalities, then, as though he were sure that when the time came he would have a quite sufficient stock of coldness to meet these debts. Yet he had known from the first that he had not. Eventually he would have to evade them or succumb. The flourishes of the hand and mind had caused Bertha's mute and mournful attitude. She thought she knew him, but was amazed at his ignorance or pretence.

So he had now brought this new element into relief. For the last hour he had been accumulating difficulties, or rather unearthing some new one at every step. Impossible to tackle *en masse*, they were all there before him. The thought of "settling everything before he went," now appeared monstrous. He had, anyhow, started these local monsters and demons, fishing them to the light. Each had a different vocal explosiveness or murmur, inveighing unintelligibly against each other. The only thing to be done was to herd them all together and march them away for inspection at leisure.

Sudden herdsman, with the care of a delicate and antediluvian flock; well!—But what was Bertha to be told? Nothing. He would file out silently with his flock, without any hornblasts or windings such as he customarily affected.

"I am going now," he said at last, getting up.

She looked at him with startled interest.

"You are leaving me, Sorbet?"

"No. At least, now I am going." He stooped down for his hat and cane. "I will come and see you to-morrow or the day after."

Closing the door quietly, with a petty carefulness, he crossed the passage, belittled and guilty. He did not wish to escape this feeling. It would be better to enhance it. For a moment it occurred to him to go back and offer marriage. It was about all he had to offer. He was ashamed of his only gift! But he did not stop, he opened the front door and went downstairs. Something raw and uncertain he seemed to have built up in the room he had left. How long would it hold together? Again he was acting in secret, his errand and intentions kept to himself. Something followed him like a restless dog.

PART II
DOOMED, EVIDENTLY. THE "FRAC"

CHAPTER I

From his window in the neighbouring boulevard Kreisler's eye was fixed blankly on a spot thirty feet above the scene of the Hobson-Tarr dialogue. He was shaving himself, one eye fixed on Paris. It beat on this wall of Paris drearily. Had it been endowed with properties of illumination and been directed there earlier in the day, it would have served as a desolate halo for Tarr's ratiocination. For several days Kreisler's watch had been in the Mont de Piété. Until some clock struck he was in total ignorance of the time of day.

The late spring sunshine flooded, like a bursted tepid star, the pink boulevard. The people beneath crawled like wounded insects of cloth. A two-story house terminating the Boulevard Pfeiffer covered the lower part of the Café Berne.

Kreisler's room looked like some funeral vault. Shallow, ill-lighted, and extensive, it was placarded with nude and archaic images, painted on strips of canvas fixed to the wall with drawing-pins. Imagining yourself in some Asiatic dwelling of the dead, with the portraits of the deceased covering the holes in which they had respectively been thrust, you would, following your fancy, have turned to Kreisler seeking to see in him some devout recluse who had taken up his quarters there.

Kreisler was in a sense a recluse (although almost certainly the fancy would have gasped and fallen at his contact). But cafés were the luminous caverns where he could be said, most generally, to dwell; with, nevertheless, very little opening of the lips and much *recueillement* or meditation; therefore not unworthy of some rank among the inferior and less fervent solitudes.

A bed like an overturned cupboard, dark, and with a red billow of cloth and feathers covering it entirely; a tesselated floor of dark red tile; a little rug, made with paint, carpet, cardboard, and horse-hair, to represent a leopard—these, with chair, washstand, easel, and several weeks' of slowly drifting and shifting garbage, completed its contents.

Kreisler flicked the lather on to a crumpled newspaper, with an irresponsible gesture. Each time his razor was raised he looked at himself with a peering vacancy. His face had long become a piece of troublesome meat. Life did not each day deposit an untidiness that could be whisked off by a Gillette blade, as Nature did its stubble.

His face, it is true, wore like a uniform the frowning fixity of the Prussian warrior. But it was such a rig-out as the Captain of Koepenich must have worn, and would take in nobody but a Teutonic squad. The true German seeks every day, by little acts of boorishness, to keep fresh this trenchant Prussian attitude; just as the German student, with his weekly routine of duels, keeps courage simmering in times of peace, that it may instantly boil up to war pitch at the least sign from his Emperor.

He brushed his clothes in a sulky, vigorous way, like a silent, discontented domestic of a shabby, lonely master. He cleaned his glasses with the absorption and tenderness of the short-sighted. Next moment he was gazing through them, straddled on his flat Slav nose—brushing up whimsical moustaches over pouting mouth. This was done with two tiny ivory brushes taken out of a small leather case—present from a fiancée who had been alarmed that his moustaches showed an unpatriotic tendency to droop.

This old sweetheart just then disagreeably occupied his mind. But he busied himself about further items of toilet with increased precision. To a knock he answered with careful "Come in." He did not take his eyes from the glass, spotted blue tie being pinched into position. He watched with impassibility above and around his tie the entrance of a young woman.

"Good morning. So you're up already," she said in French.

He treated her as coolly as he had his thoughts. Appearing just then, she gave his manner towards the latter something human to play on, with relief. Imparting swanlike undulations to a short stout person, eye fixed quizzingly on Kreisler's in the glass, she advanced. Her manner was one seldom sure of welcome, a little deprecatingly aggressive. She owned humorously a good-natured face with protruding eyes, gesticulated with, filling her silences with explosive significance. Brows always raised. A soul made after the image of injuries. A skin which would become easily blue in cold weather was matched with a taste in dress inveterately blue. The Pas de Calais had somehow produced her. Paris, shortly afterwards, had put the mark of its necessitous millions on a mean, lively child.

"Are you going to work to-day?" came in a minute or two.

"No," he replied, putting his jacket on. "Do you want me to?"

"It would be of certain use. But don't put yourself out," with grin tightening all the skin of her face, making it pink and bald and her eyes drunken.

"I'm afraid I can't." Watched with sort of appreciative raillery, he got down on his knees and dragged a portmanteau from beneath the bed. "Susanna, what can I get on that?" he asked simply, as of an expert.

"Ah, that's where we are? You want to pawn this? I don't know, I'm sure. Perhaps they'd give you fifteen francs. It's good leather."

"Perhaps twenty?" he asked. "I must have them!" he clamoured of a sudden, with energy that astonished her.

She grimaced, looked very serious; said, "Je ne sais pas, vous savez!" with several vigorous, yet rhythmical and rich, forward movements of the head. She became the broker: Kreisler was pressing for a sum in excess of regulations. Not for the world, any more than had she been the broker in fact, would she have valued it at a penny over what it seemed likely to fetch.

"Je ne sais pas, vous savez!" she repeated. She looked even worried. She would have liked to please Kreisler by saying more, but her business conscience prevented her.

"Well, we'll go together."

This conversation was carried on strictly in dialect. Suzanne understood him, for she was largely responsible for the lingo in which Kreisler carried on conversation with the French. This young woman had no fixed occupation. She disappeared for periods to live with men. She sat as a model.

"Your father hasn't sent yet?" He shook his head.

"Le cochon!" she stuttered.

"But it will come to-morrow, or the day after, anyway." The idiosyncrasies of these monthly letters were quite familiar to her. The dress-clothes had been pawned by her on a former occasion.

"What do you need twenty francs for?"

"I must have, not twenty, but twenty-five."

Her silence was as eloquent as face-muscles and eye-fluid could make it.

"To get the dress-clothes out," he explained, fixing her stolidly with his eye.

She first smiled slowly, then allowed her ready mirth to grow, by mechanical stages, into laughter. The presence of this small, indifferent, and mercenary acquaintance irritated him. But he remained cool. Just then a church clock began striking. He foreboded it was already ten, but not later. It struck ten and then eleven. He leapt the hour—the clock seemed rushing with him, in a second, to the more advanced hour—without any flurry, quite calmly. Then it struck twelve. He at once absorbed that further hour as he had the former. He lived an hour as easily and carelessly as he would have lived a second. Could it have gone on striking he would have swallowed, without turning a hair, twenty, thirty strokes!

Going out with Suzanne, he turned the key carefully in the door. The concierge or landlord might slip in and fire his things out in his absence.

The portmanteau, whisked up from the floor, flopped along with him like a child's slack balloon. He frowned at Suzanne and, prepared for surprises, went warily down the stairs.

He had felt a raw twinge of anger as he had opened the door, looking down at the first boards of his room. A half an hour before, on waking, he had sat up in bed and gazed at the crevice at its foot where a letter, thrust underneath by the concierge, usually lay. He had stared as though it had been a shock to find nothing. That little square of rich bright white paper was what he had counted on night to give him—that he had expected to find on waking, as though it were a secretion of those long hours. It made him feel that there had been no night—long, fecund, rich in surprises—but merely a barren moment of sleep. A stale and garish continuation of yesterday, no fresh day at all, had dawned. The chill and phlegmatic appearance of his room annoyed him. It was its inhospitable character that repelled the envelope pregnant with revolutionary joy and serried German marks. Its dead unchangeableness must preclude all innovation. This spell of monotony on his life he could not break. The room cut him off from the world. He gazed around as a man may eye a wife whom he suspects of intercepting his correspondence. There was no reason why the letter with his monthly remittance should have come on that particular morning, already eight days overdue.

"If I had a father like yours!" said Suzanne in menacing, humorous sing-song, eyes bulging and head nodding. At this vista of perpetual blackmail she fell into a reverie.

"Never get your father off on your fiancée, Suzanne!" Kreisler advised in reply.

"Comment?" Suzanne did not understand, and pulled a sour face.

"I had a fiancée."

"Oui. Très bien. Tu t'es brouillé avec elle?"

"I have quarrelled with her; yes. She married my father. Or I married her, I may say, to my father. That was a mistake."

"I believe you! That, as you say, was careless! You don't get on well with her?"

"I never see her."

"You never go home?"

Kreisler was too proud to reply to Suzanne very often. He marched on, staring severely ahead.

"How long ago is it that you—how long have you had that stepmother?"

"My father married four years ago."

"Married your—girl—?"

"That's it."

"And that's why you have trouble? She makes the trouble. She is at the bottom of the trouble? Ah! You never told me that. Now I understand why. What's she like? Is she nice?"

"Not bad."

They got near the Berne.

"Let's have a cup of coffee," Kreisler said.

Suzanne sat down—with the hiding of her red hands, her guilty lofty silence, eyebrows raised as though with a slimy pescine enamel, inducing an impression of nefarious hurry and impermanence. Kreisler was sour and full of himself. His bag looked as though it should hold the properties or merchandise of some illicit trade or amusement.

Suzanne seemed to triumph at this information.

She pressed and pressed in breathless undertone, fascinated by something. Family dramas, of all dramas, she had the expertest interest in.

"You remember the time I had to send three letters to the old devil—?"

"Of course! Three months ago, you mean?" Suzanne had taken a near and serious interest in Otto's financial arrangements. She remembered dates well, apart from that.

Otto did not proceed for some time. She stared quizzingly and patiently past the tip of his nose.

"He then asked me to give up art. He told me of two posts in German firms that were vacant. That was her doing, the swine! One was a station-restaurant business."

"You refused!"

"I didn't reply at all."

In this his methods were very similar to his father's. The elder Kreisler had repeatedly infuriated his son, calculating on such effect, by sending his allowance only when written for, and even then neglecting his appeal for several days. It came frequently wrapped up in bits of newspapers, and his letters of demand and expostulation were never answered. On two occasions forty marks and thirty marks respectively had been deducted, merely as an irritative measure.

"Dîtes! Why don't you write to your stepmother?"

"Write to her? No, I won't write to her."

"P'raps she wants you to. I should. Why don't you write to her?"

"I shall before—I shall some day!"

"Before what?"

"Oh, before—"

Suzanne once more glimmered into the absurd distance.

"He will send, I suppose?"

"Now—? Yes, I suppose sooner or later it will turn up."

"If it didn't what would you do? You think it's your stepmother who does it? Why don't you manage her? You are stupid. You must allow me to tell you that."

Kreisler knew the end was not far off; this might be it. So much the better!

Kreisler's student days—a lifetime in itself—had unfitted him, at the age of thirty-six, for practically anything. He had only lost one picture so far. This senseless solitary purchase depressed him whenever he thought of it. How dreary that cheque for four pounds ten was! Who could have bought it? It sold joylessly and fatally one day in an exhibition.

CHAPTER II

Nine months previously Kreisler had arrived in Paris at the Gare de Lyon, from Italy. He had left Rome, according to his account, because the Italian creditor is such a bad-tempered fellow, and he could never get any sleep after 8—or latterly 7.30—even, in the morning.

> "Dear Colleague,—Expect me Thursday. I am at last quitting this wretched city. I hope that the room you mentioned is still free. Will come at once to your address. With many hearty greetings,—Yours,
>
> Otto Kreisler."

He had dispatched this note before leaving to a Herr Ernst Volker.—For some time he stood on the Paris platform, ulster thrown back, smoking a lean cigar, with a straw stuck in it. He was glad to be in Paris. How busy the women, intent on travel, were! Groups of town-folk, not travellers, stood like people at a show. Each traveller was met by a phalanx of uninterested faces beyond the gangway.

His standing on the platform was a little ceremonious and military. He was taking his bearings. Body and belongings with him were always moved about with certain strategy. At last, with racial menace, he had his things swept together, saying heavily:

"Un viagre!"

Ernst Volker was not in, but had left word he would be there after dinner. It was in a pension. He rented a studio as well in the garden behind. The house was rather like a French Public Baths, two-storied, of a dirty purple colour. Kreisler looked up at it and felt that a very public sort of people must live there, looking big and idle in their rooms and constantly catching the eye of the stranger on the pavement. He was led to the studio in rear of the house, and asked to wait.

He turned round several long canvases and was astonished to find dashing ladies in large hats before him.

"Ha ha! Well, I'm damned! Bravo, Ernst!" he exploded in his dull solitude, extremely amused.

Volker had not done this in Rome.—Even there he had given indications of latent virtuosity, but had been curbed by classic presences. Since arriving in Paris he had blossomed prodigiously. He dealt out a vulgar vitality by the peck to each sitter, and they forgave him for making them comparatively "ugly." He flung a man or woman on to nine feet of canvas and pummelled them on it for a couple of hours, until they promised to remain there or were incapable of moving, so to speak. He had never been able to treat people like this in any other way of life, and was grateful to painting for the experience. He always appeared to feel he would be expected to apologize for his brutal behaviour as an artist, and was determined not to do so.

A half-hour later, on his return, the servant told him somebody was waiting in the studio. With face not exhibiting joyful surprise, but rather the collected look of a man of business arriving at his office, he walked out quickly across the garden.

When he saw Kreisler the business look disappeared. Nothing of his private self remained for the moment, all engulfed in his friend's personality.

"But, Ernst! What beautiful pictures! What pleasant company you left me to wait amongst!—How are you? I am glad to see you again!"

"Had a good journey? Your letter amused me!—So Rome became too hot?"

"A little! My dear chap, it was eine ganz verdammte klemme! In this last scuffle I lost—but I *lost*!—half the clothes off my back! But chiefly Italian clothes; that is fortunate!"

"Why didn't you write?"

"Oh, it wasn't serious enough to call for help." He dismissed the out-of-date notion at once!—"This is a nice place you've got."—Kreisler looked round as though measuring it. He noticed Volker's discomfort. He felt he was examining something more intimate than the public aspect of a dwelling. It was as though his friend were expecting a wife, whom Kreisler had not met, to turn up suddenly.

"Have you dined?—I waited until eight. Have you...?"

"I should like something to eat. Can we get anything here?"

"I'm afraid not.—It's rather late for this neighbourhood. Let's take these things to your room—on the way—and go to the Grands Boulevards."

They stayed till the small hours of the morning, in the midst of "Paris by Night" of the German bourgeois imagination, drinking champagne and toasting the creditors Kreisler had left behind in Rome.

Kreisler, measured by chairs or doors, was of immoderate physical humanity. He was of that select section, corporally, that exceed the mean. His long round thighs stuck out like poles. This large body lounged and poised beside Volker in massive control and over-reaching of civilized matter. It was in Rome or in Paris. It had an air of possession everywhere. Volker was stranger in Paris than his companion, who had only just arrived. He felt a little raw and uncomfortable, almost a tourist. He was being shown "Paris by Night"; almost literally, for his inclinations had not taken him much to that side of the town.

Objects—cocottes, newsvendors, waiters—flowed through Kreisler's brain without trouble or surprise. His heavy eyes were big gates of a self-centred city. It was just a procession. There was no trade in the town.

He was a property of Nature, or a favourite slave, untidy and aloof. Kreisler so real and at home was like a ghost sitting there beside him, for Ernst Volker. He had not had the time to solidify yet in Paris by all rights, and yet was so solid and accustomed at once. *This body was in Paris now!*—with an heroic freedom.

Volker began looking for himself. He was only made of cheap thin stuff. He picked up the pieces quietly. This large rusty machine of a man smashed him up like an egg-shell at every meeting. His shell grew quickly again, but never got hard enough.

He was glad to see him again! Kreisler was a good fellow.—Despite himself Ernst Volker was fidgety at the lateness of the hour. The next day Fräulein Bodenaar, who was sitting for him, was due at 9.30. But the first night of seeing his friend again—He drank rather more than usual, and became silent, thinking of his Westphalian home and his sister who was not very well. She had had a bicycle accident, and had received a considerable shock. He might spend the summer with her and his mother at Berck-sur-Mer or Calais. He would have gone home for a week or so now, only an aunt he did not like was staying there.

"Well, let's get back!" said Kreisler, rather thoughtful, too, at all the life he had seen.

CHAPTER III

In Paris Ernst Volker had found himself. It seemed especially constructed for him, such a wonderful, large, polite institution. No one looked at him because he was small. For money in Paris represented delicate things, in Germany chiefly gross ones. His money lent him more stature than anything else could, and in a much more dignified and subtle way than elsewhere. His talent benefited for the first time by his money. Heavy temperament, primitive talent, had their big place, but money had at last come into its own and got into the spiritual sphere. A very sensible and soothing spirit reigned in this seat of intelligence. A very great number of sensible, well-dressed figures perambulated all over these suave acres. Large tribes of "types" prosecuted their primitive enthusiasms in certain cafés, unannoyed by either the populace or the differently minded élite. The old romantic values he was used to in his Fatherland were all deeply modified. Money—that is luck and its power—was the genius of the new world. American clothes were adapted for the finer needs of the Western European.

On the evening following Kreisler's arrival Volker had an engagement. The morning after that Kreisler turned up at half-past twelve. Volker was painting Fräulein Bodenaar. She was very smartly dressed, in a tight German way. He displayed a disinclination to make Kreisler and his sitter acquainted. He was a little confused. They arranged to meet at dinner-time. He was going to lunch with Fräulein Bodenaar.

Kreisler the night before had spent a good deal of money in the German paradise beyond the river. Volker understood by the particular insistent blankness of Kreisler's eye that money was needed. He was familiar with this look. Kreisler owed him fifteen hundred marks. He had at first made an effort to pay back Volker money borrowed, when his allowance arrived. But in Rome, and earlier for a short time in Münich, his friend's money was not of so much value as it was at present. Ernst waived repayment in an eager, sentimental way. The debt grew. Kreisler had felt keenly the financial void caused by Volker's going off to Paris. He had not formulated to himself the real reason of his following Volker. Nor had he taken the trouble to repudiate it. He was now in the position of a man separated for some months from his wife. He was in a luxurious hurry to see once more the colour of Volker's gold.

Kreisler was very touchy about money, like many borrowers. He sponged with discrimination. He had not for some time required to sponge at all, as Volker amply met his needs. So he had got rather out of practice. He found this reopening of his account with little friend Ernst a most delicate business. It was worse than tackling a stranger. He realized there might be a modification of Volker's readiness to lend. He therefore determined to ask for a sum in advance of actual needs, and by boldness at once re-establish continuity.

After dinner he said:

"You remember Ricci? Where I got my paints the first part of the time. I had some trouble with that devil before I left. He came round and made a great scandal on the staircase. He shouted 'Bandit! Ha! ha! Sporca la tua Madonna!'—how do you say it?—'Sporco Tedesco.' Then he called the neighbours to witness. He kept repeating he was 'not afraid of me.' I took him by the ear and kicked him out!" he ended with florid truculence.

Volker laughed obsequiously but with discomfort. Kreisler solicited his sympathetic mirth with a masterful eye. He laughed himself, unnecessarily heartily. A scene of violence in which a small man was hustled, which Volker would have to applaud, was a clever prelude. Then Otto began to be nice.

"I am sorry for the little devil! I shall have the money soon. I shall send it him. He shall not suffer. Antonio, too. I don't owe much. I had to settle most before I left. Himmel! My landlord!" He choked mirthfully over his coffee a little, almost upsetting it, then mincingly adjusted the cup to his moustached lips.

If he had to *settle up* before he left, he could not have much now, evidently! There was a disagreeable pause.

Volker stirred his coffee. He immediately showed his hand, for he looked up and with transparent innocence asked:

"By the way, Otto, you remember Blauenstein at Münich—?"

"You mean the little Jew from whom everybody used to borrow money?" Kreisler fixed him severely and significantly with his eye and spoke with heavy deliberation.

"Did people borrow money from him? I had forgotten. Yes, that's the man. He has turned up here; who do you think with? With Irma, the Bohemian girl. They are living together—round the corner there."

"Hum! Are they? She was a pretty little girl. Do you remember the night Von Gerarde was found stripped and tied to his door handle? He assured me Irma had done it and had pawned his clothes."

Was Volker thinking that Blauenstein's famous and admitted function should be resorted to as an alternative for himself by Kreisler?

"Volker, I can speak to you plainly; isn't that so? You are my friend. What's more, already we have—" he laughed strongly and easily. "My journey has cost the devil of a lot. I shall be getting my allowance in a week or so. Could you lend me a small sum of money. When my money comes—"

"Of course! But I am hard up. How much—?" These were three jerky efforts.

"Oh, a hundred and fifty or two hundred marks."

Volker's jaw dropped.

"I am afraid, my dear Kreisler, I can't—just now—manage that. My journey, too, cost me a lot. I'm very sorry. Let me see. I have my rent next week? I don't see how I can manage—"

Volker had a clean-shaven, depressed, and earnest face. He had always been honest and timid.

Kreisler looked sulkily at the tablecloth and knocked the ash sharply off his cigarette into his cup.

He said nothing. Volker became nervous.

"Will a hundred marks be of any use?"

"Yes." Kreisler drew his hand over his chin as though stroking a beard down and then pulled his moustaches up, fixing the waitress with an indifferent eye. "Can you spare that?"

"Well—I can't really. But if you are in such a position that—"

This is how he lost Volker. He felt that hundred marks, given him as a favour, was the last serious bite he would get. He only gradually realized of how much more worth Volker's money now was, and what before was an unorganized mass of specie, in which the professional borrower could wallow, was now a sound and suitably conducted business. He met that night the new manager.

He was taken round to the Berne after dinner. He did not realize what awaited him. He found himself in the head-quarters of many national personalities. Politeness reigned. Kreisler was pleased to find a permanent vat of German always on tap. His roots mixed sluggishly with Ernst's in this living lump of the soil of the Fatherland dumped down at the head of the Boulevard Pfeiffer.

The Germans he met here spoke a language and expressed opinions he could not agree with, but with which Volker evidently did. They argued genially over glasses of beer and champagne. He found his ticket at once. He was the *vielle barbe* of the party.

"Yes, I've seen Gauguins. But why go so far as the South Sea Islands unless you are going to make people more beautiful? Why go out of Europe? Why not save the money for the voyage?" he would bluster.

"More beautiful? What do you understand by the word 'beautiful,' my dear sir?" would answer a voice in the service of new movements.

"What do I call beautiful? How would you like your face to be as flat as a pancake, your nostrils like a squashed strawberry, one of your eyes cocked up by the side of your ear? Would not you be very unhappy to look like that? Then how can you expect any one but a technique-maniac to care a straw for a picture of that sort—call it Cubist or Fauve or whatever you like? It's all spoof. It puts money in somebody's pocket, no doubt."

"It's not a question, unhappily, of how we should *like* our faces to be. *It is how they are.* But I do not consider the actual position of my eyes to be any more *beautiful* than any other position that might have been chosen for them. The almond eye was long held in contempt by the hatchet-eye—"

Kreisler peered up at him and laughed. "You're a modest fellow. You're not as ugly as you think! Nach! I like to find—"

"But you haven't told us, Otto, what you call *beautiful.*"

"I call this young lady here"—and he turned gallantly to a blushing cocotte at his side—"*beautiful*, very beautiful!" He kissed her amid gesticulation and applause.

"That's just what I supposed," his opponent said with appreciation.

He did not get on well with Soltyk. Louis Soltyk was a young Russian, half Polish, who occasionally sat amongst the Germans at the Berne. Volker saw more of him than anybody. It was he who had superseded Kreisler in the position of influence as regards Volker's purse. Soltyk did not borrow a hundred marks. His system was far more up to date. Ernst had experienced an unpleasant shock in coming into contact with Kreisler's clumsy and slovenly, small-scale money habits again! Soltyk physically bore, distantly and with polish, a resemblance to Kreisler. His handsome face and elegance were very different. Kreisler and he disliked each other for obscure physiological reasons: they had perhaps scrapped in the dressing-rooms of creation for some particular fleshly covering, and each secured only fragments of a coveted garment. In some ways, then, Soltyk was his efficient and more accomplished counterpart, although as empty and unsatisfactory as himself.

"Aber wo ist der deutsche Student?" Soltyk would ask, referring to him usually like that.

"He's in good company somewhere!" Volker revealed Kreisler as a lady's man. This satisfied Soltyk's antipathy. The Russian kept an eye on Volker's pocket while Kreisler was about. He had not only recognized in him a mysterious and vexing kinship, with his instinct; his sharper's sense, also, noted the signs of the professional borrower, the most contemptible and slatternly member of the crook family. In an access of sentiment Ernst asked his new friend to try and sell a painting of Kreisler's. Soltyk dealt in paintings and art objects. But Soltyk took him by the lapel of the coat and in a few words steadied him into cold sense.

"Non! Sois pas bête! Here," he pulled out a handful of money and chose a dollar-piece. "Here—give him this. You buy a *picture*—if it's a picture you want to buy—of Krashunine's. Kreisler has nothing but *Kreisler* to offer. C'est peu!"

Ernst introduced Kreisler next to another sort of Paris compatriot. It was a large female contingent this time. He took him round to Fräulein Lipmann's on her evening, when these ladies played the piano and met.

Kreisler felt that he was a victim of strategy. He puffed and swore outside, complained of their music, the coffee, their way of dressing.

The Lipmann circle could have stood as a model for Tarr's Bourgeois-Bohemians, stood for a group.

For chief characteristic this particular Bourgeois-Bohemian set had the inseparability of its members. Should a man, joining them, wish to flirt with one particularly, he must flirt with all—flatter all, take all to the theatre, carry the umbrellas and paint-boxes of all. Eventually, should he come to that, it is doubtful if a proposition of marriage could be made otherwise than before the assembled band! And marriage alone could wrench the woman chosen away from the clinging bunch.

Kreisler, despite his snorting, went again with Volker. The female charm had done its work. This gregarious female personality had shown such frank invitation to Volker that had any separate woman exhibited half as hospitable a front he would have been very alarmed. As it was, it had at first just fulfilled certain bourgeois requirements of his lonely German soul. Kreisler came a few weeks running to the Lipmann soirée. Never finding Volker there, he left off going as well. He felt he had been tricked and slighted. The ladies divined what had happened. Fräulein Lipmann, the leader, put a spiteful little mark down to each of their names.

CHAPTER IV

Kreisler pocketed Ernst's hundred marks and made no further attempt on the formerly hospitable income of his friend. Debts began accumulating. Only he found he had grown suddenly timid with his creditors. The concierge frightened him. He conciliated the garçon at the café, to whom he owed money. He even paid several debts that it was quite unnecessary to pay, in a moment of panic and weakness. A straitened week ensued. At the Berne he had lost his nerve in some way; he clowned obsequiously on some evenings, and, depressed and slack the next, perhaps, resented his companions' encores.

Next he gradually developed the habit of sitting alone. More often than not he would come into the café and go to a table at the opposite side of the room to that at which the Germans were sitting.

Ridicule is sighted at twenty yards, the spectator then, without the sphere of average immediate magnetism. For once it does not matter, but if persisted in it inevitably results in humour. Those who keep to themselves awaken mirth as a cartwheel running along the road by itself would. People feel with the "lonely" man that he is going about with some eccentric companion—that is himself. Why did he choose this deaf-and-dumb companion? What do they find to say? He is ludicrous as two men would be who, perpetually in each other's company, were never seen to exchange a word—who dined together, went to theatre or café, without ever looking at each other or speaking.

So Kreisler became a lonely figure. It was a strange feeling. He must be quiet and not attract attention. He was marked in some way as though he had committed a theft. Perhaps it was merely the worry of perpetual "tick" beginning to tell. For the moment he would just put himself aside and see what happened. He was afraid of himself too. Always up till then immersed in that self, now for the first time he stood partly outside it. This slight divorce made him less sure in his actions. A little less careful of his appearance, he went sluggishly about, smoking, reading the paper a great deal, working at the art school fairly often, playing billiards with an Austrian cook whose acquaintance he had made in a café and who disappeared owing him seven francs.

Volker had been a compendious phenomenon in his life, although his cheery gold had attracted him to the more complete discovery. He had ousted women, too, from Kreisler's daily needs. He had become a superstition for his tall friend.

It was Kreisler's deadness, his absolute lack of any reason to be confident and yet perfect aplomb, that mastered his companion. But this acquired eventually its significance as well, for Kreisler. The inertia and phlegm, outward sign of depressing everyday Kreisler, had found some one for whom they were a charm and something to be envied. Kreisler's imagination woke shortly after Volker's. It was as though a peasant who had always regarded his life as the dullest affair, were suddenly inspirited about himself by realizing some townsman's poetic notion of him. Kreisler's moody wastefulness and futility had found a *raison d'être* and meaning.

Ernst Volker had remained for three vague years becalmed on this empty sea. Kreisler basked round him, never having to lift his waves and clash them together as formerly he had been forced sometimes to do. There had been no appeals to life. Volker had been the guarantor of his peace. His failure was the omen of the sinking ship, the disappearance of the rats!

Then they had never arrived at terms of friendship. It had been only an epic acquaintanceship, and Kreisler had taken him about as a parasite that he pretended not to notice.

There was no question, therefore, of a reproach at desertion. He merely hopped off on to somebody else. Kreisler was more exasperated at this than at the defection of a friend, who could be fixed down, and from whom at last explanation must come. It was an unfair advantage taken. A man had no right to accompany you in that distant and paradoxical fashion, get all he could, become ideally useful, unless it was for life.

He watched Soltyk's success with distant mockery. Volker's loves were all husks, of illogical completeness.

A man appeared one day in the Berne who had known Kreisler in Münich. The story of Kreisler's marrying his fiancée to his father then became known. Other complications were alleged in which Otto's paternity played a part. The dot of the bride was another obscure matter. It was during his aloofness. He looked the sort of man, the party agreed, who would splice his sweetheart with his papa or reinforce his papa's affairs with a dot he did not wish to pay for at last with his own person. The Berne was also informed that Kreisler had to keep seventeen children in Münich alone; that he only had to look at a woman for her to become pregnant. It was when the head of the column, the eldest of the seventeen, emerged into boyhood, requiring instruction, that Kreisler left for Rome. Since then a small society had been founded in Bavaria to care for Kreisler's offsprings throughout Germany. This great capacity of Otto's was, naturally, not admired; at the best it could be considered as a misdirected and disordered efficiency. The stories pleased, nevertheless. When he appeared that night his friends turned towards his historic figure with cries of welcome. But he was not gregarious. He missed his opportunity. He took a seat in the passage-way leading to the Bureau de Tabac. As their laughter struck him through his paper he was unstrung enough to be annoyed.

He frowned and puckered up his eyes, and two flushed lines descended from his eyes to his jaw. On their way out one or two of his compatriots greeted him:

"Sacred Otto! Why so unsociable?"

"Hush! He has much to think about. You don't understand what the cares of—"

"Come, old Otto, a drink!"

He shook them off with mixture of affected anger and genuine spitting oaths. He avoided their eyes and spat blasphemously at his beer. He avoided the café for some days.

Kreisler then recovered.

At first nothing much happened. He had just gone back again into the midst of his machinery like a bone slipped into its place, with a soft crick. He became rather more firm with his creditors. He changed his rooms (moving then to the Boulevard Pfeiffer), passed an occasional evening with the Germans at the Berne, and started a portrait of Suzanne, who had been sitting at the school.

"How is Herr Volker? Is he out of Paris?" Fräulein Lipmann asked him when they met. "Come round and see us."

People's actual or possible proceedings formed in very hard-and-fast mould in Kreisler's mind, seen not with realism, but through conventions of his suspicious irony. This solicitude as to Volker he contrasted with their probable indifference as regards his old, shabby, and impolite self.

But he went round, his reception being insipid. He had shown no signs of animation or interest in them. Both he and the ladies were rather doubtful as to why he came at all. No pleasure resulted on either side from these visits, yet they doggedly continued. A distinct and steady fall in the temperature could be observed. He sneered, as though the aimlessness of his visits were an insult that had at last been taken up. They would have been for ever discontinued except for a sudden necessity to reopen that channel of bourgeois intercourse.

CHAPTER V

On the first day of his letter being overdue, a convenient way of counting, Otto rose late, from a maze of shallow dreams, and was soon dressed, wanting to get out of his room.

As the clock struck one he slammed his door and descended the stairs alertly. The concierge, on the threshold of her "loge," peered up at him.

"Good morning, Madame Leclerc; it's a fine day," said Kreisler, in his heavy French, his cold direct gaze incongruously ornamented by a cheerful smile.

"Monsieur has got up late this morning," replied the concierge, with very faint amiability.

"Yes, I have lost all sense of time. J'ai perdu le temps! Ha ha!" He grinned mysteriously. The watch had gone the way of the dress clothes some days already.

She followed him slowly along the passage, become extremely grave. "Quel original! quel genre!" With a look of perplexed distrust she watched him down the street.—This German good humour and sudden expansiveness has always been a portentous thing to French people. Latin races are as scandalized at northern amenities, the badness of our hypocrisies or manners and total immodesty displayed, as the average man of Teutonic race is with the shameful perfection of and ease in deceit shown by the French neighbour. Kreisler, still beneath the eye of the concierge, with his rhythmic martial tread, approached the restaurant. A few steps from the threshold he slowed down, dragging his long German boots, which acted as brakes.

The Restaurant Lejeune, like many others in Paris, had been originally a clean, tranquil little creamery, consisting of a small shop a few feet either way.—Then one customer after another had become more gluttonous. He had asked, in addition to his daily glass of milk, for beefsteak and spinach, or some other terrific nourishment, which the decent little business at first supplied with timid protest. But perpetual scenes of sanguine voracity—weeks of compliance with the most brutal and unbridled appetites of man—

gradually brought about a change in its character.—It became frankly a place where the most carnivorous palate might be palled. As trade grew, the small business had burrowed backwards into the house—the victorious flood of commerce had burst through walls and partitions, flung down doors, discovered many dingy rooms in the interior that it instantly filled with serried cohorts of eaters. It had driven out terrified families, had hemmed the apoplectic concierge in her "loge," it had broken out on to the court at the back in shed-like structures. And in the musty bowels of the house it had established a broiling, luridly-lighted, roaring den, inhabited by a rushing and howling band of slatternly savages.—The chef's wife sat at a desk immediately fronting the entrance door. When a diner had finished, adding up the bill himself on a printed slip of paper, he paid it there on his way out. In the first room a tunnel-like and ill-lit recess furnished with a long table formed a cul-de-sac to the left. Into this Kreisler got. At the right-hand side the passage led to the inner rooms.

A mind feeling the need for things clean and clear cut would have been better content, although demurring, with Kreisler's military morning suit, slashed with thick seams; carefully cut hair, short behind, a little florid and bunched on the top; his German high-crowned bowler hat, and plain cane, than the Charivari of the Art-fashion and uniform of The Brush in those about him, chiefly students from the neighbouring Art schools.

He was staring at the bill of fare when some one took the seat in front of him.—He looked up, put down the card. A young woman was sitting there, who now seemed waiting, as though Kreisler might be expected, after a rest, to take up the menu again and go on reading it.

"Have you done with—? May I—?"

At the sound of her voice he moved a little forward, and in handing it to her, spoke in German.

"Danke schön," she said, smiling with a German nod of racial recognition.

He ordered his soup.—Usually this meal passed in surly impassible inspection of his neighbours and the newspaper. Staring at and through the figure in front of him, he spent several minutes. He seemed making up his mind.

"Monsieur est distrait aujourd'hui," Jeanne said, who was waiting to take his order.

Contrary to custom, he sought for some appetizing dish, to change the routine. Appetite had not woken, but he had become restless before the usual dull programme. There were certain tracts of menu he never explored. His eye always guided him at once to the familiar place where the "plat du jour" was to be found, and the alternative sweets heading the list. He now plunged his eye down the long line of unfamiliar dishes.

He fixed his eye on Jeanne with indecision too, and picked up the menu. "My vis-à-vis is pretty!" he thought.

"Lobster salad, mayonnaise, and a pommes à l'huile, Jeanne," he called out.

This awakening to beauties of the menu brought with it a survey of his neighbour. Vaguely, she must be connected with lobster salad. How could that be?

First he was surprised that such a beautiful girl should be sitting there. Beautiful people wander dangerously about in life, just like ordinary folk. He appeared to think that they should be isolated like powder magazines or lepers. This man could never leave good luck alone, or reflect that that, too, was a dangerous vagrant. He could not quite grasp that it was a *general* good luck and easily explained phenomenon.

He had already been examined by the beautiful girl. Throwing an absent far-away look into her eyes, she let them wander over him. Afterwards she cast them down into her soup. As a pickpocket, after brisk work in a crowd, hurries home to examine and evaluate his spoil, so she then examined collectedly what her dreamy eyes had noted. This method was not characteristic of her, but of the category of useful habits bequeathed us, each sex having its own. Perhaps in her cloudy soup she beheld something of the storm and shock that inhabited her neighbour.

Without preliminary reflection Kreisler found himself addressing her, a little abashed when he suddenly heard his voice, and with eerie feeling when it was answered.

"From your hesitation in choosing your lunch, gnädiges Fräulein, I suppose you have not been long in Paris?"

"No, I only arrived a week ago, from America." She settled her elbows on the table for a moment.

"Allow me to give you some idea of what the menu of this restaurant is like." This was like a lesson. He started ponderously. "At the head of each list you will find simple dishes; elemental dishes, I might call them! (Elementalische plätter!) This is the rough material from which the others are evolved. Each list is like an oriental dance. It gets wilder as it goes along. In the last dish you can be sure that the potatoes will taste like tomatoes, and the pork like a sirloin of beef."

"*So!*" laughed the young woman, with good German guttural. "I'm glad to say I have ordered dishes that head the list."

"Garlic is an enemy usually ambushed in gigot.—That is his only quite certain haunt."

"Good; I will avoid gigot." She was indulgent to his clowning, and drawled a little in sympathy. Between language and feeding, Kreisler sought to gain the young lady's confidence, adhering conventionally to the progress of Creation.

He found his neighbour inclined to slight Nature. He, too, was a little overlooked; in waiving of conventions being blandly forestalled. There was something uncomfortable about all this. He must brace himself. He realized with the prophetic logic of his hysteria, racing through the syllogisms his senses divined, sensations now anachronisms, afterwards recognized as they burst out in due course. This precocity in the restaurant took him to the solution of what their coming together might mean.

One plethoric impression of her was received—although *from* her—instalment of a senseless generosity.

She wore a heavy black burnous, very voluminous and severe; a large ornamental bag was on the chair at her side, which you expected to contain herbs and trinkets, paraphernalia of the witch, rather than powder, lip-cream, and secrets. Her hat was immense and sinuous; generally she implied an egotistic code of advanced order, full of insolent strategies.

Other women in the restaurant appeared dragged down and drained of vitality by their clothes beside her, Kreisler thought, although she wore so much more than they did. Her large square-shouldered and slim body swam in hers like a duck.

When she laughed, this commotion was transmitted to her body as though sharp, sonorous blows had been struck on her mouth. Her lips were long, hard bubbles risen in the blond heavy pool of her face, ready to break, pitifully and gaily. Grown forward with ape-like intensity, they refused no emotion noisy egress if it got so far. Her eyes were large, stubborn, and reflective, brown coming out of blondness. Her head was like a deep white egg in a tobacco-coloured nest. She exuded personality with alarming and disgusting intensity. It was an ostentation similar to diamonds and gold watch-chains. Kreisler felt himself in the midst of a cascade, a hot cascade.

She seemed to feel herself a travelling circus of tricks and wonders, beauty shows and monstrosities. Quite used to being looked at, she had become resigned to inability to avoid performing. She possessed the geniality of public character and the genius of sex. Kreisler was a strange loafer talked to easily, without any consciousness of condescension.

Just as he was most out of his depth, Kreisler had run up against all this! It all had the mellowness of sunset, and boomed in this small alcove infernally.—By the fact of sex this figure seems to offer him a traditional substantiality. He clutches at it eagerly as at something familiar and unmetamorphosed—and somewhat unmetamorphosable—by Fate.

In the first flush he revolves with certain skill in this new *champ de manœuvres*, executing one or two very pretty gymnastics. He has only to flatter himself on the excellent progress, really, that he makes.

"My name is Anastasya," she says irrelevantly to him, as if she had stupidly forgotten, before, this little detail.

Whew! his poor ragged eyelashes flutter, a cloud of astonishment passes grotesquely over his face; like the clown of the piece, he looks as though he were about to rub his head, click his tongue, and give his nearest man-neighbour an enthusiastic kick. "Anastasya!" It will be "Tasy" soon!

He outwardly becomes more solemn than ever, like a merchant who sees an incredible dupe before him, and would in some way conceal his exhilaration. But he calls her carefully at regular intervals, Anastasya!

"I suppose you've come here to work?" he asked.

"I don't want to work any more than is absolutely necessary. I am overworked as it is, by living merely." He could well believe it; she must do some overtime! "If it were not for my excellent constitution—"

This was evidently, Kreisler felt, the moment to touch on the heaviness of life's burden; as her expression was perfectly even and non-committal.

"Ah, yes," he sighed heavily, one side of the menu rising gustily and relapsing, "Life gives one work enough."

She looked at him and reflected, "What work does 'cet oiseau-là' perform?"

"Have you many friends here, Anastasya?"

"None."—She laughed with ostentatious satisfaction at his funniness. "I came here, as a matter of fact, to be alone. I want to see only fresh people. I have had all the gusto and illusion I had lent all round steadily handed back to me where I come from. 'I beg your pardon! Your property, ma'am!' The result is that I am amazingly rich!—I am tremendously rich!" She opened her eyes wide; Kreisler pricked up his ears and wondered if this were to be taken in another sense. He cast down his eyes respectfully. "I have the sort of feeling that I have enough to go all round.—But perhaps I haven't!"

Kreisler lingered over her first observation: "wanted to be alone." The indirect compliment conveyed (and he felt, when it was said, that he was somewhere near the frontier, surely, of a German confidence) was rather mitigated by what followed. The "having enough to go all round"; that was very universal, and included him too easily in its sweep.

"Do you want to go all round?" he asked, with heavy plagiarism of her accent, and solemn sentimental face.

"I don't want to be mean."

His eyes struggled with hers; he was easily thrown.

But she had the regulation feminine foible of charity, he reassured himself, by her answer.

Kreisler's one great optimism was a belief in the efficacy of women.—You did not deliberately go there—at least, he usually did not—unless you were in straits. But there they were all the time, vast dumping-ground for sorrow and affliction—a world-dimensioned pawnshop, in which you could deposit not your dress-suit or garments, but yourself, temporarily, in exchange for the gold of the human heart. Their hope consisted, no doubt, in the reasonable uncertainty as to whether you would ever be able to take yourself out again. Kreisler had got in and out again almost as many times as his "smokkin" in *its* pawnshop.

Women were Art or expression for him in this way. They were Man's Theatre. The Tragedies played there purged you periodically of the too violent accumulations of desperate life. There its burden of laughter as well might be exploded.—Woman was a confirmed *Schauspielerin* or play-actress; but coming there for illusion he was willingly moved. Much might be noticed in common between him and the drunken navvy on Saturday night, who comes home bellicosely towards his wife, blows raining gladly at the mere sight of her. He may get practically all the excitement and exertion he violently needs, without any of the sinister chances a more real encounter would present. His wife is "his little bit" of unreality, or play. He can declaim, be outrageous to the top of his bent; can be maudlin too; all conducted almost as he pleases, with none of the shocks of the real and too tragic world. In this manner woman was the æsthetic element in Kreisler's life. Love, too, always meant unhappy love for him, with its misunderstandings and wistful separations. He issued forth solemnly and the better for it. He approached a love affair as the *deutscher Student* engages in a student's duel—no vital part exposed, but where something spiritually of about the importance of a nose might be lost; at least stoically certain that blood would be drawn.

A casual observer of the progress of Otto Kreisler's life might have said that the chief events, the crises, consisted of his love affairs—such as that unfortunate one with his present stepmother.—But, in the light of a careful analysis, this would have been an inversion of the truth. When the events of his life became too unwieldy or overwhelming, he converted them into love, as he might have done, with specialized talent, into some art or other. He was a sculptor—a German sculptor of a mock-realistic and degenerate school—in the strange sweethearting of the "free-life." The two or three women he had left about the world in this way—although perhaps those symbolic statues had grown rather characterless in Time's weather and perhaps lumpish—were monuments of his perplexities. After weeks of growing estrangement, he would sever all relations suddenly one day—usually on some indigestible epigram, that worried the poor girl for the rest of her days. Being no adept in the science of his heart, there remained a good deal of mystery for him about the appearance of "Woman" in his life. He felt that she was always connected with its important periods; he thought, superstitiously, that his existence was in some way implicated with *dem Weib*. She was, in any case, for him, a stormy petrel. He would be killed by a woman, he sometimes thought. This superstition had flourished with him before he had yet found for it much *raison d'être*.—A serious duel having been decided on in his early student days, this reflection, "I am quite safe; it is not thus that I shall die," had given him a grisly coolness. His opponent nearly got himself killed, because he, for his part, had no hard and fast theory about the sort of death in store for him.

This account, to be brought up to date, must be modified. Since knowing Volker, no woman had come conspicuously to disturb him. Volker had been the ideal element of balance in his life.

But between this state—the minimum degree of friendship possible—a distant and soothing companionship—and more serious states, there was no possible foothold for Kreisler.

Friendship usually dates from unformed years. But Love still remains in full swing long after Kreisler's age at that time; a sort of spurious and intense friendship.

An uncomfortable thing happened now. He realized suddenly all the possibilities of this chance acquaintanceship, plainly and cinematographically.—He was seized with panic.—He must make a good impression.—From that moment he ran the risk of doing the reverse. For he was unaccustomed to act with calculation.—There he was like some individual who had gone nonchalantly into the presence of a prince; who—just in the middle of the audience—when he would have been getting over his first embarrassment—is overcome with a tardy confusion, the imagination in some way giving a jump. It is the imagination, repressed and as it were slighted, revenging itself.

Casting about desperately for means of handling the situation, he remembered she had spoken of getting a dog *to guide her*.—What had she meant? Anyway, he grasped at the dog. He could regain possession of himself in romantic stimulus of this figure. He would be her dog! Lie at her feet! He would fill with a merely animal warmth and vivacity the void that *must* exist in her spirit. His imagination, flattered, came in as ally. This, too, exempted him from the necessity of being victorious. All he asked was to be her dog!—only wished to impress her as a dog! Even if she did not feel much sympathy for him now, no matter.—He would humbly follow her up, put himself at her disposal, not be exigent. It was a rôle difficult to refuse him. Sense of security the humility of this resolution brought about caused him to regain a self-possession. Only it imposed the condition, naturally, of remaining a dog.—Every time he felt his retiring humbleness giving place to another sensation, he anew felt qualms.

"Do you intend studying here, Fräulein?" he asked, with a new deference in his tone—hardly a canine whine, but deep servient bass of the faithful St. Bernard.—She seemed to have noticed this something new already, and Kreisler on all fours evidently astonished her. She was inclined to stroke him, but at the same time to ask what was the matter.

"A year or two ago I escaped from a bourgeois household in an original manner. Shall I tell you about that, Otto?"

Confidence for confidence, he had told Anastasya that he was Otto.

"Please!" he said, with reverent eagerness.

"Well, the bourgeois household was that of my father and mother.—I got out of it in this way.—I made myself such a nuisance to my family that they had to get rid of me." Otto flung himself back in his chair with dramatic incredulity. "It was quite simple.—I began scribbling and scratching all over the place—on blotting-pads, margins of newspapers, on my father's correspondence, the wall-paper. I inundated my home with troublesome images. It was like vermin; my multitude of little figures swarmed everywhere. They simply *had* to get rid of me.—I said nothing. I pretended to be possessed. I got a girl-friend in Münich to write enthusiastic letters: her people lived quite near us when we were in Germany."

Kreisler looked at her rather dully, and smiled solemnly, with really something of the misplaced and unaccountable pathos and protest of dogs (although still with a slavish wagging of the tail) at some pleasantry of the master.—Her expansiveness, as a fact, embarrassed him very much at this point. He was divided between his inclination to respond to it in some way, and mature their acquaintance at once, and his determination to be merely a dog. Yet he felt that her familiarity, if adopted, in turn, by him, might not be the right thing. And yet, as it was, he would appear to be holding back, would seem "reserved" in his mere humility. He was a very perplexed dog for some time.

He remained dumb, smiling up at her with appealing pathos from time to time. She wondered if he had indigestion or what. He made several desperate dog-like sorties. But she saw he was clearly in difficulties—As her lunch was finished, she called the waitress.—Her bill was made out, Kreisler scowling at her all the while. Her attitude, suggesting, "Yes, you *are* funny, you know you are. I'd better go, then you'll be better," was responded to by him with the same offended dignity as the drunken man displays when his unsteadiness is observed. He repudiated sulkily the suggestion that there was anything wrong. Then he grew angry with her. His nervousness was her doing.—All was lost. He was very near some violence.—But when she stood up, he was so impressed that he sat gaping after her. He remained cramped in his place until she had left the restaurant.

He moved in his chair stiffly; he ached as though he had been sitting for his portrait. The analogy struck him. Had he been sitting for his portrait? These people dining near him as though they had suddenly appeared out of the ground—he was embarrassed at finding himself alone with them. They knew all that had happened, but were pretending not to. He had not noticed that they were there all round him, overbearing and looking on. It was as though he had been talking to himself, and had just become aware of it. A tide of magnetism had flowed away, leaving him bare and stranded.—He cursed his stupidity. He then stopped this empty mental racket abruptly.—Only a few minutes had passed since Anastasya's departure. He seized hat and stick and hurried up to the desk.—Once outside he gave his glasses an adjusting pull, gazed up and down the boulevard in all directions. No sign of the tall figure he was pursuing. He started off, partly at a run, in the likeliest direction.—At the Café Berne corner, where several new vistas opened, there she was, some way down the Boulevard du Paradis, on the edge of the side-walk, waiting till a tram had passed to cross. Having seen so much, should he not go back? For there was nothing else to be done. To catch her up and force himself on her could have only one result, he thought. He might, perhaps, follow a little way. That was being done already.

They went on for some hundred yards, she a good distance ahead on the other side of the boulevard. Walking for a moment, his eyes on the ground, he looked up and caught her head pivoting slowly round. She no doubt had seen him.—With shame he realized what was happening.—"Here I am following this girl as though we were strangers! This is what I began in the restaurant. I am putting the final touch by following her in the street, as though we had never spoken!" Either he must catch her up at once or vanish. He promptly turned up a side street, and circled round to his starting-point.

CHAPTER VI

His nature would probably have sought to fill up the wide, shallow gap left by Ernst and earlier ties either by another Ernst or, more likely, a variety of matter. It would have been only a temporary stopping. Now a gold crown, regal person, had fallen on the hollow.

But his nature was an effete machine and incapable of working on all that glory. Desperate at dullness, he betook himself to self-lashings. He would respond to utmost of weakened ability; with certainty of failure, egotistically, but not at a standstill. Kreisler was a German who, by all rights and rules of the national temperament, should have committed suicide some weeks earlier. Anastasya became an *idée fixe*. He was a machine, dead weight of old iron, that, started, must go dashing on. His little-dog simile was veritably carried out in his scourings of the neighbourhood, in hope of crossing Anastasya. But these "courses" gave no result. Benignant apparition, his roughness had scared it away, and off the earth, for ever. He entered, even infested, all painting schools of the quarter. He rapidly pursued distant equivocal figures in streets and gardens. Each rendered up its little quota of malignant hope, then presented him with a face of monotonous strangeness.

It was Saturday when Kreisler was found preparing to take his valise to the Mont de Piété. On the preceding evening he had paid one of his unaccountable calls on Fräulein Lipmann, the first for some time. He had a good reason for once. This *salon* was the only place of comparatively public assembly in the quarter he had not visited. Entering with his usual slight air of mystification, he bent to kiss Fräulein Lipmann's hand in a vaguely significant fashion.

The blank reciprocal indifference of these calls was thus relieved. It awoke a vague curiosity on one side, a little playful satisfaction on the other. This might even have ripened into a sort of understanding and bonhomie. He did not pursue it or develop the rôle. After a half-hour of musing on the brink of a stream of conversation and then music, he suddenly recognized something, flotsam bobbing past. It had bobbed past before several times. He gradually became steadily aware of it. A dance at the Bonnington Club, that would take place the following evening, was the event that arrested him. Why was this familiar? Anastasya! Anastasya had spoken of it. That was all he could remember. Would she be there? He at once, and as though he had come there to do so, fished delicately in this same stream of tepid chatter for an invitation to the dance. Fräulein Lipmann, the fish he particularly angled for, was backward. They did not seem to want him very much at the dance. Nevertheless, after an hour of indefatigable manœuvring, the exertion of many powers seldom put forth in that *salon*, he secured the form, not the spirit, of an invitation.

Kreisler saw, in his alarmed fancy, Anastasya becoming welded into this gregarious female personality. The energy and resource of the Devil himself would be required to extricate her. She must be held back from this slough for the moment he needed.

Was it too late to intercept her? But he felt he might do it. The eyes of these ladies, so far dull with indifference, would open. He would be seen as a being with a new mysterious function. He felt that Volker's absence from their *réunions* was due to his not wishing to meet him. They, too, must see that. Now the enigmatical and silent doggedness of these visits would seem explained. He would appear like some unwieldy, deliberate parasite got on to their indivisible body. The invitation given, he made haste to go. If he stayed much longer it would be overlaid with all sorts of offensive and effacing matter, and be hardly fit for use. A defiant and jeering look on his face, he withdrew with an "Until to-morrow."

It was at this point that the "smokkin" came into prominence.

CHAPTER VII

"Impossible, my poor Kreisler! Five francs. No more!"

Suzanne stood at attention before him in the hall of the Mont de Piété. If she had been inexorable before, she was now doubly so beneath the eyes of the veritable officials. The sight of them, and the half-official status of go-between and interpreter, urged her to ape-like importance.

With flushed and angry face, raised eyebrows, shocked at his questioning the verdict, she repeated, "Five francs; it's the most."

"No, that's no good; give me the portmanteau," he said.

She gave it him in silence, eyebrows still raised, eyes fixed, staring with intelligent disapproval right in front of her. She did not look at her eminent countrymen behind the large counter. But her intelligent and significant stare, lost in space, was meant to meet and fraternize with probable similar stares of theirs, lost in the same intelligent void.

Her face fixed in distended, rubicund, discontentedly resigned mask, she walked on beside him, the turkey-like backward-forward motion of fat neck marking her ruffled state. Kreisler sat down on a bench of the Boulevard du Paradis, she beside him.

"Dis! couldn't you have borrowed the rest?" she said at last.

Kreisler was tired. He got up.

"No, of course I couldn't. I hate people who lend money as I hate pawnbrokers."

Suzanne listened, with protesting grin. Her head nodded energetically.

"Eh bien! si tout le monde pensait comme toi—!"

He pushed his moustache up and frowned pathetically.

"Où est Monsieur Volker?" she asked.

"Volker? I don't know. He has no money."

"Comment! Il n'a pas d'argent? C'est pas vrai! Tu ne le vois plus?"

"Good-bye." Kreisler left Suzanne seated, staring after him.

The portmanteau dragged along, he strode past a distant figure. Suzanne saw him turn round and examine the stranger's face. Then she lost sight of them round a corner of the boulevard.

"Quel type!" she exclaimed to herself, nearly as the concierge had done. She sauntered back home, giving Kreisler the benefit of several sour reflections.

In a little room situated behind the Rue de la Gaieté, she pulled open one of two drawers in her washstand, which contained a little bread, tea, potatoes, and a piece of cold fish. She spread out a sheet of the *Petit Parisian* beside the basin. Having peeled the potatoes and put them on the gas, she took off those outdoor things that just enabled her to impart a turkey-like movement to her person. Then, dumpy, in a salmon-check petticoat, her legs bowed backwards and her stomach stuck out, she stood moodily at the window. A man she knew, now in the Midi, sent her now and then a few francs.

This rueful spot, struck in image of this elementary dross of humanity, was Kreisler's occasional haunt. Cell of the unwieldy, tragic brain of the city, with million other similar cells, representing overwhelming uniform force of brooding in that brain, attracted him like a desert or ocean.

He would listen solemnly, like a great judge, to Suzanne's perpetual complaints, sitting on the edge of her bed, hat on head. She was so humble and so pretentious. Her imagination was arrogant and constantly complaining. The form her complaints took was always that of lies—needless, dismal lies. She could not grumble without inventing and she never stopped grumbling. This, then, was one of Kreisler's dwellings. He lived at large. Some of his rooms, such as this, the Café de Berne, and Juan Soler's School of Art, he shared with others. On very troubled days his body, like the finger of a weather-glass, would move erratically. When found in Suzanne's room it might be taken as an indication of an unsettled state. A tendency to remain at home, on the contrary, denoted mostly a state of equilibrium and peace.

CHAPTER VIII

The portmanteau fell under the bed; he crushed into the red bulbous cover. Kreisler never sat on his bed except when going to get into it. For another man it would have replaced the absent armchair. In those moments of depression in which he did so he always, at once, felt more depressed, or quite hopeless. Head between hands, he now stared at the floor. Four or five hours! He must raise money, else he could not go to the dance. How absurd, this fuss about such a sum! All the same, how the devil could he get it?

"Small as it is, I shan't get it," he thought to himself. He began repeating this stupidly, and stuck at word "shan't." His brain and mouth clogged up, he stuttered thickly in his mind. He sprang up. But the slovenly, hopeless quality of the bed clung to him. This was a frivolous demonstration. He wandered to the window; stood staring out, nose flattened against the pane.

The sudden quiet and idleness of his personality was an awakening after the little nightmare of Suzanne. But it was not a refreshing one.

His portmanteau had always received certain consideration, as being, next the dress-suit, the most dependable article among those beneath his sway—to come to his aid if their common existence were threatened. He had now thrown it under the bed with disgust. He and all his goods were rubbish for the streets.

He sauntered from the window to the bed and back. Whenever he liked, in a sense, he would open the door and go out; but still, *until* then (and *when* would he "like"?) he was a poor prisoner. Outside, he took some strength and importance from others. In here he touched bottom and realized what the Kreisler-self was, with four walls round it.

His muscles were still full. They symbolized his uselessness. The thought, so harsh and tyrannical, of his once more going to the window and gazing down at the street beneath made him draw back his chair. He sat midway in the room, looking steadily out at the housetops. But, like his vigorous muscles and his deadness, there was the same contradiction; his mechanical obstinacy as regards Anastasya and his comic activity at present to get to a dance.

Comrades at painting school, nodding acquaintances, etc., were once more run through. None valued his acquaintance at more than thirty centimes, if that.

Perhaps Anastasya had left Paris? This solution, occurring sometimes, had only made his activity during the last few days more mad and mechanical—the pursuit of a shadow.

Ten minutes later, through a series of difficult clockwork-like actions, he had got once more to Lejeune's to have lunch. With disgust he took what had been his usual seat latterly, at the table in the recess; the one place, he was sure, Anastasya would never be found in again, wherever else she might be found.

Lunch nearly over, he caught sight of Lowndes. "Hi, Master Lowndes!" he called out—always assuming great bluffness and brutality, as he called it, with English people, and laborious opposite to "stiffness." "How do you do?"

The moment his eye had fallen on "Master" Lowndes this friend's probable national opulence had occurred to him as a tantalizing fact. No gross decision could be come to in that moment. Lowndes was called to be kept there a little bit, while he turned things over and made up his mind. This was an acquaintance existing chiefly on chaff and national antithesis. It meant nothing to him. What matter if he were refused? Lowndes not being a compatriot made it easier. Something must be sacrificed. Lowndes' acquaintanceship was a possession something equivalent to a cheap ring, a souvenir. He must part with it, if necessary.

Lowndes grinned at sight of Kreisler. He had finished his own lunch and was just going off. He had almost forgotten his idea in coming to the restaurant, that of seeing his German acquaintance. Swaying from side to side on his two superlatively elastic calves, he sat down opposite the good Otto, who leered back, blinking. He spoke German better than Kreisler any other language, so they used that, after a little flourish of English.

"Well, what have you been doing? Working?"

"No," replied Kreisler. "I'm giving up painting and becoming a business man. My father has offered me a position!"

This subject seemed no more important than his speech made it, and yet it filled his life. Lowndes smiled correctly, not suspecting realities.

"Have you seen Douglas?" This was a friend through whom they had known each other in Italy.

Why should this fellow lend him thirty francs? The grin would not be there, he felt, had he been conscious that the other was thinking of the contents of his pocket. Not humour, but a much colder stuff no doubt mounted guard over his pocket-book, guarantee of this easiness and health. Oh, the offensive prosperity of the English, smugness of middle-class affluence! etc. etc.

Kreisler imagined the change that would come over this face when there was question of thirty francs. Estrangement set in on his side already, anger and humiliation at the imagined expression. This was of help. Here was his chance of borrowing that very insignificant but illusive sum. The man was already an enemy. He would willingly have knocked him on the head and taken his money had they been in a quiet place.

The complacent health and humoristic phlegm with which he grinned and perambulated through life charged Kreisler with the contempt natural to his more stiff and human education. His relations with him hinging on mild racial differences, he saw behind him the long line of all the Englishmen he had ever known. "Useless swine," he thought, "so pleased with his cursed English face, and mean as a peasant!"

"Oh, I was asked for my opinion on a certain matter this morning. I was asked what I thought of German women!"

"What reply did you make, Mr. Lowndes?"

"I didn't know what to say. I suggested that my friend should come along and get your opinion."

"My opinion as an *expert*? My fees as an expert are heavy. I charge thirty francs a consultation!"

"I'm sure he'd have paid that," Lowndes laughed innocently. Kreisler surveyed him unsympathetically.

"What, then, is your opinion of our excellent females?" he asked.

"Oh, I have no opinion. I admire your ladies, especially the pure Prussians."

Kreisler was thinking: "If I borrow the money, there must be some time mentioned for paying back—next week, say. He would be more likely to lend it if he knew where to find me. He must have my address."

"Come and see me—some time," he blinked. "52 Boulevard Pfeiffer, fourth floor, just beside the restaurant here. You see? Up there."

"I will. I looked you up at your old address a month or so ago; they didn't know where you'd gone."

Kreisler stared fixedly at him—a way of covering discomfiture felt at this news. The old address reminded him of several little debts there. For this reason he had not told them where he was going. The concierge would complain of her old tenant; probably, even, Lowndes might have been shown derelict tradesmen's bills. Not much encouragement for his proposed victim!

Lowndes was writing on a piece of paper.

"There's my address: Rue des Flammes."

Kreisler looked at it rather fussily and said over: "5 Rue des Flammes. Lowndes." He hesitated and repeated the name.

"R. W.—Robert Wooton. Here, I'll write it down for you."

"Are you in a hurry? Come and have a drink at the Berne," Kreisler suggested when he had made up his bill.

On the way Lowndes continued a discourse.

"A novelist I knew told me he changed the names of the characters in a book several times in the course of writing it. It freshened them up, according to him. He said that the majority of people were killed by their names. I think a name is a man's soul."

Kreisler forged ahead, rhythmically and sullenly.

"If we had numbers, for instance, instead of names, who would take the number thirteen?" Lowndes wondered in German.

"I," said Kreisler.

"Would you?"

Every minute Kreisler delayed increased the difficulty. His energy was giving out. They were now sitting on the *terrasse* at the Berne. He had developed a particular antipathy to borrowing. An immense personal neurasthenia had grown up round this habit of his, owing to his late discomfitures. He already heard an awkward voice, saw awkward eyes. Then he suddenly concluded that the fact that Lowndes was not a German made it more difficult, instead of less so, as he had thought. Why could he not take?—why petition? He knew that if Lowndes refused he would break out; he nearly did so as it was. With disgust and fatigue he lay back in his chair, paying no attention to what Lowndes was saying. His mind was made up. He would not proceed with his designs on this dirty pocket. He became rough and monosyllabic. He wished to purify himself in rudeness of his preceding amiability.

Lowndes had been looking at a newspaper. He put it down and said he must go back to "work." His "morning" had, of course, been interrupted by Tarr!

Kreisler still saw the expression on the Englishman's face he had imagined, and restrained with difficulty the desire to spit in it. The nearness they had been to this demand must have affected, he thought, even his impervious companion. He *had* asked and been refused, to all intents and purposes. He got up, left Lowndes standing there, and went into the lavatory at the side of the café, where he had a thorough wash in cold water.

Back at his table, he saw no sign of the Englishman, and sat down to finish his drink, considering what his next move should be.

Various pursuits suggested themselves. He might go and offer himself as model at some big private studios near the Observatoire. He could get a week's money advanced him? He would dress as a woman and waylay somebody or other on the boulevards. He might steal some money. Volker was the last. He came just after murder. He would go to Ernst Volker—he with his little obstinate resolve in obscurity of his mind no longer to be Kreisler's acquaintance. Obstinacy in people of weak character is the perfectly exasperating thing. They have no right to their resoluteness—appearing weaker and meaner than ever in anomalous tenacity. Volker, naturally submissive, had broken away and was posing somewhere as a stranger. He felt physical disgust; this proceeding was indecent.

A spirit that has mingled with another, suddenly covering itself and wishing to regain its strangeness, can be as indecent as a strange being suddenly baring itself. A man's being is never divined so completely and pungently as when his friendship cools and he becomes once more a stranger. This is one of the moments when the imagination, most awake, sees best.

This little rat's instinctive haste to separate from him was an ill omen: what did he care for omens? he clamoured impatiently.

At this juncture in his reflections, from where he sat on the café terrace he saw Volker's back, as he supposed, disappearing round a corner, as though trying to avoid a meeting. Blood came to his head with a shock. He nearly sprang forward in pursuit of this unsociable form. Rushing words of insult rose to his lips, he fidgeted on his seat, gazed blankly at the spot where he had seen the figure. That it was no longer there exasperated him beyond measure. It was as though he considered that Ernst should have remained at the corner, immobile, with his back towards him, a visible mark and fuel for anger. He made a sign to the waiter, indicating that his drink would go into his "tick." He then hurried off in the direction of Volker's house—the direction also that the back had taken—determined to get something out of him. Kreisler, letting instinct guide his steps, took the wrong turning—following, in fact, his customary morning's itinerary. He found himself suddenly far beyond the street Volker lived in, near Juan Soler's atelier. He gazed down the street towards the atelier, then took off his glasses and began carefully wiping them. While doing this he heard words of greeting and found Volker at his elbow.

"Hallo! You look pretty hot. You nearly knocked me over a minute ago in your haste," he was saying.

Kreisler jumped—as the bravest might if, having stoutly confronted an apparition, it suddenly became a man of flesh and blood. Had his glasses been firmly planted on his nose things might have gone differently. He frowned vacantly at Ernst and went on rubbing them.

Volker saw that something was wrong. It would have been to his advantage also to "have out" anything that was there and have done with it. But in his attitude German sluggishness seemed appealing to the same element in Kreisler's nature, claiming its support and sympathy.

"It's dreadfully hot!" he said uneasily, looking round as though examining the heat. He stepped up on to the pavement out of the way of a horse-meat cart. The large-panelled conveyance, full of enormous outlandish red carcases, went rushing down the street, carrying an area of twenty yards of deafness with it. This explosion of sound had a pacifying effect on Kreisler; it made him smile for some reason or other. Volker went on: "I don't know whether I told you about my show."

"What show?" Kreisler asked rudely.

"In Berlin, you know. It has not gone badly. Our compatriots improve. I've got a commission to paint the Countess Wort. What have you been doing lately?" There was a forbidding pause. "I've intended coming round to see you; but I've been sticking at home working. Have you been round at the Berne?" He spoke rapidly and confidentially, as two business men meeting in the street and always in a hurry might try and compress into a few minutes, between two handshakes, a lot of personal news. He seemed to wish to combine conviction that he was very anxious to tell Kreisler all about himself and (by his hurried air) paralysis of the other's intention to have an explanation.

"I am glad you are going to paint the Countess Wort. I congratulate you, Mr. Volker! I am in a hurry. Good day."

Kreisler turned and walked towards the Atelier Juan Soler. For no reason (except that it was impossible) he could not get money from Volker. It was as though that money would not be real money at all. Supposing he got it; the first place he tried to pass it the man would say, "This is not money." As for taking him to task, his red, correct face made it impossible; it had suddenly become a lesson and exercise that it would be ridiculous to repeat. He was not a schoolboy.

Volker walked away ruffled. He was mortified that, by apprehension of a scene, he had been so friendly. The old Otto had scored. He, Volker, had humiliated himself needlessly, for it was evident Kreisler's manner had been misinterpreted by him.

Kreisler had not intended going to Soler's that day. Yet there he was, presumably got there now to avoid Ernst Volker. He saw himself starting up from the Berne a quarter of an hour before, steaming away in pursuit of a skulking friend—impetus of angry thought carrying him far beyond his destination; then Volker comes along and runs him into the painting school. He compared himself to one of those little steam toys that go straight ahead without stopping; that any one can take up and send puffing away in the opposite direction. Humouring this fancy, he entered the studio with the gaze a man might wear who had fallen through a ceiling and found himself in a strange room in midst of a family circle. The irresponsible, resigned, and listless air signified whimsical expectancy. Some other figure would rise up, no doubt, and turn him streetwards again?

A member of the race which has learnt to sleep standing up posed on the throne. He had suddenly come amongst brothers. He was as torpid as she, as indifferent as these mechanical students. The clock struck. With a glance at the *massier*, the model slowly and rhythmically abandoned her rigid attitude, coming to life as living statues do in ballets; reached stiffly for her chemise. The dozen other figures, who had been slowly pulsing—advancing or retreating, suspended around her yellowness—now laboriously moved, relapsing aimlessly here and there, chiefly against walls.

He had been considering a fat back and especially a parting carried half-way down the back of the head. Why should not its owner, and gardener, he had reflected, continue it the whole distance down, dividing his head in half with a line of white scalp? This man now turned on him sudden, unsurprised, placid eyes. Had he *eyes*, as well as a parting, at the back of his head? Kreisler felt on the verge of courteous discussion as to whether that parting should or should not be gone on with till it reached the neck.

Three had struck. He left and returned to the neighbourhood of the Berne by the same and longest route, as though to efface in some way his previous foolish journey.

Every three or four hours vague hope recurred of the delayed letter, like hunger recurring at the hour of meals. He went up to the loge of his house and knocked.

"Il n'y a rien pour vous!"

Four hours remained. The German party was to meet at Fräulein Lipmann's after dinner.

CHAPTER IX

Otto's compatriots at the Berne were sober and thoughtful, with discipline in their idleness. Their monthly moneys flowed and ebbed, it was to be supposed, small regular tides frothing monotonously in form of beer. This rather desolate place of chatter, papers, and airy, speculative business had the charm of absence of gusto.

Kreisler was ingrainedly antiquated, purer German. He had experienced suddenly home-sickness, that often overtakes voluntary exiles at the turn of their life—*his* being, not for Germany, exactly, but for the romantic, stiff ideals of the German student of his generation. It was a home-sickness for his early self. Like knack of riding a bicycle or anything learnt in youth, this character was easily assumed. He was gradually discovering the foundations of his personality. Many previous moods and phases of his nature were mounting to the surface.

Arrived in front of the Café Berne, he stood for fifteen minutes looking up and down the street, at the pavement, his watch, the passers-by. Then he chose the billiard-room door to avoid the principal one, where he usually entered.

All the ugly familiarity of this place, he hated with methodic, deliberate hatred; taking things one by one, as it were, persons and objects. The *garçon's* spasmodic running about was like a gnat's energy over stagnation.

Passing from the billiard-room to a gangway with several tables, his dull, exasperated eye fell on something it did not understand. How could it be expected to understand? It was an eye and it stuck. It was simple, though. It was amazed and did not understand.

Anastasya.

Set in the heart of this ennui, it arrested the mind like a brick wall some carter drowsed on his wagon. Stopping dead, Kreisler stared stupidly. Anastasya was sitting there with Soltyk. With Soltyk! He seemed about to speak to them—they, at least, were under this impression. Quite naturally he was about to do this, like a child. As though in intense abstraction, he fixed his eyes on them. Then he took a step towards them, possibly with the idea of sitting down beside them. Consciousness set in, with a tropic tide of rage, and carried him at a brisk pace towards the door, corresponding to the billiard-room door, on the other side of the café. Yet in the midst of this he instinctively raised his hat a little, his eyes fixed now on his feet.

He was in a great hurry to get past the two people sitting there. This could not be done without discovering two inches of the scalp for a moment—as an impatient man in a crush, wishing to pass, pushes another aside, raising his hat at the same time to have the right to be rude.

Same table on *terrasse* as an hour before. But Kreisler seemed sitting on air, or one of those wooden whirling platforms in the fêtes.

The *garçon*, with a femininely pink, virile face which, in a spirit of fun, he kept constantly wooden and solemn except when, having taken your order, he winked or smiled—came up hastily.

"Was wünschen Sie?" he asked, wiping the table with a serviette. He had learned a few words of German from the customers. Supposing Kreisler rather a touchy man, he always attempted to put him at his ease, as the running of bills was valuable to him. He had confidence in this client, and wished the bill to assume vague and profitable proportions.

Kreisler's thoughts dashed and stunned themselves against this waiter. His mind stood stock-still for several minutes. This pink wooden face paralysed everything. As its owner thought "the young man" was having a joke with him, it became still more humorously wooden. The more wooden it became, the more paralysed became Kreisler's intelligence. He stared at him more and more oddly, till the *garçon* was forced to laugh. As a matter of fact, Kreisler mentally was steadying himself on this hard personality. As he had appeared to walk deliberately with hot intention to his seat, so he seemed gazing deliberately at the waiter and choosing his drink. Then the dam gave way. He hated this familiar face; his thought smashed and buffeted it. Such commercial modicum of astute good nature was too much. It was kindness that only equilibrium could ignore. The expression of his own face became distorted. The *garçon* fixed him with his eye and took a step back, with dog-like doubt, behind the next table.

Anastasya had smiled in a very encouraging way as he passed. This had offended him extremely. Soltyk—Anastasya; Soltyk—Anastasya. That was a bad coupling! His sort of persecution mania seized him by the throat. This had done it! Soltyk, who had got hold of Volker and was the something that had interfered between that borrowable quantity and himself, occupied a position not unsimilar to his stepmother. Volker and his father, who had kept him suspended in idleness, and who now both were withdrawing or had withdrawn like diminishing jets of water, did not attract the full force of his indolent, tragic grumpiness.

Behind Ernst and his parent Soltyk and his stepmother stood.

A certain lonely and comic ego all people carry about with them, who is always dumb except when they get drunk or become demented. It then talks, never sincerely, but in a sort of representative, pungent way. This ego in Kreisler's case would not have been shameless and cynical if it had begun to grumble about Volker. It would have said, "Hang that little Ernst! I come to Paris, I am ashamed to say, partly for him. But the little swine-dog has given me the go-by. Hell take his impudence! I don't like that swine-dog Soltyk! He's a slimy Russian rascal!" It would not have said: "I've lost the access to Ernst's pocket. The pig-dog Soltyk is sitting there!"

In any case his vanity too was hurt.

Anastasya now provided him with an acceptable platform from which his vexation might spring at Soltyk. There was no money or insignificant male liaison to stuff him down into grumpiness. "Das Weib" was there. All was in order for unbounded inflammation.

He wanted to bury his fear in her hot hair; he wanted to kiss her lips as he had never kissed any woman's; all the things he wanted—! But what would Soltyk be doing about it? He had met her alone, and that was all right and not impossible with a world made by their solitary meeting in the restaurant. He had lived with her instinctively in this solitary world of he and she. It was quite changed at present. Soltyk had got into it. Soltyk, by implication, brought a host of others, even if he did not mean that he was a definite rival there himself. What was he saying to her now? Sneers and ridicule, oceans of sneers directed at himself, more than ten thousand men could have discharged, he felt, certainly were inundating her ear. His stepmother-fiancée, other tales, were being retailed. *Everything* that would conceivably prejudice Anastasya, or would not, he accepted as already retailed. There he sat, like a coward. He was furious at their distant insulting equanimity.

A breath of violent excitement struck him, coming from within. He stirred dully beneath it. She was there; he had only put a thin partition between them. His heart beat slowly and ponderously. "On hearing what the swine Soltyk has to say she will remember my conduct in the restaurant and my appearance. She will make it all fit in. And, by God, it does fit in! Himmel! Himmel! there's nothing to be done! Anything I did, every movement, would only be filling out the figure my ass-tricks have cut for her!"

He was as conscious of the interior, which he could not see from his place on the street, as though, passing through, he had just found the walls, tables, chairs, painted bright scarlet. He felt he had left a wake of seething agitation in his passage of the café. Passing the two people inside there had been the affair of a moment, not yet grasped. This experience, apparently of the past, was still going on. The sense's picture, even, was not yet complete. New facts, details, were added every moment. He was still passing Anastasya and Soltyk. He sat on, trembling, at the door. There were other exits. She might be gone. But he forgot about them.

How he had worried himself about the pawned suit. Fate had directed him there to the café to save him the trouble of further racking his brains about it. Should he leave Paris? But he was mutinous. The occurrence of this idea filled him with suspicions.

The fit was over; reaction had set in. He was eyeing himself obliquely in the looking-glass behind his head.

He almost jumped away at two voices beside him, and the thrilling sound of a dress; it was as though some one had spoken with his own voice. It seemed all round him, attacking him. The thin, ordinary brushing of a skirt was like the low breathing of a hidden animal to a man in the forest. He felt they were coming to speak to him—just as they had thought that he was. The nerves on that side of his head twitched as though shrinking from a touch.

They were crossing the *terrasse* to the street. His heart beat a slow march. Her image there had become used. The reality, in its lightning correction of this, dug into his mind. There once more the real figure had its separate and foreign life. He was disagreeably struck by a certain air of depression and cheerlessness in the two figures before him. This one thing that should have been pleasant, displeased him. He was angry as though she had been shamming melancholy.

They were not talking, the best proof of familiarity. A strange figure occurred to him; he felt like a man, with all organs, bones, tissues complete, but made of cheap perishable stuff, who could only live for a day and then die of use.

This image, reality now before him, had drawn out all his energy, like a distinct being nourished by him. The image, intact in his mind, had returned him more or less the vigour spent. Her listlessness seemed a complement of the weakness he now felt. Energy was ebbing away from both.

He stared with bloodshot eyes. Then he got up and began walking after her. Soltyk, on hearing steps, turned round; but he made no remark to

Anastasya. They crossed the street and got into a passing tram. Otto Kreisler went back to the café.

It was like returning to some hall where there had been a banquet to find empty chairs, empty bottles, and disorder. The vacant seats around seemed to have been lately vacated. Then there was the sensation of being left behind. The Café Berne was a solitary and antediluvian place. Everything began to thrust itself upon him—the people, street, insignificant incidents—as though this indifferent life of facts, in the vanishing of the life of the imagination, had now become important, being the only thing left. Common life seemed rushing in and claiming him, and emphasizing his defeat and the new condition thus inaugurated. He went to Lejeune's for dinner. During the whole day he had been in feverish hurry, constantly seeing time narrowing in upon him. Now he had a sensation of intolerable leisure.

The useless ennui of his life presented itself to him for the thousandth time, but now clearly. This fact seemed to have been waiting with irritating calm, as though to say, "As soon as you can give me your attention?—Well, what are you going to do with me?" For he had compromised himself irretrievably. He knew that sooner or later he must marry and settle down with this stony fact, multiply its image. Things had gone too far.

And how about his father? What was that letter going to contain? His father had got a certain amount of pleasure out of him. Otto had satisfied in him in turn the desire of possession (that objects such as your watch, your house, which could equally well belong to anybody, do not satisfy), of authority (that servants do not satisfy), of self-complacency (that self does not): had been to him, later, a kind of living cinematograph and travel-book combined; and, finally, had inadvertently lured with his youth a handsome young woman into the paternal net. But he knew that he could procure no further satisfaction to this satiated parent. He could be henceforth a source only of irritation and expense.

After dinner he walked along the boulevard. The dark made him adventurous. He peered into cafés as he passed. He noticed it was already eight. Supposing he should meet some of the women on the way to Fräulein Lipmann's? He made a movement as though to turn down a side-street and hide himself at thought of possible confrontation. Next moment he was walking on obstinately in the direction of the Lipmann's house. His weakness drew him on, back into the vortex. Anything, death, and annihilation, was better than going back into that terrible colourless mood. His room, the café, waited for him like executioners. He had escaped from it for a time. Late agitations had given him temporary freedom, to which he was now committed. Dressed as he was, extremely untidy, he would go to Fräulein Lipmann's flat. Only humiliation he knew awaited him in that direction. If Anastasya were there (he would have it that she would be found wherever he least would care to see her) then anything might happen. But he wanted to suffer still more by her; *physically*, as it were, under her eyes. That would be a relief from present suffering. He must look in her eyes; he must excite in her the maximum of contempt and dislike. He wanted to be in her presence again, with full consciousness that his mechanical idyll was barred by Fate. Not strong enough to leave things as they were, he could not go away with this incomplete and, physically, uncertain picture behind him. It was as though a man had lost a prize and wanted written and stamped statement that he had lost it. He wished to shame her. If he did not directly insult her, he would at least insult her by thrusting himself on her. Then, at height of her disgust, he would pretend again to make advances.

As to the rest of the party, a sour glee possessed him at thought of *their* state by the time he had done with them. He already saw their faces in fancy when he should ring their bell and present himself, old morning suit, collar none too clean, dusty boots. All this self-humiliation and suffering he was preparing for himself was wedded with the thought of retaliation. Kreisler's schooldays could have supplied him with a parallel if he could have thought just then. He saw a curious scene proceeding beneath a desk in class. The boy next to him had jabbed his neighbour in the hand with a penknife. The latter, pale with fury, held his hand out in sinister invitation, hissing, "Do it again! do it again!" The boy next to Kreisler complied. "Do it again!" came still fiercer. He seemed to want to see his hand a mass of wounds and delect himself with the awful feeling of his own rage. Kreisler did not know how he should wipe out this debt with the world, but he wanted it bigger, more crushing. The bitter fascination of suffering drew him on to substitute real wounds for imaginary.

Near Fräulein Lipmann's house he rubbed his shoulder against a piece of whitewashed wall with a grin. He went rapidly up the stairs leading to her flat on the entresol, considering a scheme for the commencement of the evening. This seemed so happy that he felt further resourcefulness in misconduct would not be wanting.

PART III
BOURGEOIS-BOHEMIANS

CHAPTER I

Kreisler pressed the bell. It was a hoarse low z-like blast, braying softly into the crowded room. Kreisler still stood safely outside the door.

There was a rush in the passage: the hissing and spitting sounds inseparable from the speaking of the German tongue. Some one was spitting louder than the rest, and squealing dully as well. They were females disputing among themselves the indignity of door-openers. The most anxious to please gained the day.

The door was pulled ajar; an arch voice said:

"Wer ist das?"

"Ich bin's, Fräulein Lunken."

The roguish and vivacious voice died away, however. The opening of the door showed in the dark vestibule Bertha Lunken with her rather precious movements and German robustness.

His disordered hair, dusty boots and white patch on the jacket had taken effect.

"Who is it?" a voice cried from within.

"It's Herr Kreisler," Bertha answered with dramatic quietness. "Come in Herr Kreisler; there are still one or two to come." She spoke in a businesslike way, and bustled to close the door, to efface politely her sceptical reception of him by her handsome, wondering eyes.

"Ah, Herr Kreisler! I wonder where Fräulein Vasek is?" he heard some one saying.

He looked for a place to hang his hat. Fräulein Lunken preceded him into the room. Her expression was that of an embarrassed domestic foreseeing horror in his master's eye. Otto appeared in his turn. The chatter seemed to him to swerve a little bit at his right. Bowing to two or three people he knew near the door, he went over to Fräulein Lipmann, and bending respectfully down, kissed her hand. Then with a naïve air, but conciliatory, began:

"A thousand pardons, Fräulein Lipmann, for presenting myself like this. Volker and I have been at Fontenay-aux-Roses all the afternoon. We made a mistake about the time of the trains and I have only just got back; I hadn't time to change. I suppose it doesn't matter? It will be quite *intime* and bohemian, won't it? Volker had something to do. He's coming on to the dance later if he can manage it."

This cunning, partly affected, with a genuinely infantile glee, served him throughout the evening. While waiting at the door he had hit on this ridiculous fib. Knowing how welcome Volker was and almost sure of his not turning up, he would use him to cover the patch from the whitewashed wall. But he would get other patches and find other lies to cover them up till he could hardly move about for this plastering of small falsehoods.

Fräulein Lipmann had been looking at him with indecision.

"I am glad Herr Volker's coming. I haven't seen him for some weeks. You've plenty of time to change, you know, if you like. Herr Ekhart and several others haven't turned up yet. You live quite near, don't you, Herr Kreisler?"

"Yes, third to the right and second to the left, and keep straight on! But I don't think I'll trouble about it. I will do like this. I think I'll do, don't you, Fräulein Lipmann?" He took a couple of steps and looked at himself complacently in a glass.

"You are the best judge of that."

"Yes, that is so, isn't it, Fräulein? I have often thought that. How curious the same notion should come to you!" Again Kreisler smiled, and affecting to consider the question as settled turned to a man standing near him, with whom he had worked at Juan Soler's. His hostess moved away, in doubt as to whether he intended to go and change or not. He was, perhaps, just talking to his friend a moment before going.

The company was not "mondain" but "interesting." It was rather on its mettle on this occasion, both men and women in their several ways, dressed. An Englishwoman who was friendly with Fräulein Lipmann was one of the organizers of the Bonnington Club. Through her they had been invited there. Five minutes later Kreisler found Fräulein Lipmann in his neighbourhood again.

This lady had a pale fawn-coloured face, looking like the protagonist of a *crime passionel*. She multiplied her social responsibilities at every turn. But her manner implied that the quite ordinary burdens of life were beyond her strength. The two rooms with folding doors, which formed her salon and where her guests were now gathered, had not been furnished at haphazard. The "Concert" of Giorgione did not hang there for nothing. The books lying about had been flung down by a careful hand. Fräulein Lipmann required a certain sort of admiration. But she had a great contempt for other people, and so drew up, as it were, a list of her attributes, carefully and distinctly underlining each. With each new friend she went over again the elementary points, as a schoolmistress would go over with each new pupil the first steps of grammar or geography, position of his locker, where the rulers were put, etc. She took up her characteristic attitudes, one after the other, as a model might; that is, those simplest and easiest to grasp.

Her room, dress and manner were a sort of chart to the way to admire Fräulein Lipmann; the different points in her soul one was to gush about, the different hints one was to let fall about her "rather" tragic life-story, the particular way one was to regard her playing of the piano. You felt that there was not a candlestick, or antimacassar in the room but had its lesson for you. To have two or three dozen people, her "friends," repeating things after her in this way did not give her very much satisfaction. But she had a great many of the characteristics of the "school-marm," and she continued uninterruptedly with her duties teaching "Lipmann" with the solemnity, resignation and half-weariness, with occasional bursts of anger, that a woman would teach "twice two are four, twice three are six." Her best friends were her best pupils, of course.

The rooms were furnished with somewhat the severity of the schoolroom, a large black piano—for demonstrations—corresponded more or less to the blackboard.

"Herr Schnitzler just tells me that dress is *de rigueur*. Miss Bennett says it doesn't matter; but it would be awkward if you couldn't get in." She was continuing their late conversation. "You see it's not so much an artists' club as a place where the English *Société permanente* in Paris meet."

"Yes, I see; of course, that makes a difference! But I asked, I happened to ask, an English friend of mine to-day—a founder of the club, Master Lowndes" (this was a libel on Lowndes), "he told me it didn't matter a bit. You take my word for it, Fräulein Lipmann, it won't matter a bit," he reiterated a little boisterously, nodding his head sharply, his eyelids flapping like metal shutters rather than winking. Then, in a maundering tone, yawning a little and rubbing his glasses as though they had now idled off into gossip and confidences:

"I'd go and dress only I left my keys at Soler's. I shall have to sleep out to-night, I shan't be able to get my keys till the morning." Suddenly in a new tone, the equivalent of a vulgar wink:

"Ah, this life, Fräulein! It's accidents often separate one from one's 'smokkin' for days; sometimes weeks. My 'smokkin' leads a very independent life. Sometimes it's with me, sometimes not. It was a very expensive suit. That has been its downfall."

"Do you mean you haven't got a *frac*?"

"No, not that. You misunderstand me." He reflected a moment.

"Ah, before I forget, Fräulein Lipmann! If you still want to know about that little matter: I wrote to my mother the other day. In her reply she tells me that Professor Heymann is still at Karlsruhe. He will probably take a class in the country this summer as usual. The remainder of the party!" he added as the bell again rang.

He could not be brutally prevented from accompanying them to the dance. But with his remark about Volker he felt as safe as if he had a ticket or *passe-partout* in his pocket.

Kreisler was standing alone nearly in the middle of the room, his arms folded and staring at the door. He would use this fictitious authority and licence to its utmost limit. Some of the others were conscious of something unusual in his presence besides his dress and the disorder even of that. They supposed he had been drinking.

There were rustlings and laughter in the hall for some minutes. Social facts, abstracted in this manner, appealed to the mind with the strangeness of masks, each sense, isolated, being like a mask on another. Anastasya appeared. She came out of that social flutter astonishingly inapposite, like a mask come to life. The little fanfare of welcome continued. She was much more outrageous than Kreisler could ever hope to be: bespangled and accoutred like a princess of the household of Peter the Great jangling and rumbling like a savage showman through abashed capitals.

Her amusement often had been to disinter in herself the dust and decorations of some ancestress. She would float down the windings of her

Great Russian and Little Russian blood, living in some imagined figure for a time as you might in towns on a stream.

"We are new lives for our ancestors, not theirs a playground for us. We are the people who have the Reality." Tarr lectured her later, to which she replied:

"But they had such prodigious lives! I don't like being anything out and out, life is so varied. I like wearing a dress with which I can enter into any *milieu* or circumstances. That is the only real self worth the name."

Anastasya regarded her woman's beauty as a bright dress of a harlot; she was only beautiful for that. Her splendid and bedizened state was assumed with shades of humility. Even her tenderness and peculiar heart appeared beneath the common infection and almost disgrace of that state.

The Bonnington Club was not far off and they had decided to walk, as the night was fine. It was about half-past nine when they started. Seven or eight led the way in a suddenly made self-centred group; once outside in the spaciousness of the night streets the party seemed to break up into sections held together in the small lighted rooms within—Soltyk and his friend, still talking, and a quieter group, followed.

Fräulein Lunken had stayed behind with another girl, to put out the lights. Instead of running on with her companion to join the principal group, she stopped with Kreisler, whom she had found bringing up the rear alone.

"Not feeling gregarious to-night?" she asked.

Kreisler walked slowly, increasing, at every step, the distance between them and the next group, as though hoping that, should he draw her far enough back in the rear, like an elastic band she would in panic shoot forward. "Did he know many English people?" and she continued in a long eulogy of that race. Kreisler murmured and muttered sceptically. And she seemed then to be saying something about Soler's, and eventually to be recommending him a new Spanish professor of some sort.

Kreisler cursed this chatterer and her complaisance in accompanying him.

"I must get some cigarettes," he said briskly, as a *bureau de tabac* came in sight. "But don't you wait, Fräulein. Catch the others up."

Having purposely loitered over his purchase, when he came out on the Boulevard again there she was waiting for him. "Aber! aber! what's the matter with her?" Kreisler asked himself in impatient astonishment.

What was the matter with Bertha? Many things, of course. Among old general things was a state hardly of harmony with the Lipmann circle. She was rather suspect for her too obvious handsomeness. It was felt that she was perhaps a little too interested in the world. She was not quite obedient enough in spirit to the Lipmann. Even nuances of disrespect had been observed. Then Tarr had turned up nearly at the commencement of her incorporation. This was an eternal thorn in their sides, and chronic source of difficulty. Tarr was uncompromisingly absent from all their gatherings, and bowed to them, when met in the street, as it seemed to them, *narquoisement*, derisively, even. He had been excommunicated long ago, most loudly by Fräulein Van Bencke.

"Homme sensuel!" she had called him. She averred she had caught his eye resting too intently on her well-filled-out bosom.

"Homme égoiste!" (this referred to his treatment of Bertha, supposed and otherwise).

Tarr considered that these ladies were partly induced to continue their friendship for Bertha in a hope of disgusting her of her fiancé, or doing as much harm to both as possible.

Bertha alternately went to them a little for sympathy, and defied them with a display of his opinions.

Kreisler had lately been spoken about uncharitably among them. By inevitable analogy he had, in her mind, been pushed into the same boat with Tarr. She always *felt* herself a little *without* the circle.

So, Bertha, still in this unusual way clinging to him (although she had ceased plying him with conversation) they proceeded along the solitary backwater of Boulevard in which they were. Pipes lay all along the edge of excavations to their left, large flaccid surface-machinery of the City. They tramped on under the small uniform trees Paris is planted with, a tame and insipid obsession.

Kreisler ignored his surroundings. He was transporting himself, self-guarded Siberian exile, from one cheerless place to another. To Bertha Nature still had the usual florid note. The immediate impression caused by the moonlight was implicated with a thousand former impressions: she did not discriminate. It was the moon illumination of several love affairs. Kreisler, more restless, renovated his susceptibility every three years or so. The moonlight for him was hardly nine months old, and belonged to

Paris, where there was no romance. For Bertha the darkened trees rustled with the delicious and tragic suggestions of the passing of time and lapse of life. The black unlighted windows of the tall houses held within, for her, breathless and passionate forms, engulfed in intense eternities of darkness and whispers. Or a lighted one, in its contrast to the bland light of the moon, so near, suggested something infinitely distant. There was something fatal in the rapid never-stopping succession of their footsteps—loud, deliberate, continual noise.

Her strange companion's dreamy roughness, this romantic enigma of the evening, suddenly captured her fancy. The machine and indiscriminate side of her awoke.

She took his hand—rapid, soft and humble, she struck the deep German chord, vibrating rudimentarily in the midst of his cynicism.

"You are suffering! I know you are suffering. I wish I could do something for you. Cannot I?"

Kreisler began tickling the palm of her hand slightly. When he saw it interrupted her words, he stopped, holding her hand solemnly as though it had been a fish slipped there for some unknown reason. Having her hand—her often-trenchant hand with its favourite gesture of sentimental over-emphasis—captive, made her discourse almost quiet.

"I know you have been wronged and wounded. Treat me as a sister: let me help you. You think my behaviour odd: do you think I'm a funny girl? But, ah! we walk about and torment each other enough! I knew you were not drunk, but were half-cracked with something—Perhaps you had better not come on to this place—"

He quickened his steps, and still gazing stolidly ahead, drew her by the hand.

"I only should like you to feel I am your friend," she said.

"Right!" with promptness came through his practical moustache.

"You're afraid I—" she looked at the ground, he ahead.

"No," he said, "but you shall know my secret! Why should not I avail myself of your sympathy? You must know that my *frac*—useful to waiters, that is why I get so much for the poor suit—this *frac* is at present *not* in my lodgings. No. That seems puzzling to you? Have you ever noticed an imposing edifice in the Rue de Rennes, with a foot-soldier perpetually on guard? Well, he mounts guard, night and day, over my suit!" Kreisler pulled his moustache with his free hand—"Why keep you in suspense? My *frac* is not on my back because—it is *in pawn*! Now, Fräulein, that you are acquainted with the cause of my slight, rather wistful, *meditative* appearance, you will be able to sympathize adequately with me!"

She was crying a little, engrossed directly, now, in herself.

He thought he should console her.

"Those are the first tears ever shed over my *frac*. But do not distress yourself, Fräulein Lunken. The *garçons* have not yet got it!"

Kreisler did not distinguish Bertha much from the others. At the beginning he was distrustful in a mechanical way at her advances. If not "put up" to doing this, she at least hailed from a quarter that was conspicuous for Teutonic solidarity. Now he accepted her present genuineness, but ill-temperedly substituted complete boredom for mistrust, and at the same time would use this little episode to embellish his programme.

He had not been able to shake her off: it was astonishing how she had stuck: and here she still was; he was not even sure yet that he had the best of it. His animosity for her friends vented itself on her. He would anyhow give her what she deserved for her disagreeable persistence. He shook her hand again. Then suddenly he stopped, put his arm round her waist, and drew her forcibly against him. She succumbed to the instinct to "give up," and even sententiously "destroy." She remembered her resolve—a double one of sacrifice—and pressed her lips, shaking and wettened, to his. This was not the way she had wished: but, God! what did it matter? *It mattered so little, anything,* and above all *she*! This was what she had wanted to do, and now she had done it!

The "resolve" was a simple one. In hazy, emotional way, she had been making up her mind to it ever since Tarr had left that afternoon. He wished to be released, did not want her, was irked, not so much by their formal engagement as by his liking for her (this kept him, she thought she discerned). A stone hung round his neck, he fretted the whole time, and it would always be so. Good. This she understood. Then *she* would release him. But since it was not merely a question of *words*, of saying "we are no longer engaged" (she had already been very free with them), but of acts and facts, she must bring these substantialities about. By putting herself in the most definite sense out of his reach and life—far more than if she should leave Paris, their continuance of relations must be made impossible. Somebody else—and a somebody else who was at the same time *nobody*, and who would evaporate and leave no trace the moment he had served her purpose—must be found. She must be able to stare pityingly and resignedly, but silently, if he were mentioned. Kreisler exactly filled this ticket. And he arose not too unnaturally.

This idea had been germinating while Tarr was still with her that morning.

So, a prodigality and profusion of self-sacrifice being offered her in the person of Kreisler, she behaved as she did.

This clear and satisfactory action displayed her Prussian limitation; also her pleasure with herself, that done. *Should Tarr wish it undone*, it could easily be so. The smudge on Kreisler's back was a guarantee, and did the trick in more ways than he had counted on. But in any case his whole personality was a perfect alibi for the heart, to her thinking. At the back of her head there may have been something in the form of a last attempt here. With the salt of jealousy, and a really big row, could Tarr perhaps he landed and secured even now?

In a moment, the point so gained, she pushed Kreisler more or less gently away. It was like a stage-kiss. The needs of their respective rôles had been satisfied. He kept his hands on her biceps. She was accomplishing a soft withdrawal. They had stopped at a spot where the Boulevard approached a more populous and lighted avenue. As they now stood a distinct, yet strangely pausing, female voice struck their ears.

"Fräulein Lunken!"

Some twenty yards away stood several of her companions, who, with fussy German sociableness, had returned to carry her forward with them, as they were approaching the Bonnington Club. Finding her not with them, and remembering she had lagged behind, with some wonderment they had walked back to the head of the Boulevard. They now saw quite plainly what was before them, but were in that state in which a person does not believe his eyes, and lets them bulge until they nearly drop out, to correct their scandalous vision. Kreisler and Bertha were some distance from the nearest lamp and in the shade of the trees. But each of the spectators would have sworn to the identity and attitude of their two persons.

Bertha nearly jumped out of her skin, broke away from Kreisler, and staggered several steps. He, with great presence of mind, caught her again, and induced her to lean against a tree, saying curtly: "You're not quite well, Fräulein. Lean—so. Your friends will be here in a moment."

Bertha accepted his way out. She turned, indeed, rather white and sick, and even succeeded so far as to half believe her lie, while the women came up. Kreisler called out to the petrified and quite silent group at the end of the avenue. Soon they were surrounded by big-eyed faces. Hypocritical concern soon superseded the masks of scandal.

"She was taken suddenly ill." Kreisler coughed conventionally as he said this, and flicked his trousers as though he had been scuffling on the ground.

Indignant glances were cast at him. Whatever attitude they might take up towards their erring friend, there was no doubt as to their feeling towards *him*. He was to blame from whichever way you looked at it. They eventually, with one or two curious German glances into her eyes, slow, dubious, incredulous questions, with a drawing back of the head and dying away of voice, determined temporarily to accept her explanation. To one of them, very conversant with her relations with Tarr, vistas of possible ruptures and commotions opened. Here was a funny affair! With Kreisler, of all people—Tarr was bad enough!

Bertha would at once have returned home, carrying out the story of sudden indisposition. But she felt the only thing was to brave it out. She did not want to absent herself at once. The affair would be less conspicuous with her not away. Her friends must at once ratify their normal view of this little happening. The only thing she thought of for the moment was to hush up and obliterate what had just happened. Her heroism disappeared in the need for action. So they all walked on together, a scandalized silence subsisting in honour chiefly of Kreisler.

Again he was safe, he thought with a chuckle. His position was precarious, only he held Fräulein Lunken as hostage! Exception could not *openly* be taken to him, without reflecting on their friend. He walked along with perfect composure, mischievously detached and innocent.

Fräulein Lipmann and the rest had already gone inside. Several people were arriving in taxis and on foot. Kreisler got in without difficulty. He was the only man present not in evening-dress.

CHAPTER II

One certain thing amongst many uncertainties about the English club, the Bonnington Club, was that it had not yet found itself quite. Its central room (and that was all there was of it—a shell of a house) reminded you of a public swimming-bath when it was used as a ballroom, and when used as a studio you thought of a concert-hall. But one had a respect for it. It had cost a good deal to build. It was quite phenomenally handsome as seen from the street, and was graceful. It made a cheerful show, with pink, red, and pale blue paper-chains and Chinese lanterns, one week for some festivity; and the next, sparely robed in dark red curtains, would settle its walls gravely to receive some houseless quartet. In this manner it paid its way. Some phlegmatic but obstinate power had brought it into existence. "Found a club, found a club!" it had reiterated in the depths of certain anonymous minds, with sleepy tenacity. Some one sighed, got up and went round to another, and said perhaps a club had better be founded. The other assented and subscribed something, to get rid of the other. In the course of time a young French architect had been entrusted with the job. A club. Yes. What sort of a club? The architect could not find out. Something to be used for drawing-classes, social functions, a reading-room, etc. He saw he was on the wrong tack. He went away and made his arrangements accordingly. He produced a design of an impressive and to all appearance finished house. It was a sincerely ironic masterpiece, but with a perfect gravity, and even stateliness, of appearance. It was the most non-committing façade, the most absolutely unfinal interior, the most tentative set of doors, ever seen: a monster of reservation.

Not only had it been put to every conceivable use itself, but it dragged the club with it, as it were. The club changed and metamorphosed itself with its changes. The club became athletic or sedentary according to the shifts and exigencies of the building's existence. The members turned out in dress-clothes or gymnasium get-ups as the building's destiny prompted, to back it up. One month they would have to prove that it *was* a gymnasium, the next that it *was* a drawing-school.

The inviting of the German contingent was a business move. They might be enticed into membership, and would in any event spread the fame of the club, getting and subsequently giving some conception of the resources of the club-house building. The *salle* was arranged very prettily. The adjoining rooms were hung with the drawings and paintings of the club members.

Kreisler ever since the scene on the boulevard had felt a reckless gaiety and irresponsibility, which he did not conceal.

With his abashed English hostess he carried on a strange conversation full of indirect references to the "stately edifice in the Rue de Rennes." He had spoken of it to Bertha: "That stately edifice in the Rue de Rennes—but of course you don't know it!"

With smiling German ceremoniousness, with ingenious circumlocutions, he bent down to his hostess's nervously smiling face and poured into her startled ear symbols and images of pawnshops, usury, three gold balls, "pious mountains," "smokkin" or "frac" suits, etc., which he seemed a little to confuse, overwhelmed her with a serious terminology, all in a dialect calculated to bewilder the most acute philologist.

"Yes, it *is* interesting," she said with strained conviction.

"Isn't it?" Kreisler replied. It was a comparative estimate of the facilities for the disposing of a watch in Germany and France.

"I'm going to introduce you, Herr Kreisler, to a friend of mine—Mrs. Bevelage."

She wanted to give the German guests a particularly cordial reception. Kreisler did not seem, superficially, a great acquisition to any club, but he was with the others. As a means of concluding this very painful interview—he was getting nearer every minute to the word that he yet solemnly forbade himself the use of—she led him to a self-controlled remnant of beautiful womanhood who had a reputation with her for worldliness. Mrs. Bevelage could listen to all this, and would be able to cope with a certain disquieting element she recognized in the German.

He saw the reason of this measure; and, looking with ostentatious regret at a long-legged flapper seated next door, cast a reproachful glance at his hostess.

Left alone with the widow, he surveyed her ample and worldly form.

"Get thee to a nunnery!" he said dejectedly.

"I beg your pardon?"

"Yes. You have omitted 'my lord.'"

Mrs. Bevelage looked pleased and puzzled. Possibly he was a count or baron.

"Do you know that stingy but magnificent edifice—"

"Yes—?"

"That handsome home of precarious 'fracs' in the Rue de Rennes—?"

"I'm afraid I don't quite understand—" The widow had not got used to his composite tongue. She liked Kreisler, however.

"Shall we dance?" he said, getting up quickly.

He clasped her firmly in the small of the back and they got ponderously in motion, he stamping a little bit, as though he mistook the waltz for a more primitive music.

He took her twice, with ever-increasing velocity, round the large hall, and at the third round, at breakneck speed, spun with her in the direction of the front door.

The impetus was so great that she, although seeing her peril, could not act sufficiently as a break on her impetuous companion to avert the disaster. Another moment and they would have been in the street, amongst the traffic, a disturbing meteor, whizzing out of sight, had they not met the alarmed resistance of a considerable English family entering the front door as Kreisler bore down upon it. It was one of those large, featureless, human groups built up by a frigid and melancholy pair, uncannily fecund, during interminable years of blankness. They received this violent couple in their midst. The rush took Kreisler and his partner half-way through, and there they stood embedded and unconscious for many seconds. The English family then, with great dignity, disgorged them and moved on.

The widow had come somewhat under the fascination of Kreisler's mood. She was really his woman, had he known it. She felt wrapt in the midst of a simoon—she had not two connected thoughts. All her worldliness and measured management of her fat had vanished. Her face had become coarsened in a few minutes. But she buzzed back again into the dance and began a second, mad, but this time merely circular career.

Kreisler was very careful, whatever he did, to find a reason for it. "He was abominably short-sighted; he had mistaken the front door for one leading into the third room, merely." His burden, not in the best condition, was becoming more and more puffed, and heavier every moment. When satisfied with this part of his work he led Mrs. Bevelage into a sort of improvised conservatory and talked about pawnshops for ten minutes or so—in a mixture of French, English, and German. He then reconducted her, more dead than alive, to her seat, and strode off from her with great sweeps of his tall figure.

He had during this incident regained complete impassivity. He stalked away to the conservatory.

Bertha had soon been called on to dance vigorously without much intermission. In the convolutions of the valse, however, she matured a bold and new plan. She whirled and trotted with a preoccupied air.

Would Tarr hear of all this? She was alarmed, now it was done. Also she was cowed and sorry for her action at the thought of Lipmann and Van Bencke's attitude towards the Kreisler kissing. She undoubtedly must secure herself. The plan she hit on offered a "noble" rôle that she could not, in any circumstances, have resisted.

Her scheme was plain and clever. She would simply "tell the truth."

"She had recognized something distracting in Kreisler's life, the presence of crisis. *On an impulse*, she had offered him her sympathy. He had taken up her offer immediately in an astonishing and brutal manner. (One against him: two for her!) Such direct and lurid sympathy he claimed."

So she jogged out her strategies in exhilaration of the waltzes.

At this point of her story she would hint, by ambiguous hesitation, that she, in truth, had been ready even for this sacrifice: had made it, if her hearers wished! She would imply rather that from modesty—not wanting to appear *too* "noble"—she refrained from telling them.

It is true that for such a confession she had many precedents. Only a week ago Fräulein Van Bencke herself, inflating proudly her stout handsome person, had told them that while in Berlin she had allowed a young painter to kiss her: she believed "that the caresses of a pure woman would be helpful to him at that juncture of his life." But this had not been, it was to be supposed, in the middle of the street. No one had ever seen, or ever would see, the young painter in question, or the kiss.

Busy with these plans, Bertha had not much time to notice Kreisler's further deportment. She came across him occasionally, and keyed her solid face into an intimate flush and such mask as results from any sickly physical straining. "*Poor* mensch!"

Soltyk surprised one Anglo-Saxon partner after another with his wonderful English—unnecessarily like the real thing. He went about surprising people in a cold, tireless way, exhibiting no signs of pleasure, except as much as was testified to by his action, merely.

Kreisler saw him with Anastasya only twice. On those occasions he could not, on the strength of Soltyk's attitude, pin him down as a rival. Yet he was thirsting for conventional figures. His endless dissatisfaction and depression could only be satisfied by *active* things, *unlike* itself. Soltyk's self-possessed and masterly signs of distinguished camaraderie depressed Kreisler very much. The Russian *had been there once* at the critical moment, and was, more distantly, an attribute of Volker. He did not like him. How it would satisfy him to dig his fingers into that flesh, and tear it like thick cloth! He was "for it"; he was going out. He was being helped off by things. Why did he not *shout*? He longed to *act*: the rusty machine had a thirst for action. His energies were repudiating their master.

Soltyk's analogies with Kreisler worked in the dark to some end of mutual destruction. The nuance of possibility Soltyk liked his friendships with women to have, was a different affair to Kreisler's heady and thorough-going intrigues. But he liked his soul to be marked with little delicate wounds and wistfulnesses. He liked an understanding, a little melancholy, with a woman. They would just divine in each other possibilities of passion, that was yet too *lasse* and sad to rise to the winding of Love's horns that were heard, nevertheless, in a *décor Versaillesque* and Polonais. They were people who looked forward as others look back. They would say farewell to the future as most men gaze at the past. At the most they played the slight dawning and disappearing of passion, cutting, fastidiously, all the rest of the piece. So he was often found with women. Life had no lethargic intervals as with Kreisler. It at all times needed "expression" of such sort.

For Anastasya, Soltyk was one of her many impresarios, who helped her on to and off the scene of Life. He bored her usually, but they had something equivalent to pleasant business relations. She appreciated him as an Impresario.

These things arraying themselves in reality after this ordinary unexciting fashion, conventional figures of drama lacked. Kreisler was in the wrong company. But he conformed for the sake of the Invisible Audience haunting life. He emulated the matter-of-factness and aplomb that impressed him in the others *à outrance*. So much was this so that the Audience took some time to notice him, the vein of scandal running through the performance.

In the conservatory he established his head-quarters.

From there he issued forth on various errands. All his errands showed the gusto of the logic of his personality, and not despair. He might have been enjoying himself. He invented outrage that was natural to him, and enjoyed slightly the licence and scope of his indifference.

He, for instance, at the first sortie, noticed a rather congested, hot, and spectacled young woman, rather constantly fluttered over her womanhood, but overworked by her conscience, her features set by duty. He succeeded in getting her for a partner, and soon won her confidence by his scrupulous German politeness. He then, while marking time in a crush, disengaged his hand, and appeared to wish to alter the lie of her bosom, very apologetically.

"Excuse me! It's awkward. More to the left—so! Clumsy things and women are so proud of them! (No: I'm sure you're not!) No. Let it hang to the left!" The young lady, very red, and snorting almost in his face, left him brusquely.

Several young women, and notably a flapper, radiant with heavy inexperience and loaded with bristling bronze curls, he lured into the conservatory. They all came out with scarlet faces.

For the first hour he paid no attention to Anastasya, but prosecuted his antics as though he had forgotten all about her. He knew she was there and left her alone, even in thought, in a grim spirit. He hid coquettishly behind his solemn laughter-in-action, the pleasant veil of his hysteria.

He had become generally noticed in the room, although there were a great many people present. Fräulein Lipmann hesitated. She thought at length that he was mad. In speaking to him and getting him removed, she feared a scandalous scene.

As he appeared on the threshold of the conservatory an expectant or anxious tremor invaded several backs. But he just stalked round this time on a tour of inspection, as though to see that all was going along as it should. He stared heavily and significantly at those young ladies who had been his partners, when he came across them. One he stopped in front of and gazed at severely. He then returned to the conservatory.

In his deck chair, his head stretched back, glasses horizontal and facing the ceiling, he considered the graceless Hamlet that he was.

"Go to a nunnery, Widow!"

He should have been saying that to his Ophelia.

Why did he not *go to her*? *Contact* was the essential thing, but so difficult to bring about.

He must make her angry, insult her: that would bare her soul. Then he would spit on it. Then he really could insult her. But Soltyk offered a conventional target for violence. Soltyk was evading him with his contempt. Soltyk! What should be done with him? Why (a prolonged and stormily rising "why"), there was no difficulty about *that*. He got up from his chair, and walked deliberately and quickly into the central room. But Soltyk was nowhere to be seen.

The dancers were circling rapidly past with athletic elation, talking in the way people talk when they are working. Their intelligences floated and flew above the waves of the valse, but with frequent drenchings, as it were, and cessations. The natural strangeness for him of all these English people together did not arrest his mind or lead him to observation, but yet got a little in the way. Couple followed couple, the noise of their feet, or dress, for a moment queerly distinct and near above the rest, as though a yard or two of quiet surrounded Kreisler. They came into this area for a moment, everything distinct and clear cut, and then went out again. Each new pair of dancers seemed coming straight for him. Their voices were loud for a moment. A hole was cut out of the general noise, as it were opening a passage into it. Each new face was a hallucination of separate energy, seeming very distant, laughs, words, movements. They were like trunkless, living heads rolling and bobbing past, a sea of them. The two or three instruments behind the screen of palms produced the necessary measures to keep this throng of people careering, like a spoon stirring in a saucepan. It stirred and stirred and they jerked and huddled insipidly round and round.

Kreisler was drawn up at the first door for a minute. He was just taking a step forward to work his way round to the next, when he caught sight of Anastasya dancing with (he supposed) some Englishman.

He stopped, paralysed by her appearance. This reality intercepted the course of his imaginary life (of which his pursuit of Soltyk was a portion). He stood like somebody surprised in a questionable act. He had not reckoned on being met by her before his present errand was finished. The next moment he was furious at this interference; at her having the power to draw him up. This imaginary life *should* grow. Hell and Heaven! he was not going to stop there looking at her. She and her partner had drawn up for a moment just in his way, being stopped by other couples marking time. She had not seen him. He took her partner roughly by the arm, pushing him against her, hustling him, fixing him with his eye. He passed beyond them then, through the passage he had made. His blood was flooding him, and making him expand and sink like a Russian dancer. The young man handled in this manner, shy and unprompt, stared after Kreisler with a "What the devil!" People are seldom so rude in England. Preparation for outbursts of potential rudeness form a part of the training of a German. Kreisler also, without apology, but as if waiting for more vigorous expostulation, was also looking back, while he stepped slowly along the wall towards a door beyond, the one leading to the refreshment-room.

Anastasya freed herself at once from her partner and pale and frowning (but as though waiting) was looking after Kreisler curiously. She would have liked him to stop. He had done something strange and was as suddenly going away. That was unsatisfactory. They looked at each other blankly. He showed no sign of stopping: she just stared. Suddenly it was comic. She burst out laughing. But they had clashed, like people in the dance, and were both disappearing from each other again, the shock hardly over. The *contact* had been brought about. He was still as surprised at his action, which had been done "in a moment," as she was. Anastasya felt, too, in what way this had been *contact*. She felt his hand on her arm as though it had been she he had seized. This rough figure disappeared in the doorway, as incapable of explaining anything. She shivered nervously as she grasped her partner's arm again, at this merely physical *contact*. "What's the matter with that chap?" her partner asked, conscious of a lameness, but of something queer going on. This question had been asked a few minutes before elsewhere. "Herr Kreisler is behaving very strangely. Do you think he's been drinking?" Fräulein Lipmann had asked Eckhart.

Eckhart was a little drunk himself. He took a very decided view of Kreisler's case.

"Comme toute la Pologne! As drunk as the whole of Poland!" he affirmed. But he only gave it as an opinion, adding no sign of particular indignation. He was beaming with greedy generosity at his great Amoureuse.

"Ah! here he comes again!" said Fräulein Lipmann at the door. (It was when Kreisler had started up in search of Soltyk).

So Kreisler disappeared in the doorway. He passed through the refreshment-room. In a small room beyond he sat down by an open window.

Anastasya had at last got into line with him. She had been startled, awakened, and had also laughed. This was an exact and complete response to Kreisler at the present. Something difficult to understand and which should have been alarming for a woman, the feel of the first tugs of the maelstrom he was producing and conducting all on his own, and which required her for its heart: and then laughter, necessarily, once one was in that atmosphere, like laughing gas, with its gusty tickling.

But this was not how Kreisler felt about it. He was boiling and raging. That laugh had driven him foaming, fugitive and confused, into the nearest chair. He could not turn round and retaliate at the time. The door being in front of him, he vanished as Mephistopheles might sink with suddenness into the floor, at the receipt of some affront, to some sulphurous regions beneath, in a second; come to a stop alone, upright; stick his fingers in his mouth, nearly biting them in two, his eyes staring: so stand stock still, breathless and haggard for some minutes: then shoot up again, head foremost, in some other direction, like some darting and skulking fish, to the face of the earth.

He did not even realize that the famous *contact* was established, so furious was he. He would go and strike her across the mouth, spit in her face, kiss her in the middle of the dance, where the laugh had been! Yet he didn't move, but sat on staring in front of him, quite forgetful where he was and how long he had sat there, in the midst of a hot riot of thoughts.

He suddenly sat up and looked round, like a man who has been asleep and for whom work is waiting; got up with certain hesitation, and again made for the door. Well, life and work (*his* business) must he proceeded with all the same. He glanced reflectively and solemnly about, and perceived the Widow talking to a little reddish Englishman.

"May I take the Widow away for a little?" he asked her companion.

He always addressed her as "Widow": he began all his discourses with a solemn "Widow!" occasionally alternating it with "*Derelict!*" But this, all uttered in a jumbled tongue, lost some of its significance.

The little Englishman on being addressed gave the English equivalent of a jump—a sudden moving of his body and shuffling of his feet, still looking at the floor, where he had cast his eyes as Kreisler approached.

"What? I—"

"Widow! permit me—" said Kreisler.

Manipulating her with a leisurely gusto, he circled into the dance.

The band was playing the "Merry Widow" valse.

"*Merry* Widow!" he said smilingly to his partner. "Yes, *Merry* Widow!" shaking his head at her.

The music seemed fumbling in a confused mass of memory, but finding nothing definite. All it managed to bring to light was a small cheap photograph, taken at a Bauern Bal, with a flat German student's cap. The man remained just his photograph. Their hostess also was dancing. Kreisler noted her with a wink of recognition. Dancing very slowly, almost mournfully, he and his partner bumped into her each time as they passed. The Widow felt the impact, but it was only at the third round that she perceived the method and intention inducing these bumps. She realized they were going to collide with the other lady. The collision could not be avoided. But she shrank away, made herself as small and soft as possible, bumped gently and apologized over her shoulder, with a smile and screwing up of the eyes, full of meaning. At the fourth turn of the room, however, Kreisler having increased her speed sensibly, she was on her guard, and in fact already suggesting that she should be taken back to her seat. He pretended to be giving their hostess a wide berth this time, but suddenly and gently swerved, and bore down upon her. The Widow veered frantically, took a false step, tripped on her dress, tearing it, and fell to the ground. They caused a circular undulating commotion throughout the neighbouring dancers like a stone falling in a pond. Several people bent down to help Mrs. Bevelage—Kreisler's assistance was angrily rejected. His partner scrambled to her feet and went to the nearest chair, followed by one or two people.

"Who is he?"

"He's drunk."

"What happened?"

"He ought to be turned out!" people said who had seen the accident.

Kreisler regained the conservatory with great dignity.

But now Fräulein Lippmann, alone, appeared before him as he lay stretched in his chair, and said in a tight, breaking voice:

"I think, Herr Kreisler, you would do well now, as you have done nothing all the evening but render yourself objectionable, to relieve us of your company. I don't know whether you're drunk. I hope you are, for—"

"You hope I'm drunk, Fräulein?" he asked in an astonished voice.

He remained lolling at full length.

"A lady I was dancing with fell over, owing entirely to her own clumsiness and intractability—but perhaps she was drunk; I didn't think of that."

"So you're not going?"

"Certainly, Fräulein—when you go! We'll go together."

"Scheusal!" Hurling hotly this epithet at him—her breath had risen many degrees in temperature at its passage, and her breast heaved in dashing it out (as though, in fact, the word "scheusal" had been the living thing, and she were emptying her breast of it violently), she left the room. His last exploit had been accomplished in a half disillusioned state. He merely went on farcing because he could think of nothing else to do. Anastasya's laughter had upset and ended everything of his "imaginary life." He told himself now that he *hated* her. "Ich hasse dich! Ich hasse dich!" he hissed over to himself, enjoying the wind of the "hasse" in his moustaches. But (there was no doubt about it) the laugh had crushed him. Ridiculous and hateful had been his goal. But now that he had succeeded he thought chiefly in the latter affair, he was overwhelmed. His vanity was wounded terribly. In *laughing* at him she had puffed out and transformed in an extraordinary way, also, his infatuation. For the first time since he had first set eyes on her he realized her sex. His sensuality had been directly stirred. He wanted to *kiss* her now. He must get his mouth on hers—he must revel in the laugh, where it grew! She was *néfaste*. She was in fact evidently *the devil*.

So his *idée fixe* having suddenly taken body and acquired flesh, now allied to his senses, the vibration became more definitely alarming. He began thinking about her with a slow moistening of the lips. "I *shall possess* her!" he laid to himself, seeing himself in the rôle of the old Berserker warrior, ravening and irresistible. The use of the word *shall* in that way was enough.

But this *infernal* dance! With the advent of the *real* feeling all the artificial ones flew or diminished at once. He was no longer romantically "desperate," but bored with his useless position there. All his attention was now concentrated on a practical issue, that of the "possession" of Anastasya.

He was tired as though he had been dancing the whole evening. He got up and threw his cigarette away; he even dusted his coat a little with his hand. He then, not being able to get at the white patch on the shoulder, took it off and shook it. A large grey handkerchief was used to flick his boots with.

"So!" he grunted, smartly shooting on his coat.

The central room, when he got into it, appeared a different place. People were standing about and waiting for the next tune. It had been completely changed by his novel and material feeling for Anastasya. Everything, for a second time, was quite ordinary, but *not* electrically ordinary, almost hushed, this time. He had become a practical man, surrounded by facts. But he was much more worried and tired than at the beginning of the evening.

To get away was his immediate thought. But he felt hungry. He went into the refreshment-room. On the same side as the door, a couple of feet to the right, was a couch. The trestle-bar with the refreshments ran the length of the opposite wall. The room was quiet and almost empty. Out of the tail of his eye, as he entered, he became conscious of something. He turned towards the couch. Soltyk and Anastasya were sitting there, and looking at him with the abrupt embarrassment people show when an absentee under discussion suddenly appears. He flushed and was about to turn back to the door. But he flushed still more next moment, at thought of his hesitation. This humiliating full-stop beneath their eyes must be wiped out, anyhow. He walked on steadily to the bar.

A shy consciousness of his physique beset him. He felt again an outcast—of an inferior class, socially. He must not show this. He must be leisurely.

He *was* leisurely. He thought when he stretched his hand out to take his cup of coffee that it would never reach it. Reduced to posing nude for Anastasya and the Russian was the result of the evening! Scores of little sensations, like troublesome imps, herded airily behind him. They tickled him with impalpable fingers.

He munched sandwiches without the faintest sense of their taste. Anastasya's eyes were scourging him. He felt like a martyr. Suddenly conscious of an awkwardness in his legs, he changed his position. His arms were ludicrously disabled. The sensation of standing neck deep in horrid filth beset him. Compelled to remain in soaking wet clothes and unable to change them, his body gradually drying them, would have been a similar discomfort. The noise of the dancing began again, filled the room. This purified things somewhat. He got red in the face as though with a gigantic effort, but went on staring in front of him.

His anger kept rising. He stood there deliberately longer; in fact on and on, almost in the same position. She should wait his pleasure till he liked to turn round, and—then. He allowed her laughter to accumulate on his back, like a coat of mud. In his illogical vision he felt her there behind him laughing and laughing interminably. Had he gone straight up to her, in a moment of passion, both disembodied as it were, anything in the shape of objective observation disappearing, he could have avoided this scrutiny. He had preferred to plank himself there in front of her, inevitably ridiculous, a mark for that laugh of hers. Soltyk was sharing it. More and more *his* laughter became intolerable. The traditional solution again suggested itself. Laugh! Laugh! He would stand there letting the debt grow, letting them gorge themselves on his back. The attendant behind the bar began observing him with severe curiosity. He had stood in almost the same position for five minutes and kept staring darkly past her, very red in the face. Then suddenly a laugh burst out behind him—a blow, full of insult, in his ears—and he nearly jumped off the ground. After his long immobility the jump was of the last drollery. His fists clenched, his face emptied of every drop of colour, in the mere action he had almost knocked a man, standing beside him, over. The laugh, for him, had risen with tropic suddenness, a simoom of intolerable offence. It had carried him off his legs, or whirled him round rather, in a second. A young English girl, already terrified at Kreisler's appearance, and a man, almost as much so, stood open-mouthed in front of him. As to Anastasya and Soltyk, they had very completely disappeared, long before, in all probability.

To find that he had been struggling and perspiring in the grasp of a shadow was a fresh offence, merely, for the count of the absentees. Obviously, shadow or not, there or not there, it was they. He felt this a little; but they had disappeared into the *Ewigkeit* for the moment. He had been again beating the air. This should have been a climax, of blows, words, definite things. But things remained vague. The turmoil of the evening remained his, the solid part of it, unshared by anybody else. He smiled, rather hideously and menacingly, at the two English people near him, and walked away. He was not going in search of Anastasya. They would be met somewhere or other, no doubt. All he wanted now was to get away from the English club as soon as possible.

While he was making towards the vestibule he was confronted again with Fräulein Lipmann. "Herr Kreisler, I wish to speak to you," he heard her say.

"Go to the devil!" he answered without hesitation or softness.

"Besotted fool! if you don't go at once, I'll get—"

Turning on her like lightning, with exasperation perfectly meeting hers, his right hand threatening, quickly raised towards his left shoulder, he shouted:

"Lass mich doch—gemeine alte Sau!"

The hissing, thunderous explosion was the last thing in vocal virulence. The muscles all seemed gathered up at his ears like reins, and the flesh tightened and white round his mouth.

Fräulein Lipmann took several steps back. Kreisler with equal quickness turned away, rapped on the counter, while the attendant looked for his hat, and left the Club. Fräulein Lippmann was left with the heavy, unforgettable word "sow" deposited in her boiling spirit, that, boil as it might, would hardly reduce this word to tenderness or digestibility.

PART IV
A JEST TOO DEEP FOR LAUGHTER

CHAPTER I

With a little scratching (as the concierge pushed it) with the malignity of a little, quiet, sleek animal, the letter from Germany crept under the door the next morning, and lay there through the silence of the next hour or two, until Kreisler woke. Succeeding to his first brutal farewells to his dreams, no hopes leapt on his body, a magnificent stallion's, uselessly refreshed. Soon he saw the letter. It lay there quiet, unimportant, rather matter of fact and sly.

Kreisler felt it an indignity to have to open it. Until his dressing was finished, it remained where it was. He might have been making some one wait. Then he took it up, and opening it, drew out between his forefinger and thumb, the cheque. This he deposited with as much contempt as possible, and a "phui" on the edge of his washhand stand. Then he turned to the letter. He read the first few lines, pumping at a cigarette, reducing it mathematically to ash. Cold fury entered his mind with a bound at the first words. They were the final words giving notice of a positive stoppage of supplies. This month's money was sent to enable him to settle up his affairs and come to Germany at once.

He read the first three lines over and over again, going no further, although the news begun in these first lines was developed throughout the two pages of the letter. Then he put it down beside the cheque, and crushing it under his fist, said monotonously to himself, without much more feeling than the sound of the word contained: "Schwein, Schwein, Schwein!"

He got up, and pressed his hand on his forehead; it was wet: he put his hands in his pockets and these came into contact with a cinquante centime piece. He took them out again slowly, went to his box and underneath an old dressing-gown found writing paper and envelopes. Then, referring to his father's letter for the date, he wrote the following lines:

"7th June 19—

"Sir,—I shall not return as you suggest in person, but my body will no doubt be sent to you about the middle of next month. If—keeping to your decision—no money is sent, it being impossible to live without money, I shall on the seventh of July, this day next month, shoot myself.

"Otto Kreisler."

Within half an hour this was posted. Then he went and had breakfast with more tranquillity and relish than he had known for some days. He sat up stiffly like a dilapidated but apparently in some way satisfied rooster at his café table. This life was now settled, pressure ceased. He had come to a conventional and respectable decision. His conduct the night before, for instance, had not been at all respectable. Death—like a monastery—was before him, with equivalents of a slight shaving of the head merely, a handful of vows, some desultory farewells, very restricted space, but none the worse for that; with something like the disagreeableness of a dive for one not used to deep water. But he had got into life, anyhow, by mistake; *il s'était trompé de porte*. His life might almost have been regarded as a long and careful preparation for voluntary death. The nightmare of Death, as it haunted the imaginations of the Egyptians, had here been conjured in another way. Death was not to be overcome with embalmings and Pyramids, or fought within the souls of children. It was confronted as some other more uncompromising race (and yet also haunted by this terrible idea) might have been.

Instead of rearing smooth faces of immense stone against it, you imagine an unparalleled immobility in life, a race of statues, throwing flesh in Death's path instead of basalt. Kreisler would have undoubtedly been a high priest among this people.

CHAPTER II

In a large fluid but nervous handwriting, the following letter lay, read, as it were: Bertha still keeping her eye on it from a distance:

> "Dear Bertha,—I am writing at the Gare St. Lazare, on my way to England. You have made things much easier for me in one way of course, far more difficult in another. Parenthetically, I may mention that the whimsical happenings between you and your absurd countryman in full moonlight are known to me. They were recounted with a wealth of detail that left nothing to the imagination, happily for my peculiar possessive sensitiveness, known to you. I don't know whether that little red-headed bitch—the colour of Iscariot, so perhaps she is—is a friend of yours? Kreisler! I was offered an introduction to him the other day, which I refused. It seems he has introduced himself!
>
> "Before, I had contemplated retiring to a little distance for the purpose of reflection. This last *coup* of yours necessitates a much further *recul*, withdrawal—a couple of hundred miles at least, I have judged. And as far as I can see I shall be some months—say ten—away. I am not wise enough to take your action *au pied de la lettre*; nevertheless, you may consider yourself free as women go. What I mean is you need not trouble to restrain the exuberance of your exploits in future. (What rubbish!) Let them develop naturally, right up to *fiançailles*, or elsewhere. I have a very German idea. Why should not girls have two or three fiancés? Not two or three husbands. But fiancé, especially nowadays, is an elastic term. Why shouldn't fiancé take the place of husband? It is a very respectable word: a very respectable state. But my idea was that of a club, organized around the fiancée. You seem to me cut out for such a club. A man might spend

quite a pleasant time with the other fiancés. A fine science of women would be developed, perhaps along Oriental lines a little. Then a man would remember the different clubs he had belonged to. Some very beautiful women might have a sort of University settled near them. To have belonged to one of these celebrated but ephemeral institutions would insure a man success with less illustrious queens. 'He was a fiancé of Fräulein Stück's, you know,' would carry prestige. You have Germanized me in a horrible way! Anyhow, you may count on me should you think of starting a little institution of that sort. My address for the next few months will be 10 Waterford Street, London, W.C.—Yours,

"Sorbett."

He spelt his name with two T's because Bertha had never disciplined herself to suppress final consonants.

Bertha was in her little kitchen. It was near the front door. Next to it was her studio or *salon*, then bedroom: along a passage at right angles the rooms rented by Clara Goenthner, her friend.

The letter had been laid on the table, by the side of which stood the large gas-stove, like a safe, its gas stars, on top, blasting away luridly at pans and saucepans with Bertha's breakfast. While busying herself with eggs and coffee, she gazed over her arm reflectively at the letter. It was a couple of inches too far away for her to be able to read it.

The postman had come ten minutes before. It was now four days after the dance, and since she had last seen Tarr. She had "felt" he would come on that particular morning. The belief in woman's intuition is not confined, of course, to men. "Could he have heard anything of the Kreisler incident?" she had asked herself. The possibility of this was terrifying. But perhaps it would be as well if he had. It might at any future time crop up. And what things had happened when other older things had come to light suddenly! She would tell him if he had not already heard. He should hear it from her. The great boulevard sacrifice of the other night had appeared folly, long ago. But peculiarly free from any form of spite—she did not feel unkindly towards Kreisler.

So Sorbert was expected to breakfast, on the authority of her intuition. Bread was being fried in fat. What manner of man would appear, how far *renseigné*—or if *not* informed, still all their other difficulties were there inevitably enough? Experience, however, suggested such breakfast as pleased him. Could fried toast and honey play a part in such troubles? Ah, yes. Troubles often reduced themselves to fried bread and honey: they could sow troubles, why not help to quell troubles? But she had had a second intuition that he *knew*. Not knowing how stormy their interview might be she neglected no minute precautions—and these were the touching ones—any more than the sailor would neglect to stow away even the smallest of his sails, I suppose, at the sulky approach of a simoom. The simoom, however, had left her becalmed and taken the train for Dieppe instead of coming in her direction.

CHAPTER III

Bertha went on turning the bread over in the pan, taking the butter from its paper and dropping it into its dish: rinsing and wiping a knife or two, regulating the gas. Frequent truculent exclamations spluttered out if anything went wrong. "Verdammtes Streichholz!" "Donnerwetter!" She used the oaths of Goethe. One eyebrow was raised in humorous reflective irritation. She would flatten the letter out and bend down to examine a sentence, stopping her cooking for a moment.

"Sâlot!" she exclaimed, after having read the letter, all through again, putting it down. She turned with coquettish contemptuousness to her frying-pan. "Sâlot" was, with her, a favourite epithet. Clara's door opened, and Bertha crumpled the letter into her pocket. Clara entered sleepy-eyed and affecting ill-humour. Her fat body was a softly distributed burden, which she carried with the aplomb and indifference of habit. She had a gracefully bumpy forehead, a nice whistling mouth, soft, good and discreet orbs. Her days were passed in the library of the Place Saint Sulpice.

"Ach, lasse! lass mich doch! Get on with your cooking!" she exclaimed as Bertha began her customary sociable and playful greeting. Bertha always was conscious of her noise, of shallowness and worldliness, with this shrewd, indifferent, slow, and monosyllabic bookworm. She wanted to caper round it, inviting it to cumbrous play, like a small lively dog around a heavy one. She was much more *femme* as she said, but aware that Clara did not regard this as an attainment. Being *femme* had taken up so much of her energy and life that she could not expect to be so complete in other ways as Clara. With this other woman, who was much less "woman" than she, she always felt impelled to ultra-feminine behaviour. She was childish to the top of her bent. This was insulting to the other: it showed too clearly Bertha's way of regarding her as not so much *femme* as herself. Clara felt this and would occasionally show impatience at Bertha's skittishness: a gruff man-like impatience entering grimly but imperturbably into the man-part, but claiming at the same time its prerogatives.

Clara had had no known love affairs. She regarded Bertha, sometimes, with much curiosity. This "woman's temperament," so complacently displayed, soothed and tickled her.

"Clara, Soler has told me to send a picture to the Salon d'Automne."

"Oh!" Clara was not impressed by "success." She was preparing her own breakfast and jostled Bertha, usurping more than half the table. Bertha, delighted, retorted with trills of shrill indignation and by recapturing the positions lost by her plates. Her breakfast ready she carried it into her room, pretending to be offended with Clara.

Breakfast over she wrote to Tarr. The letter was written quite easily and directly. She was so sure in the convention of her passion that there was no scratching out or hesitation. "I feel so far away from you." There was nothing more to be said; as it had been said often before, it came easily and promptly with the pen. All the feeling that could find expression was fluent, large and assured, like the handwriting, and went at once into these conventional forms.

"Let Englishmen thank their stars—the good stars of the Northmen and early seamen—that they have such stammering tongues and such a fierce horror of grandiloquence. They are still primitive and true in their passions, because they are afraid of them, like children. The shocks go on *underneath*; they trust their unconsciousness. The odious facility of the South, whether it be their, at bottom, very shrewdly regulated anger (*l'art de s'engueuler*) or their picture post card perfection of amorous expressiveness; such things these Island mutterers and mutes have escaped. But worst of all is the cult of the 'Tempera*ment*,' all the accent on that poor last syllable, whose home is that dubious middle Empire, so incorrigibly banal. The lacerating and tireless pricking and pushing of this hapless 'temperament' is a more harrowing spectacle than the use of dogs in Belgium or women in England."

This passage, from an article in the *English Review*, Tarr had shown to Bertha with great pleasure. Bertha had a good share of impoverished and overworked tempera*ment*, but in a very genial fashion. It had not, with her, grown crooked and vicious with this constant ill-treatment. It was strenuous but friendly. It served in any case a mistress surprisingly disinterested and gentle.

On the receipt of Tarr's letter she had felt, to begin with, very indignant and depressed at his having had the strength to go away without coming to see her. So her letter began on that complaint. He had at last, this was certain, gone away, with the first likelihood of permanence since they had known each other. Despite her long preparation for this, and her being even deliberately the cause of it, she was mortified and at the same time unhappy at the sight of her success.

The Kreisler business had been more for herself than anything, for her own private edification. She would free Sorbert by an act, in a sort of impalpable way. It was not destined as yet for publicity. The fact of the women surprising Kreisler and her on the boulevard had put everything at once out of perspective, damaged her illusion of sacrifice. Compelled at once to be practical again, find excuses, repudiate immediately what she had done before she had been able to enjoy or digest it, was like a man being snatched away from table, the last mouthful hardly swallowed. She was the person surprised before some work doing is completed—it still in a rudimentary unshowable state. For once Tarr was not only in the right, but, to her irritation, he had proofs, splendid ocular proofs, a cloud of witnesses.

To end nobly, on her own initiative, had been her idea; to make a last sacrifice to Sorbert in leaving him irrevocably, as she had sacrificed her feelings all along in allowing their engagement to drag suspiciously on, in making her position slightly uncomfortable with her friends (and these social things meant so much to her in addition). And now, instead, everything had been turned into questionable meanness and ridicule; when she had intended to behave with the maximum of swagger, she suddenly found herself relegated to a skulking and unfortunate plane.

Considerations about Fate beset her. Everything was hopelessly unreliable. The best thing to do was to do nothing. She was not her usual energetic too spiritually bustling self. She wrote her letter quite easily and as usual, but she did not (very unusually) believe in its efficacy. She even wrote it a trifle *more* easily than usual for that reason.

It was only a momentary rebellion against the ease with which this protest was done. Perhaps had it not been for the fascination of habit, then some more adequate words would have been written. His letter had come. Empty and futile she had done her task, answered as she must do; "As we all must do!" she would have thought, with an exclamation mark after it. She sealed up her letter and addressed it.

In the drawer where she was putting Sorbert's latest letter away were some old ones. A letter of the year before she took out and read. With its two sentences it was more cruel and had more meaning than the one she had just received: "Put off that little Darmstadt woman. Let's be alone."

It was a note she had received on the eve of an expedition to a village near Paris. She had promised to take a girl down with them, to show her the place, its hotel and other possibilities—she had stayed there once or twice herself. The Darmstadt girl had not been taken. Sorbert and she had spent the night at an inn on the outskirts of the forest. They had come back in the train next day without speaking, having quarrelled somehow or other in the inn. Chagrin and regret for him struck her a series of sharp blows. She started crying again suddenly, quickly, and vehemently as though surprised by some thought.

The whole morning her work worried her, dusting and arranging. She experienced a revolt against her ceaseless orderliness, a very grave thing in such an exemplary prisoner. At four o'clock in the afternoon, as often happened, she was still dawdling about in her dressing-gown and had not yet had lunch.

The *femme de ménage* came at about eight in the morning, doing Clara's rooms first. Bertha was in the habit of discussing politics with Madame Vannier. Sorbert too was discussed.

"Mademoiselle est triste?" this good woman said, noticing her dejection. "C'est encore Monsieur Sorbert qui vous a fait du chagrin?"

"Oui madame, c'est un Sâlot!" Bertha replied, half crying.

"Oh, il ne faut pas dire ça, mademoiselle. Comment, il est un Sâlot?" Madame Vannier worked silently with soft quiet thud of felt slippers. She appeared to regard work as not without dignity. Bertha was playing at life. She admired and liked her as an emblem of Fortune; she respected herself as an emblem of Misfortune. Madame Vannier was given the letter to post at two.

CHAPTER IV

Bertha's friends looked for her elsewhere, nowadays, than at her rooms. Tarr was always likely to be found there in impolite possession. She made them come as often as she could; her coquetry as regards her carefully arranged rooms needed satisfaction. She suffered in the midst of her lonely tastefulness. But Tarr had certainly made these rooms a rather deserted place. Since the dance none of her women friends had come. She had spent an hour or two with them at the restaurant.

At the dance she had kept rather apart. Dazed, after a shock, and needing self-collection, was the line sketched. Her account of things could not, of course, be blurted out anyhow. It had to grow out of circumstances. It, of course, must be given. She had not yet given it. But haste must be avoided. For its particular type, as long a time as possible must be allowed to elapse before she spoke of what had happened. It must almost seem as though she were going to say nothing; sudden, perfect, and very impressive silence on her part. To accustom their minds to her silence would make speech all the more imposing, when it came. At a café after the dance her account of the thing flowered grudgingly, drawn forth by the ambient heat of the discussion.

They were as yet at the stage of exclamations, no *malveillant* theory yet having been definitely formed about Kreisler.

"He came there on purpose to create a disturbance. Whatever for, I wonder!"

"I expect it was the case of Fräulein Fogs over again." (Kreisler had, on a former occasion, paid his court to a lady of this name, with resounding unsuccess.)

"If I'd have known what was going on, I'd have dealt with him!" said one of the men.

"Didn't you say he told a pack of lies, Renée—?"

Fräulein Lipmann had been sitting, her eyes fixed on a tram drawn up near by, watching the people evacuating the central platform, and others restocking it. The discussion and exclamations of her friends did not, it would appear, interest her. It would have been, no doubt, scandalously unnatural if Kreisler had not been execrated. But anything they could say was negligible and inadequate to cope with the "Gemeine alte Sau." The tameness of their reflections on and indignation against Kreisler when compared with the terrific corroding of this epithet (known only to her) made her sulky and impatient.

Applied to in this way directly about the lies, she turned to the others and said, as it were interposing herself regally at last in their discussion:

"Ecoutez—listen," she began, leaning towards the greater number of them, seeming to say, "It's really simple enough, as simple as it is disagreeable: I am going to settle the question for you. Let us then discuss it no more." It would seem a great effort to do this, too, her lips a little white with fatigue, her eyes heavy with disgust at it all: fighting these things, she was coming to their assistance.

"Listen: we none of us know anything about that man"; this was an unfortunate beginning for Bertha, as thoughts, if not eyes, would spring in her direction no doubt, and Fräulein Lipmann even paused as though about to qualify this: "we none of us, I think, want to know anything about him. Therefore why this idiot—the last sort of beer-drinking brute—treated us to his bestial and—and—wretched foolery—"

Fräulein Lipmann shrugged her shoulders with blank, contemptuous indifference. "I assure you it doesn't interest me the least little bit in the world to know *why* such brutes behave like that at certain times. I don't see any mystery. It seems odd to you that Herr Kreisler should be an offensive brute?" She eyed them a moment. "To me not!"

"We do him too much honour by discussing him, that's certain," said one of them. This was in the spirit of Fräulein Lipmann's words, but was not accepted by her just then as she had something further to say.

"When one is attacked, one does not spend one's time in considering *why* one is attacked, but in defending oneself. I am just fresh from the *souillures de ce brute*. If you knew the words he had addressed to me."

Ekhart was getting very red, his eyes were shining, and he was moving rhythmically in his chair something like a steadily rising sea.

"Where does he live, Fräulein Lipmann?" he asked.

"Nein, Ekhart. One could not allow anybody to embroil themselves with that useless brute." The "Nein, Ekhart" had been drawled fondly at once, as though that contingency had been weighed, and could be brushed aside lightly in advance. It implied as well an "of course" for his red and dutiful face. "I myself, if I meet him anywhere, shall deal with him better than you could. This is one of the occasions for a woman—"

So Bertha's story had come uncomfortably and difficultly to flower. She wished she had not waited so long. But it was impossible now, the matter put in the light that Fräulein Lipmann's intervention had caused, to delay any longer. She was, there was no doubt about it, vaguely responsible for Kreisler. It was obviously her duty *to explain* him. And now Fräulein Lipmann had just put an embargo on explanations. There were to be no more explanations. In Kreisleriana her *apport* was very important: much more definite than the indignation or hypothesis of any of the rest. She had been *nearer to him*, anyway. She had waited too long, until the sea had risen too high, or rather in a direction extremely unfavourable for launching her contribution. It must be in some way, too, a defence of Kreisler. This would be a very delicate matter to handle.

Yet could she sit on there, say nothing, and let the others in the course of time drop the subject? They had not turned to her in any way for further information or as to one peculiarly susceptible of furnishing interesting data. Maintaining this silence was a solution. But it would be even *bolder* than her first plan. This would be a still more vigorous, more insolent development of her plan of confessing—*in her way*. But it rather daunted her. They might easily mistake, if they pleased, her silence for the silence of acknowledged, very eccentric, guilt. The subject was drawing perilously near the point where it would be dropped. Fräulein Lipmann was summing up, and doing the final offices of the law over the condemned and already unspeakable Kreisler. No time was to be lost. The breaking in now involved inevitable conflict of a sort with Fräulein Lipmann. She was going to "say a word for Kreisler" *after* Fräulein Lipmann's words. (How much better it would have been before!)

So at this point, looking up from the table, Bertha (listened to with uncomfortable unanimity and promptness) began. She was smiling with an affectedly hesitating, timid face, smiling in a flat strained way, the neighbourhood of her eyes suffused slightly with blood, her lips purring the words a little:

"Renée, I feel that I ought to say something—" Her smile was that made with a screwing up of the eyes and slow flowering of the lips, noticed on some people's faces when some snobbery they cannot help has to be allowed egress from their mouth.

Renée Lipmann turned towards her composedly. This interruptic would require argument; consciousness of the peculiar nature of Bertha's qualifications was not displayed.

"I had not meant to say anything—about what happened to me, that is. I, as a matter of fact, have something particularly to complain of. But I had nothing to say about it. Only, since you are all discussing it, I thought you might not quite understand if I didn't—I don't think, Renée, that Herr Kreisler was quite in his right mind this evening. He doesn't strike me as *méchant*. I don't think he was really in any way accountable for his actions. I don't, of course, know any more about him than you do. This evening was the first time I've ever exchanged more than a dozen words with him in my life."

This was said in the sing-song of quick parentheses, eyebrows lifted, and with little gestures of the hand.

"He caught hold of me—like this." She made a quick snatching gesture at Fräulein Lipmann, who did not like this attempt at intimidation or velvety defiance. "He was kissing me when you came up," turning to one or two of the others. This was said with dramatic suddenness and "determination," as it were: the "kissing" said with a sort of deliberate sententious brutality, and luscious disparting of the lips.

"We couldn't make out *whatever* was happening—" one of them began.

"When you came up I felt quite dazed. I didn't feel that it was a man kissing me. He was mad. I'm sure he was. It was like being mauled by a brute." She shuddered, with rather rolling eyes. "He *was* a brute to-night—not a man at all. He didn't know what he was doing."

They were all silent, answerless at this unexpected view of the case. It only differed from theirs in supposing that he was not *always* a brute. She had spoken quickly and drew up short. Their silence became conscious and septic. They appeared as though they had not expected her to stop speaking, and were like people surprised naked, with no time to cover themselves.

"I think he's in great difficulties—money or something. But all I know for certain is that he was *really* in need of somebody—"

"But what makes you think, Bertha—" one of the girls said, hesitating.

"I let him in at Renée's. He looked strange to me: didn't you notice? I noticed him first there."

Anastasya Vasek was still with them. She had not joined in the talk about Kreisler. She listened to it with attention, like a person newly arrived in some community, participating for the first time at one of their discussions

on a local and stock subject. Kreisler would, from her expression, hav seemed to be some topic peculiar to this gathering of people—they engagec in a characteristic occupation. Bertha she watched as one would watch a very eloquent chief airing his views at a clan-meeting.

"I felt he was *really* in need of some hand to help him. He seemed just like a child. He was ill, too. He can't have eaten anything for some time. I am sure he hasn't. He was walking slower and slower—that's how it was we were so far behind. It was my fault, too—what happened. At least—"

The hungry touch was an invention of the moment. "You make him quite a romantic character. I'm afraid he has been working on your feelings, my dear girl. I didn't see any signs of an empty stomach myself," said Fräulein van Bencke.

"He refreshed himself extensively at the dance, in any case. You can put your mind at rest as to his present emptiness," Renée Lipmann said.

Things languished. The Lipmann had taken her stand on boredom. She was committed to the theory of the unworthiness of this discussion. The others not feeling quite safe, Bertha's speeches raised no more comment. It was all as though she had been putting in her little bit of abuse of the common enemy. Bertha might have interrupted with a "Yes. He outraged me too!"—and this have been met with a dreary, acquiescing silence!

She was exculpating herself, then (heavily), at his expense. The air of ungenerosity this had was displeasing to her.

The certain lowering of the vitality of the party when she came on the scene with her story offended her. There should have been noise. It was not quite the lifelessness of scepticism. But there was an uncomfortable family likeness to the manner of people listening to discourses they do not believe. She persevered. She met with the same objectionable flaccid and indifferent opposition. Her intervention had killed the topic, and they seemed waiting till she had ended her war-dance on its corpse.

The red-headed member of the party had met Tarr by chance. Hearing he had not seen Bertha since the night of the ball, she had said with roguish pleasantness: "He'd better look after her better; why hadn't he come to the ball?" Tarr did not understand.

"Bertha had had an adventure. All of them, for that matter, had had an adventure, but especially Bertha. Oh, Bertha would tell him all about it." But, on Tarr insisting, Bertha's story, in substance, had been told.

So with Bertha, the *fact* was still there. Retrospectively, her friends insisted upon passing by the two remarkably unanimous-looking forms on the boulevard in stony silence. She shouted to them and kissed Kreisler loudly. But they refused to take any notice. She sulked. They had been guilty of catching her. She kept to herself day after day. She would make a change in her life. She might go to Germany; she might go to another *quartier*. To go on with her life just as though nothing had happened, *that was out of the question*. Demonstration of some sort must follow, and change compatible with grief.

Her burly little clock struck four. Hurrying on reform-clothes, she went out to buy lunch. The dairy lay nearly next door to Lejeune's restaurant. Crossing the road towards it, she caught sight of Kreisler's steadily marching figure approaching. First she side-stepped and half turned. But the shop would be reached before they met, so she went on, merely quickening her pace. Her eye, covertly fixed on him, calculating distances and speeds, saw him hesitate—evidently having just caught sight of *her*—and then turn down a side street nearly beside the dairy she was making for. Unwise pique beset her at this.

CHAPTER V

Kreisler, on his side, had been only a few paces from his door when he caught sight of Bertha. As his changed route would necessitate a good deal of tiresome circling to bring him back practically to the spot he had started from, he right-about-faced in a minute or two, the danger past, as he thought. The result was that, as she left the shop, there was Kreisler approaching again, almost in the same place as before.

She was greeted affably, as though to say "Caught! both of us!" He was under the impression, however, that she had lain in wait for him. He was so accustomed to think of her in that character! If she had been in full flight he would have imagined that she was only decoying him. She was a woman who could not help adhering.

"How do you do? I've just been buying my lunch."

"So late?"

"I thought you'd left Paris!" She had no information of this sort, but was inclined to rebuke him for *not* leaving Paris.

"I? Who told you that, I should like to know. I shall never leave Paris; at least—"

There was heavy enigmatic meaning in this, said lightly. It did not escape her, sensible to such nuances.

"How are our fair friends?" he asked.

"Our? Oh, Fräulein Lipmann and—Oh, I haven't seen them since the other night."

"Indeed! Not since the other night—?"

She made her silence swarm with significant meanings, like a glassy shoal with innumerable fish: her eyes even, stared and darted about, glassily.

It was very difficult, now she had stopped, to get away. The part she had more or less played with her friends, of his champion, had imposed itself on her. She could not leave her protégé without something further said. She was flattered, too, at his showing no signs now of desire to escape.

His more plainly brutal instincts woke readily in these vague days. Various appetites had been asserting themselves. So the fact that she was a pretty girl did its work on a rather recalcitrant subject. He felt so modest now, ideals things of the past. Surely for a quiet ordinary existence pleasant little distinctions were suitable?

Without any anxiety about it, he began to talk to Bertha with the idea of a subsequent meeting. He had wished to avoid her because she had embodied for him the evening of the dance, and appeared to him in its disquieting colours. What he sought unconsciously now was a certain quietude, enlivened by healthy appetites. He had disconnected her with his great Night.

"I was cracked the other night. I'm not often in that state," he said. Bertha's innuendoes had to be recognized.

"I'm glad of that," she answered.

As to Bertha, to have been kissed and those things, under however eccentric circumstances, gave a man certain rights on your interest.

"I'm afraid I was rather rude to Fräulein Lipmann before leaving. Did she tell you about it?"

"I think you were rude to everybody!"

"Ah, well—"

"I must be going. My lunch—"

"Oh, I'm so sorry! Have I kept you from your lunch? I wonder if you would procure me the extreme pleasure of seeing you again?"

Bertha looked at him in doubtful astonishment, taking in this sensational request.

See Kreisler again! The result as regards the Lipmann circle! But this pleaded for Kreisler. It would be carrying out her story. It would be insisting on it, and destroying that subtle advantage, now possessed by her friends, in presenting them with somewhat the same uncompromising spectacle again. In *deliberately* exposing herself to criticism she would be effacing, in some sense, the extreme *involuntariness* of the boulevard incident. He asked her simply if he might see her again. The least pretentious request. Would the refusal to do this simple thing be a concession to Lipmann and the rest? Did she want to at all? But it was in a jump of deliberate defiance or "carelessness" that she concluded:

"Yes, of course, if you wish it."

"You never go to cafés? Perhaps some day—"

"Good! Very well!" she answered very quickly, in her trenchant tone, imparting all sorts of particular unnecessary meanings to this simple acceptance. She had answered as men accept a bet or the Bretons clinch a bargain in the fist.

Kreisler was still leisurely. He appeared to regard her vehemence with amusement.

"I should like then to go with you to the Café de l'Observatoire to-morrow evening. I hope I shall be able to efface the rather unusual impression I must have made on you the other night!" (The tone of this remark did not ignore or condemn, however, the kisses.) "When can I meet you?"

"Will you come and fetch me at my house?"

But shivers went down her back as she said it.

She was now thoroughly committed to this new step. She was delighted, or rather excited, at each new further phase of it. Its horrors were scores off her friends. These details of *meeting*!—these had not been reckoned on. Of course they would have to *meet*. Kreisler seemed like a physician conducting a little unpleasant operation in a genial, ironical, unhurrying way.

"Well, it's understood. We shall see each other to-morrow," he said. And with a smile of half raillery at her rather upset expression, he left her. So much fuss about a little thing, such obstinacy in doing it! What was the terrible thing? Meeting him! His smiling was only natural. She showed without disguise in her face the hazardous quality, as she considered it, of this consent. She would wish him to feel the largeness of the motive that prompted her, and for him to participate too in the certain horror of meeting himself!

CHAPTER VI

Back in her rooms, she examined, over her lunch, with stupefaction, the things she had been doing—conversations, appointments, complementary sensations, and all the rest, as she might have sat down before some distinctly expensive, troubling purchase that she had not dreamt of making an hour before. "What a strange proceeding!"—as it might have been—"what sudden disease in my taste made me buy that!"

Had she been enveloped, in a way, by that idle Teutonically smiling manner of his? But at the bottom of her (for her) dramatic consent was the instantaneous image of Fräulein Lipmann and Company's disapprobation. The *carrying out* and so substantiating her story, that notion turned the scale. Kreisler's easy manner (he *was* unmistakably "a gentleman!") contrasted with her friend's indignant palaver gave him the advantage. He cannot, cannot have behaved *so* outrageously as they pretended!

These activities as well distracted her from brooding over Sorbert's going.

Of Kreisler she thought very little. Her women friends held the centre of the stage.

In her thoughts they stared at her supersession: Tarr to Kreisler. From bad to worse, for her friends. There was a strange continuity in her troubled friendship with these women. Always (only more so) at the same point, stretching the cord.

So this was the key to her programme; *a person has made some slip in grammar, say*. He makes it again deliberately, so that his first involuntary speech may appear deliberate.

She began her customary pottering about in her rooms. Fräulein Elsa Kinderbach, one of the Dresden sisters already spoken of, interrupted her. At the knock she thought of Tarr and Kreisler simultaneously, and welded in one.

"Isn't it hot? It's simply broiling outside. I left the studio quite early." Fräulein Kinderbach sat down, giving her hat a toss and squinting up at it.

The most evident thing about these sisters was dirt, anæmia, and a sort of soiled, insignificant handsomeness. They explained themselves, roughly, by describing in a cold-blooded lazy way their life at home.

A stepmother, prodigiously smart, well-to-do, neglecting them; sent first to one place then another (now Paris) to be out of the way. Yet the stepmother supplies them superfluously from her superfluity.—They talked about themselves with a consciously dramatic matter-of-factness, as twin parcels, usually on the way from one place to another, expensively posted here and there, without real destination. They enjoyed nothing at all; painted well (according to Juan Soler); had a sort of wild uncontrollable attachment for the Lipmann.

"Oh! Bertha, I didn't know your dear 'Sorbert' was going to England." "Dein Sorbet" was the bantering formula for Tarr. Bertha was perpetually talking about him, to them, to the charwoman, to the greengrocer opposite, to everybody she met. Tarr did not quite bask in this notoriety.

"Didn't you? Oh, yes; he's gone."

"You've not quarrelled—with your Sorbert?"

"What's that to do with you, my dear?" Bertha gave a brief, indecent laugh she sometimes had. "By the way, I've just seen Herr Kreisler. We've arranged to go out somewhere to-morrow."

"Go out—Kreisler! Liebes Kind!—What on earth possessed you—!—Herr—*Kreisler*!"

"What's the matter with Herr Kreisler? You were all friendly enough with him a week ago."

Elsa looked at her with the cold-blooded scrutiny of the precocious urchin.

"But he's a vicious brute. Besides, there are other reasons for avoiding Herr Kreisler. You know the reason of his behaviour the other night? It was it appears, because Anastasya Vasek snubbed him. He was nearly the same when the Fogs wouldn't take an interest in him. He can't leave women alone. He follows them about and annoys them, and then becomes—well, as you saw him the other night—when he's shaken off. He is impossible. He is not a person who can be accepted by anybody."

"Where did you hear all that? I don't think that Fräulein Vasek's story is true. I am certain—"

"Well, he once was like that with me. He began hanging round, and—You know the story of his engagement?"

"What engagement?"

"He was engaged to a girl and she married his father instead of marrying him."

Bertha struggled a moment, a little baffled.

"Well, what is there in that? I've known several cases—"

"Yes. That *by itself*—"

Elsa Kinderbach was quite undisturbed. Her information had been coldly given. She had argued sweepingly, as though talking to a child, and following some reasonable resolve formed during her earlier silent scrutiny.—In a few moments Bertha returned to the charge.

"Did Fräulein Vasek give that particular explanation of Herr Kreisler's behaviour?"

"No. We put two and two together. She did say something—yes, she did as a matter of fact say that she thought she had been the cause of Kreisler's behaviour."

"How funny! I can't stand that girl; she's so unnatural, she's such a *poseuse*. Don't you think, Elsa?—What a funny thing to say? You can depend on it that *that*, anyhow, is not the explanation."

"Sorbert has a rival perhaps?"

This remark was met in staring silence. It was a mixing of elements, an unnecessary bringing in of something as unapropos, as unmanageable; that deserved only no words at all. She did not wish to concede the light tone required.

Elsa had admitted that Fräulein Vasek was responsible for the statement, "*I* was the cause of Kreisler's behaviour," etc. That was one of those things (there being no evidence to confirm or even suggest it) which at once puts a woman on a peculiar pinnacle of bad taste, incomprehensibleness, and horridness. Bertha's personal estimation of Kreisler received a complex fillip. This ridiculous version—coming after her version—was a *rival version*, believed in by her friends.

Bertha took some minutes to digest Elsa's news. She flushed. The more she thought of this rival version of Fräulein Vasek's, the more reprehensible it appeared. It was a startlingly novel and uncompromising version, giving proof of a perfect immodesty. It charged hers full tilt.

This *version* of hers had been the great asset of existence for three days. Some one had coolly set up shop next door, to sell an article in which she, and she alone, had specialized. Here was an unexpected, gratuitous, *new* inventor of versions coming along. And what a version to begin with!

Bertha's version had been a vital matter, Fräulein Vasek's evidently was a matter of vanity. The contempt of the workman, sweating for a living, for the amateur, possessed her.

But there was a graver aspect to the version of this poaching Venus. In discrediting Bertha's suggested account of how things happened, it attacked indirectly her action, proceeding, ostensibly, from these notions.

Her meeting Kreisler at present depended for its reasonableness and existence even on the "hunger" theory; or, if that should fail, something equally touching and primitive. Were she forced, as Elsa readily did, to accept the snub-by-Anastasya theory, with its tale of ridiculous reprisals, further dealings with Kreisler would show in a bare and ugly light. Her past conduct also would have its primitive slur renewed.

Her defiance to Elsa had been delivered with great satisfaction. "I am meeting Herr Kreisler to-morrow!" The shine had soon been taken off that.

All Bertha's past management of the boulevard scene had presupposed that she was working in an element destined to obscurity: malleable, therefore, to any extent. Anastasya had risen up calm, contradictory, a formidable and perplexing enemy, with her cursed *version*. The weak point in it was the rank immodesty of the form it took.

Her obstinacy awoke. This new turn coming from the other camp solidified two or three degrees more, in a twinkling, her partisanship of Kreisler. She had a direct interest now in their meeting. She was curious to hear what he had to say as to his alleged attempt in Fräulein Vasek's direction.

"Well, I'm going to Renée's now, to fetch her for dinner. Are you coming?" Elsa said, getting up.

"No. I'm going to dine here to-night," and Bertha accompanied her to the door.

CHAPTER VII

People appear with a startling suddenness sometimes out of the fog of Time and Space. Bertha did not visualize Kreisler very readily. She was surprised when she saw him below her windows the next day. He stared up at the house with an eager speculation. He considered the house and studio opposite. Behind the curtains Bertha stood with emotions of an ambushed soldier. She felt on her face the blankness of the wall of the house, its silence and unresponsiveness. He appeared almost to be looking at her face, magnified and exposed.—Then it appeared to her that it was *he*, the enemy getting in. She wished to stop him there, before he came any further.

In the processes of his uncertainty he was so innocuous and distant, for the moment. His first visit. There he was: so far, a stranger. Why should these little obstacles of strangeness—which gate to enter, which bell to ring—be taken away from this particular individual? He should remain "stranger" for her, where he came from. But he had burrowed his way through, was at the bell already, and would soon be at herself. *She* found here, in her room, was very different from *she* found outside, in restaurant or street. The clothing of this *décor* was a nakedness.

She struggled for a moment up from the obstinate dream, made of artificial but tenacious sentiments, shaped by contretemps of all sorts that had been accumulating like a snowball ever since her last interview with Tarr. Still somewhat wrapt in this interview she rolled in its nightmarish, continually metamorphosed, substance through space. Where would it land her, this electric, directionless, vital affair? This invasion of Indifference and Difference had floated her, successfully, away in *some* direction.

The bell rang again. She could see him, almost, through the wall, standing phlegmatic and erect. They had not spoken yet. But they had been some minutes "in touch."

Perhaps he was *mad*! Elsa, cold, matter-of-fact, but with warnings for her, came into her mind. However much she resisted the facts, there was very little reason for this meeting. It was a now unnecessary, exploded, and objectless impulse, sapped by Anastasya. She was going through with something from laziness and obstinacy mixed, that no longer meant anything.

Already dressed, she walked to the door as the bell rang a third time. Kreisler was serious and a little haggard; different from the day before. He had expected to be asked in. Instead, hardly saying anything, she came out on the narrow landing and closed the door behind her. Surprised, he felt for the first stair. It was eight in the evening, very dark on the staircase, and he stumbled several times. Bertha felt she *could* not say a single word to him. It was just as though some lawyer's clerk had come to fetch her for a tragic disagreeable interview, and she, having been sitting fully dressed for unnecessary hours in advance, were now urging him silently and violently before her, following.

That afternoon she had received a second letter from Sorbert.

> "My dear Bertha.—Excuse me for the *blague* I wrote the other day. There is nothing to be gained in conforming to our old convention of vagueness. I think we had better say, finally, that we will try and get used to not seeing each other, and give up our idea of marriage. Do you agree with me? As you will see, I am still here, in Paris. I am going to England this afternoon.
>
> "Toujours affectueusement,
>
> "Votre Sorbert."

On the receipt of this letter—as on the former occasion a little—she first of all behaved as she would have done had Sorbert been there. She acted silent resignation and going about her work as usual for the benefit of the letter, as though it had been a living person. The reply to this, written an hour or so before Kreisler arrived, had been an exaggerated acquiescence. "Of course, Sorbert: far better that we should part!" But soon this letter began to worry her and threaten her mannerisms. She was just going to take up a book and read, when, as though something had called her attention, she put it down, got up, her head turned over her shoulder, and then suddenly flung herself on the sofa as though it had been rocks and she plunging on them from a high cliff. She sobbed until she had tired herself out.

So Kreisler and she walked up the street as though compelled by some very strange circumstances, only, to be in each other's company.

He appeared depressed, and to have come also under the spell of some sort of meaningless duty. His punctuality suggested, too, fatigued and senseless waiting, careful timing. His temporary destination reached, he delivered himself up indifferently into her hands. He said something about its being hot. They said hardly anything, but walked on away from her house. They showed no *pudeur* about this peculiar state of mind and their manners.

Before they got to the Café de l'Observatoire Kreisler was attempting to make up for his lapse into strangeness, discovering, however, in a little, that he had not been alone.

Bertha looked at the clock inside as they took up their place on the quieter *terrasse*. When she asked herself how long she would stop she was astonished.

"Who is that, then?" Kreisler asked, after some moments of gradually changing silence, when Anastasya began to be mentioned by Bertha. He showed no interest.

This meeting had been the only event of the day for him. He had looked forward to it a little at first. But as it approached he got fidgety, began counting the time, and from being a blessed *something*, it became a burden. The responsibility of this meeting even seemed too much for him. He began to ask himself what useless errand he was on now? The effort of this simple affair worked lamentably on his nerves. He would not have gone, only the appointment being made and fixed in his mind, and he having felt it in the distance all day, he knew it would irk him more if he did *not* go. He was compelled, in short, to go, to have done with it. The worrying obsession of not having done it intimidated him. In the empty evening he would have been at the mercy of this thing-not-done, like an itch.

Bertha, for her part, recovered. Kreisler's complete abstraction and indifference were soothing. He seemed to know as little why he was there as she, or less, and be only waiting for her to disappear again. No slight was implied. Her vanity stirred a little. She perhaps came through this to bring Fräulein Vasek on the boards as she had originally intended. As to there being anything compromising in this meeting, that might be disposed of. He did not look like suggesting another.—His manner on the day before would not have warranted complete calm. And Elsa's description of his conduct with women had stuck in her mind. As the hour of meeting approached it helped her uneasiness. But now she felt refreshingly relieved. *This* was the man who had caused her fresh misgivings! When a dog or cow has passed a trembling child without any signs of mischief, the child sometimes is inclined to step after it and put forth a caressing hand.

By his manner and its reflection on her feelings he had created a situation not unlike that of the dance night. There they sat, she pressing a little, he civilly apathetic. It seemed for all the world as though Bertha had run after him somewhere and forced a meeting on him, to which he had grudgingly come. She was back in what would always be for him her characteristic rôle. And so now—and again later continually—she appeared to be following him up, to the discomfort of both, for some unguessable reason.

"No, I don't know who you mean," he said, replying to descriptions of Anastasya. "A tall girl you say? No, I can't bring to mind—"

He liked fingering over listlessly the thought of Anastasya, but as a stranger. This subject gave him a little more interest in Bertha, just as, for her, it had a similar effect in his favour. She was immediately convinced that Fräulein Vasek had been guilty of the most offensive, self-complacent mistake.

Kreisler had not energy enough left to continue his pursuit of his bespangled dream.

Bertha now had achieved a simplification of the whole matter as follows:

Anastasya, a beautiful and swankily original girl, had arrived, bespangled and beposed, on the scene of her (Bertha's) simple little life. She had discovered her kissing and being kissed by a ridiculous individual in the middle of the street. Bertha had disengaged herself rapidly, and explained that she had been doing that because he had awoken her pity by his miserable and half-starved appearance; that, even then, he had assaulted her, and she had been found in that delicate situation entirely independent of her own will. Anastasya's lip had curled, and she had received these explanations in silence. Then, at their nervous repetition, she had said negligently: "You were no doubt being hugged by Herr Kreisler in the middle of the pavement, the motives the ordinary ones. You might have waited till—But that's your own business. On the other hand, the reason of his eccentric appearance this evening was *this*. He had the incredible impudence to wish to make up to me. I sent him about his business, and he 'manifested' in the way you know."

Reducing all the confused material of this affair to such essential situation, Bertha saw clearly the essence of her action.

Definite withdrawal from the circle of her friends was now essential. It was accomplished with as much style as possible. Kreisler provided the style.

Her instinct now was to wallow still more in the unbecoming situation in which she had been found, with defiance. She wanted to be seen with Kreisler. The meanness, strangeness, and certain *déchéance* or come-down, in consorting with this sorry bird, must be heightened into poetry and thick and luscious fiction. *They had driven her to this. They were driving her!* Very well. She was *lasse*! She would satisfy them. She would satisfy Sorbert. It was what he wanted, was it not?

Kreisler, of course, was the central, irreducible element in this mental pie. He was the egg-cup that kept up the crust. She tried to interest herself in Kreisler and satisfy Tarr, her friends, *the whole world*, more thoroughly.

CHAPTER VIII

Destiny has more power over the superstitious. They attract constantly bright fortunes and disasters within their circle. Destiny had laid its trap in the unconscious Kreisler. It fixed it with powerful violent springs. Eight days later (dating from the Observatoire meeting), it snapped down on Bertha.

Kreisler's windows had been incandescent with steady saffron rays, coming over the roofs of the quarter. His little shell of a room had breasted them with pretence of antique adventure. The old boundless yellow lights streamed from their abstract El Dorado. They were a Gulf Stream for our little patch of a world, making a people as quiet as the English. Men once more were invited to be the motes in the sunbeam, to play in the sleepy surf on the edge of remoteness.

Now, from within, his windows looked as suddenly harsh and familiar. Unreasonable limitation gave its specific colour to thin glass.

The clock was striking eight. Like eight metallic glittering waves dashing discordantly together in a cavern, its strokes rushed up and down in Bertha's head. She was leaning on the mantelshelf, head sunk forward, with the action of a person about to be sick. She had struggled up from the bed a moment before—the last vigour at her disposal being spent in getting away from the bed at all costs.

"Oh schwein! schwein! Ich hass es—ich hass dich! Schwein! Scheusal! schenesslicher Mensch!"

All the hatred and repulsion of her being, in a raw, indecent heat, seemed turned into this tearful sonority, gushing up like blood. An exasperated falling, deepening sing-song in the "schensslicher Mensch!" something of the disgusting sound of the brutal relishing and gobbling of food. Hatred expresses itself like the satisfaction of an appetite. The outrage was spat out of her body on to him. As she stood there she looked like some one on whom a practical joke had been played, of the primitive and physical order, such as drenching, in some amusing manner, with dirty water. She had been decoyed into swallowing something disgusting. Her attitude was reminiscent of the way people are seen to stand bent awkwardly forward, neck craned out, slowly wiping the dirt off their clothes, or spitting out the remains of their polluted drink, cursing the joker.

This had been, too, a desperate practical joke in its madness and inconsequence. But it was of the solemn and lonely order. At its consummation there had been no chorus of intelligible laughter. An uncontrolled Satyr-like figure had leapt suddenly away: Bertha, in a struggle that had been outrageous and extreme, fighting with the silence of a confederate beneath the same ban of the world. A joke too deep for laughter, parodying the phrase, alienating sorrow and tears, had been achieved. The victim had been conscious of an eeriness.

A folded blouse lay on the corner of Kreisler's trunk. Bertha's arms and shoulders were bare, her hair hanging in wisps and strips, generally—a Salon picture was the result. For purposes of work (he had asked her to sit for him), the blouse had been put aside. A jagged tear in her chemise over her right breast also seemed the doing of a Salon artist of facile and commercial invention.

Kreisler stood at the window. His eyes had a lazy, expressionless stare, his lips were open. Nerves, brain and the whole body were still spinning and stunned, his muscles teeming with actions not finished, sharp, when the actions finished. He was still swamped and strung with violence. His sudden immobility, as he stood there, made the riot of movement and will rise to his brain like wine from a weak body. Satisfaction had, however, stilled everything except this tingling prolongation of action.

The inanity of what had happened to her showed as her unique, intelligible feeling. Her being there at all, her eccentric conduct of the last week, what disgusting folly! Ever since she had known Tarr, her "sentiment" had been castigating her. A watchful fate appeared to be inventing morals to show her the folly of her perpetual romancing. And now *this* had happened. It was senseless. There was not a single atom of compensation anywhere. She was not one of those who, were there any solid compensation of sentiment and necessity (such as, in the most evident degree, was the case with Tarr), would draw back from natural conclusions. Then conclusive physical matters were a culmination of her romance, and not a separate and disloyal gratification. It never occurred to her that they could be arrived at without traversing the romance.

Was this to be explained as the boulevard incident had been explained by her? Was she to proceed with her explanations and her part? But this time it would be to herself that the explanations would have to be made. That was a different audience; a dim feeling found its way into her, with a sort of sickening malice. She had a glimpse too of Kreisler's Bertha—the woman that you couldn't shake off, who, for some unimaginable reason, was always hanging on to you. She even had the strength to admit, distantly, the logic of this act—what had happened to her—still more disgusting and hateful than its illogic. The only thing that might have been found to mitigate, in some sense, the dreary, sudden madness of it, was that she felt practically nothing at all for Kreisler. It was like some violent accident of the high road, the brutality of a tramp. And—as that too would—it partook of the unreality of nightmare.

A few minutes before he had been tranquilly working away at a drawing, she sitting in some pose she had taken up with quick ostentatious intelligence. Startled at his request to draw her shoulders she had immediately condemned this feeling. She had come to sit for him; the mere idea that there was any danger was so repulsive that she immediately consented. He was an artist, too, of course. While he was working they had not talked. Then he had put down his paper and chalk, stretched, and said:

"Your arms are like bananas!" A shiver of warning had penetrated her at this. But still he was an artist: it was natural—even inevitable—that he should compare her arms to bananas.

"Oh! I hope you've made a good drawing. May I see?" She intended to emphasize the reason of this exposure.

He had got up, and before she knew what he was doing caught hold of her above the elbow, chafing her arm, saying:

"You have pins and needles, Fräulein?" The "Fräulein" used here had some disquieting sound. She drew herself away, now serious and on the defence.

"No, thank you. Now I will put my blouse on, if you have finished."

They had looked at each other uncertainly for a moment, he with a flushed rather silly fixed smile. She was afraid, somehow, to move away.

"Let me rub your arm." Then with the fury of a man waking up to some insult, he had seized her. Her tardy words, furious struggling and all her contradictory emotions disappeared in the whirlpool towards which they had, with a strange deliberateness and yet aimlessness, been steering.

He was standing there at the window now as though wishing to pretend that he had done nothing; she "had been dreaming things" merely. The long silence and monotony of the posing had prepared her for the strangeness now. It had been the other extreme out of which she had been flung and into which, at present, she was again flung. She saw side by side and unconnected the silent figure drawing her and the other one full of blindness and violence.

Then there were two other figures, one getting up from the chair, yawning, and the present lazy one at the window—four in all, that she could not bring together somehow, each in a complete compartment of time of its own. It would be impossible to make the present idle figure at the window interest itself in these others. A loathsome, senseless event, of no meaning, naturally, to that figure there. It had quietly, indifferently, talked: it had drawn: it had suddenly flung itself upon her and taken her, and now it was standing idly there. It could do all these things. It appeared to her in a series of precipitate states. It resembled in this a switchback, rising slowly, in a steady insouciant way to the top of an incline, and then plunging suddenly down the other. Or a mastiff's head turning indolently for some seconds and then snapping at a fly, detached again the next moment. Her fury and animal hostility did not last more than a few minutes. She had come there, got what she did not expect, and now must go away again. There was positively nothing more to be said to Kreisler. She had spasmodic returns of raging. They did not pass her dourly active mind. There never had been anything to say to him. He was a mad beast.

She now had to go away as though nothing had happened. It was nothing. After all what did it matter what became of her now? Her body was of little importance—ghosts of romantic consolations here! What was the good (seeing what she knew and everything) of storming against this man? She saw herself coming there that afternoon, talking with amiable affectation of interest in his work, in him (in him!), sitting for him; a long, uninterrupted stream of amiability, talk, suddenly the wild few minutes, then the present ridiculous hush.

The moral, heavily, too heavily, driven in by her no doubt German fate, found its mark in her mind. What Tarr laughed at her for—that silly and vulgar mush, was the cause of all this. Well!

She had done up her hair; her hat was once more on her head. She went towards the door, her face really haggard, inevitable consciousness of drama too in it. Kreisler turned round, went towards the door also, unlocked it, let her pass without saying anything, and, waiting a moment, closed it indifferently again. She was let out as a workman would have been, who had been there to mend a shutter or rectify a bolt.

CHAPTER IX

Bertha made her way home in a roundabout fashion to avoid the possibility of meeting any one she knew. The streets were loftily ignorant of her affairs. Thin walls dyked in affairs and happenings. Ha ha! the importance of our actions! Is it more than the kissing of the bricks?

She came out with mixed feelings; gratefulness for the enormous indifference and ignorance flowing all round us; anger and astonishment at finding herself walking away in this matter-of-fact manner; suffering at the fact that the customary street scene would not mix with the obsession of her late experience.

No doubt Nature was secret enough. But not to tell this experience of hers to *anybody* also would be shutting her in with Kreisler, somehow for good. She would never be able to escape the contamination of that room of his. It was one of those things that in some form one should be able to tell. She had a growing wish to make it known at once somewhere, in some shape.

That is, at bottom, she still was inclined to *continue* things—dreams, fancies, explanations, sacrifices. Would nothing cure her? The first feeling that *this was finally the end of those things,* that there was nothing further to be said or thought, was modified. She did not definitely think of telling any one—the moral was wearing off more quickly than it should. But the thought of this simple, unsensational walking away and ending up of everything in connexion with Kreisler irked her more and more. Anger revived spasmodically. *Kreisler, by doing this, had made an absolute finishing with Kreisler perhaps impossible.*

There was nobody now in any sense on her side, or on whose side she could range herself. Kreisler had added himself to the worrying list of her women friends, Tarr, etc., in a disgusting, dumbfounding way, the list of people preying on her mind and pushing her to perpetual fuss, all sorts of explicative, defiant, or other actions. She had stuck Kreisler up as a "cause" against her friends. In a manner of his own, he had betrayed her and placed himself beside her friends. In any case, he had carried out in the fullest fashion their estimate of him. In being virtuous a libelled man can best attack his enemies; in being "blackguardly," awaken a warmth of sympathy in corroborating them. Kreisler had acted satanically for her friends.

She had seen Elsa and her sister twice that week, but none of the others. Ungregariousness, keeping to herself, was explained by indisposition. Sorbert was meant by this. Her continued seeing of Kreisler was known to all now, and she could imagine their reception of that news. Now she could hardly go on talking about Kreisler. This would at once be interpreted as "something having happened." So more scandal against her name. In examining likelihoods of the future she concluded that she would have to break still more with her friends, to make up for having to retire from her Kreisler positions. To squash and counteract their satisfaction she must accentuate her independence in their direction to insult and contempt.

The last half-hour of senseless outrage still took up all the canvas. Attempts to adjust her mind to a situation containing such an element as this was difficult. What could be done with it? It took up too much space. Everything must come back and be referred to that. She wanted to tell this somewhere. This getting closed in with Kreisler—a survival, perhaps, of her vivid fear of a little time before, when he had locked the door, and she knew that resisting him would be useless—must be at all costs avoided.

Who could she tell? Clara? Madame Vannier?

Once home, she lay down and cried for some time, but without conjuring any of her trouble.

Kreisler seemed to have suddenly brought confusion everywhere. There was *nothing* that would quite fit in with that ridiculous, disgusting event. He had even, in the end, driven her friends out of her mind, too. She would have said nothing had one turned up then.

Having left Kreisler so simply and undramatically worried her. *Something* should have been done. *There* would have been the natural relief. But her direct human feelings of revenge had been paralysed. She thought of going back at once to his room. She could not begin life clearly again until something had been done against him, or in some way where he was.

He had been treated by her as a cypher, as something vague to put up against her friends. All along for the last week he had been a shadowy and actually unimportant figure. He had shown no consciousness of this.

Rather dazed and machine-like himself, Bertha had treated him as she had found him. Suddenly, without any direct articulateness, he had revenged himself as a machine might do, in a nightmare. At a leap he was in the rigid foreground of her life. He had absorbed all the rest in an immense clashing wink. But the moment following this "desperateness" he stood, abstracted, distant and baffling as before. It was difficult to realize he was there.

Tarr had been the real central and absorbing figure all along, of course, but purposely veiled. He had been as really all-important, though to all appearance eliminated, as Kreisler had been of no importance, though propped up in the foreground. Sorbert at last could no longer be suppressed and kept from coming forward now in her mind. But his presence, too, was perplexing. She had become so used to regarding him, though seeing him daily, as an uncertain and departing figure, that now he had really gone that did not make much difference. His proceedings, a carefully prepared anæsthesia for himself, had had its effect on her as well, serving for both.

The bell rang. She stood up in one movement and stared towards the door. She looked as though she were waiting for the bell to ring two or three times to find resolution in that, one way or the other. It rang a second and third time. She did not know *how* much persistence would draw her to the door. But she knew that any definite show of energy would overcome her. Was it Elsa? She had lighted her lamp, and her visitor could therefore have seen that she was at home.

Bertha went to the door at length with affected alacrity, in a pretence of not having heard the bell before, and opened it sharply. Kreisler was there. The opening of the door had been like the tearing of a characterless mask off a face. Had he not been looking at her through it all the time? There did not seem room for them where they were standing. He looked to her like a great terrifying poster, cut out on the melodramatic stairway. She remained stone-still in front of him with a pinched expression, as though about to burst out crying, and something deprecating in her paralysed gesture, like a child. There was an analogy to a laugh struck dead on a child's face at a rebuff, souring and twisting all the features.

Caricatured and enlarged to her eyes, she wanted to laugh for a moment. The surprise was complete. "What, what—" Her mind formed his image, rather like a man compelled to photograph a ghost. Kreisler! It was as though the world were made up of various animals, each of a different kind and physique even, and this were the animal Kreisler, whose name alone conjured up certain peculiar dangerous habits. A wild world, not of uniform men and women, but of very divergent and strangely living animals—Kreisler, Lipmann, Tarr. This man, about to speak to her again, on the same square foot of ground with her: he was not an apparition from any remote Past, but from a Past almost a Present, a half-hour old, much more startling. He had the too raw and too new colours of an image hardly digested, much less faded. When she had last seen him she had been still in the sphere of an intense agitation. His ominous and sudden appearance, so hardly out of that, seemed to swallow up the space and time in between. It was like the chilly return of a circling storm. She had imagined that it depended on her to see him or not, that he was pensive except when persistently approached. But here he was, this time, at last, *following*!

CHAPTER X

He took a step forward, her room evidently his destination.

"Mistvich!" Bertha said, at the same time retreating into the passage-way.—"Go!"

Got into the room, he did not seem to know what next to do. So far he had been evidently quite clear as to his purpose. He had been feeling the same necessity as her—he, to see his victim. He had not known what he wanted with her, but the obvious pretext and road for the satisfaction of this impulse was the seeking of pardon.

She had a moment before felt that she *must* see him again, at once, before going further with her life.—He, more vague but more energetic, had come at the end of twenty minutes. They were now together, quite tongue-tied. Once he was there, the pretext appeared unnecessary. The *real* reason might be found. The real reason no doubt was an intuition not to lose her absolutely, the wisdom of his appetite counselling.

He stood leaning on his cane, and staring in front of him.—Bertha stood quite still, as she would sometimes do when a wasp entered the room, waiting to see if it would blunder about and then fly out again. He was a dangerous animal, he had got in there, and might in the same manner go off again in a minute or two.

Now was the chance she had been fretting for to wipe out in some way what had happened;—not to seem, anyhow, to have taken it all as a matter of course.—But it was *too* convenient. She had never reckoned on his actually coming and putting himself at her disposition in this way. He stood there without saying anything, just as though he had been sent for and it were for her to speak.—She would have been inclined to send him back to his room, and *then*, perhaps, go to *him*.

Constantly on the point of "throwing him out," as her energetic German idiom put it, it yet evidently would then, in the first place, be the same as before. Secondly, she was a good deal intimidated by his unexplained presence. She had a curiosity about him,—curiosity rather as to how what had happened to her could be straightened out or a little sense in some way got into it. The material of this modification was in him and only there.—

She hated him thoroughly now. But this new and distinct feeling gave him at last some reality.—Her way of regarding Kreisler was that of the girl a man "has got into trouble," and to whom she looks to get her out of it.

So she stood, anxious as to what he might have come there to do, gradually settling down into a "proud and silent indignation," behind which her curiosity might wait and see what would transpire.

Kreisler had at length, having allowed her to stay unexplained by his side for a week or so, divined some complication. Her case might possibly be similar to his? She did not interest him any the more for this. But communication would not be, perhaps, absolutely useless.

His only possibility of action at present was to act violently, in gusts. He did not know, when he began an action, whether he would be able to go through with it.—He could not now prevail upon himself to go through the senseless form of apology or anything else. He had got there, that would have to be sufficient.

But the situation for Bertha became urgent, too. The difficulty was that there was *nothing adequate* to be done, that she could think of, in any way in proportion to the enormity of the occasion. Yet, to escape from the memory of Kreisler, what had happened must be wiped out, checkmated, by some action. She was still stunned and overwhelmed with the normal feminine feelings proper to the case. But yet even here there was an irregularity. Another source of infinite discomfort was that she could not even *feel*, as she should normally, the extent of the outrage, although it was evident enough. She had an hysterical inclination, in waves of astonishment, to accept its paradoxical and persistent appearance. This appearance Kreisler's peculiar manner, her own present mind and the unexampled circumstances gave it. It was nothing,—a bagatelle!—Pooh! it is nothing, after all! How *can* it be of any importance, seeing that—?—This was one of those things that seem to have got into the category of waking by mistake. It had nothing to do with life's context. And yet it *was* life. She must deal with it.

She had wished to *free* Sorbert. *That* had been the beginning of all this. It was with idea of sacrifice in her mind that she had committed the first folly on the boulevard.—Well, *she had succeeded*. What did Kreisler mean?—At last his significance was as clear as daylight. He meant *always* and *everywhere* merely that *she could never see Tarr again*!

She now faced him with fresh strength, her face illuminated with happy tragic resolve.—Supposing she had *given* herself to a man to compass this sacrifice? As it was, everything, except the hatefulness and violence of the act, had been spared her. And in telling Sorbert that there was something, now, between them, she had been driven to something, she would be nobly lying, and turning an involuntary act into a voluntary one.

She could now, too, be tragically forbearing even with Kreisler.

"Herr Kreisler, I think I have waited long enough. Will you please leave my room?"

He stirred gently like a heavy flower in a light current of wind. But he turned towards her and said:

"I don't know what to say to you.—Is there nothing I can do to make up to you—? I shall go and shoot myself, Fräulein! I cannot stand the thought of what I have done!"

This was perplexing and made her angry. He appeared to possess a genius for making things complicated and more difficult.

"All I ask you is to go. That will be the best thing you can do for me."

"Fräulein, I *can't*!—Do listen to me for a moment.—I cannot even refer to what has happened without insult in the mere direction of the words.—I am mad—mad—mad!—You have showed yourself a good friend to me. And that is the way I repay you! Were you anywhere but here and unprotected, there would be a man to answer to for this outrage. I will be that man myself!—I come to ask your permission!"

His appetite, waking afresh, was the only directing thing in Kreisler at present. With hypocritical—almost palpably mock—eloquence, he was serving that.

This talk alone would have been of little use or consequence to Bertha. But coming in conjunction with her new independent reinforcement, which alone would have been enough to shape things to a specious ending, it was in a way effective.—The new contradiction and struggle in her mind was between her natural aversion for Kreisler now and her feeling of clemency towards him in his now beautiful usefulness.

She was very dignified, wise, and clement when she answered:

"Let us leave all that, if you please.—It was my fault.—I should have known better what I was doing. You must have been mad, as you say. But if you wish to show yourself a gentleman now, the only obvious thing is to go away, as I have said, and not to molest or remind me any further of what has passed. There is nothing more to say, is there?—Go, now, please!"

Kreisler flung himself on his knees, and seized her hand, she receiving this with astonished, questioning protestation.

"Fräulein, you are an angel! You don't know how much *good* you do me! You are *so* good, so good! There is nothing you can ask of me too much. I have done something I can never undo. It is as though you had saved my life.—Otto Kreisler you can always count on!—The greatest service you can do me, that I humbly beg you may—is to ask some service of me, the more difficult the better!—Good-bye, Fräulein."

Giving her hand a last hug, he sprang up, and Bertha heard him next stormily descending the stairs, and then farther away passing rapidly down the avenue.

Bertha was distinctly affected by this demonstration. It put a last brilliant light of grateful confusion on all the emotions emanating from Kreisler. The sort of notion he had evoked in parting that they had been doing something splendid together—a life-saving, a heroism—found a hospitable ground in her spirit. Taking everything together, things had been miraculously turned round. Her late blackness of depression and perplexity now merged in steadily growing relieved exaltation.

CHAPTER XI

Tarr had not gone to England. Kreisler had not been sufficient to accomplish this. He still persisted in his self-indulgent system of easy stages. A bus ride distant, he would be able to keep away. But in any case he did not wish to go to England, nor anywhere else, for that matter. Paris was much the most suitable domicile, independently of Bertha, with his present plans.

In the neighbourhood of the Place Clichy, in an old convent, he found a room big enough for four people. There, on the day of the second of the letters, he arrived in a state of characteristic misgiving. It was the habitual indigestion of Reality. He was very fond of reality. But he was like a man very fond of what did not agree with him. It usually ended, however, by his assimilating it.

The insouciant, adventurous, those needing no preparation to live, he did not admire, but felt he should imitate.—A new room was a thing that had to be fitted into as painfully as a foot into some new and too elegant boot. The things deposited on the floor, the door finally closed on this new area to be devoted exclusively to himself, the blankest discomfort descended on him. To undo and let loose upon the room his portmanteau's squashed and dishevelled contents—like a flock of birds, brushes, photographs and books flying to their respective places on dressing-table, mantelpiece, shelf or bibliothèque; boxes and parcels creeping dog-like under beds and into corners, taxed his character to the breaking-point. The unwearied optimism of these inanimate objects, the way they occupied stolidly and quickly room after room, was appalling. Then they were *packed up* things, with the staleness of a former room about them, and the souvenir of a depressing time of tearing up, inspecting, and interring.

This preliminary discomfort was less than ever spared him here. He had cut his way to this decision (to go and live in Montmartre), through a bristling host of incertitudes. A place would have had to be particularly spacious to convince him. This large studio-room was worse than any desert. It had been built for something else, and would never be right.—A large square whitewashed box was what he wanted to pack himself into. This was an elaborate carved chest of a former age. He would no doubt pack it eventually with consoling memories of work. He started work at once, in fact. This was his sovereign cure for new rooms.

Half an hour after his taking possession, it being already time for the *apéritif,* he issued forth into the new quarter. There were a few clusters of men. The Spanish men dancers were coloured earth-objects, full of basking and frisking instincts; the atmosphere of the harlot's life went with them, and Spanish reasonableness and civility. He chose a café on the Place Clichy. The hideous ennui of large gimcrack shops and dusty public offices pervaded other groups of pink, mostly dark-haired Frenchmen drinking appetizers. They responded with their personalities on the café terraces to the emptiness of the boulevard.

He had not any friends in Montmartre. But he had not been at the café above a few minutes, when he saw a familiar face approaching. It was a model (Berthe, by name, though bringing no reminder with her of the other "Berthe" he knew) with an English painter he saw for the first time, but whom he had just heard about in connexion with this girl. Berthe knew Tarr very slightly. But she chose a table near him, with a nod, and shortly opened conversation. She meant to talk to him evidently. She asked about one or two people Tarr knew.

"Do you wish me to present you?" she said, looking towards her protector. "This is Mr. Tarr, Dick."

So it was done.

"Why don't you come and sit here?" That too was done, partly from inquisitiveness.

The young Englishman annoyed Tarr by pretending to be alarmed every time he was addressed. He had a wide-open, wondering eye, fixed on the world in timid serenity. It did not appear at first to understand what you said, and rolled a little alarmedly, even so only to be filled the next moment with some unexpected light of whimsical intelligence. It had understood all the time! It was only its art to surprise you, and its English affectation of unreadiness and childishness.

He was a great big child, wandering through life! The young Latin wishes to impress you with his ability to look after himself. General idiocy of demeanour, on the other hand, is the fashionable English style. This young man was six feet one, with a handsome beak in front of his face, meant for a super-Emersonian mildness. His "wide awake" was large, larger than Hobson's. Innumerable minor Tennysons had planted it on his head, or bequeathed a desire for it to this ultimate Dick of long literary line. His family was allied to much Victorian talent. But, alas, thought Tarr, how much worse it is when the mind gets thin than when the blood loses its body, in merely aristocratic refinement. Intellectual aristocracy in the fifth generation!—but Tarr gazed at the conclusive figure in front of him, words failing. Words failed, too, for maintaining conversation with it. He soon got up, and left, his first *apéritif* at Montmartre unsatisfactory.

He did not take possession of his new life with very much conviction. After dinner he went to a neighbouring music hall, precariously amused, soothed by the din. But he eventually left with a headache. The strangeness of the streets, cafés, and places of entertainment depressed him deeply. Had it been an absolutely novel scene, he would have found stimulus in it. But it was like a friend grown indifferent, or something perfectly familiar with the richness of habit taken out of it. Tarr was gregarious in the sense that usually he liked his room and some familiar streets with their traces of familiar men. And where more energetic spirit suggested some truer solitude to him, he would never have sought it where a vestige of inanimate friendship remained.

Here, where he had chosen to live, he appeared as though fallen in some intermediate negative existence. Unusually for him, he felt alone. *To be alone* was essentially a nondescript, lowered, and unreal state for him.

The following morning Tarr woke, his legs rather cramped and tired, and not thoroughly rested. But as soon as he was up, work came quite easily.

He got his paints out, and without beginning on his principal canvas, took up a new and smaller one by way of diversion. Squaring up a drawing of three naked youths sniffing the air, with rather worried Greek faces and heavy nether limbs, he stuck it on the wall with pins and drew his camp easel up alongside it. He squared up his canvas on the floor with a walking-stick, and fixed it on the easel. To get a threadlike edge a pencil had to be sharpened several times.

By the end of the afternoon he had got a witty pastiche on the way. Two colours principally had been used, mixed in piles on two palettes: a smoky, bilious saffron, and a pale transparent lead. The significance of the thing depended first on the psychology of the pulpy limbs, strained dancers' attitudes and empty faces; secondly, the two colours and the simple yet contorted curves.

Work over, his depression again grasped him, like an immensely gloomy companion who had been idling impatiently while he worked. He promenaded this companion in "Montmartre by Night," without improving his character. Nausea glared at him from every object met. Sex surged up and martyrized him, but he held it down rather than satisfy himself with its elementary servants.

The next day, *même jeu*. He sat for hours in the fatiguing evening among a score of relief ships or pleasure boats, hesitating, but finally rejecting relief or pleasure. And the next day it was the same thing.

Meantime his work progressed. But to escape these persecutions he worked excessively. His eyes began to prick, and on the sixth day he woke up with a headache. He was sick and unable to work.

Tarr decided he had been mistaken in remaining in Paris. The fascination of the omnibuses bound for the *Rive gauche* was almost irresistible. Destiny had granted him the necessary resolution to break. He could have gone away—anywhere, even. His will had then offered him a free ticket, as it were, to any end of the earth. Or simply, and most sensibly, to London. And yet he had decided to go no farther than Montmartre, in the unwisdom of his sense of energy and freedom of that moment. Now the "free ticket" was not any more available. His Will had changed. It offered all sorts of different bus tickets, merely, which would conduct him, *avec* and *sans* correspondence, in the direction of the *Quartier du Paradis*.

Why not go back again, simply, in fact? The mandates of the governing elements in our nature, resolves, etc., were childish enough things. His resentment against Bertha, and resolve to quit, would always be there. There was room in life for the satisfaction of this impulse, and the equally strong one to see her again. The road back to the *Quartier du Paradis* would probably have been taken quite soon, only it needed in a way as much of an effort in the contrary direction to get back as it had to get away. He did not know what might await him either. She might really have given him up and changed her life. He had not the necessary experience to dismiss that possibility.

But at last one evening he did go. He went deliberately up to an omnibus "Clichy—St. Germain," and took his seat under its roof. He was resolved to glut himself, without any atom of self-respect or traces of "resolve" remaining, in what he had been wanting to do for a week. He would go to Bertha's rooms, even find out what had been happening in his absence. He might even, perhaps, hang about a little outside, and try to surprise her in some manner. Then he would behave *en maître*, there would be no further question of his having given her up and renounced his rights. He would behave just as though he had never gone away or the letters been sent. He would claim her again with all the appeals he knew to her love for him. He would conduct himself without a scrap of dignity or honesty. Once the "resolution" and pride of his retiring had been broken down, it was thenceforth immaterial to what length he went. In fact, better be frankly weak and unprincipled in his actions and manner, go the whole length of his defeat and confusion. In such completeness there remains a grain of superiority and energy.

But once started in his bus, a wave of excitement and anxiety surged in him with hot gushes.—What awaited him? He fancied all sorts of strange developments.—Perhaps, after all, his journey would not satisfy his weaker movement, but confirm and establish definitely his more sensible resolves. Perhaps weaknesses would find at last the door closed against them.

He smiled at the city as they passed through it, with the glee of a boy on a holiday excursion.

PART V
A MEGRIM OF HUMOUR

CHAPTER I

Some days later, in the evening, Tarr was to be found in a strange place. Decidedly his hosts could not have explained how he got there. He displayed no consciousness of the anomaly.

He had introduced himself—now for the second time—into Fräulein Lipmann's æsthetic saloon, after dining with her and her following at Flobert's Restaurant. As inexplicable as Kreisler's former visits, these ones that Tarr began to make were not so perfectly unwelcome. There was a glimmering of meaning in them for Bertha's women friends. He had just walked in two nights before, as though he were an old and established visitor there, shaken hands and sat down. He then listened to their music, drank their coffee and went away apparently satisfied. Did he consider that his so close connexion with Bertha entitled him to this? It was at all events a prerogative he had never before availed himself of, except on one or two occasions at first, in her company.

The women's explanation of this eccentric sudden frequentation was that Tarr was in despair. His separation from Bertha (or her conduct with Kreisler) had hit him hard. He wished for consolation or mediation.

Neither of these guesses was right. It was really something absurder than that that had brought him there.

Only a week or ten days away from his love affair with Bertha, Tarr was now coming back to the old haunts and precincts of his infatuation. He was living it all over again in memory, the central and all the accessory figures still in exactly the same place. Suddenly, everything to do with "those days," as he thought of a week or two before (or what had ended officially then) had become very pleasing. Bertha's women friends were delightful landmarks. Tarr could not understand how it was he had not taken an interest in them before. They had so much of the German savour of that life lived with Bertha about them!

But not only with them, but with *Bertha herself* he was likewise carrying on this mysterious retrospective life. He was so delighted, as a fact, to be free of Bertha that he poetized herself and all her belongings.

On this particular second visit to Fräulein Lipmann's he met Anastasya Vasek. She, at least, was nothing to do with his souvenirs. Yet, not realizing her as an absolute new-comer at once, he accepted her as another proof of how delightful these people in truth were.

He had been a very silent guest so far. They were curious to hear what this enigma should eventually say, when it decided to speak.

"How is Bertha?" they had asked him.

"She has got a cold," he had answered. It was a fact that she had caught a summer cold several days before.—"How strange!" they thought.—"So he sees her still!"

"She hasn't been to Flobert's lately," Renée Lipmann said. "I've been so busy, or I'd have gone round to see her. She's not in bed, is she?"

"Oh, no, she's just got a slight cold. She's very well otherwise," Tarr answered.

Bertha disappears. Tarr turns up tranquilly in her place. Was he a substitute? What could all this mean? Their first flutter over, their traditional hostility for him reawakened. He had always been an arrogant, eccentric, and unpleasant person: "Homme égoïste! Homme sensuel!" in Van Bencke's famous words.

On seeing him talking with new liveliness, not displayed with them, to Anastasya, suspicions began to germinate. Even such shrewd intuition, a development from the reality, as this: "*Perhaps getting to like Germans, and losing his first, he had come here to find another.*" Comfortable in his liberty, he was still enjoying, by proxy or otherwise, the satisfaction of slavery.

The arrogance implied by his infatuation for the commonplace was taboo. He must be more humble, he felt, and take an interest in his equals.

He had been "Homme égoïste" so far, but "Homme sensuel" was an exaggeration. His concupiscence had been undeveloped. His Bertha, if she had not been a joke, would not have satisfied him. She did not succeed in waking his senses, although she had attracted them. There was no more reality in their sex relations than in their other relations.

He now had a closer explanation of his attachment to stupidity than he had been able to give Lowndes. It was that his artist's asceticism could not support anything more serious than such an elementary rival, and, when sex was in the ascendant, it turned his eyes away from the highest beauty and dulled the extremities of his senses, so that he had nothing but rudimentary inclinations left.

But in the interests of his animalism he was turning to betray the artist in him. For he had been saying to himself lately that a more suitable lady-companion *must* be found; one, that is, he need not be ashamed of. He felt that the time had arrived for Life to come in for some of the benefits of Consciousness.

Anastasya's beauty, bangles, and good sense were the very thing.

Despite himself, Sorbert was dragged out of his luxury of reminiscence without knowing it, and began discriminating between the Bertha enjoyment felt through the pungent German medium of her friends, and this novel sensation. Yet this sensation was an intruder. It was as though a man having wandered sentimentally along an abandoned route, a tactless and gushing acquaintance had been discovered in unlikely possession.

Tarr asked her from what part of Germany she came.

"My parents are Russian. I was born in Berlin and brought up in America. We live in Dresden," she answered.

This accounted for her jarring on his maudlin German reveries.

"Lots of Russian families have settled latterly in Germany, haven't they?" he asked.

"Russians are still rather savage. The more bourgeois a place or thing is the more it attracts them. German watering places, musical centres and so on, they like about as well as anything. They often settle there."

"Do you regard yourself as a Russian—or a German?"

"Oh, a Russian. I—"

"I'm glad of that," said Tarr, quite forgetting where he was, and forgetting the nature of his occupation.

"Don't you like Germans then?"

"Well, now you remind me of it, I do:—Very much, in fact," He shook himself with self-reproach and gazed round benignantly and comfortably at his hosts. "Else I shouldn't be here! They're such a nice, modest, assimilative race, with an admirable sense of duty. They are born servants; excellent mercenary troops, I understand. They should always be used as such."

"I see you know them *à fond*." She laughed in the direction of the Lipmann.

He made a deprecating gesture.

"Not much. But they are an accessible and friendly people."

"You are English?"

"Yes."

He treated his hosts with a warm benignity which sought, perhaps, to make up for past affronts. It appeared only to gratify partially. He was treating them like part and parcel of Bertha. They were not ready to accept this valuation, that of chattels of her world.

The two Kinderbachs came over and made an affectionate demonstration around and upon Anastasya. She got up, scattering them abruptly and went over to the piano.

"What a big brute!" Tarr thought. "She would be just as good as Bertha to kiss. And you get a respectable human being into the bargain!" He was not intimately convinced that she would be as satisfactory. Let us see how it would be; he considered. This larger machine of repressed, moping senses did attract. To take it to pieces, bit by bit, and penetrate to its intimacy, might give a similar pleasure to undressing Bertha!

Possessed of such an intense life as Anastasya, women always appeared on the verge of a dark spasm of unconsciousness. With their organism of fierce mechanical reactions, their self-possession was rather bluff. So much more accomplished socially than men, yet they were not the social creatures, but men. Surrender to a woman was a sort of suicide for an artist. Nature, who never forgives an artist, would never allow *her* to forgive. With any "superior" woman he had ever met, this feeling of being with a parvenu never left him. Anastasya was not an exception.

On leaving, Tarr no longer felt that he would come back to enjoy a diffused form of Bertha there. The prolongations of his Bertha period had passed a climax.

On leaving Renée Lipmann's, nevertheless, Tarr went to the Café de l'Aigle, some distance away, but with an object. To make his present frequentation quite complete, it only needed Kreisler. Otto was there, very much on his present visiting list. He visited him regularly at the Café de l'Aigle, where he was constantly to be found.

This is how Tarr had got to know him.

CHAPTER II

Tarr had arrived at Bertha's place about seven in the evening on his first return from Montmartre. He hung about for a little. In ten minutes' time he had his reward. She came out, followed by Kreisler. Bertha did not see him at first. He followed on the other side of the street, some fifteen yards behind. He did this with sleepy gratification. All was well.

Relations with her were now, it must be clear, substantially at an end. A kind of good sensation of alternating jealousy and regret made him wander along with obedient gratitude. Should she turn round and see him, how uncomfortable she would be! How naturally alike in their mechanical marching gait she and the German were! He was a distinct third party. Being a stranger, with very different appearance, thrilled him agreeably. By a little manœuvre of short cuts he would get in front of them. This he did.

Bertha saw him as he debouched from his turning. She stopped dead, and appeared to astonished Kreisler to be about to take to her heels. It was flattering in a way that his mere presence should produce this effect. He went up to her. Her palm a sentimental instrument of weak, aching, heavy tissues, she gave him her hand, face fixed on him in a mask of regret and reproach. Fascinated by the intensity of this, he had been staring at her a little too long, perhaps with some of the reflection of her expression. He turned towards Kreisler. He found a, to him, conventionally German indifferent countenance.

"Herr Kreisler," Bertha said with laconic energy, as though she were uttering some fatal name. Her "Herr Kreisler" said hollowly, "It's done!" It also had an inflexion of "What shall I do?"

A sick energy saturated her face, the lips were indecently compressed, the eyes wide, dull, with red rims.

Tarr bowed to Kreisler as Bertha said his name. Kreisler raised his hat. Then, with a curious feeling of already thrusting himself on these people, he began to walk along beside Bertha. She moved like an unconvinced party to a bargain, who consents to walk up and down a little, preliminary to a final consideration of the affair. "Yes, but walking won't help matters," she might have been saying. Kreisler's indifference was absolute. There was an element of the child's privilege in Tarr's making himself of the party ("Sorbet, tu es *si jeane*"). There was the claim for indulgence of a spirit not entirely serious! The childishness of this turning up as though nothing had happened, with such wilful resolve not to recognize the seriousness of things, Bertha's drama, the significance of the awful words, "Herr Kreisler!" and so on, was present to him. Bertha must know the meaning of his rapid resurrection—she knew him too well not to know that. So they walked on, without conversation. Then Tarr inquired if she were "quite well."

"Yes, Sorbert, quite well," she replied, with soft tragic banter.

As though by design, he always found just the words or tone that would give an opening for this sentimental irony of hers.

But the least hint that he had come to reinstate himself must not remain. It must be clearly understood that *Kreisler* was the principal figure now. He, Tarr, was only a privileged friend.

With unflattering rapidity somebody else had been found. Her pretension to heroic attachment was compromised. Should not he put in for the vacated berth?

He had an air of welcoming Kreisler. "Make yourself at home; don't mind me," his manner said. As to showing him over the premises he was taking possession of—he had made the inspection, himself, no doubt!

"We have a mutual friend, Lowndes," Tarr said to Kreisler, pleasantly. "A week or two ago he was going to introduce me to you, but it was fated—"

"Ah, yes, Lowndes," said Kreisler, "I know him."

"Has he left Paris, do you know?"

"I think not. I thought I saw him yesterday, there, in the Boulevard du Paradis." Kreisler nodded over his shoulder, indicating precisely the spot on which they had met. His gesture implied that Lowndes might still be found thereabout.

Bertha shrank in "subtle" pantomime from their affability. From the glances she pawed her German friend with, he must deserve nothing but horrified avoidance. Sorbert's astute and mischievous way of saddling her with Kreisler, accepting their being together as the most natural thing in life, roused her combativity. Tarr honoured him, clearly out of politeness to her. Very well: all she could do for the moment was to be noticeably distant with Kreisler. She must display towards him the disgust and reprobation that Tarr should feel, and which he refused, in order to vex her.

Kreisler during the last few days had persisted and persisted. He had displayed some cleverness in his choice of means. As a result of overtures and manœuvres, Bertha had now consented to see him. Her demoralization was complete. She could not stand up any longer against the result, personified by Kreisler, of her idiotic actions. At present she transferred her self-hatred from herself to Kreisler.

Tarr's former relations with Bertha were known to him. He resented the Englishman's air of proprietorship, the sort of pleasant "handing-over" that was going on. It had for object, he thought, to cheapen his little success.

"I don't think, Herr Kreisler, I'll come to dinner after all." She stood still and rolled her eyes wildly in several directions, and stuck one of her hands stiffly out from her side.

"Very well, Fräulein," he replied evenly.—The dismissal annoyed him. His eyes took in Tarr compendiously in passing. Was this a resuscitation of old love at his expense? Tarr had perhaps come to claim his property. This was not the way that is usually done.

"Adieu, Herr Kreisler," sounded like his dismissal. A "let me see you again; understand that here things end!" was written baldly in her very bald eyes. With irony he bid good day to Tarr.

"I hope we shall meet again": Tarr shook him warmly by the hand.

"It is likely," Kreisler replied at once.

As yet Kreisler was undisturbed. He intended not to relinquish his acquaintance with Bertha Lunken. If the Englishman's amiability were a polite way of reclaiming property left ownerless and therefore susceptible of new rights being deployed as regards it, then in time these *later* rights would be vindicated. Kreisler's first impression of Tarr was not flattering. But no doubt they would meet again, as he had said.

CHAPTER III

Bertha held out her hand brutally, in a sort of spasm of will: said, in the voice of "finality,"

"Good-bye, Sorbet: good-bye!"

He did not take it. She left it there a moment, saying again, "Good-bye!"

"Good-bye, if you like," he said at length. "But I see no reason why we should part in this manner. If Kreisler wouldn't mind"—he looked after him—"we might go for a little walk. Or will you come and have an *apéritif*?"

"No, Sorbert, I'd rather not.—Let us say good-bye at once; will you?"

"My dear girl, don't be so silly!" He took her arm and dragged her towards a café, the first on the boulevard they were approaching.

She hung back, prolonging the personal contact, yet pretending to be resisting it *with wonder*.

"I can't, Sorbert. Je ne *peux* pas!" purring her lips out and rolling her eyes. She went to the café in the end. For some time conversation hung back.

"How is Fräulein Lipmann getting on?"

"I don't know. I haven't seen her."

"Ah!"

Tarr felt he had five pieces to play. He had played one. The other four he toyed with in a lazy way.

"Van Bencke?"

"I have not seen her."

That left three.

"How is Isolde?"

"I don't know."

"Seen the Kinderbachs?"

"One of them."

"How is Clara?"

"Clara? She is quite well, I think."

The solder for the pieces of this dialogue was a dreary grey matter that Bertha supplied. Their talk was an unnecessary column on the top of which she perched herself with glassy quietude.

She turned to him abruptly as though he had been hiding behind her, and tickling her neck with a piece of feather-grass.

"Why did you leave me, Sorbert?—*Why* did you leave me?"

He filled his pipe, and then said, feeling like a bad actor:

"I went away at that particular moment, as you know, because I had heard that Herr Kreisler—"

"Don't speak to me about Kreisler—don't mention his name, I *beg* you.—I hate that man.—Ugh!"

Genuine vehemence made Tarr have a look at her. Of course she would say that. She was using too much genuineness, though, not to be rather flush of it for the moment.

"But I don't see—"

"Don't; don't!" She sat up suddenly in her chair and shook her finger in his face. "If you mention Kreisler again, Sorbert, I shall *hate you too*! I especially *pray* you not to mention him."

She collapsed, mouth drawn down at corners.

"As you like." In insisting he would appear to be demanding an explanation. Any hint of exceptional claims on her confidence must be avoided.

"*Why* did you leave me?—You don't know.—I have been mad ever since. One is as helpless as can be—When you are here once more, I feel how weak I am without you. It has not been fair. I have felt just as though I had got out of a sick-bed. I am not blaming you."

They went to Flobert's from the café. It was after nine o'clock, and the place was empty. She bought a wing of chicken; at a dairy some salad and eggs; two rolls at the baker's, to make a cold supper at home. It was more than she would need for herself. Sorbert did not offer to share the expense. At the gate leading to her house he left her.

Immediately afterwards, walking towards the terminus of the Montmartre omnibus, he realized that he was well in the path that led away, as he had not done while still with her. He was glad and sorry, doing homage to her and the future together. She had a fascination as a moribund

Bertha. The immobile short sunset of their friendship should be enjoyed. A rich throwing up and congesting of souvenirs on this threshold were all the better for the weak and silly sun. Oh what a delightful, imperturbable clockwork orb!

The next day he again made his way across Paris from Montmartre at a rather earlier hour. He invited himself to tea with her. They talked as though posing for their late personalities.

He took up deliberately one or two controversial points. In a spirit of superfluous courtesy he went back to the subject of several of their old typical disputes, and argued against himself.

All their difficulties seemed swept away in a relaxed humid atmosphere, most painful and disagreeable to her. He agreed entirely with her, now agreeing no longer meant anything! But the key was elsewhere. Enjoyment of and acquiescence in everything Berthaesque and Teutonic was where it was to be found. Just as now he went to see Bertha's very German friends, and said "How delightful" to himself, so he appeared to be resolved to come back for a week or two and to admire everything formerly he had found most irritating in Bertha herself. Before retiring definitely, like a man who hears that the rind of the fruit he has just been eating is good, and comes back to his plate to devour the part he had discarded, Tarr returned to have a last tankard of German beer.

Or still nearer the figure, his claim in the unexceptionable part of her now lapsed, he had returned demanding to be allowed to live *just a little while longer* on the absurd and disagreeable section.

Bertha suffered, on her side, more than all the rest of the time she had spent with him put together. To tell the whole Kreisler story might lead to a fight. It was too late now. She could not, she felt, in honour, seek to re-entangle Tarr, nor could she disown Kreisler. She had been found with Kreisler: she had no means of keeping him away for good. An attempt at suppressing him might produce any result. Should she have been able, or desired to resume her relations with Tarr, Kreisler would not have left him uninformed of things that had happened, shown in the most uncongenial light. If left alone, and not driven away like a dog, he might gradually quiet down and disappear. Sorbert would be gone, too, by that time!

Their grand, never-to-be-forgotten friendship was ending in shabby shallows. Tarr had the best rôle, and did not deserve it. Kreisler was the implacable remote creditor of the situation.

CHAPTER IV

Tarr left Bertha punctually at seven. She looked very ill. He resolved not to go there any more. He felt upset. Lejeune's, when he got there, was full of Americans. It was like having dinner among a lot of canny children. Kreisler was not there. He went on a hunt for him afterwards, and ran him to earth at the Café de l'Aigle.

Kreisler was not cordial. He emitted sounds of surprise, shuffled his feet and blinked. But Tarr sat down in front of him on his own initiative. Then Kreisler, calling the *garçon*, offered him a drink. Afterwards he settled down to contemplate Bertha's Englishman, and await developments. He was always rather softer with people with whom he could converse in his own harsh tongue.

The causes at the root of Tarr's present thrusting of himself upon Kreisler were the same as his later visits at the Lipmann's. A sort of bath of Germans was his prescription for himself, a voluptuous immersion. To heighten the effect, he was being German himself: being Bertha as well.

But he was more German than the Germans. Many aspects of his conduct were so un-German that Kreisler did not recognize the portrait or hail him as a fellow. Successive lovers of a certain woman fraternizing; husbands hobnobbing with their wives' lovers or husbands of their unmarried days is a commonplace of German or Scandinavian society.

Kreisler had not returned to Bertha's. He was too lazy to plan conscientiously. But he concluded that she had better be given scope for anything the return of Tarr might suggest. He, Otto Kreisler, might be supposed no longer to exist. His mind was working up again for some truculent action. Tarr was no obstacle. He would just walk through Tarr like a ghost when he saw fit to "advance" again.

"You met Lowndes in Rome, didn't you?" Tarr asked him.

Kreisler nodded.

"Have you seen Fräulein Lunken to-day?"

"No." As Tarr was coming to the point Kreisler condescended to speak: "I shall see her to-morrow morning."

A space for protest or comment seemed to be left after this sentence, in Kreisler's still very "speaking" expression.

Tarr smiled at the tone of this piece of information. Kreisler at once grinned, mockingly, in return.

"You can get out of your head any idea that I have turned up to interfere with your proceedings," Tarr then said. "Affairs lie entirely between Fräulein Lunken and yourself."

Kreisler met this assurance truculently.

"You could not interfere with my proceedings. I do what I want to do in this life!"

"How splendid. *Wunderbar!* I admire you!"

"Your admiration is not asked for!"

"It leaps up involuntarily! Prosit! But I did not mean, Herr Kreisler, that my desire to interfere, had such desire existed, would have been tolerated. Oh, no! I meant that no such desire existing, we had no cause for quarrel. Prosit!"

Tarr again raised his glass expectantly and coaxingly, peering steadily at the German. He said, "Prosit" as he would have said, "Peep-oh!"

"Pros't!" Kreisler answered with alarming suddenness, and an alarming diabolical smile. "Prosit!" with finality. He put his glass down. "That is all right. I have no *desire*," he wiped and struck up his moustaches, "to *quarrel* with anybody. I wish to be left alone. That is all."

"To be left alone to enjoy your friendship with Bertha—that is your meaning? Am I not right? I see."

"That is my business. I wish to be left *alone*."

"Of course it's your business, my dear chap. Have another drink!" He called the *garçon*. Kreisler agreed to another drink.

Why was this Englishman sitting there and talking to him? It was in the German style and yet it wasn't. Was Kreisler to be shifted, was he meant to go? Had the task of doing this been put on Bertha's shoulders? Had Tarr come there to ask him, or in the hope that he would volunteer a promise, never to see Bertha again?

On the other hand, was he being approached by Tarr in the capacity of an old friend of Bertha's, or in her interests or at her instigation?

With frowning impatience he bent forward quickly once or twice, asking Tarr to repeat some remark. Tarr's German was not good.

Several glasses of beer, and Kreisler became engagingly expansive.

"Have you ever been to England?" Tarr asked him.

"England?—No—I should like to go there! I like Englishmen! I feel I should get on better with them than with these French. I hate the French! They are all actors."

"You should go to London."

"Ah, to London. Yes, I should go to London! It must be a wonderful town! I have often meant to go there. Is it expensive?"

"The journey?"

"Well, life there. Dearer than it is here, I have been told." Kreisler forgot his circumstances for the moment. The Englishman seemed to have hit on a means of escape for him. He had never thought of England! A hazy notion of its untold wealth made it easier for him to put aside momentarily the fact of his tottering finances.

Perhaps this Englishman had been sent him by the *Schicksal*. He had always got on well with Englishmen!

The peculiar notion then crossed his mind that Tarr perhaps wanted *to get him out of Paris,* and had come to make him some offer of hospitality in England. In a bargaining spirit he began to run England down. He must not appear too anxious to go there.

"They say, though, things have changed. England's not what it was," he said.

"No. But it has changed for the better."

"I don't believe it!"

"Quite true. The last time I was there it had improved so much that I thought of stopping. Merry England is *foutu*! There won't be a regular Pub. in the whole country in fifty years. Art will flourish! There's not a *real* gipsy left in the country. The sham art-ones are dwindling!"

"Are the *Zigeuner* disappearing?"

"Je vous crois! Rather!"

"The only Englishmen I know are very *sympathisch.*"

They pottered about on the subject of England for some time. Kreisler was very tickled with the idea of England.

"English women—what are they like?" Kreisler then asked with a grin. Their relations made this subject delightfully delicate and yet, Kreisler thought, very natural. This Englishman was evidently a description of pander, and no doubt he would be as inclined to be hospitable with his countrywomen in the abstract as with his late fiancée in material detail.

"A friend of mine who had been there told me they were very 'pretty'"—he pronounced the English word with mincing slowness and mischievous interrogation marks in his distorted face.

"Your friend did not exaggerate. They are like languid nectarines! You would enjoy yourself there."

"But I can't speak English—only a little. 'I spik Ingleesh a leetle,'" he attempted with pleasure.

"Very good! You'd get on splendidly!"

Kreisler brushed his moustaches up, sticking his lips out in a hard gluttonous way. Tarr watched him with sympathetic curiosity.

"But—my friend told me—they're not—very easy? They are great flirts. So far—and then *bouf*! You are sent flying!"

"You would not find anything to compare with the facilities of your own country. But you would not wish for that?"

"No?—But, tell me, then, they are cold?—They are of a calculating nature?"

"They are practical, I suppose, up to a certain point. But you must go and see."

Kreisler ruminated.

"What do you find particularly attractive about Bertha?" Tarr asked in a discursive way. "I ask you as a German. I have often wondered what a German would think of her."

Kreisler looked at him with resentful uncertainty for a moment.

"You want to know what I think of the Lunken?—She's a sly prostitute, that's what she is!" he announced loudly and challengingly.

"Ah!"

When he had given Tarr time for any possible demonstration, he thawed into his sociable self. He then added:

"She's not a bad girl! But she tricked you, my friend! She never cared *that*"—he snapped his fingers inexpertly—"for you! She told me so!"

"Really? That's interesting.—But I expect you're only telling lies. All Germans do!"

"All Germans *lie*?"

"'*Deutsches Volk*—the folk that deceives!' is your philosopher Nietzsche's account of the origin of the word Deutsch."

Kreisler sulked a moment till he had recovered.

"No. We don't lie! Why should we? We're not *afraid of the truth*, so why should we?"

"Perhaps, as a tribe, you lied to begin with, but have now given it up?"

"What?"

"That may be the explanation of Nietzsche's etymology. Although he seemed very stimulated at the idea of your national certificate of untruthfulness. He felt that, as a true patriot, he should react against your blue eyes, beer, and childish frankness."

"*Quatsch!* Nietzsche was always paradoxal. He would say anything to amuse himself. You English are the greatest liars and hypocrites on this earth!"

"'See the Continental Press'! You should not swallow that rubbish. I only dispute your statement because I know it is not first-hand. What I mean about the Germans was that, like the Jews, they are extremely proud of success in deceit. No enthusiasm of that sort exists in England. Hypocrisy is usually a selfish stupidity, rather than the result of cunning."

"The English are *stupid* hypocrites then! We agree. Prosit!"

"The Germans are uncouth but zealous liars! Prosit!"

He offered Kreisler a cigarette. A pause occurred to allow the acuter national susceptibilities to cool.

"You haven't yet given me your opinion of Bertha. You permitted yourself a truculent flourish that evaded the question."

"I wish to evade the question.—I told you that she has tricked you. She is very *malin*! She is tricking me now; or she is trying to. She will not succeed with *me*! 'When you go to take a woman you should be careful not to forget your *whip*!' *That* Nietzsche said too!"

"Are you going to give her a beating?" Tarr asked.

Kreisler laughed in a ferocious and ironical manner.

"You consider that you are being fooled, in some way, by Fräulein Lunken?"

"She would if she could. She is nothing but deceit. She is a snake. *Pfui!*"

"You consider her a very cunning and double-faced woman?"

Kreisler nodded sulkily.

"With the soul of a prostitute?"

"She has an innocent face, like a Madonna. But she is a prostitute. I have the proofs of it!"

"In what way has she tricked *me*?"

"In the way that women always trick men!"

With resentment partly and with hard picturesque levity Kreisler met Tarr's discourse.

This solitary drinker, particularly shabby, who could be "dismissed" so easily, whom Bertha with accents of sincerity, "hated, hated!" was so different to the sort of man that Tarr expected might attract her, that he began to wonder. A certain satisfaction accompanied these observations.

For that week he saw Kreisler nearly every day. A *partie à trois* then began. Bertha (whom Tarr saw constantly too) did not actually refuse admittance to Kreisler (although he usually had first to knock a good many times), yet she prayed him repeatedly not to come any more. Standing always in a drooping and desperate condition before him, she did her best to avert a new outburst on his part. She sought to mollify him as much as was consistent with the most absolute refusal. Tarr, unaware of how things actually stood, seconded his successor.

Kreisler, on his side, was rendered obstinate by her often tearful refusal to have anything more whatever to do with him. He had come to regard Tarr as part of Bertha, a sort of masculine extension of her. At the café he would look out for him, and drink deeply in his presence.

"I *will* have her. *I will have her!*" he once shouted towards the end of the evening, springing up and calling loudly for the *garçon*. It was all Tarr could do to prevent him from going, with assurances of intercession.

His suspicions of Tarr at last awoke once more. What was the meaning of this Englishman always there? What was he there for? If it had not been for him, several times he would have rushed off and had his way. But he was always there between them. And in secret, too, probably, and away from him—Kreisler—he was working on Bertha's feelings, and preventing her from seeing him. Tarr was anyhow the obstacle. And yet there he was, talking and palavering, and offering to act as an intermediary, and preventing him from acting. He alone was the obstacle, and yet he talked as though he were nothing to do with it, or at the most a casually interested third party. That is how Kreisler felt on his way home after having drunk a good deal. But so long as Tarr paid for drinks he staved him off his prey.

CHAPTER V

Tarr soon regretted this last anti-climax stage of his adventure. He would have left Kreisler alone in future, but he felt that by frequenting him he could save Bertha from something disagreeable. With disquiet and misgiving every night now he sat in front of his Prussian friend. He watched him gradually imbibing enough spirits to work him up to his pitch of characteristic madness.

"After all, let us hear really what it all means, your Kreisler stunt, and Kreisler?" he said to her four or five days after his reappearance. "Do you know that I act as a dam, or rather a dyke, to his outrageous flood of liquorous spirits every night? Only my insignificant form is between you and destruction, or you and a very unpleasant Kreisler, at any rate.—Have you seen him when he's drunk?—What, after all, does *Kreisler* mean? Satisfy my curiosity."

Bertha shuddered and looked at him with dramatically wide-open eyes, as though there were no answer.

"It's nothing, Sorbert, nothing," she said, as though Kreisler were the bubonic plague and she were making light of it.

Yet a protest had to be made. He had rather neglected the coincidence of his arrival and Bertha's refusal to see Kreisler. He must avoid finding himself manœuvred into appearing the cause. A tranquil and sentimental revenant was the rôle he had chosen. Up to a point he encouraged Bertha to see his boon companion and relax her sudden exclusiveness. He hesitated to carry out thoroughly his part of go-between and reconciler. At length he began to make inquiries. After all, to have to hold back his successor to the favours of a lady, from going and seizing those rights (presumably temporarily denied him), was a strange situation. At any moment now it seemed likely that Kreisler would turn on him. This would simplify matters. Better leave lovers to fight out their own quarrels and not take up the ungrateful rôle of interferer and voluntary policeman. All his retrospective pleasure was being spoilt. But he was committed to remain there for the present. To get over his sensation of dupe, he was more sociable with Kreisler than he felt. The German interpreted this as an hypocrisy. His contempt and suspicion of the peculiar revenant grew.

Bertha was tempted to explain, in as dramatic a manner as possible, the situation to Tarr. But she hesitated always because she thought it would lead to a fight. She was often, as it was, anxious for Tarr.

"Sorbert, I think I'll go to Germany at once," she said to him, on the afternoon of his second visit to Renée Lipmann's.

"Why, because you're afraid of Kreisler?"

"No, but I think it's better."

"But why, all of a sudden?"

"My sister will be home from Berlin, in a day or two—"

"And you'd leave me here to 'mind' the dog."

"No.—Don't see Kreisler any more, Sorbert. Dog is the word indeed! He is mad: *ganz verucht!*—Promise me, Sorbert"—she took his hand—"not to go to the café any more!"

"Do you want him at your door at twelve to-night?—I feel I may be playing the part of—gooseberry, is it—?"

"Don't, Sorbert. If you only knew!—He was here this morning, hammering for nearly half an hour. But all I ask you is to go to the café no more. There is no need for you to be mixed up in all this. I only am to blame."

"I wonder what is the real explanation of Kreisler?" Sorbert said, pulled up by what she had said. "Have you known him long—before you knew me, for instance?"

"No, only a week or two—since you went away."

"I must ask Kreisler. But he seems to have very primitive notions about himself."

"Don't bother any more with that man, Sorbert. You don't do any good. Don't go to the café to-night!"

"Why to-night?"

"Any night."

Kreisler certainly was a "new link"—too much. The chief cause of separation had become an element of insidious *rapprochement*.

He left her silently apprehensive, staring at him mournfully.

So that night, after his second visit to Fräulein Lipmann's, he did not seek out Kreisler at his usual head-quarters with his first enthusiasm.

CHAPTER VI

Already before a considerable pile of saucers, representing his evening's menu of drink, Kreisler sat quite still, his eyes very bright, smiling to himself. Tarr did not at once ask him "what Kreisler meant." "Kreisler" looked as though it meant something a little different on that particular evening. He acknowledged Tarr's arrival slightly, seeming to include him in his reverie. It was a sort of silent invitation to "come inside." Then they sat without speaking, an unpleasant atmosphere of police-court romance for Tarr.

Tarr still kept his retrospective luxury before him, as it maintained the Kreisler side of the business in a desired perspective. Anastasya, whom he had seen that evening, had come as a diversion. He got back, with her, into the sphere of "real" things again, not fanciful retrospective ones.

This would be a reply to Kreisler (an Anastasya for your Otto) and restore the balance. At present they were existing on a sort of three-legged affair. This inclusion of the fourth party would make things solid and less precarious again.

To maintain his rôle of intermediary and go on momentarily keeping his eye on Kreisler's threatening figure, he must himself be definitely engaged in a new direction, beyond the suspicion of hankerings after his old love.

Did he wish to enter into a new attachment with Anastasya? That could be decided later. He would make the first steps, retain her if possible, and out of this, charming expedient pleasant things might come. He was compelled to requisition her for the moment. She might be regarded as a travelling companion. Thrown together inevitably on a stage-coach journey, anything might happen. Delight, adventure, and amusement was always achieved: as his itch to see his humorous concubine is turned into a "retrospective luxury," visits to the Lipmann circle, mysterious relationship with Kreisler. This, in its turn, suddenly turning rather prickly and perplexing, he now, through the medium of a beautiful woman, turns it back again into fun; not serious enough for Beauty, destined, therefore, rather for her subtle, rough, satiric sister.

Once Anastasya had been relegated to her place rather of expediency, he could think of her with more freedom. He looked forward with gusto to his work in her direction.

There would be no harm in anticipating a little. She might at once be brought on to the boards, as though the affair were already settled and ripe for publicity.

"Do you know a girl called Anastasya Vasek? She is to be found at your German friend's, Fräulein Lipmann's."

"Yes, I know her," said Kreisler, looking up with unwavering blankness. His introspective smile vanished. "What then?" was implied in his look. What a fellow this Englishman was, to be sure! What was he after now? Anastasya was a much more delicate point with him than Bertha.

"I've just got to know her. She's a charming girl, isn't she?" Tarr could not quite make out Kreisler's reception of these innocent remarks.

"Is she?" Kreisler looked at him almost with astonishment.

There is a point in life beyond which we must hold people responsible for accidents and their unconsciousness. Innocence then loses its meaning. Beyond this point Tarr had transgressed. Whether Tarr knew anything or not, the essential reality was that Tarr was beginning to get at him with Anastasya, just having been for a week a problematic and officious figure suddenly appearing between him and his prey of the Rue Martine. The habit of civilized restraint had kept Kreisler baffled and passive for a week. Annoyance at Bertha's access of self-will had been converted into angry interest in his new self-elected boon companion. He had been preparing lately, though, to borrow money from him. Anastasya brought on the scene was another kettle of fish.

What did this Tarr's proceedings say? They said: "Bertha Lunken will have nothing more to do with you. You mustn't annoy her any more. In the meantime, I am getting on very well with Anastasya Vasek!"

A question that presented itself to Kreisler was whether Tarr had heard the whole story of his assault on his late fiancée? The possibility of his knowing this increased his contempt for Tarr.

Kreisler was disarmed for the moment by the remembrance of Anastasya. By the person he had regarded as peculiarly accessible becoming paradoxically out of his reach, the most distant and inaccessible—such as Anastasya—seemed to be drawn a little nearer.

"Is Fräulein Vasek working in a studio?" he asked.

"She's at Serrano's, I think," Tarr told him.

"So you go to Fräulein Lipmann's?"

"Sometimes."

Kreisler reflected a little.

"I should like to see her again."

Tarr began to scent another mysterious muddle. Would he never be free of Herr Kreisler? Perhaps he was going to be followed and rivalled in this too? With deliberate meditation Kreisler appeared to be coming round to Tarr's opinion. For his part too, Fräulein Vasek was a nice young lady. "Yes, she is nice!" His manner began to suggest that Tarr had put her forward as a substitute for Bertha!

For the rest of the evening Kreisler insisted upon talking about Anastasya. How was she dressed? Had she mentioned him? etc. Tarr felt inclined to say, "But you don't understand! She is for *me*. *Bertha* is your young lady now!" Only in reflecting on this possible remark, he was confronted with the obvious reply, "But *is* Bertha my young lady?"

CHAPTER VII

Tarr had Anastasya in solitary promenade two days after this. He had worked the first stage consummately. He swam with ease beside his big hysterical black swan, seeming to guide her with a golden halter. They were swimming with august undulations of thought across the Luxembourg Gardens on this sunny and tasteful evening about four o'clock. The Latins and Scandinavians who strolled on the Latin terrace were each one a microscopic hero, but better turned out than the big doubtful heroes of 1840.

The inviolate, constantly sprinkled and shining lawns by the Lycée Henri Trois were thickly fringed with a sort of seaside humanity, who sat facing them and their coolness as though it had been the sea. Leaving these upland expanses to the sedentary swarms of Mammas and Papas, Tarr and Anastasya crossed over beneath the trees past the children's carousels grinding out their antediluvian lullabies.

This place represented the richness of four wasted years. Four incredibly gushing, thick years; what had happened to this delightful muck? All this profusion had accomplished for him was to dye the avenues of a Park with personal colour for the rest of his existence.

No one, he was quite convinced, had squandered so much stuff in the neighbourhood of these terraces, ponds, and lawns. So this was more nearly *his Park* than it was anybody else's. He should never walk through it without bitter and soothing recognition from it. Well: that was what the Man of Action accomplished. In four idle years he had been, when most inactive, trying the man of action's job. He had captured a Park!—Well! he had spent himself into the Earth. The trees had his sap in them.

He remembered a day when he had brought a book to the bench there, his mind tearing at it in advance, almost writing it in its energy. He had been full of such unusual faith. The streets around these gardens, in which he had lodged alternately, were so many confluents and tributaries of memory, charging it on all sides with defunct puissant tides. The places, he reflected, where childhood has been spent, or where, later, dreams of energy have been flung away, year after year, are obviously the healthiest spots for a person. But perhaps, although he possessed the Luxembourg Gardens so completely, they were completely possessed by thousands of other people! So many men had begun their childhood of ambition in this neighbourhood. His hopes, too, no doubt, had grown there more softly because of the depth and richness of the bed. A sentimental miasma made artificially in Paris a similar good atmosphere where the mind could healthily exist as was found by artists in brilliant complete and solid times. Paris was like a patent food.

"Elle dit le mot, Anastase, né pour d'éternels parchemins." He could not, however, get interested. Was it the obstinate Eighteenth Century animal vision? When you plunge into these beings, must they be all quivering with unconsciousness, like life with a cat or a serpent?—But her sex would throw clouds over her eyes. She was a woman. It was no good. Again he must confess Anastasya could only offer him something too *serious*. He could not *play* with that. Sex-loyalty to his most habitual lips interfered.

He had the protective instinct that people with a sense of their own power have for those not equals with whom they have been associated. He would have given to Bertha the authority of his own spirit, to prime her with himself that she might meet on equal terms and vanquish any rival. He experienced a slight hostility to Anastasya like a part of Bertha left in himself protesting and jealous. It was chiefly vanity at the thought of this superior woman's contempt could she see his latest female effort.

"I suppose she knows all about Bertha," he thought. Kreisler-like, he looked towards the Lipmann women. "Homme sensuel! Homme égoïste!"

She seemed rather shy with him.

"How do you like Paris?" he asked her.

"I don't know yet. Do you like it?" She had a flatness in speaking English because of her education in the United States.

"I don't like to be quite so near the centre of the world. You can see all the machinery working. It makes you a natural sceptic. But here I am. I find it difficult to live in London."

"I should have thought everything was so perfected here that the machinery did not obtrude—"

"I don't feel that. I think that a place like this exists for the rest of the world. It works that the other countries may live and create. That is the rôle France has chosen. The French spirit seems to me rather spare and impoverished at present."

"You regard it as a mother-drudge?"

"More of a drudge than a mother. We don't get much really from France, except tidiness."

"I expect you are ungrateful."

"Perhaps so. But I cannot get over a dislike for Latin facilities. Suarès finds a northern rhetoric of ideas in Ibsen, for instance, exactly similar to the word-rhetoric of the South. But in Latin countries you have a democracy of vitality, the best things of the earth are in everybody's mouth and nerves. *The artist has to go and find them in the crowd.* You can't have 'freedom' both ways. I prefer the *artist* to be free, and the crowd not to be 'artists.' What does all English and German gush or sentiment, about the wonderful, the artistic French nation, etc., amount to? They gush because they find thirty-five million little Bésnards, little Botrels, little Bouchers, or little Bougereaus living together and prettifying their towns and themselves. Imagine England an immense garden city, on Letchworth lines (that is the name of a model Fabian township near London), or Germany (it almost has become that) a huge nouveau-art, reform-dressed, bestatued State. Practically every individual Frenchman of course has the filthiest taste imaginable. You are more astonished when you come across a sound, lonely, and severe artist in France than elsewhere. His vitality is hypnotically beset by an ocean of artistry. His best instinct is to become rather aggressively harsh and simple. The reason that a great artist like Rodin or the Cubists to-day arouse more fury in France than in England, for instance, is not because the French are *more interested in Art*! They are less interested in art, if anything. It is because they are all 'artistic' and all artists in the sense that a cheap illustrator or Mr. Brangwyn, R.A., or Mr. Waterhouse, R.A., are. They are *scandalized* at good art; the English are inquisitive about and tickled by it, like gaping children. Their social instincts are not so developed and logical."

"But what difference does the attitude of the crowd make to the artist?"

"Well, we were talking about Paris, which is the creation of the crowd. The man thinking in these gardens to-day, the man thinking on the quays of Amsterdam three centuries ago, think much the same thoughts. Thought is like climate and chemistry. It even has its physical type. But the individual's *projection of himself* he must entrust to his *milieu*. I maintain that the artist's work is nowhere so unsafe as in the hands of an 'artistic' vulgarly alive public. The other question is his relation to the receptive world, and his bread and cheese. Paris is, to begin with, no good for bread and cheese, except as a market to which American and Russian millionaire dealers come. Its intelligence is of great use. But no friendship is a substitute for the blood-tie; and intelligence is no substitute for the response that can only come from the narrower recognition of your kind. This applies to the best *type* of art rather than work of very personal genius. Country is left behind by that. Intelligence also."

"Don't you think that work of very personal genius often *has* a country? It may break through accidents of birth to perfect conditions somewhere; not necessarily contemporary ones or those of the country it happens in?"

"I suppose you could find a country or a time for almost *anything*. But I am sure that the *best* has in reality *no* Time and no Country. That is why it accepts without fuss any country or time for what they are worth; thence the seeming contradiction, that it is always *actual*. It is alive, and nationality is a portion of actuality."

"But *is* the best work always 'actual' and up to date?"

"It always has that appearance. It's manners are perfect."

"I am not so sure that manners cannot be overdone. A personal code is as good as the current code."

"The point seems to me to be, in that connexion, that manners are not very important. You use them as you use coins."

"The most effectual men have always been those whose notions were diametrically opposed to those of their time," she said carefully.

"I don't think that is so; except in so far as all effectual men are always the enemies of every time. With that fundamental divergence, they give a weight of impartiality to the supreme thesis and need of their age. Any opinion of their fellows that they adopt they support with the uncanny authority of a plea from a hostile camp. *All activity* on the part of a good mind has the stimulus of a paradox. To produce is the sacrifice of genius."

They seemed to have an exotic grace to him as they promenaded their sinuous healthy intellects in this eighteenth-century landscape. There was no other pair of people who could talk like that on those terraces. They were both of them barbarians, head and shoulders taller than the polished stock around. And they were highly strung and graceful. They were out of place.

"Your philosophy reminds me of Jean-Jacques," she said.

"Does it? How do you arrive at that conclusion?"

"Well, your hostility to a tidy rabble, and preference for a rough and uncultivated bed to build on brings to mind 'wild nature' and the doctrine of the natural man. You want a human landscape similar to Jean-Jacques' rocks and water falls."

"I see what you mean. But I also notice that the temper of my theories is the exact opposite of Jean-Jacques'.—He raved over and poetized his wild nature and naturalness generally and put it forward as an ideal. My point of view is that it is a question of expediency only. I do not for a moment sentimentalize crudeness. I maintain that that crude and unformed *bed,* or backing, is absolutely essential to maximum fineness; just as crudity in an individual's composition is necessary for him to be able to create. There is no more absolute value in stupidity and formlessness than there is in dung. But they are just as necessary. The conditions of creation and of life disgust me. The birth of a work of art is as dirty as that of a baby. But I consider that my most irremediable follies have come from fastidiousness; not the other thing. If you are going to work or perform, you must make up your mind to have dirty hands most part of the time. Similarly, you must praise chaos and filth. *It is put there for you.* Incense is, I believe, camels' dung. When you praise, you do so with dung. When you see men fighting, robbing each other, behaving meanly or breaking out into violent vulgarities, you must conventionally clap your hands. If you have not the stomach to do that, you cannot be a creative artist. If people stopped behaving in that way, you could not be a creative artist."

"So you would discourage virtue, self-sacrifice, and graceful behaviour?"

"No, praise them very much. Also praise deceit, lechery, and panic. Whatever a man does, praise him. In that way you will be acting as the artist does; If you are not an artist, you will not act in that way. An artist should be as impartial as God."

"Is God impartial?"

"We disintegrate. His dream is no doubt ignorant of our classifications."

"Rousseau again—?"

"If you really want to saddle me with that Swiss, I will help you. My enthusiasm for art has made me fond of chaos. It is the artist's fate almost always to be exiled among the slaves. *The artist who takes his job seriously gets his sensibility blunted.* He is less squeamish than other people and less discriminating."

"He becomes in fact less of an artist?"

"An artist is a cold card, with a hide like a rhinoceros."

"You are poetizing him! But if that is so, wouldn't it be better to be something else?"

"No, I think it's about the best thing to be."

"With his women companions, sweethearts, he is also apt to be undiscriminating."

"He is notorious for that!"

"I think that is a pity. Then that is because I am a woman, and am conscious of not being a slave."

"But then such women as you are condemned also to find themselves surrounded by slaves!"

"Your frequentation of the abject has not caused you to forget one banal art!"

"You tempt me to abandon art. Art is the refuge of the shy."

"Are you shy?"

"Yes."

"You need not be."

Her revolving hips and thudding skirts carried her forward with the orchestral majesty of a simple ship. He suddenly became conscious of the monotonous racket.

At that moment the drums beat to close the gardens. They had dinner in a Bouillon near the Seine. They parted about ten o'clock.

CHAPTER VIII

For the first time since his "return" Tarr found no Kreisler at the café. "I wonder what that animal's up to," he thought. The *garçon* told him that Kreisler had not been there at all that evening. Tarr reconsidered his responsibilities. He could not return to Montmartre without just informing himself of Kreisler's whereabouts and state of mind. The "obstacle" had been eluded. It must be transported rapidly "in the way" again, wherever and in whatever direction the sluggish stream was flowing.

Bertha's he did not intend to go to if he could help it. A couple of hours at tea-time was what he had instituted as his day's "amount" of her company. *Kreisler's* room would be better. This he did. There was a light in Kreisler's room. The window had been pointed out to him. This perhaps was sufficient, Tarr felt. He might now go home, having located him. Still, since he was there he would go up and make sure. He lighted his way up the staircase with matches. Arrived at the top floor he was uncertain at which door to knock. He chose one with a light beneath it and knocked.

In a moment some one called out "Who is it?" Recognizing the voice Tarr answered, and the door opened slowly. Kreisler was standing there in his shirt-sleeves, glasses on, and a brush in his hand.

"Ah, come in," he said.

Tarr sat down, and Kreisler went on brushing his hair. When he had finished he put the brush down quickly, turned round, and pointing to the floor said, in a voice suggesting that that was the first of several questions:

"Why have you come *here*?"

Tarr at once saw that he had gone a step too far, and either shown bad calculation or chanced on his rival at an unfortunate time. It was felt, no doubt, that—acting more or less as "keeper," or check, at any rate—he had come to look after his charge, and hear why Kreisler had absented himself from the café.

"Why have you come, here?" Kreisler asked again, in an even tone, pointing again with his forefinger to the centre of the floor.

"Only to see you, of course. I thought perhaps you weren't well."

"Ah, so! I want you, my dear English friend, now that you are here, to explain yourself a little. Why do you honour me with so much of your company?"

"Is my company disagreeable to you?"

"I wish to know, sir, why I have so much of it!" The Deutscher-student was coming to the top. His voice had risen and the wind of his breath appeared to be making his moustaches whistle.

"I, of course, have reasons, besides the charm of your society, for seeking you out."

Tarr was sitting stretched on one of Kreisler's two chairs looking up frowningly. He was annoyed at having let himself in for this interview. Kreisler stood in front of him without any expression in particular, his voice rather less guttural than usual. Tarr felt ill at ease at this sudden breath of storm and kept still with difficulty.

"You have reasons? You have reasons! Heavens! Outside! Quick! Out!"

There was no doubt this time that it was in earnest. He was intended rapidly to depart. Kreisler was pointing to the door. His cold grin was slightly on his face again, and an appearance of his hair having receded on his forehead and his ears gone close against his head warned Tarr definitely where he was. He got up. The absurdity in the situation he had got himself into chiefly worried him. He stood a moment in a discouraged way, as though trying to remember something. His desire for a row had vanished with the arrival of it. It had come at such an angle that it was difficult to say anything, and he had a superstition of the vanity about the marks left by hands, or rather his hands.

"Will you tell me what on earth's the matter with you to-night?" he asked.

"Yes! I don't want to be followed about by an underhand swine like you any longer! By what devil's impudence did you come here to-night? For a week I've had you in the café. What did you want with me? If you wanted your girl back, why hadn't you the courage to say so? I saw you with another lady to-night. I'm not going to have you hovering and slavering around me.

Be careful I don't come and pull your nose when I see you with that other lady! You're welcome, besides, to your girl—"

"I recommend you to hold your mouth! Don't talk about *my girl*. I've had enough of it. Where her sense was when she alighted on a specimen like you—" Tarr's German hesitated and suddenly struck, as though for the rest of the night. He had stepped forward with a suggestion of readiness for drama:

"Heraus, schwein!" shouted Kreisler, in a sort of incredulous drawling crescendo, shooting his hand towards the door and urging his body like the cox of a boat. Like a sheep-dog he appeared to be collecting Tarr together and urging him out.

Tarr stood staring doubtfully at him.

"What—"

"Heraus! Out! Quicker! Quicker!! Quick!"

His last word, "Schnell!" dropped like a plummet to the deepest tone his throat was capable of. It was short and so absolutely final that the grace given, even after it had been uttered, for this hateful visitor to remove himself, was a source of astonishment to Tarr. For a man to be ordered out of a room that does not belong to him always puts him at a disadvantage. Should he insist, forcibly and successfully, to remain, it can only be for a limited time. He will have to go sooner or later, and make his exit, unless he establish himself there and make it his home henceforth; a change of lodging most people are not, on the spur of the moment, prepared to decide on. The room, somehow, too, seems on its owner's side, and to be vomiting forth the intruder. The civilized man's instinct of ownership makes it impossible for any but the most indelicate to resist a feeling of hesitation before the idea of resistance in another man's shell! All Tarr's attitude to this man had been made up of a sort of comic hypocrisy. Neither comedy nor hypocrisy were usable for the moment.

Had Tarr foreseen this possible termination of his rôle of "obstacle?" And ought he, he would ask himself, to have gone on with this half-farce if he were not prepared to meet the ultimate consequences? Kreisler was quite unworthy to stand there, with perfect reason, and to be telling him to "get out." It was absurd to exalt Kreisler in that way! But Tarr had probably counted on being equal to any emergency, and baffling or turning Kreisler's violence in some genial manner.

He stood for a few seconds in a tumultuous hesitation, when he saw Kreisler run across the room, bend forward and dive his arm down behind his box. He watched with uncomfortable curiosity this new move, as one might watch a surgeon's haste at the crisis of an operation, searching for some necessary implement, mislaid for the moment. He felt schoolboy-like, left waiting there at Kreisler's disposition. It was as a reaction against this unpleasant feeling that he stepped towards the door. The wish not to "obey" or to seem to turn tail either had alone kept him where he was. He had just found the door when Kreisler, with a bound, was back from his box, flourishing an old dog-whip in his hand.

"Ah, you go? Look at this!" He cracked the whip once or twice. "This is what I keep for hounds like you!" Crack! He cracked it again in rather an inexperienced way with a certain difficulty. He frowned and stopped in his discourse, as though it had been some invention he were showing off, that would not quite work at the proper moment, necessitating concentration.

"If you wish to see me again, you can always find me here. You won't get off so easily next time!" He cracked the whip smartly and then slammed the door.

Tarr could imagine him throwing it down in a corner of the room, and then going on with his undressing.

When Kreisler had jumped to the doorway Tarr had stepped out with a half-defensive, half-threatening gesture and then gone on with strained slowness, lighting a match at the head of the stairs. He felt like a discomfited pub-loafer as he raised the match to an imaginary clay pipe rising in his mind. There was the ostentatious coolness of the music-hall comedian.

The thing that had chiefly struck him in Kreisler under this new aspect was a kind of nimbleness, a pettiness in his behaviour and movements, where perhaps he had expected more stiffness and heroics; the clown-like gibing form his anger took, a frigid disagreeable slyness and irony, a juvenile quickness and coldness.

Tarr was extremely dissatisfied with the part he had played in this scene. First of all he felt he had withdrawn too quickly at the appearance of the whip, although he had in fact got under way before it had appeared. Then, he argued, he should have stopped at the appearance of this instrument of disgrace. To stop and fight with Kreisler, what objection was there to that, he asked himself? A taking Kreisler too seriously? But what *less* serious than fighting? He had saved himself an unpleasantness, something ridiculous, merely to find himself outside Kreisler's door, a feeling of primitive dissatisfaction in him. Had he definitely been guilty of a lack of pluck or pride, it would have been better.

There was something mean and improper in all this that he could not reason away or mistake. He had undoubtedly insulted this man by his attitude, *s'en était fiche de lui*; and when the other turned, whip in hand, he had walked away. What really should he have done? He should, no doubt, he thought, having humorously instituted himself Kreisler's keeper, have humorously struggled with him, when the idiot became obstreperous. At that point his humour had stopped. Then his humour had limitations?

Once and for all and certainly: he had no right to treat a man as he had treated Kreisler and yet claim, when he turned and resented this treatment, immunity from action on the score of Kreisler's idiocy. In allowing the physical struggle any importance he allowed Kreisler an importance, too, that made his former treatment of him unreal and unjustified. In Kreisler's eyes he was a *blagueur*, without resistance at a pinch, who walks away when turned on. This opinion was of no importance, since he had not a shadow of respect for Kreisler. Again he turned on himself. If he was so weak-minded as to care what trash like Kreisler thought or felt! He wandered in the direction of the Café de l'Aigle, gripped in this ratiocination.

His unreadiness, his dislike for action, his fear of ridicule, he treated severely in turn. He thought of everything he could against himself. And he laughed at himself. But it was no good. At last he gave way to the urgency of his vanity and determined not to leave the matter where it was. At once plans for retrieving this discomfort came crowding on him. He would go to the café as usual on the following evening, sit down smilingly at Kreisler's table as though nothing had happened. In short, he would altogether endorse the opinion that Kreisler had formed of him. And yet why this meanness, even assumed, Tarr asked himself, even while arranging realistically his to-morrow evening's purification? Always in a contemptuous spirit, some belittlement or unsavoury rôle was suggesting itself. His contempt for everybody degraded him.

Still, for a final occasion and since he was going this time to accept any consequences, he would follow his idea. He would be, to Kreisler's mind for a little, the strange "slaverer and hoverer" who had been kicked out on the previous night. He would even have to "pile it on thick" to be accepted at all, exaggerate in the direction of Kreisler's unflattering notion of him. Then he would gradually aggravate Kreisler, and with the same bonhomie attack him with resolution. He laughed as he came to this point, as a sensible old man might laugh at himself on arriving at a similar decision.

Soothed by the prospect of this rectification of the evening's blunder, Tarr once more turned to reflect on it, and saw more clearly than ever the parallel morals of his Bertha affair and his Kreisler affair. His sardonic dream of life got him, as a sort of Quixotic dreamer of inverse illusions, blows from the swift arms of windmills and attacks from indignant and perplexed mankind. He, instead of having conceived the world as more chivalrous and marvellous than it was, had conceived it as emptied of all dignity, sense, and generousness. The drovers and publicans were angry at not being mistaken for legendary chivalry or châtelaines. The very windmills resented not being taken for giants! The curse of humour was in him, anchoring him at one end of the see-saw whose movement and contradiction was life.

Reminded of Bertha, he did not, however, hold her responsible. But his protectorate would be wound up. Acquaintance with Anastasya would be left where it was, despite the threatened aggression against his nose.

PART VI
HOLOCAUSTS

CHAPTER I

Tarr's character at this time performed repeatedly the following manœuvre: his best energies would, once a farce was started, gradually take over the business from the play department and continue it as a serious line of its own. It was as though it had not the go to initiate anything of its own accord. It was content to exploit the clown's discoveries.

The bellicose visit to Kreisler now projected was launched to a slow blast of Humour, ready, when the time came, to turn into a storm. His contempt for the German would not allow him to enter into anything seriously against him. Kreisler was a joke. Jokes, it had to be admitted (and in that they became more effective than ever), were able to make you sweat.

That Kreisler could be anywhere but at the Café de l'Aigle on the following evening never entered Tarr's head. As he was on an unpleasant errand, he took it for granted that Fate would on this occasion put everything punctually at his disposal. Had it been an errand of pleasure, he would have instinctively supposed the reverse.

At ten, and at half-past, his rival had not yet arrived. Tarr set out to make rapidly a tour of the other cafés. But Kreisler might be turning over a new leaf. He might be going to bed, as on the previous evening. He must not be again sought, though, on his own territory. The moral disadvantage of this position, on a man's few feet of most intimate floor space, Tarr had clearly realized.

The Café Souchet, the most frequented café of the Quarter, entered merely in a spirit of German thoroughness, was, however, the one. More alert, and brushed up a little, Tarr thought, Kreisler was sitting with another man, with a bearded, naïf, and rather pleasant face, over his coffee. No pile of saucers this time attended him.

The stranger was a complication. Perhaps the night's affair should be put off until the conditions were more favourable. But Tarr's vanity was impatient. His wait in the original café had made him nervous and hardly capable of acting with circumspection. On the other hand, it might come at once. This was an opposite complication. Kreisler might open hostilities on the spot. This would rob him of the subtle benefits to be derived from his gradual strategy. This must be risked. He was not very calm. He crudely went up to Kreisler's table and sat down. The feeling of the lack of aplomb in this action, and his disappointment at the presence of the other man, chased the necessary good humour out of his face. He had carefully preserved this expression for some time, even walking lazily and quietly as if he were carrying a jug of milk. Now it vanished in a moment. Despite himself, he sat down opposite Kreisler as solemn as a judge, pale, his eyes fixed on the object of his activity with something like a scowl.

But, his first absorption in his own sensations lifted and eased a little, he recognized that something very unusual was in the air.

Kreisler and his friend were not speaking or doing anything visibly. They were just sitting still, two self-possessed malefactors. Nevertheless, Tarr's arrival to all appearance disturbed and even startled them, as if they had been completely wrapped up in some engrossing game or conspiracy.

Kreisler had his eyes trained across the room. The other man, too, was turned slightly in that direction, although his eyes followed the tapping of his boot against the ironwork of the table, and he only looked up occasionally.

Kreisler turned round, stared at Tarr without at once taking in who it was; then, as though saying to himself, "It's only Bertha's Englishman," he took up his former wilful and patient attitude, his eyes fixed.

Tarr had grinned a little as Kreisler turned his way, rescued from his solemnity. There was just a perceptible twist in the German's neck and shade of expression that would have said "Ah, there you are? Well, be quiet, we're having some fun. Just you wait!"

But Tarr was so busy with his own feelings that he didn't understand this message. He wondered if he had been seen by Kreisler in the distance, and if this reception had been concerted between him and his friend. If so, why?

Sitting, as he was, with his back to the room, he stared at his neighbour. His late boon companion distinctly was waiting, with absurd patience, for something. The poise of his head, the set of his yellow Prussian jaw, were truculent, although otherwise he was peaceful and attentive. His collar looked *new* rather than clean. His necktie was one not familiar to Tarr. Boots shone impassibly under the table.

Tarr screwed his chair sideways, and faced the room. It was full of people—very athletically dressed American men, all the varieties of the provincial in American women, powdering their noses and ogling Turks, or sitting, the younger ones, with blameless interest and fine complexions. And there were *plenty* of Turks, Mexicans, Russians and other "types" for the American ladies! In the wide passage-way into the further rooms sat the orchestra, playing the "Moonlight Sonata," Dvorak and the "Machiche."

In the middle of the room, at Tarr's back, he now saw a group of eight or ten young men whom he had seen occasionally in the Café Berne. They looked rather German, but smoother and more vivacious. Poles or Austrians, then? Two or three of them appeared to be amusing themselves at his expense. Had they noticed the little drama that he was conducting at his table? Were they friends of Kreisler's, too?—He was incapable of working anything out. He flushed and felt far more like beginning on them than on his complicated idiot of a neighbour, who had become a cold task. This genuine feeling illuminated for him the tired frigidity of his present employment.

He had moved his chair a little to the right, towards the group at his back, and more in front of Kreisler, so that he could look into his face. On turning back now, and comparing the directions of the various pairs of eyes engaged, he at length concluded that he was without the sphere of interest; *just* without it.

At this moment Kreisler sprang up. His head was thrust forward, his hands were in rear, partly clenched and partly facilitating his passage between the tables by hemming in his coat tails. The smooth round cloth at the top of his back, his smooth head above that with no back to it, struck Tarr in the way a momentary smell of sweat would. Germans had no backs to them, or were like polished pebbles behind. Tarr mechanically moved his hand upwards from his lap to the edge of the table on the way to ward off a blow. He was dazed by all the details of this meeting, and the peculiar miscarriage of his plan.

But Kreisler brushed past him with the swift deftness of a person absorbed with some strong movement of the will. The next moment Tarr saw the party of young men he had been observing in a sort of noisy blur of commotion. Kreisler was in among them, working on something in their midst. There were two blows—smack—smack; an interval between them. He could not see who had received them.

Tarr then heard Kreisler shout in German:

"For the *second* time to-day! Is your courage so slow that I must do it a *third* time?"

Conversation had stopped in the café and everybody was standing. The companions of the man smacked, too, had risen in their seats. They were expostulating in three languages. Several were mixed up with the *garçons*, who had rushed up to do their usual police work on such occasions. Over Kreisler's shoulder, his eyes carbonized to a black sweetness, his cheeks a sweet sallow-white, with a red mark where Kreisler's hand had been, Tarr saw the man his German friend had singled out. He had sprung towards the aggressor, but by that time Kreisler had been seized from behind and was being hustled towards the door. The blow seemed to hurt his vanity so much that he was standing half-conscious till the pain abated. He seemed to wish to brush the blow off, but was too vain to raise his hands to his cheek. It was left there like a scorching compress. His friends, Kreisler wrenched away from them, were left standing in a group, in attitudes more or less of violent expostulation and excitement.

Kreisler receded in the midst of a band of waiters towards the door. He was resisting and protesting, but not too much to retard his quick exit. The *garçons* had the self-conscious unconcern of civilian braves.

The young man attacked and his friends were explaining what had happened, next, to the manager of the café. A *garçon* brought in a card on a plate. There was a new outburst of protest and contempt from the others. The plate was presented to the individual chiefly concerned, who brushed it away, as though he had been refusing a dish that a waiter was, for some reason, pressing upon him. Then suddenly he took up the card, tore it in half, and again waived away the persistent platter. The *garçon* looked at the manager of the café and then returned to the door.

So this was what Kreisler and the little bearded man had been so busy about! Kreisler had laid his plans for the evening as well! Tarr's scheme was destined not to be realized; unless he followed Kreisler at once, and got up a second row, a more good-natured one, just outside the café? Should he go out now and punch Kreisler's head, fight about a little bit, and then depart, his business done, and leave Kreisler to go on with his other row? For he felt that Kreisler intended making an evening of it. His companion had not taken part in the fracas, but had followed on his heels in his ejection, protesting with a vehemence that was intended to hypnotize.

Just at the moment when he had felt that he was going to be one of the principal parties to a violent scene, Tarr had witnessed, not himself at all, but another man snatched up into his rôle. He felt relieved. As he watched the man Kreisler had struck, he seemed to be watching himself. And yet he felt rather on the side of Kreisler. With a mortified chuckle he prepared to pay for his drink and be off, leaving Kreisler for ever to his very complicated, mysterious and turbulent existence. He noticed just then that Kreisler's friend had come back again, and was talking to the man who had been struck. He could hear that they were speaking Russian or Polish. With great collectedness, Kreisler's emissary, evidently, was meeting their noisy expostulations. He could not at least, like a card, be torn in half! On the other hand, in his person he embodied the respectability of a visiting card. He was dressed with perfect "correctness" suitable to such occasions and such missions as his appeared to be. By his gestures (one of which was the taking an imaginary card between his thumb and forefinger and tearing it) Tarr could follow a little what he was saying.

"That, sir," he seemed to assert, "is not the way to treat a gentleman. That, too, is an insult no gentleman will support." He pointed towards the door. "Herr Kreisler, as you know, cannot enter the café; he is waiting there for your reply. He has been turned out like a drunken workman."

The Russian was as grave as he was collected, and stood in front of the other principal in this affair, who had sat down again now, with the evident determination to get a different reply. The talking went on for some time. Then he turned towards Tarr, and, seeing him watching the discussion, came towards him, raising his hat. He said in French:

"You know Herr Kreisler, I believe. Will you consent to act for him with me, in an affair that unfortunately—? If you would step over here, I will put you 'au courant.'"

"I'm afraid I cannot act for Herr Kreisler, as I am leaving Paris early to-morrow morning," Tarr replied.

But the Russian displayed the same persistence with him as he had observed him already capable of with the other people.

At last Tarr said, "I don't mind acting temporarily for a few minutes, now, until you can find somebody else. But you must understand that I cannot delay my journey—you must find a substitute at once."

The Russian explained with businesslike gusto and precision, having drawn him towards the door (seemingly to cut off a possible retreat of the enemy), that it was a grave affair. Kreisler's honour was compromised. His friend Otto Kreisler had been provoked in an extraordinary fashion. Stories had been put about concerning him, affecting seriously the sentiments of a girl he knew regarding him; put about with that object by another gentleman, also acquainted with this girl. The Russian luxuriated emphatically on this point. Tarr suggested that they should settle the matter at once, as he had not very much time. He was puzzled. Surely the girl mentioned must be Bertha? If so, had Bertha been telling more fibs? Was the Kreisler mystery after all to her discredit? Perhaps he was now in the presence of *another* rival, existing, unknown to him, even during his friendship with her.

In this heroic, very solemnly official atmosphere of ladies' "honour" and the "honour" of gentlemen, that the little Russian was creating, Tarr unwillingly remained for some time. Noisy bursts of protest from other members of the opposing party met the Russian's points. "It was all nonsense;" they shouted; "there could be no question of honour here. Kreisler was a quarrelsome German. He was drunk." Tarr liked his own farces. But to be drawn into the service of one of Kreisler's was a humiliation. Kreisler, without taking any notice of him, had turned the tables.

The discussion was interminable. They were now speaking French. The entire café appeared to be participating. Several times the principal on the other side attempted to go, evidently very cross at the noisy scene. Then Anastasya's name was mentioned. Tarr found new interest in the scene.

"You and Herr Kreisler," the Russian was saying patiently and distinctly, "exchanged blows, I understand, this afternoon, before this lady. This was as a result of my friend Herr Kreisler demanding certain explanations from you which you refused to give. These explanations had reference to certain stories you are supposed to have circulated as regards him."

"Circulated—as regards—that chimpanzee you are conducting about?

"If you please! By being abusive you cannot escape. You are accused by my friend of having at his expense—"

"Expense? Does he want money?"

"If you please! You cannot buy off Herr Kreisler; but he might be willing for you to pay a substitute if you find it—inconvenient—?"

"I find you, bearded idiot!—"

"We can settle all that afterwards. You understand me? I shall be quite ready! But at present it is the affair between you and Herr Kreisler—"

In brief, it was the hapless Soltyk that Kreisler had eventually got hold of, and had just now publicly smacked, having some hours before smacked him privately.

CHAPTER II

Kreisler's afternoon encounter with Anastasya and Soltyk had resembled Tarr's meeting with him and Bertha. Kreisler had seen Anastasya and his new café friend one day from his window. His reference to possible nose-pulling was accounted for by this. The next day he had felt rather like seeing Anastasya again somewhere. With this object, he had patrolled the neighbourhood. About four o'clock, having just bought some cigarettes at the "Berne," he was standing outside considering a walk in the Luxemburg, when Fräulein Vasek appeared in this unshunnable circus of the Quartier du Paradis. Soltyk was with her. He went over at once. With urbane timidity, as though they had been alone, he offered his hand. She looked at Soltyk, smiling. But she showed no particular signs of wanting to escape. They began strolling along the Boulevard, Soltyk showing every sign of impatience. She then stopped.

"Mr. Soltyk and I were just going to have the 'five o'clock' somewhere," she said.

Soltyk looked pointedly down the Boulevard, as though that had been an improper piece of information to communicate to Kreisler.

"If you consent to my accompanying you, Fräulein, it would give me the greatest pleasure to remain in your company a little longer."

She laughed. "Where were we going, Louis? Didn't you say there was a place near here?"

"There is one over there. But I'm afraid, Fräulein Vasek, I must leave you.—I have—"

"Oh, must you? I'm sorry."

Soltyk was astonished and mortified. He did not go, looking at her doubtfully. At this point Kreisler had addressed him.

"I said nothing, sir, when a moment ago, you failed to return my salute. I understand you were going to have tea with Fräulein Vasek. Now you deprive her suddenly of the pleasure of your company. So there is no further doubt on a certain point. Will you tell me at once and clearly what objection you have to me?"

"I don't wish to discuss things of that sort before this lady."

"Will you then name a place where they may be discussed? I will then take my leave?"

"I see no necessity to discuss anything with you."

"Ah, you see none. I do. And perhaps it is as well that Fräulein Vasek should hear. Will you explain to me, sir, how it is that you have been putting stories about having reference to me, and to my discredit, calculated to prejudice people against me? Since this lady no doubt has heard some of your lies, it would be of advantage that you take them back at once, or else explain yourself."

Before Kreisler had finished, Soltyk said to Anastasya, "I had better go at once, to save you this—" Then he turned to Kreisler,

"I should have thought you would have had sufficient decency left—"

"Decency, liar? Decency, *lying swine*? Decency—? What do you mean?" said Kreisler, loudly, in crescendo.

Then he crossed quickly over in front of Anastasya and smacked Soltyk first smartly on one cheek and then on the other.

"There is liar branded on both your cheeks! And if you should not wish to have coward added to your other epithets, you or your friends will find me at the following address before the day is out." Kreisler produced a card and handed it to Soltyk.

Soltyk stared at him, paralysed for the moment at this outrage, his eyes burning with the sweet intensity Tarr noticed that evening, taking in the incredible fact. He got the fact at last. He lifted his cane and brought it down on Kreisler's shoulders. Kreisler snatched it from him, broke it in three and flung it in his face, one of the splinters making a little gash in his under lip.

Anastasya had turned round and begun walking away, leaving them alone. Kreisler also waited no longer, but marched rapidly off in the other direction.

Soltyk caught Anastasya up, and apologized for what had occurred, dabbing his lip with a handkerchief.

Kreisler after this felt himself fairly launched on a satisfactory little affair. Many an old talent would come in useful. He acted for the rest of the day with a gusto of professional interest. For an hour or two he stayed at home. No one came, however, to call him to account. Leaving word that he would soon be back, he left in search of a man to act for him. He remembered a Russian he had had some talk with at the Studio, and whom he had once visited. He was celebrated for having had a duel and blinded his opponent. His instinct now led him to this individual, who has already been seen in action. His qualifications for a second were quite unique.

Kreisler found him just finishing work. He had soon explained what he required of him. With great gravity he set forth his attachment for a "beautiful girl," the discreditable behaviour of the Russian in seeking to prejudice her against him. In fact, he gave an entirely false picture of the whole situation. His honour *must* now be satisfied. He would accept nothing less than reparation by arms. Such was Kreisler, but he was *himself* very cynically. He had explained this to Volker after the following manner: "I am a hundred different things; I am as many people as the different types of people I have lived amongst. I am a 'Boulevardier' (he believed that on occasion he answered fully to that description), I am a 'Rapin'; I am also a 'Korps-student.'"

In his account of how things stood he had, besides, led the Russian to understand that there was more in it all than it was necessary to say, and, in fact, than he *could* say. Whatever attitude Soltyk might take up, this gentleman too knew, he hinted, that they had come to the point in their respective relations towards this "beautiful girl" at which one of them must disappear. In addition, he, Kreisler, had been grossly insulted in the very presence of the "beautiful girl" that afternoon. The Russian's compatriot had used his cane. These latter were facts that would be confirmed later, for the physical facts at least could not be got round by Soltyk.

The Russian, Bitzenko by name, a solemnly excitable bourgeois of Petrograd, recognized a situation after his own heart. Excitement was a food he seldom got in such quantities, and pretending to listen to Kreisler a little abstractedly and uncertainly to start with, he was really from the first very much his man.

So Kreisler and his newly found henchman, silently and intently engaged on their evening's business, have been accounted for. Soltyk had been discovered some quarter of an hour before Tarr's appearance, and stared out of countenance for the whole of the time by Kreisler.

CHAPTER III

The indignation and flurry subsided; but the child of this eruption remained. The Polish party found the legacy of the uproar as cold as its cause had been hot. Bitzenko inspired respect as he scratched his beard, which smelt of Turkish tobacco, and wrinkled up imperturbably small grey eyes.

Then, the excitement over, the red mark on Soltyk's cheek became merely a fact. One or two of his friends found themselves examining it obliquely, as a relic, with curiosity.

He had had his face smacked earlier in the day, as well. How much longer was his face going to go on being smacked? Here was this Russian still there. There *was* the chance of an affair. A duel—a duel, for a change, in our civilized life; *c'était une idée.*

Who was the girl the Russian kept mentioning? Was she that girl he had been telling them about who had a man-servant? Kreisler was a Frei-Herr? The Russian had referred to him as "my friend the Frei-Herr."

"Herr Kreisler does not wish to take further measures to ensure himself some form of satisfaction," the Russian said monotonously.

"There is always the police for drunken blackguards," Soltyk answered.

"If you please! That is not the way! It is not usually so difficult to obtain satisfaction from a gentleman."

"But then I am not a gentleman in the sense that your friend Kreisler is."

"Perhaps not, but a blow on the face—"

The little Russian said "blow on the face" in a soft inviting way, as though it were a titbit with powers of fascination of its own.

"But it is most improper to ask me to stand here wrangling with you," he next said.

"You please yourself."

"I am merely serving my friend Herr Kreisler. Will you oblige me by indicating a friend of yours with whom I can discuss this matter?"

The waiter who had brought in the card again approached their table. This time he presented Soltyk with a note, written on the café paper and folded in four.

Tarr had been watching what was going on with as much interest as his ruffled personal dignity would allow him to take. He did not believe in a duel. But he wondered what would happen, for he was certain that Kreisler would not let this man alone until something had happened. What would he have done, he asked himself, in Soltyk's place? He would have naturally refused to consider the idea of a duel as a possibility. If you had to fight a duel with any man who liked to hit you on the head—Kreisler, moreover, was not a man with whom a duel need be fought. He was in a weak position in that way, in spite of the additional blacking on his boots. Tarr himself, of course, could have taken refuge in the fact that Englishmen do not duel. But what would have been the next step, this settled, had he been in Soltyk's shoes? Kreisler was waiting at the door of the café. If his enemy got up and went out, at the door he would once more have his face smacked. His knowledge of Kreisler convinced him that that face would be smacked all over the *quartier*, at all hours of the day, for many days to come. Kreisler, unless physically overwhelmed, would smack it in public and in private until further notice. He would probably spit in it, after having smacked it, occasionally. So Kreisler must be henceforth fought by his victim wherever met. Would this state of things justify the use of a revolver? No. Kreisler should be maimed. It all should be prepared with great thoroughness; exactly the weight of stick, etc. The French laws would allow quite a bad wound. But Tarr felt that the sympathetic young Prussian-Pole would soon have Bitzenko on his hands as well. Bitzenko was very alarming.

Kreisler, although evicted from the café, had been allowed by the waiters to take up his position on a distant portion of the terrace. There he sat with his legs crossed and his eye fixed on the door with a Scottish solemnity. He was an object of considerable admiration to the *garçons*. His coolness and persistence appeared to them amusing and typical. His solemnity aroused their wonder and respect. He meant business. He was behaving correctly.

Soltyk opened the note at once.

On it was written in German:

> *"To the cad Soltyk*
>
> "If you make any more trouble about appointing seconds, and delay the gentlemen who have consented to act for me, I shall wait for you at the door and try some further means of rousing you to honourable action."

A little man sitting next to Soltyk with an eloquent, sleek lawyer's face took the letter as though it had been a public document and read it. He bent towards his friend and said:

"What is really the matter with this gentleman?"

Soltyk shrugged his shoulders.

"He's a brute, and he is a little crazy as well. He wants to pick a quarrel with me, I don't know why."

"He means trouble. Doesn't he want to be taken seriously, only? Let his shaggy friend here have a chat with a friend of yours. He may be a nuisance—"

"What rot! Why should one, Stephen? If he comes for me at the door, let him! I wish that little man there would go away. He has annoyed us quite enough."

"Louis, will you give me permission to speak to him on your behalf?"

"If that will give you any satisfaction."

Stephen (Staretsky) got up and put himself at Bitzenko's disposition. The whole party became tumultuous at this.

"What the devil are you up to, Stephen? Let them alone."

"You're not going—?"

"Tell them to go to hell!"

"Stephen, come back, you silly fool!"

Stephen Staretsky smiled at this with a sort of worldly indulgence. "You don't understand. This is the best thing to do," he seemed to say.

"Do you want this to last the whole evening?" he asked the man nearest him.

He followed Bitzenko out, and Tarr followed Bitzenko.

CHAPTER IV

They went over to a small, gaudy, quiet café opposite, Kreisler watching them, but still with his eye on the door near at hand.

Tarr was amused now at his position of dummy. He enjoyed crossing the road under Kreisler's eye, in his service. The evening's twists were very comic.

Imaginative people are easy to convince of the naturalness of anything; and the Russian was the prophet of the necessity of this affair. Stephen was not convinced; but he soon made up his mind that Bitzenko was either Kreisler's accomplice in some scheme or at least had made up his mind that there could only be one ending to the matter.

He went back to the café and, sitting down beside Soltyk again, said:

"I'm afraid I was mistaken, Louis. Your German means to fight you or else he has some little game. If you're sure there's nothing in it, you must tell him and his little Russian to go to the devil."

While Stephen Staretsky had been away one of Soltyk's friends told them about Bitzenko.

"Don't you know him, Louis? Maiewski used to know him. He lives in one of those big studios, Rue Ulm, near the Invalides. Il a du pognon, il parait."

Soltyk began patting his cheek gently. But his vanity ached steadily inside.

"What is his name?" asked another.

"Bitzenko. He once had a duel and blinded a man."

Soltyk looked up and stopped patting his cheek.

"How? Blinded him?" somebody asked.

"Yes, blinded him."

The blows began to take effect, the atmosphere becoming somehow congenial to them. When Stephen Staretsky delivered his message Soltyk was losing his self-control. The opportunity of killing this obnoxious figure offered him so obstinately by Bitzenko—whom he disliked even more—began to recommend itself to him. This *commis voyageur* sent to press the attractions of destruction had won his point.

Soltyk had been silent. He had been twisting up the corners of a newspaper on the table before him, and appeared struck lazy, into a kind of sullen sleepiness and detachment resembling despair.

"Ask him," he said suddenly to Staretsky, "what he wants."

"What do you mean?"

Soltyk answered irritably, "Why, what they want: what sort of a duel he wants and when." "Duel" was said as though it were a common object. "Settle it quickly and let's get all this nonsense over, since you have begun negotiations."

Stephen Staretsky stared at him.

"You don't mean—? I have not been negotiating. I simply—"

The others once more clamoured, after a moment of astonishment.

"You don't mean to say, Louis, you're going—?"

"What nonsense, what utter nonsense! What can you be thinking of?"

"If Bitzenko comes in again, pay no attention to him! What possesses you, Louis! Whatever possesses you, Louis!"

Soltyk looked angrily at his friends without replying.

"Staretsky, arrange that, do you mind?" he said when the exclamations stopped. "But for Heaven's sake get it finished quickly. This is becoming boring."

Staretsky said, leaning on the back of Soltyk's chair, with authority:

"Don't be absurd, Louis: don't be absurd. You must refuse to listen to him. All that rot about libelling and the 'beautiful girl': my God, man, you're not going to take that seriously?"

"Of course not. But I shall fight the German clown. I want to. This is becoming ridiculous."

Soltyk had made up his mind. He would never have armed himself and shot Kreisler in the street. That would have been too ridiculous. It would have had the touch of passion and intimacy of a *crime passionel*. It would only have been dignified for an inhabitant of Nevada.

He did not regard this as a duel, but a brawl, ordered by the rules of "affairs of honour." If a drunken man or an *apache* attacked you the best thing to do would be to fight. If he offered to "fight you fair"—putting it in that way—then *that* would be the best thing, too, no doubt.

But Bitzenko really had brought him to this. Kreisler alone could never have hoped to compass anything approaching a duel with him.

Stephen Staretsky overwhelmed him with expostulation—even reproaches. His voice rose and fell in a microscopic stream of close-packed sound. His face became shiny and the veins appeared in it. He begged Soltyk to think of his friends! He gathered his arguments up in the tips of his fingers in little nervous bunches and held them under his friend's nose, as though asking him to smell them. And then, with a spasm of the body, a vibrating twang on some deep chord in his throat, he dashed his gathered fingers towards the floor.

In face of this attack it was impossible, even had he wished to do so, for Soltyk to reconsider his decision. The others, too, sat for the most part watching him.

Bitzenko appeared again. Soltyk became pale at the sight of this sinister figure, so bourgeois, prepossessing, and bearded, with its legend of blindings and blood and uncanny tenacity as a second.

He turned to a good-looking, sleek, sallow companion at his elbow.

"Khudin, will you act for me, as Stephen won't?"

Stephen Staretsky rose. A superfine sweat moistened his skin. His extraordinary volubility was tucked away somewhere in him in a flash, in a satisfied and polished acrobatic, and he faced the Russian. Khudin rose at the same time. Bitzenko had won.

Tarr was astonished at the rapid tragic trend of these farcical negotiations.

"How angry that man must be to do that," he thought. But he had not been smacked the evening before; yet he remembered he had been passably angry.

CHAPTER V

Otto Kreisler, when he had entered the Café Souchet, had been anxious. His eyes had picked out Soltyk in a delicate flurry. He had been afraid that he might escape him. Soltyk looked so securely bedded in life, and he wanted to wrench him out. He was not at all bad-tempered at the moment. He would have extracted him quite "painlessly" if required. But bleeding and from the roots, he must come out! (Br-r-rr. The Bersaker rage!)

He was quite quiet and well-behaved; above all things, *well-behaved*! The mood he had happened on for this particular phase of his action was a virulent snobbery. He was a painful and blushing snob! He had, at his last public appearance, taken the rôle of a tramp-comedian. He had invited every description of slight and indignity. The world seemed to wish to perpetuate this part for him. But he would not play! He refused! A hundred times, he refused!

He remembered with eagerness that he was a German gentleman, with a *university education*; who had never worked; *a member of an honourable family*! He remembered each detail socially to his advantage, realizing methodically things he had from childhood accepted and never thought of examining. But he had gone a step further. He had arbitrarily revived the title of Frei-Herr that, it was rumoured in his family, his ancestors had borne. With Bitzenko he had referred to himself as the Frei-Herr Otto Kreisler. Had the occasion allowed, he would have been very courteous and gentle with Soltyk, merely to prove what a gentleman he was! But, alas, nothing but brutality (against the grain—the noble grain—as this went!) would achieve his end.

And the end was still paramount. His snobbery was the outcome of this end, of his end. It was, in this obsession of disused and disappearing life, the wild assertion of vitality, the clamour for recognition that life and the beloved self were still there, that brought out the reeking and brand-new snob. He was almost dead (he had promised his father his body for next month, and must be punctual), but people already had begun treading on him and striking matches on his boots. As to fighting with a man who was practically dead, to all intents and purposes, one mass of worms—a worm, in short—that was not to be expected of anybody.

So he became a violent snob.

It was Soltyk's rude behaviour on the day before in the presence of Anastasya that had set him raving on this subject. The Russian Pole was up against a raving snob whose social dignity he had wounded.

Bitzenko and Kreisler came out to get Louis Soltyk like two madmen, full of solemn method and with miraculous solidarity. Their schemes and energies flew direct from mind to mind, without the need for words. Bitzenko with his own hand had brushed the back of Kreisler's coat; on tiptoe doing this he looked particularly childlike. They were together there in Kreisler's room before they started like two little boys dressing up in preparation for some mischief.

Kreisler had fixed his eyes on Soltyk from his table with alert offensiveness. The prosperous appearance of the Poles annoyed him deeply. Their watches were all there, silk handkerchiefs slipped up their sleeves; they looked sleek and new. A gentle flame of social security and ease danced in their eyes and gestures. He was out in the dark, they were in a lighted room! He wished their fathers' affairs might deteriorate and their fortunes fall to pieces; that their watches could be stolen, and their restaurant-tick attacked by insidious reports! And as he watched them he felt more and more an outcast, shabbier and shabbier. He saw himself the little official in a German provincial town that his father's letter foreshadowed.

One or two of them pointed him out to Soltyk, and it was a wounding laugh of the latter's that brought him to his feet.

As he was slapping his enemy he woke up out of his nightmare. He was like a sleeper having the first inkling of his solitude when he is woken by the climax of his dream, still surrounded by tenacious influences. But had any one struck him then, the blow would have had as little effect as a blow aimed at a waking man by a phantom of his sleep. The noise around him was a receding accompaniment.

Then he felt hypnotized by Soltyk's quietness. The sweet white of the face made him sick. To overcome this he stepped forward again to strike the dummy once more, and then it moved suddenly. As he raised his hand his glasses almost slipped off, and at that point he was seized by the *garçons*. Hurried out on to the pavement, he could still see, at the bottom of a huge placid mirror just inside the café, the wriggling backs of the band of Poles. Drawing out his card-case, he had handed the waiter a visiting-card. The waiter at first refused it. He turned his head aside vaguely, as a dog does when doubtful about some morsel offered him; then he took it. Kreisler saw in the mirror the tearing up of his card. Fury once more—not so much because it was a new slight as that he feared his only hope, Soltyk, might escape him.

The worry of this hour or so in which Bitzenko was negotiating told on him so much that when at last his emissary announced that an arrangement had been come to in the sense he wished, he questioned him incredulously. He felt hardly any satisfaction, reaction setting in immediately.

Bitzenko went back to Kreisler's door with him and, promising to return within half an hour, left him. Tarr having, as he had stipulated, left when the talking was over, Bitzenko first went in search of a friend to serve as second. The man he decided on was already in bed, and at once, half asleep, without preparation of any sort, consented to do what was asked of him.

"Will you be a second in a duel to-morrow morning at half-past six?"

"Yes."

"At half-past six?"

"Yes." And after a minute or two, "Is it you?"

"No, a German friend of mine."

"All right."

"You will have to get up at five."

Bitzenko's friend was a tall, powerfully built young Russian painter, who, with his great bow-legs, would take up some straggling and extravagantly twisted pose of the body and remain immobile for minutes together, with an air of ridiculous detachment. This combination of a tortured, restless attitude, and at the same time statuesque tendency, suggested something like a contemplative acrobat or contortionist. A mouth of almost anguished attention and little calm indifferent eyes, produced similar results in the face.

Bitzenko's next move was to go to his rooms, put a gently ticking little clock, with an enormous alarum on the top, under his arm, and then walk round once more to Otto Kreisler's. He informed his friend of these last arrangements made in his interests. He suggested that it would be better for him to sleep there that night, to save time in the morning. In short, he attached himself to Kreisler's person. Until it were deposited in the large cemetery near by, or else departed from the Gare du Nord in a deal box for burial in Germany, it should not leave him. In the event of victory, and he being no longer responsible for it, it should disappear as best it could. The possible subsequent conflict with the police was not without charm for Bitzenko. He regarded the police force, its functions and existence, as a pretext for adventure.

The light was blown out. Bitzenko curled himself up on the floor. He insisted on this. Kreisler must be fresh in the morning and do him justice. The Russian could hear the bed shaking for some time. Kreisler was trembling violently. A sort of exultation at the thought of his success caused this nervous attack. He had been quite passive since he had heard that all was well.

At about half-past four in the morning Kreisler was dreaming of Volker and a pact he had made with him in his sleep never to divulge some secret, which there was never any possibility of his doing in any case, as he had completely forgotten what it was. He was almost annihilated by a terrific explosion. With his eyes suddenly wide open, he saw the little clock quivering in the mantelpiece beneath its large alarum. When it had stopped Kreisler could hardly believe his ears, as though this sound had been going to accompany life, for that day at least, as a destructive and terrifying feature. Then he saw the Russian, already on his feet. His white and hairy little body had apparently risen energetically out of the scratch bedclothes simultaneously with the "going off" of his clock, as though it were a mechanism set for the same hour.

They both dressed without a word. Kreisler wrote a short letter to his father, entrusting it to his second.

Kreisler's last few francs were to be spent on a taxi to take them to the place arranged on, outside the fortifications.

They found the other second sound asleep. Bitzenko more or less dressed him. They set out in their taxi to the rendezvous by way of the Bois.

The chilly and unusual air of the early morning, the empty streets and shuttered houses, destroyed all feeling of reality of what was happening for Kreisler. Had the duel been a thing to fear it would have had an opposite effect. His errand did not appear as an inflexible reality, either, following upon events that there was no taking back. It was a whim, a caprice, they were pursuing, as though, for instance, they had woken up in the early morning and decided to go fishing. They were carrying it out with a dogged persistency, with which our whims are often served.

He kept his thought away from Soltyk. He seemed a very long way off; it would be fatiguing for the mind to go in search of him.

When the scientist's nature, with immense *fugue,* has induced a man to marry some handsome young lady—this feat accomplished, Nature leaves him practically alone, only coming back to give him a prod from time to time—assured that, like a little trickling stream, his life will go steadily on in the bed gauged for it by this upheaval. Nature, in Kreisler's case, had done its work of another description. But she had left the Russian with him to see that all was carried out according to her wishes. Kreisler's German nature that craved discipline, a course marked out, had got more even than it asked for. It had been presented with a mimic Fate.

But Bitzenko evidently took his pleasure morosely. The calm and assurance of the evening before had given place to a brooding humour. He was only restored to a silent and intense animation on hearing his "Browning" speak. He produced this somewhere in the Bois, and insisted on his principal having a little practice as they had plenty of time to spare. This was a very imprudent step. It might draw attention to their movements. Kreisler proved an excellent shot. Then the Russian himself, with impassible face, emptied a couple of chambers into a tree-trunk. He put his "Browning" back into his pocket hastily after this, as though startled at his own self-indulgence.

A piece of waste land, on the edge of a wood, well hidden on all sides, had been chosen for the duel.

The enemy was not on the ground. Kreisler's passivity still subsisted. So far he had felt that Accident had been dealt a shrewd blow and brought to its knees. He was in good hands. Until this was all over he had nothing to worry about.

Fresh compartment. The duel became for him, as he stood on the damp grass, conventional. It was a duel like another. He was seeking reparation by arms. He had been libelled and outraged. "A beautiful woman" was at the bottom of it. Life had no value for him! *Tant pis* for the other man who had been foolhardy enough to cross his path. His coat-collar turned up, he looked sternly towards the road, his moustaches blowing a little in the wind.

He asked Bitzenko for a cigarette. That gentleman did not smoke, but the other Russian produced a khaki cigarette with a long mouthpiece. He struck a light. As Kreisler lit his cigarette at it, his hand resting against the other's, a strange feeling shot through him at the contact of this flesh. He moistened his lips and spat out a piece of the mouthpiece he had bitten through.

The hour arranged came round and there was still no sign of anybody. The possibility of a hitch in the proceedings dawned on Kreisler. Personal animosity for Soltyk revived. That idea of obstinacy in a caprice, instead of merely carrying out something prearranged and unavoidable, despite his passivity, had proved really the wakefulness of his will. He looked towards his companions, alone there on the ground of the encounter. They were an unsatisfactory pair, after all. They did not look a winning team. He reproached himself for having hit just on this Russian for assistance.

Bitzenko, on the other hand, was deep in thought. He was rehearsing his part of second. The duel in which he had blinded his adversary was a figment of his boyish brain, confided with tears in his voice one evening to a friend. His only genuine claim to activity was that, in a perfect disguise, he had assisted the peasants of his estate to set fire to his little Manor House during the revolution of 1906 for the fun of the thing and in an access of revolutionary sentiment. Afterwards he had assisted the police with information in the investigation of the affair, also anonymously. All this he kept to himself. He referred to his past in Russia in a way that conjured up more luridness than the flames of his little château (which did not burn at all well) warranted.

Bitzenko was quite in his element climatically; whereas Kreisler felt his hands getting so cold that he thought they might fail him in the duel.

But a car was heard beyond the trees on the Paris road. This sound in the listless blur of nature was masterful in its significance. It struck steadily and at once into brutish apathy. It so plainly knew what it wanted. It had perhaps outstripped men in that. Men in their soft bodies still contained the apathy of the fields. Their mind had burst out of them and taken these crawling pulps up on its rigid back.

It was Staretsky's car. With its load of hats it drew up. The four members of the other party came on to the field, the fourth a young Polish doctor. They walked quickly. Bitzenko went to meet them. Staretsky protested energetically that the duel must not proceed.

"It must—not—go—on! Should anything happen—you must allow me to say, should anything happen—the blood of whoever falls will be at your door!" But he felt all the same that the prospect of having a little pond of blood at his door was an alluring one for Bitzenko.

"Has not your principal seen that in accepting this duel, M. Soltyk had proved his respect for Herr Kreisler's claim? The attitude your principal attributed to him is *not* his attitude—"

Bitzenko stiffened.

"Is there anything in Herr Kreisler that would justify M. Soltyk in considering that he was condescending—?"

The little Russian kept up his cunning and baffling wrangle. Soltyk's eyes steadily avoided Kreisler's person. He hoped this ridiculous figure might make some move enabling them to abandon the duel. But the idea of a favour coming from such a quarter was repellent. His stomach had been out of order the day before—he wondered if it would surge up, disgrace him. He might be sick at any moment. He saw himself on tiptoe, in an ignominious spasm, the proceedings held up, friends and enemies watching. He kept his eyes off Kreisler as a man on board ship keeps his eyes off a dish of banana fritters or a poached egg.

Kreisler, from twenty yards off, stared through his glasses at the group of people he had assembled, as though he had been examining the enemy through binoculars. Obediently, erect and still, he appeared rather amazed at what was occurring. Soltyk, in rear of the others, struggled with his bile. He slipped into his mouth a sedative tablet, oxide of bromium and heroin. This made him feel more sick. For a few moments he stood still in horror, expecting to vomit at every moment. The blood rushed to his head and covered the back of his neck with a warm liquid sheet.

Kreisler's look of surprise deepened. He had seen Soltyk slipping something into his mouth, and was puzzled and annoyed, like a child. What was he up to? Poison was the only guess he could give. What on earth—?

Having taken part in many *mensurs* he knew that for this very serious duel his emotions were hardly adequate. His nervous system was as quiescent as a corpse's. He became offended with his phlegm. All this instinctive resistance to the idea of Death, the indignity of being nothing, was rendered empty by his premature insensitiveness. He tried to visualize and feel. In a few minutes he might be dead! That had so little effect that he almost laughed.

Then he reflected that that man over there might in a few minutes be wiped out. He would become a disintegrating mess, uglier than any vitriol or syphilis could make him. All that organism he, Kreisler, would be turning into dung, as though by magic. He, Kreisler, is insulted. The sensations and energies of that man deny him equality of existence. He, Kreisler, lifts his hand, presses a little bar of steel, and the other is swept away into the earth. Heaven knows where the insulting spirit goes to. But the *physical disfigurement* at least is complete. He went through it laboriously. But it fell flat as well. He was too near the event to benefit by his fancy. Possibilities were weakened by the nearness of Certainty.

His momentary resentment with Bitzenko survived, and he next became annoyed at being treated like an object, as he felt it. He was not deliberately conscious of much. But, try as he would to elude the disgraces and besmirchings of death, people refused to treat him as anything but a sack of potatoes.

There four or five men had been arguing about him for the last five minutes, and they had not once looked his way. But clearly Bitzenko was defending *his* duel.

Why should Bitzenko go on disposing of him in this fashion? He took everything for granted; he never so much as appealed to him, even once. Had Bitzenko been commissioned to hustle him out of existence?

But Soltyk. There was that fellow again slipping something into his mouth! A cruel and fierce sensation of mixed real and romantic origin rose hotly round his heart. He *loved* that man! But because he loved him he wished to plunge a sword into him, to plunge it in and out and up and down! Why had pistols been chosen?

He would let him off for two pins! He would let him off if—Yes! He began pretending to himself that the duel might after all not take place. That was the only way he could get anything out of it.

He laughed; then shouted out in German:

"Give me one!"

They all looked round. Soltyk did not turn, but the side of his face became crimson.

Kreisler felt a surge of active passion at the sight of the blood in his face.

"Give me one," Kreisler shouted again, putting out the palm of his hand, and laughing in a thick, insulting, hearty way. He was now a *Knabe*. He was young and cheeky. His last words had been said with quick cleverness. The heavy coquetting was double-edged.

"What do you mean?" Bitzenko called back.

"I want a jujube. Ask Herr Soltyk!"

They all turned towards the other principal to the duel, standing some yards on the other side of them.

Head thrown back and eyes burning, Soltyk gazed at Kreisler. It was genuine, but not very strong. If killing could be embodied in the organ that *sees*—a new function of expression—a perfect weapon would exist. Only the intensest expression being effective, such spiritual blasting powers would be a solution of the arbitrary decisions of force. Words, glances, music are at present as indirect as hands and cannons. Such music might be written, however, that no fool, hearing it, could survive. Whether it throttled him in a spasm of disgust or of shame is immaterial. Soltyk's battery was too conventional to pierce the layers of putrifying tragedy, Kreisler's bulwark. It played to the limit of its power. His cheeks were a dull red: his upper lip was stretched tightly over the gums. The white line of teeth made his face look as though he were laughing. He stamped his foot on the ground with the impetuous grace of a Russian dancer, and started walking hurriedly up and down. He glared at his seconds as well, but although sick with impatience made no protest.

A peal of drawling laughter came from Kreisler:

"Sorry! Sorry! My mistake," he shouted.

Bitzenko came over and asked Kreisler if he still, for his part, was of the same mind, that the duel should go on. The principal stared impenetrably at the second.

"If such an arrangement can be come to as should—er—" he began slowly. He was going to play with Bitzenko too, against whom his humour had shifted. A look of deepest dismay appeared in the Russian's face.

"I don't understand. You mean—?"

"I mean, that if the enemy and you can find a basis for understanding—" and Kreisler went on staring at Bitzenko with his look of false surprise.

"You seem very anxious for me to fight, Herr Bitzenko," he then said furiously. With a laugh at Bitzenko's miserable face and evident pleasure at his quick-change temperamental, facial agility, he left him, walking towards the other assistants.

Addressing Staretsky, his face radiating affability, stepping with caution, as though to avoid puddles, he said:

"I am willing to forgo the duel at once on one condition. If Herr Soltyk will give me a kiss, I will forgo the duel!"

He smiled archly and expectantly at Staretsky.

"I don't know what you mean!"

"Why, a kiss. You know what a kiss is, my dear sir."

"I shall consider you out of your mind, if—"

"That is my condition."

Soltyk had come up behind Staretsky.

"What is your *condition*?" he asked loudly.

Kreisler stepped forward so quickly that he was beside him before Soltyk could move. With one hand coaxingly extended towards his arm, he was saying something, too softly for the others to hear.

He had immobilized everybody by his rapid action. Surprise had shot their heads all one way. They stood, watching and listening, screwed into astonishment as though by deft fingers.

His soft words, too, must have carried sleep. Their insults and their honey clogged up his enemy. A hand had been going up to strike. But at the words it stopped dead. So much new matter for anger had been poured into the ear that it wiped out all the earlier impulse. Action must be again begun right down from the root.

Kreisler thrust his mouth forward amorously, his body in the attitude of the eighteenth-century gallant, as though Soltyk had been a woman.

The will broke out frantically from the midst of bandages and a bulk of suddenly accruing fury. Soltyk tore at *himself* first, writhing upright, a statue's bronze softening, suddenly, with blood. He became white and red by turns. His blood, one heavy mass, hurtled about in him, up and down, like a sturgeon in a narrow tank.

All the pilules he had taken seemed acting sedatively against the wildness of his muscles. The bromium fought the blood.

His hands were electrified. Will was at last dashed all over him, an Arctic douche. The hands flew at Kreisler's throat. His nails made six holes in the flesh and cut into the tendons beneath. Kreisler was hurled about. He was pumped backwards and forwards. His hands grabbed a mass of hair; as a man slipping on a precipice gets hold of a plant. Then they gripped along the coat-sleeves, connecting him with the engine he had just overcharged with fuel. A sallow white, he became puffed and exhausted.

"Acha—acha—" a noise, the beginning of a word, came from his mouth. He sank on his knees. A notion of endless violence filled him. "Tchun—tchun—tchun—tchun—tchun—tchun!" He fell on his back, and the convulsive arms came with him. The strangling sensation at his neck intensified.

Meanwhile a breath of absurd violence had smitten everywhere.

Staretsky had said:

"That *crapule* is beneath contempt! Pouah!—I refuse to act. Whatever induced us—"

Bitzenko had begun a discourse. Staretsky turned on him, shrieking, "Foute-moi la paix, imbécile!"

At this Bitzenko rapped him smartly on the cheek. Staretsky, who spent his mornings sparring with a negro pugilist, gave him a blow between the eyes, which laid him out insensible.

Bitzenko's friend, interfering when he saw this, seized Staretsky round the waist, and threw him down, falling with him.

The doctor and the other second, Wenceslas Khudin, went to separate Soltyk and Kreisler, scuffling and exhorting. The field was filled with cries, smacks, and harsh movements.

This Slav chaos gradually cleared up.

Soltyk was pulled off; Staretsky and the young Russian were separated. Bitzenko once more was on his feet. Then they were all dusting their trousers, arranging their collars, picking up their hats.

Kreisler stood stretching his neck to right and left alternately. His collar was torn open; blood trickled down his chest. He had felt weak and unable to help himself against Soltyk.

Actual fighting appeared a contingency outside the calculations or functioning of his spirit. Brutal by rote and in the imagination, if action came too quickly before he could inject it with his dream, his forces were disconnected. This physical *mêlée* had been a disturbing interlude. He was extremely offended at it. His eyes rested steadily and angrily on Soltyk. This attempt on his part to escape into physical and secondary things he must be made to pay for! He staggered a little, with the dignity of the drunken man.

His glasses were still on his nose. They had weathered the storm, tightly riding his face, because of Soltyk's partiality for his neck.

Staretsky took Soltyk by the arm.

"Come along, Louis. Surely you don't want any more of it? Let's get out of this. I refuse to act as second. You can't fight without seconds!"

Soltyk was panting, his mouth opening and shutting. He first turned this way, then that. His action was that of a man avoiding some importunity.

"C'est bien, c'est bien!" he gasped in French. "Je sais. Laisse-moi."

All his internal disorganization was steadily claiming his attention.

"Mais dépêche-toi donc! Filons. Nous avons plus rien à faire ici." Staretsky slipped his arm through his. Half supporting him, he began urging him along towards the car. Soltyk, stumbling and coughing, allowed himself to be guided.

Khudin and the doctor had been talking together, as the only two men on the field in full possession of their voices and breath. When they saw their friends moving off, they followed.

Bitzenko, recuperating rapidly, started after them.

Kreisler saw all this at first with indifference. He had taken his handkerchief out and was dabbing his neck. Then suddenly, with a rather plaintive but resolute gait, he ran after his second, his eye fixed on the retreating Poles.

"Hi! A moment! Your Browning. Give me your Browning!" he said hoarsely. His voice had been driven back into the safer depths of his body. It was a new and unconvincing one.

Bitzenko did not appear to understand.

Kreisler plucked the revolver out of his pocket with the deftness of an animal. There was a report. He was firing in the air.

Staretsky had faced quickly round, dragging Soltyk. Kreisler was covering them with the Browning.

"Halt!" he shouted. "Stop there! Not so quickly! I will shoot you like a dog if you will not fight!"

Still holding them up, he ordered Bitzenko to take over to them one of the revolvers provided for the duel.

"That will be murder! If you assist in this, sir, you will be participating in a murder! Stop this—"

Staretsky was jabbering at Bitzenko, his arm through his friend's. Soltyk stood wiping his face with his hand, his eyes on the ground. His breath came heavily, and he kept shifting his feet.

Bitzenko's tall young Russian stood in a twisted attitude, a gargoyle Apollo. His mask of peasant tragedy had broken into a slight smile.

"Move and I fire! Move and I fire!" Kreisler kept shouting, moving up towards them, with stealthy grogginess. He kept shaking the revolver and pointing at them with the other hand, to keep them alive to the reality of the menace.

"Don't touch the pistols, Louis!" said Staretsky, as Bitzenko came over with his leather dispatch-case. He let go of Soltyk's arm and folded his own.

"Don't touch them, Louis. They daren't shoot!"

Louis appeared apathetic both as to the pistols and the good advice.

"Leave him both," Kreisler called, his revolver still trained on Staretsky and Soltyk.

Bitzenko put them both down, a foot away from Soltyk, and walked hurriedly out of the zone of fire.

"Will you take up one of those pistols, or both?" Kreisler said.

"Kindly point that revolver somewhere else, and allow us to go!" Staretsky said loudly.

"I'm not speaking to you, pig-face! It's *you* I'm addressing. Take up that pistol!"

He was now five or six yards from them.

"Herr Soltyk is unarmed! The pistols you want him to take only have one charge. Yours has twelve. In any case it would be murder!"

Kreisler walked up to them. He was very white, much quieter, and acted with effort. He stooped down to take up one of the pistols. Staretsky aimed a blow at his head. It caught him just in front of the ear, on the right cheek-bone. He staggered sideways, tripped, and fell. The moment he felt the blow he pulled the trigger of the Browning, which still pointed towards his principal adversary. Soltyk threw his arms up: Kreisler was struggling towards his feet: he fell face forwards on top of him.

Kreisler thought this was a new attack. He seized Soltyk's body round the middle, rolling over on top of it. It was quite limp. He then thought the other man had fainted; ruptured himself—? He drew back quickly. Two hands grasped him and flung him down on his stomach. This time his glasses went. Scrambling after them, he remembered his Browning, which he had dropped. He shot his hands out to left and right—forgetting his glasses—to recover the Browning. He felt that a blow was a long time in coming.

"He's dead! He's dead! He's dead!"

Staretsky's voice, announcing that in French, he heard at the same time as Bitzenko's saying:

"What are you looking for? Come quickly!"

"Where is the Browning?" he asked. At that moment his hand struck his glasses. He put them on and got to his feet.

At Bitzenko's words he had a feeling of a new order of things having set in, that he remembered having experienced once or twice before in life. They came in a fresh surprising tone. It was as though they were the first words he had heard that day. They seemed to imply a sudden removal, a journey, novel conditions.

"Come along, I've got the Browning. There's no time to lose." It was all over; he must embrace practical affairs. The Russian's voice was businesslike. Something had finished for him, too. Kreisler saw the others standing in a peaceful group; the doctor was getting up from beside Soltyk.

Staretsky rushed over to Kreisler, and shook his fist in his face and tried to speak. But his mouth was twisted down at the corners, and he could hardly see. The palms of his hands pressed into each of his eyes, the next moment he was sobbing, walking back to his friends.

Bitzenko's bolt was shot. Kreisler had been unsatisfactory. All had ended in a silly accident, which might have awkward consequences for his second. It was hardly a real corpse at all.

But something was sent to console him. The police had got wind of the duel. Bitzenko, his compatriot and Kreisler were walking down the field, intending to get into the road at the farther end, and walk to the nearest station. The taxi had been sent away, Kreisler having no more money, and Bitzenko's feeling in the matter being that should Kreisler fall, a corpse can always find some sentimental soul to look after it. And there was always the Morgue, dramatic and satisfactory.

They were already half-way along the field when a car passed them on the other side of the hedge at full tilt.

The Russian was once more in his element. His face cleared. He looked ten years younger. In the occupants of the car he had recognized members of the police force!

Calling "Run!" to Kreisler he took to his heels, followed by his young fellow-second, whose neck shot in and out, and whose great bow-legs could almost be heard twanging as he ran. They reached a hedge, ran along the farther side of it. Bitzenko was bent double as though to escape a rain of bullets. Eventually he was seen careering across an open space quite near the river, which lay a couple of hundred yards beyond the lower end of the field. There he lay ambushed for a moment, behind a shrub. Then he darted forward again, and eventually disappeared along the high road in a cloud of dust. His athletic young friend made straight for the railway station, which he reached without incident and returned at once to Paris. Kreisler conformed to Bitzenko's programme of flight. He scrambled through the hedge, crossed the road and escaped almost unnoticed.

The truth was that the Russian had attracted the attention of the police to such an extent by his striking flight, that without a moment's hesitation they had bolted helter-skelter after him. They contented themselves with a parting shout or two at Kreisler. Duelling was a very venial offence; capture in these cases was not a matter of the least moment. But they were so impressed by the Russian's businesslike way of disappearing that they imagined this must have been a curiously immoral sort of duel. That he was the principal they did not doubt for a moment.

So they went after him in full cry, rousing two or three villagers in their passage, who followed at their heels, pouring with frantic hullabaloo in the direction of Paris. Bitzenko, however, with great resourcefulness, easily outwitted them. He crossed the Seine near St. Cloud, and got back to Paris in time to read the afternoon newspaper account of the duel and flight with infantile solemnity and calm.

CHAPTER VI

Five days after this, in the morning, Otto Kreisler mounted the steps of the police-station of a small town near the German frontier. He was going to give himself up.

Bitzenko had pictured his principal, in the event of his succeeding against Soltyk, seeking rapidly by train the German frontier, disguised in some extraordinary manner. Had the case been suggested to him of a man in this position without sufficient money in his pocket to buy a ticket, he would then have imagined a melodramatic figure hurrying through France, dodging and dogged by the police, defying a thousand perils. Whether Kreisler were still under the spell of the Russian or not, this was the course, more or less, he took. He could be trusted not to go near Paris. That city dominated all his maledictions.

The police disturbing the last act of his sanguinary farce was a similar contretemps to Soltyk's fingers in his throat. At the last moment everything had begun to go wrong. He had not prepared for it, because, as though from cunning, the world had shown no tendency up till then to interfere.

Soltyk had died when his back was turned, so to speak. He got the contrary of comfort out of the thought that he could claim to have done the deed. The police had rushed in and broken things off short, swept everything away, ended the banquet in a brutal raid. A deep sore, a shocked and dislocated feeling remained in Kreisler's mind. He had been hurried so much! He had never needed leisure, breathing space, so much. The disaster of Soltyk's death was raw on him! Had he been given time—only a little time—he might have put that to rights. (This sinister regret could only imply a possible mutilation of the corpse.)

A dead man has no feeling. He can be treated as an object and hustled away. But a living man needs time!—time!

Does not a *living man* need so much *time* to develop his movements, to lord it with his thoughtful body, to unroll his will? *Time* is what he needs!

As a tramp being hustled away from a café protests, at each jerk the waiter gives him, that he is a human being, probably a *free* human being—yes, probably *free*; so Kreisler complained to his fate that he was a living man, that he required *time*—that above all it was *time* he needed—to settle his affairs and withdraw from life. But his fate was a harsh Prussian gendarme. He whined and blustered to no effect.

He was superstitious as well in the usual way about this decease. In his spiritless and brooding tramp he questioned if it were not he that had died and not Soltyk, and if it were not his ghost that was now wandering off nowhere in particular.

One franc and a great many coppers remained to him. As he jumped from field to road and road to field again, in his flight, they rose and fell in a little leaden wave in his pocket, breaking dully on his thigh. This little wave rose and fell many times, till he began to wait for it, and its monotonous grace. It was like a sigh. It heaved and clashed down in a foiled way.

He spent the money that evening on a meal in a village. The night was dry and was passed in an empty barge. Next day, at four in the afternoon, he arrived at Meaux. Here he exchanged his entire wardrobe for a very shabby workman's outfit, gaining seven francs and fifty centimes on the exchange. He caught the early train for Rheims, travelling thirty-five kilometres of his journey at a sou a kilometre, got a meal near the station, and took another ticket to Verdun. Believing himself nearer the frontier than he actually was, he set out on foot. At the next large town, Pontlieux, he had too hearty a meal. He had exhausted his stock of money long before the frontier was reached. For two days he had eaten hardly anything; and tramped on in a dogged and careless spirit.

The *nearness* of the German frontier began to rise like a wall in front of him. This question had to be answered: Did he want to cross it after all?

His answer was to mount the steps of the local *gendarmerie.*

His Prussian severity of countenance, now that he was dressed in every point like a vagabond, without hat and his hair disordered, five days' beard on his chin—this sternness of the German warrior gave him the appearance of a scowling ruffian. The *agent* on duty, who barred his passage brutally before the door of the inner office, scowling too, classed him as a depraved cut-throat vagabond, and considered his voluntary entrance into the police-station as an act not only highly suspicious and unaccountable in itself, but of the last insolence.

"Qu'est-ce qu'il te faut?"

"Foir le Commissaire," returned Kreisler.

"Tu ne peux pas le voir. Il n'y est pas."

A few more laconic sentences followed, the *agent* reiterating sulkily that the magistrate was not there. But he was eyeing Kreisler doubtfully and turning something over in his mind.

The day before, two Germans had been arrested in the neighbourhood as spies, and were now locked up in this building until further evidence should be collected on the affair. It is extremely imprudent for a German to loiter on the frontier on entering France. It is much wiser for him to push on at once—neither looking to right nor left—pretending especially not to notice hills, unnatural military-looking protuberances, ramparts, etc.—to hurry on as rapidly as possible to the interior. But the two men in question were carpenters by profession, and both carried huge foot-rules in their pockets. The local authorities on this discovery were in a state of the deepest consternation. They shut them up, with their implements, in the most inaccessible depths of the local police-station. And it was in the doorway of this building—all the intermittant inhabitants of which were in a state of hysterical speculation, that Kreisler had presented himself.

The *agent*, who had recognized a German by his accent and manner, at last turned and disappeared through the door, telling him to wait. He reappeared with several superiors. All of them crowded in the doorway and surveyed Kreisler blankly. One asked in a voice of triumphant suspicion:

"And what are you doing there, my good fellow?"

"I had tuel, and killed the man; I have walked for more days—"

"Yes, we know all about that!"

"So you had a duel, eh?" asked another, and they all laughed with nervous suddenness at the picture of this vagabond defending his honour at twenty paces.

"Well, is that all you have to say?"

"I would eat."

"Yes! your two friends inside also have big appetites. But come to the point. Have you anything to tell us about your compatriots inside there?"

Since his throttling by Soltyk, Kreisler had changed. He knew he was beaten. There was nothing to do but to die. His body ran to the German frontier as a chicken's does down a yard, headless, from the block.

Kreisler did not understand the official. He muttered that he was hungry. He could hardly stand. Leaning his shoulder against the wall, he stood with his eyes on the ground. He was making himself at home! "What a nerve!"

"Va t'en! If you don't want to tell us anything, clear out. Be quick about it! A pretty lot of trouble you cursed Germans are giving us. You'll none of you speak when it comes to the point. You all stand staring like boobies. But that won't pay here. Of you go!"

They all turned back into the office, and slammed the door. The *agent* stood before it again, looking truculently at Kreisler. He said:

"Passez votre chemin! Don't stand gaping there!"

Then, giving him a shake, he hustled him to the top of the steps. A parting shove sent him staggering down into the road.

Kreisler walked on for a little. Eventually, in a quiet square, near the entrance to the town, he fell on a bench, drew his legs up and went to sleep.

At ten o'clock, the town lethargically retiring, all its legs moving slowly, like a spent insect, heavily boarding itself in, an *agent* came gradually along the square. Kreisler's visit to the police-station was not known to this one. He stopped opposite the sleeping Kreisler, surveying him with lawful indignation.

"En voilà un joli gigolo!" He swayed energetically up to him.

"Eh! le copain! Tu voudrais coucher à la belle étoile?"

He shook him.

"Oh, là! Tu ne peux pas dormir ici! *Houp!* Dépêches-toi. Mets-toi debout!"

Kreisler responded only by a tired movement as though to bury his skull in the bench. A more violent jerk rolled him on the ground.

He woke up and protested in German, with a sort of dull asperity. He got on to his feet.

At the sound of the familiar gutturals of the neighbouring Empire, the *agent* became differently angry. Kreisler stood there, muttering partly in German and partly in French; he was very tired. He was telling bitterly of his attempt to get into the police-station, and of his inhospitable reception. The *agent* understood several words of German—notably "ja" and "lager beer" and "essen." The consequence was that he always thought he understood more than was really said in that language. However much might be actually intended on any given occasion by the words of that profound and teeming tongue, it could never equal in scope, intensity, and meaning what he heard.

So he was convinced that Kreisler was threatening an invasion, and scoffed loudly in reply. He understood Kreisler to assert that the town in which they stood would soon belong to Germany, and that he would then sleep, not on a bench, but in the best bed their dirty little hole of a village could offer. He approached him threateningly. And eventually the functionary distinctly heard himself apostrophized as a "sneaking 'flic'," a "dirty peeler." At that he laid his hand on Kreisler's collar, and threw him in the direction of the police-station. He had miscalculated the distance. Kreisler, weak for want of food, fell at his feet; but, getting up, scuffled a short time. Then, it occurring to him that here was an unhoped for way of getting a dinner, and being lodged after all in the *bureau de police*, he suddenly became passive and complaisant.

Arrived at the police-station—with several revolts against the brutal handling to which he was subjected—he was met at the door by the same inhospitable man. Exasperated beyond measure at this unwelcome guest turning up again, the man sent his comrade into the office to report, while he held Kreisler. He held him as a restive horse is held, and jerked him several times against the wall, as if he had been showing signs of resistance.

Two men, one that he had formerly seen, came and looked at him. No effort was made to discover if he were really at fault or not. By this time they were quite convinced that he was a desperate character, and if not a spy, then anyway a murderer, although they were inclined to regard him as a criminal mystery. At all events they no longer could question his right to a night's lodging.

Kreisler was led to a cell, given some bread and water at his urgent request, and left alone.

On the following morning he was taken up before the *commissaire de police*. When Kreisler was brought in, this gentleman had just finished cross-examining for the fifteenth time the two German carpenters who were retained as spies. They were not let alone for an instant. They would be dragged out of their cells three times in the course of an afternoon, as often as a new and brilliant idea should strike one of the numerous staff of the police-station. They would be confronted with their foot-rules, and watched in breathless silence; or be keenly cross-questioned, confused and contradicted as to the exact hour at which they had lunched the day before their arrest. The *commissaire* was perspiring all over with the intensity of his last effort to detect something. Kreisler was led in, and prevented from finishing any sentence or of becoming in any way intelligible during a quarter of an hour by the furious interruptions of the enraged officer. At last he succeeded in asserting that he was quite unacquainted with the two carpenters; moreover, that all he needed was food; that he had decided to give himself up and await the decision of the Paris authorities as regards the deed. If they were not going to take any action, he would return to Paris—at least, as soon as he had received a certain letter; and he gave his address. The *commissaire* considered him with exhausted animosity and he was sent back to his cell.

He slept the greater part of the day, but the next he spent nervous and awake. In the afternoon a full confirmation of his story reached the authorities. It was likely that the following morning he would be sent to Paris. It meant, then, that he was going to be tried as a kind of murderer. He could not allege complete accident. The thought of Paris, the vociferous courts, the ennuis of a criminal case about this affair, so thoroughly ended and boringly out of date, disturbed him extremely. Then the Russian—he would have to see him again. Kreisler felt that he was being terribly worried once more. Sorrow for himself bowed him down. This journey to Paris resembled his crossing of the German frontier. He had felt that it was impossible to see his father. That represented an effort he would do anything to avoid. Resentment against his parent had vanished. It was this that made a meeting so difficult. It was a stranger, with an ill will that had survived his own, awaiting him. Noise, piercing noise, effort, awaited him revengefully. He knew exactly what his father would do and say. If there had been a single item that he could not forecast!—But there was not the least item. Paris was the same. The energy and obstinacy of the rest of the world, the world that would question him and drag him about, these frightened him as something mad. Bitzenko appealed most to this new-born timidity. Bitzenko was like some favourite dish a man has one day eaten too much of, and will never be able again to enjoy, or even support.

On the other hand, he became quite used to his cell. His mind was sick, and this room had a clinical severity. It had all the economical elements of a place in which a human operation might be performed. He became fond of it as patients get an appetite for the leanness of convalescent life. He lay on his bed. He turned over the shell of many empty and depressing hours he had lived. He took particular pleasure in these listless concave shapes. His "good times" were avoided. Days spent with his present stepmother, before his father knew her, gave him a particularly numbing and nondescript feeling.

He sat up, listening to the noises from the neighbouring rooms and corridors. It began to sound to him like one steady preparation for his removal. Steps bustled about getting this ready and getting that ready.

The police-station had cost him some trouble to enter. But they had been attracted to each other from the start. Something in the form of an illicit attachment now existed between them. Buildings are female. There is no such thing as a male building. This practical and pretentious small modern edifice was having its romance. Otto Kreisler was its romance.

It was now warning him. It echoed sharply and insistently the feet of its policemen.

After his evening meal he took up his bed in his arms and placed it on the opposite side of the cell, under the window. He sat there for some time as though resting after this effort. The muttering of two children on a doorstep in the street below came to him on the evening light with melodramatic stops and emptiness. It bore with it an image, like an old picture, bituminous and with a graceful, queer formality. It fixed itself before him like a mirage. He watched it muttering.

He began slowly drawing off his boots. He took out the laces, and tied them together for greater strength. Then he tore several strips off his shirt, and made a short cord of them. He went through these actions deliberately and deftly, as though it were a routine and daily happening. He measured the drop from the bar of the ventilator, calculating the necessary length of cord, like a boy preparing the accessories of some game. It was only a game, too. He realized what these proceedings meant, but shunned the idea that it was serious. Just as an unmoral man with a disinclination to write a necessary letter takes up the pen, resolving to begin it merely and writes more and more until it is, in fact, completed, so Kreisler proceeded with his task.

Standing on his bed, he attached the cord to the ventilator. He tested its strength by holding it some inches from the top, and then, his shoulders hunched, swaying his whole weight languidly on it for a moment.

Adjusting the noose, he smoothed his hair back after he had slipped it over his head. He made as though to kick the bed away, playfully, then stood still, staring in front of him. The last moment must be one of realization. He was not a coward. His caution was due to his mistrust of some streaks of him, the sex streak the powerfullest.

A sort of heavy confusion burst up as he withdrew the restraint. It reminded him of Soltyk's hands on this throat. The same throttling feeling returned. The blood bulged in his head. He felt dizzy; it was the Soltyk struggle over again. But, as with Soltyk, he did not resist. He gently worked the bed outwards from under him, giving it a last steady shove. He hung, gradually choking, the last thing he was conscious of, his tongue.

The discovery of his body caused a deep-felt indignation among the staff at the police-station. They remembered the persistence with which this unprincipled and equivocal vagrant (as which they still regarded him) had attempted to get into the building. And it was clear to their minds that his sole purpose had been to hang himself on their premises. He had mystified them from the first. Now their vague suspicions were bitterly confirmed, and had taken an unpardonable form. Each man felt that this corpse had personally insulted and made a fool of him. They thrust it savagely into the earth, with vexed and disgusted faces.

Herr Kreisler paid without comment what was claimed by the landlord in Paris for his son's room; and writing to the authorities at the frontier town about the burial, paid exactly the sum demanded by this town for disposing of the body.

CHAPTER VII

The sight of Bertha's twistings and turnings, her undignified rigmarole, had irritated Anastasya. This was why she had brutally announced, as though to cut short all that, that Kreisler's behaviour was due simply to the fact that he fancied himself in love with her, Anastasya. "He was not worrying about Fräulein Lunken. He was in love with *me*;" the statement amounted to that. There was no disdainful repudiation or self-reference in her statement; only a piece of information.

Bertha's intuitions and simplifications had not been without basis. This "hostile version" had contained a certain amount of hostile intention.

But Anastasya had another reason for this immodest explicitness. She personally liked Kreisler. The spectacle of Bertha excusing herself, and in the process putting Kreisler in a more absurd and unsatisfactory light, annoyed her extremely.

How could Tarr consort with Bertha, she questioned? Her aristocratic woman's sense did not appreciate the taste for a slut, a miss or a suburban queen. The apache, the coster girl, fisher-lass, all that had *character*, oh, yes. Her romanticism, in fact, was of the same order as Butcher's only better.

Two days after the duel she met Tarr in the street. They agreed to meet at Lejeune's for dinner.

The table at which she had first come across Kreisler was where they sat.

"You knew Soltyk, didn't you?" he asked her.

"Yes. It was a terrible affair. Poor Soltyk!"

She looked at Tarr doubtfully. A certain queer astonishment in her face struck Tarr. It was the only sign of movement beneath. She spoke with a businesslike calm about his death. There was no sign of feeling or search for feeling.

She refused to regard herself as the "woman in the affair." She knew people referred to her as that. Soltyk possessed a rather ridiculous importance, being dead; a cadaveric severity in the meaning of the image,

Soltyk, for her. The fact was bigger than the person. He was like a boy in his father's clothes.

Kreisler, on the other hand, she abominated. To have killed, *he* to have killed!—and to have killed some one she knew! It was a hostile act to bring death so near her. She knew it was hostile. She hoped he might never come back to Paris. She did not want to meet Kreisler.

But these feelings were not allowed to transpire. She recognized them as personal. She was so fastidious that she refrained from using them in discussing the affair when they would have given a suspect readiness and "sincerity" to her expression. She rather went to the other extreme.

"They say Soltyk was not killed in a duel," Tarr continued. "Kreisler is to be charged with murder, or at least manslaughter."

"Yes, I have heard that Kreisler shot him before he was ready or something—"

"I heard that he was shot when he was unarmed. There was no duel at all."

"Oh, that is not the version I have heard."

She did not seem revengeful about her friend.

"I was Kreisler's second for half an hour," Tarr said in a minute.

"How do you mean, for half an hour?" She was undemonstrative but polite.

"I happened to be there, and was asked to help him until somebody else could be found. I did not suspect him, I may say, of meaning to go to such lengths."

"What was the reason of it all—do you know?"

"According to Kreisler, they had done some smacking earlier in the day—"

"Yes. Herr Kreisler met Soltyk and myself. I think that Soltyk then was a little in the wrong."

"I dare say."

Tarr's sympathies were all with Kreisler. He had never been attracted by Poles, and as such rather than a Russian he thought of Soltyk. Deep square races he preferred. And Kreisler was a clumsy and degenerate atavism bringing a peculiarity into too elastic life.

Some of Tarr's absurd friendliness for Bertha flowed over on to her fellow-countryman.

Had Anastasya more of a hand in the duel than he would naturally believe? Her indifference to Soltyk's death, and her favouring Kreisler, almost pointed to something unusual. Kreisler's ways were still mysterious!

That was all they said about the duel. As they were finishing the meal, after turning her head towards the entrance door, Anastasya remarked, with mock concern:

"There is your fiancée. She seems rather upset."

Tarr looked towards the door. Bertha's white face was close up against one of the narrow panes, above the lace curtain. There were four and a half feet of window on either side of the door. There were so many objects and lights in the front well of the shop that her face would not be much noticed in the corner it had chosen.

Her eyes were round, vacant, and dark, the features very white and heavy, the mouth steadily open in painful lines. As he looked the face drew gradually away, and then disappeared into the melodramatic night. It was a large trapped fly on the pane. It withdrew with a glutinous, sweet slowness. The heavy white jowl seemed pulling itself out of some fluid trap where it had been caught like a weighty body.

Tarr knew how the pasty flesh would nestle against the furs, the shoulders swing, the legs move just as much as was necessary for progress, with no movement of the hips. Everything about her in the chilly night would give an impression of warmth and system. The sleek cloth fitting the square shoulders tightly, the underclothes carefully tight as well, the breath from her nostrils the slight steam from a contented machine.

He caught Anastasya's eye and smiled.

"Your fiancée is pretty," she said, pretending that was the answer to the smile.

"She's not my fiancée. But she's a pretty girl."

"Oh, I understood you were engaged—"

"No."

"It's no good," he thought. But he must spare Bertha in future such discomforting sights.

PART VII
SWAGGER SEX

CHAPTER I

Bertha was still being taken in carefully prepared doses of an hour a day: from half-past four to a quarter to six. Any one else would have found this much of Bertha insupportable under any conditions. But Tarr's eccentric soul had been used to such far greater doses that this was the minimum he considered necessary for a cure.

Tarr came to her every day with the regularity of an old gentleman at a German "Bad" taking his spring water at the regulation hour. But the cure was finishing. There were signs of a new robustness, (hateful to her) equivalent to a springy walk and a contented and sunny eye, that heralded departure. His daily visits, with their brutal regularity, did her as much harm as they did him good.

The news of Soltyk's death, then Kreisler's, affected the readily melodramatic side of her nature peculiarly. Death had made himself *de la partie*. Kreisler had left her alone for a few days. This is what had occupied him. The sensational news, without actually pushing her to imitation, made her own case, and her own tragic sensations, more real. They had received, in an indirect and cousin-thrice-removed sort of way, the authority of Death. Death—real living Death—was somewhere on the scene. His presence was announced, was felt. He had struck down somebody among them.

In the meantime this disposed of Kreisler for ever. Tarr as well appeared to feel that they were left in *tête-à-tête*. A sort of chaperon had been lost in Kreisler. His official post as protector or passive "obstacle" had been a definite status. If he stayed on, it would have to be as something else. On the day on which the news of Kreisler's end arrived, he talked of leaving for England. Her more drawn face, longer silences, sharp glances, once more embarrassed him.

He did not go to England at once. In the week or two succeeding his meeting with Anastasya in the restaurant he saw her frequently. So a chaperon was found. Bertha was officially presented to her successor. When she learnt that Anastasya had been chosen, her energy reformed. She braced herself for a substantial struggle.

The apparition at the window of the restaurant was her first revived activity.

CHAPTER II

On August the tenth Tarr had an appointment with Anastasya at his studio in Montmartre. They had arranged to dine in Montmartre. It was their seventh meeting. He had just done his daily cure. He hurried back and found her lounging against the door, reading the newspaper.

"Ah, there you are! You're late, Mr. Tarr."

"Am I? I'm sorry. Have you been waiting long?"

"Not very. Fräulein Lunken—"

"She—I couldn't get away."

"No, it *is* difficult to get away, apparently."

He let her in. He was annoyed at the backwardness of his senses. His mind stepped in, determined to do their business for them. He put his arm round her waist, and planting his lips fully on hers, began kissing her. He slipped his hands sideways beneath her coat, and pressed an athletic, sinuous hulk against him. The various bulging and retreating contact of her body brought monotonous German reminders.

It was the first time he had kissed her. She showed no bashfulness or disinclination, but no return. Was she in the unfortunate position of an unawakened mass; and had she so rationalized her intimate possessions that there was no precocious fancy left until mature animal ardour was set up? He felt as though he were embracing a tiger, who was not unsympathetic, but rather surprised. Perhaps he had been too sudden. He ran his hand upwards along her body. All was statuesquely genuine. She took his hand away.

"We haven't come to that yet," she said.

"Haven't we!"

"I didn't think we had."

Smiling at each other, they separated.

"Let me take your coat off. You'll be hot in here."

Her coat was all in florid redundancies of heavy cloth, like a Tintoretto dress. Underneath she was wearing a very plain dark blouse and skirt, like a working girl, which exaggerated the breadth and straightness of her shoulders. Not to sentimentalize it, she had open-work stockings on underneath, such as the genuine girl would have worn on her night out, at one and eleven-three the pair.

"You look very well," Tarr said.

"I put these on for you."

Tarr had, while he was kissing her, found his senses again. They had flared up in such a way that the reason had been offended, and resisted. Hence some little conflict. *They* were not going to have the credit—!

He became shy. He was ashamed of his sudden interest, which had been so long in coming, and instinctively hid it. He was committed to the rôle of a reasonable man.

"I am very flattered at your thinking of me in that way. I am afraid I do not deserve—"

"I want you to *deserve*, though. You are absurd about women. You are like a schoolboy!"

"Oh, you've noticed that?"

"It doesn't require much—"

She lay staring at him in a serious way. Squashed up as she was lying, a very respectable bulk of hip filled the space between the two arms of the chair, not enough to completely satisfy a Dago, but too' much to please a dandy of the west. He compared this opulence with Bertha's and admitted that it outdid his fiancée's. He did this childish measuring in the belief that he was not observed.

"You are extremely recalcitrant to intelligence, aren't you?" she said.

"In women, you mean?"

"Yes."

"I suppose I am. My tastes are simple."

"I don't know anything about your tastes, of course. I'm guessing."

"You can take it that you are right."

He began to feel extremely attracted to this intelligent head. He had been living for the last week or so in the steady conviction that he should never get the right sensual angle with this girl. It was a queer feeling, after all, to see his sensuality speaking sense. He would marry her.

"Well," she said, with pleasant American accent in speaking English, "I feel you see some disability in sensible women that does not exist. It doesn't irritate you too much to hear a woman talking about it?"

"Of course not—*you*. You are so handsome. I shouldn't like it if you were less so. Such good looks" (he rolled his eyes appreciatively) "get us out of arty coldness. You are all right. The worst of looks like yours is that sense has about the same effect as nonsense. Sense is a delightful anomaly just as rot would be! You don't require words or philosophy. But they give one a pleasant tickling all the same."

"I am glad you are learning. However, don't praise me like that. It makes me a little shy. I know how you feel about women. You feel that good sense gets in the way."

"It interferes with the senses, you mean? I don't think I feel that altogether—"

"You feel I'm not a woman, don't you? Not properly a woman, like your Bertha. There's no mistake about her!"

"One requires something unconscious, perhaps. I've never met any woman who interested me but was ten times more stupid than I. I want *to be alone* in those things. I like it to be subterranean as well."

"Well, I have a cave! I've got all that, too. I *promise* you."

Her *promise* was slow and lisping. Tarr once more had to deal with himself.

"I—am—*a woman*; not a man. That is the fact." ("Fact" was long and American.) "You don't realize that—I assure you I am!" She looked at him with a soft, steady smile, that drew his gaze and will into her, rather than imposed itself on him.

"I know." He felt that there was not much to say.

"No, you know far less than you think. See here; I set out thinking of you in this way—'Nothing but a female booby will please that man!' I wanted to please you, but I couldn't do it on those lines. I'm going to make an effort along my own lines. You are like a youngster who hasn't got used to the taste of liquor; you don't like it. You haven't grown up yet. I want to make you drunk and see what happens!"

She had her legs crossed. Extremely white flesh showed above the black Lisle silk, amidst linen as expensive as the outer cloth was plain. This clever alternating of the humble and gorgeous! Would the body be plain? The provocation was merely a further argument. It said, "Young man, what is there you find in your Bertha that cannot be provided along with superior sense?" His Mohammedan eye did not refuse the conventional bait. His butcher's sensibility pressed his fancy into professional details. What with her words and her acts he was in a state of strong confusion.

She jumped up and put on her coat, like a ponderous curtain showering down to her heels. Peep-shows were ended!

"Come, let's have some dinner. I'm hungry. We can discuss this problem better after a beefsteak!" A Porterhouse would have fitted, Tarr thought.

He followed obediently and silently. He was glad that Anastasya had taken things into her hands. The positions that these fundamental matters got him into! Should he allow himself to be overhauled and reformed by this abnormal beauty? He was not altogether enjoying himself. He felt a ridiculous amateur. He was a butcher in his spare moments. This immensely intellectual ox, covered with prizes and pedigrees, overwhelmed him. You required not a butcher, but an artist, for that! He was not an artist in anything but oil-paint. Oil-paint and meat were singularly alike. They had reciprocal potentialities. But he was afraid of being definitely distracted.

The earlier coldness all appeared cunning; his own former coldness was the cunning of destiny.

He felt immensely pleased with himself as he walked down the Boulevard Clichy with this perfect article rolling and sweeping beside him. No bourgeoise this time! He could be proud of this anywhere! Absolute perfection! Highest quality obtainable. "The face that launched a thousand ships." A thousand ships crowded in her gait. There was nothing highfalutin about her, Burne-Jonesque, Grail-lady, or Irish-romantic. Perfect meat, perfect sense, accent of Minnesota, music of the Steppes! And all that was included under the one inadequate but pleasantly familiar heading, *German*. He became more and more impressed with what was *German* about her.

He took her to a large, expensive, and quiet restaurant. They began with oysters. He had never eaten oysters before. Prudence had prevented him. She laughed very much at this.

"You are a savage, Tarr!" The use of his surname was a tremendous caress. "You are afraid of typhoid, and your palate is as conservative as an ox's. Give me a kiss!"

She put her lips out; he kissed them with solemnity and concentration, adjusting his glasses afterwards.

They discussed eating for some time. He discovered he knew nothing about it.

"Why, man, you never think!"

Tarr considered. "No, I'm not very observant in many things. But I have a defence. All that part of me is rudimentary. But that is as it should be."

"How—as it should be?"

"I don't disperse myself. I specialize on necessities."

"Don't you call food—?"

"Not in the way you've been considering it. Listen. Life is art's rival and vice versa."

"I don't see the opposition."

"No, because you mix them up. You are the archenemy of any picture."

"I? Nonsense! But art comes out of life, in any case. What is art?"

"My dear girl—life with all the nonsense taken out of it. Will that do?"

"Yes. But what is art—especially?" She insisted with her hands on a plastic answer. "Are we in life, now? *What is art?*"

"*Life* is anything that could live and die. *Art* is peculiar; it is anything that lives and that yet you cannot imagine as dying."

"Why cannot art die? If you smash up a statue, it is as dead as a dead man."

"No, it is not. That is the difference. It is the God, or soul, we say, of the man. It always has existed, if it is a true statue."

"But cannot you say of some life that it could not die?"

"No, because in that case it is the *real* coming through. *Death* is the one attribute that is peculiar to *life*. It is the something that it is impossible to imagine in connexion with art. Reality is entirely founded on this fact, that of *Death*. All *action* revolves round that, and has it for motif. The purest thought is totally ignorant of death. Death means the perpetual extinction of impertinent sparks. But it is the key of life."

"But what is *art*? You are talking about it as though I knew what it was!"

"What is life, do you know? Well, I know what art is in the same way."

"Yes, but I ask you as a favour to define it for me. A picture is art, a living person is life. We sitting here are *life*; if we were talking on a stage we should be *art*. How would you define art?"

"Well, let's take your example. But a picture, and also the actors on a stage, are pure life. Art is merely what the picture and the stage-scene represent, and what we now, and any living person as such, only, do *not*. That is why you can say that the true statue can be smashed, and yet not die."

"Still, what *is* it? What *is* art?"

"It is ourselves disentangled from death and accident."

"How do you know?"

"I feel that is so, because I notice that that is the essential point to grasp. *Death* is the thing that differentiates art and life. Art is identical with the idea of permanence. It is a continuity and not an individual spasm. Life is the idea of the person."

Both their faces lost some of their colour, hers her white, his his yellow. They flung themselves upon each other like waves. The fuller stream came from him.

"You say that the actors on the stage are pure life, yet they represent something that *we* do not. But 'all the world's a stage,' isn't it? So how do we not also stand for that something?"

"Yes, life does generally stand for that something too; but it only emerges and is visible in art."

"*Still* I don't know what art is!"

"You ought to by this time. However, we can go further. Consider the content of what we call art. A statue is art, as you said; you are life. There is bad art and bad life. We will only consider the good. A statue, then, is a dead thing; a lump of wood or stone. Its hues and masses are its soul. Anything living, quick and changing, is bad art, always; naked men and women are the worst art of all, because there are fewer semi-dead things about them. The shell of the tortoise, the plumage of a bird, makes these animals approach nearer to art. Soft, quivering and quick flesh is as far from art as an object can be."

"Art is merely *the dead*, then?"

"No, but *deadness* is the first condition of art. A hippopotamus's armoured hide, a turtle's shell, feathers or machinery on the one hand; *that* opposed to naked pulsing and moving of the soft inside of life, along with infinite elasticity and consciousness of movement, on the other.

"Deadness, then," Tarr went on, "in the limited sense in which we use that word is the first condition of art. The second is absence of *soul,* in the sentimental human sense. The lines and masses of the statue are its soul. No restless, quick, flame-like ego is imagined for the *inside* of it. It has no inside. This is another condition of art; *to have no inside,* nothing you cannot *see.* Instead, then, of being something impelled like a machine by a little egoistic fire inside, it lives soullessly and deadly by its frontal lines and masses."

Tarr was developing, from her point of view, too much shop. She encouraged him, however, immediately.

"Why should human beings be chiefly represented in art?"

"Because what we call art depends on human beings for its advertisement. As men's ideas about themselves change, art should change too."

They had waded through a good deal of food while this conversation had been proceeding. She now stretched herself, clasping her hands in her lap. She smiled at Tarr as though to invite him to smile too, at her beautiful, heavy, hysterical anatomy. She had been driving hard inscrutable Art deeper and deeper into herself. She now drew it out and showed it to Tarr.

"Art is paleozoic matter, dolomite, oil-paint, and mathematics; also something else. Having established that, we will stick a little flag up and come back another day. I want to hear now about *life.* But do you believe in anything?"

Tarr was staring, suspended, with a smile cut in half, therefore defunct, at the wall. He turned his head slowly, with his mutilated smile, his glasses slanting in an agreeably vulpine way.

"Believe in anything? I only believe in one thing, pleasure of taste. In that way you get back though, with me, to mathematics and paleozoic times, and the coloured powders of the earth."

Anastasya ordered a *gâteau reine de Samothrace.*

"Reine de Samothrace! Reine de Samothrace!" Tarr muttered. "Donnez-moi une omelette au rhum."

Tarr looked at her for some time in a steady, depressed way. What a treat for his eyes not to be jibing! She held all the imagery of a perfect world. There was no pathos anywhere in her form. Kindness—*bestial kindness*—would be an out-of-work in this neighbourhood. The upper part of her head was massive and intelligent. The middle of her body was massive and exciting. There was no animalism out of place in the shape of a weight of jaw. The weight was in the head and hips. But was not this a complete thing by itself? How did he stand as regards it? He had always been sceptical about perfection. Did she and he need each other? His steadfast ideas of the flower surrounded by dung were challenged. She might be a monotonous abstraction, and, if accepted, impoverish his life. She was the summit, and the summit was narrow. Or in any case was not ugliness and foolishness the richest soil? Irritants were useful though not beautiful. He reached back doubtfully towards his bourgeoise. But he was revolted as he touched that mess, with this clean and solid object beneath his eyes. He was not convinced, though, that he was on the right road. He preferred a cabin to a palace, and thought that a villa was better for him than either, but did not want to order his life so rigidly as that.

"What did you make of Kreisler's proceedings?" she asked him.

"In what way do you mean?"

"Well, first—do you think he and Bertha—got on very well?"

"Do you mean was Bertha his mistress? I should think not. But I'm not sure. That isn't very interesting, is it?"

"Kreisler is interesting, not Bertha, of course."

"You're very hard on Bertha."

She put her tongue out at him and wrinkled up her nose.

A queen, standing on her throne, was obtruding her "unruly member."

"What were Kreisler's relations with you, by the way?" he asked blankly.

Her extreme freedom with himself suggested possible explanations of her manner in discussing Soltyk's death at the time.

"My relations with Kreisler consisted in a half-hour's conversation with him in a restaurant, and that was all. I spoke to him several times after that, but only for a few minutes. He was very excited the last time we met. I have a theory that his duel and general behaviour was due to unrequited passion for me. Your Bertha, on the other hand, has a theory that it was due to unrequited passion for *her*. I wondered if you had any information that might support her case or mine."

"No. I know nothing about it. I hold, myself, a quite different theory."

"What is that? That he was in love with *you*?"

"My theory has not the charming simplicity of your theory or Bertha's. I don't believe that he was in love with anybody. I believe, though, that it was a sex-tumult of sorts—"

"What is that?"

"You want to hear my theory? This is it. I believe that all the fuss he made was an attempt to get out of Art back into life again, like a fish flopping about who had got into the wrong tank. It would be more exact to say, *back into sex*. He was trying to get back into sex again out of a little puddle of Art where he felt he was gradually expiring. What I mean is this. He was an art student without any talent, and was leading a dull, slovenly existence like thousands of others in the same case. He was very hard up. Things were grim that way too. The sex-instinct of the average man, then, had become perverted into a silly false channel. Or it might be better to say that his elementary art-instinct had been rooted out of sex and one or two other things, where it was both useful and ornamental, and naturally flourished, and had been exalted into a department by itself, where it bungled and wrecked everything. It is a measure the need of which hits the eye in these days to keep the art-instinct of the run of men in its place. These art-spirits should be kept firmly embedded in *sex*, in *fighting*, and in *affairs*. The nearest the general run of men can get to Art is *Action*. Real, bustling, bloody action is what they want! Sex is *their* form of art: the battle of existence in enterprise, Commerce, is *their* picture. The moment they *think* or *dream* you get an immense weight of cheap stagnating passion that becomes a menace to the health of the world. A "cultured" nation is as great a menace as a "free" one. The answer to the men who object to this as high-handed is plain enough. You must answer: No man's claim is *individual;* the claim of an exceptional being is that of an important type or original—is an inclusive claim. The eccentric Many do not matter. They are the individuals. And anyway Goddam economy in any shape or form! Long live Waste! Curse the principle of Humanity! Mute inglorious Miltons are not mute for God-in-Heaven. They have the Silence. Bless Waste, Heaven bless Waste! Hoch Waste!"

"I'll drink to that!" said Anastasya, raising her glass. "Here's to Waste! Hoch!" Tarr drank this toast with gusto.

"Here's to Waste!" he said loudly. "Waste yourselves, pour yourselves out, let there be no High-Men except such as happen! Economy is sedition. Drink your blood if you have no wine! But *waste*; fling out into the streets; never count your yarn. Accept fools, compromise yourselves with the poor in spirit, fling the rich ones behind you; live like the lions in the forests with fleas on your back. Down with the *Efficient* Chimpanzee!"

Anastasya's eyes were bloodshot with the gulp she had taken to honour Waste. Tarr patted her on the back.

"There are no lions in the forests!" she hiccuped, patting her chest. "You're pulling my leg."

They got to their coffee more or less decorously. But Tarr had grown extremely loquacious and expansive in every way. He began slapping her thighs to emphasise his points, as Diderot was in the habit of doing with the Princesse de Clèves. After that he began kissing her, when he had made a particularly successful remark, to celebrate it. Their second bottle of wine had put many things to flight. He lay back in his chair in prolonged bursts of laughter. She, in German fashion, clapped her hand over his mouth, and he seized it with his teeth and made pale shell-shapes in its brown fat.

In a café opposite the restaurant, where they next went, they had further drinks.

They caressed each other's hands now as a matter of course! Indifferent to the supercilious and bitter natives, they became lost in lengthy kisses, their arms round each other's necks. In a little cave of intoxicated affection, a conversation took place.

"Have you had dealings with many—?"

"What's that you say, dear?" she asked with eager, sleepy seriousness. The "dear" reminded him of accostings in the streets.

"Have you been the mistress of many men?"

"No, of course not. Only one. He was a Russian."

"What's that got to do with it?"

"What did you say?"

"How much did he bag?"

"Bag?"

"What did the Russian represent?"

"Nothing at all, Tarr. That's why I took him. I wanted the experience. But now I want you! You are my first *person*!" Distant reminiscences of Bertha, grateful to him at present.

Kisses succeeded.

"I don't want *you*!" Tarr said.

"Oh! Tell me what you want?"

"I want a woman!"

"But I am a woman, stupid!"

"I want a *slave*."

She whispered in his ear, hanging on his neck.

"No! You may be a woman, but you're not a slave."

"Don't be so quarrelsome. Forget those silly words of yours—slave, woman. It's all right when you're talking about art, but you're hugging a woman at present. This is something that can die! Ha ha! We're in life, my Tarr. *We represent absolutely nothing*—thank God!"

"I realize I'm in life, darling. But I don't like being reminded of it in that way. It makes me feel as though I were in a *mauvais lieu*."

"Give me a kiss, you *efficient chimpanzee!*"

Tarr scowled at her, but did not alter the half-embrace in which they sat.

"You won't give me a kiss? Silly old *in*efficient chimpanzee!"

She sat back in her chair, and head down looked through her eyelashes at him with demure menace.

"Garçon! garçon!" she called.

"Mademoiselle?" the *garçon* said, approaching slowly, with dignified scepticism.

"This gentleman, *garçon,* wants to be a lion with fleas on his back—at least so he says! At the same time he wants a slave. I don't know if he expects the slave to catch his fleas or not. I haven't asked him. But he's a funny-looking bird, isn't he?"

The *garçon* withdrew with hauteur.

"What's the meaning of your latest tack, you little German art-tart?"

"What am I?"

"I called you German æsthetic pastry. I think that describes you."

"Oh, *tart,* is it?"

"Anything you like. Very well made, puffed out. With *one* solitary Russian, *bien entendu*!"

"And what, good God, shall we call the cow-faced specimen you spend the greater part of your days with—"

"She, too, is German pastry, more homely than you though—"

"Homely's the word!"

"But not quite so fly-blown. Less variegated creams and German pretentiousness—"

"I see! And takes you more seriously than other people would be likely to! That's what all your 'quatch' about 'woman' and 'slave' means. You know that!"

She had recovered from the effects of the drinks completely and was sitting up and talking briskly, looking at him with the same serious, rather flattened face she had had during their argument on Art and Death.

"I know you are a famous whore, who becomes rather acid in your cups!—when you showed me your legs this evening, I suppose I was meant—"

"Assez! Assez!!" She struck the table with her fist.

"Let's get to business." He put his hat on and leant towards her. "It's getting late. Twenty-five francs, I'm afraid, is all I can manage."

"Twenty-five francs for what? With you—it would be robbery! Twenty-five francs to be your audience while you drivel about art? Keep your money and buy Bertha an—*efficient chimpanzee*! She will need it if she marries you!"

Her mouth drawn tight and her hands in her coat pockets, she walked out of the door of the café.

Tarr ordered another drink.

"It's like a moral tale told on behalf of Bertha," he thought. That was the temper of Paradise! The morality, in pointing to Bertha, did her no good, but caused her to receive the *trop-plein* of his discontent.

He sat in a grim sulk at the thought of the good time he had lost. This scene had succeeded in touching the necessary spring. His vanity helping, for half an hour he plotted his revenge and satisfaction together. Anastasya had violently flung off the illusion of indifference in which she had hitherto appeared to him. The drinks of the evening were a culture in which his disappointment grew luxuriantly, but with a certain buffoonish lightness. He went back to his studio in half an hour's time with smug, thick, secretive pleasure settling down on his body's ungainly complaints.

CHAPTER III

He went slowly up the stairs feeling for his key. He arrived at the door without having found it. The door was ajar. At first this seemed natural to him, and he continued the search for the key. Then he suddenly dropped that occupation, pushed the door open and went into his studio. The moonlight came heavily through the windows. In a part of the room where it did not strike he became aware of an apparition of solid white. It was solid white flowed round by Naples yellow. It crossed into the moonlight and faced him, its hands placed like a modest statue's. The hair reached below the waist, and flowed to the right from the head. This tall nudity began laughing with a harsh sound like stone laughing.

"Close the door!" it shouted, "there's a draught. You took a long time to consider my words. I've been waiting. Forgive me, Tarr. My words were acidulated whores, but my heart"—she put her hand on the skin roughly above that organ—"my heart was completely full of sugar! The acidulated *demi-mondaine* was a trick. It occupied your mind. You didn't notice me take your key!"

His vanity was soothed. The key in her possession, which could only have been taken in the café, seemed to justify the harsh dialogue.

She stood before him now with her arms up, hands joined behind her head. This impulse to take her clothes off had the cultural hygienic touch so familiar to him. The Naples yellow of the hair was the same colour as Bertha's, only it was coarser and thicker, Bertha's being fine. Anastasya's dark face, therefore, had the appearance almost of a mask.

"Will you engage me as your model? Je fais de la réclame pour les Grecs."

"You are very Ionian—hardly Greek. But I don't require a model. I never use nude models."

"Well, I must dress again, I suppose." She turned towards a chair where her clothes were piled. But Tarr had learnt the laws of cultural emancipation.

He shouted, "I accept, I accept!" He lifted her up in his arms, kissing her in the mass, as it were, and carried her through the door at the back of the studio leading to his bedroom.

"Tarr, be my love. I don't want to give you up."

This was said next morning, the sunlight having taken the place of the moonlight, but striking on the opposite side of the house.

"You won't hear marriage talked about by me. I want to rescue you from your Bertha habits. Allow yourself to be rescued! We're very well together, aren't we? I'm not doing Bertha a bad turn, either, really. I admit my motive is quite selfish. What do you say?"

"I am your slave!"

Anastasya rolled up against him with the movement of a seal.

"Thank you, Tarr. That's better than *having a slave,* isn't it?"

"Yes, I think everything is in order."

"Then you're my efficient chimpanzee?"

"No, I'm the new animal; we haven't found a name for it yet. It will succeed the Superman. Back to the Earth!"

"Jean-Jacques Rousseau. Kiss me!"

CHAPTER IV

Tarr crawled towards Bertha that day on the back of a Place St. Michel bus. He did not like his job.

The secret of his visits to Bertha and interminable liaison was that he really never had meant to leave her at all, he reflected. He had not meant to leave her altogether. He was just playing. Or rather, a long debt of disgraceful behaviour was accumulating, that he knew would have to be met. It was deliberately increased by him, because he knew he would not repudiate it. But it would have been absurd not to try to escape.

To-day he must break the fact to Bertha that he could no longer regard himself as responsible. He was faced with the necessity, for the first time, of seriously bargaining. The debt was not to be repudiated, but he must tell her that he only had himself to pay with, and that he had been seized by somebody else.

He passed through her iron gateway with a final stealth, although making his boots sound loudly on the gravel. It was like entering a vault, the trees looked like weeds; the meaning or taste of everything, of course, had died. The concierge looked like a new one.

He had bought a flower for his buttonhole. He kept smelling it as he approached the house.

During the last week or so he had got into the habit of writing his letters at Bertha's, to fill up the time. Occasionally he would do a drawing of her (a thing he had never done formerly) to vary the monotony. This time there would be no letter-writing. This visit would be more like the old ones.

"Come in, Sorbert," she said, on opening the door. It was emphasizing the fact of the formality of the terms on which they at present met. Any prerogative of past and more familiar times was proudly rejected.

There was the same depressed atmosphere as the day before, and the days preceding that. She appeared stale, somehow deteriorated and shabby, her worth decreased, and extremely pitiable. Her "reserve" (a natural result of the new equivocal circumstances) removed her to a distance, as it seemed; it also shut her up in herself, in an unhealthy, dreary, and faded atmosphere.

She was shut up with a mass of reserves and secrets, new and old. She seemed sitting on them in rather dismal hen-like fashion, waiting to be asked to come out of herself and reveal something. It was a corpse among other things that she was sitting on, as Kreisler was one of her secrets. Mournfully reproachful, she kept guard over her secrets, a store of bric-à-brac that had gone out of fashion and were getting musty in a neglected shop.

Their meetings sometimes were made painful by activity on Bertha's part. An attempt at penetration to an intimacy once possessed can be more indecent than the same action on the part of a stranger.

This time he was greeted with long mournful glances. He felt she had thought of what she should say. This interview meant a great deal to her. His friendship meant more to her now than ever. The abject little room seemed to be thrust forward to awaken his memories and ask for pity. An intense atmosphere of Teutonic suicide permeated everything. He could not move an eyelid or a muscle without wounding or slighting something. It was like being in a dark kitchen at night, where you know at every step you will put your foot on a beetle. It had a still closer analogy to this in the disgust he felt for these too naked and familiar things he was treading on. He scowled at Beethoven, who scowled back at him like a reflection in a mirror. It was the fate of both of them to haunt this room. The *Mona Lisa* was there, and the Breton sabots and jars. She might have a change of scenery sometimes! He felt unreasonably that she must have left things in the same place to reproduce a former mood in him. His photograph was prominent on her writing-table; she seemed to say (with a sort of sickly idiocy), "You see, *he* is faithful to me!"

She preceded him to her sitting-room. As he looked at her back he thought of her as taking a set number of paces, then turning round abruptly, confronting him. From a typical and similar enervation of the will to that which was at the bottom of his troubles, he could hardly stop himself from putting his arm round her waist while they stood for a moment close to each other. He did not wish to do this as a response to any resuscitating desire. It was only because it was the one thing he must not do. To throw himself into the abyss of perplexity he had just escaped from tempted him. The dykes and simulations of conduct were perpetually threatened by his neurasthenia in this way. He kept his hands in his pockets, however.

When they had reached the room, she turned round, as he had half imagined, and caught hold of his hands.

"Sorbert, Sorbert!"

The words were said separately, each emphatic in significance. The second was a repetition only of the first. She seemed calling him by his name to conjure back his self again. Her face was a strained and anxious mask.

"What is it, Bertha?"

"I don't know!"

She dropped his hands, drooped her head to the right and turned away.

She sat down; he sat down opposite her.

"Anything new?" he asked.

"Anything new? Yes!" She gazed at him with an insistent meaning.

He concluded this was just over-emphasis, with nothing behind it; or, rather, everything.

"Well, I have something new as well!"

"Have you, Sorbert?"

"First of all, how have my visits struck you lately? What explanation have you found for them?"

"Oh, none. Why find an explanation? Why do you ask?"

"I thought I would explain."

"Well?"

"My explanation to myself was that I did not want to leave you brusquely, and I thought a blurred interlude of this sort would do no harm to either of us. Our loves could die in each other's arms."

She stared with incredulous fixity at the floor, her spirit seeming to be arched like a swan and to be gazing down hypnotically.

"The real reason was simply that, being very fond of you, I could not make up my mind to give you up. I claim that my visits were not frivolous."

"Well?"

"I would have married you, if you had considered that advisable."

"Yes? And—?"

"I find it very difficult to say the rest."

"What is difficult?"

"Well, I still like you very much. Yesterday I met a woman. I love her too. I can't help that. What must I do?"

Bertha turned a slightly stormier white.

"Who is she?"

"You know her. She is Anastasya Vasek."

The news struck through something else, and, inside, her ego shrank to an almost wizened being. It seemed glad of the protection the cocoon, the something, afforded her.

"You did not—find out what my news was."

"I didn't. Have you anything—?"

"Yes. I am enceinte."

He thought about this in a clumsy, incredulous way. It *was* a Roland for his Oliver! She was going to have a baby! With what regularity he was countered! This event rose up in opposition to the night he had just spent, his new promises and hopes of swagger sex in the future. He was beaten.

"Whose child is it?"

"Kreisler's."

"There you are!" he thought.

He got up and stepped over to her with a bright relieved look in his face.

"Poor little girl! That's a bad business. But don't worry about it. We can get married and it can always pass as mine—if we do it quickly enough."

She looked up at him obliquely and sharply, with suspicion grown a habit. When she saw the pleasant, assured expression, she saw that at last things had turned. Sorbert was denying reality! He was ending with miracles, against himself. Her instinct had always told her that generosity would not be wasted!

She did not tell him of the actual circumstances under which the child had come. That would have weakened her happiness and her case.

CHAPTER V

When he got outside Bertha's house, Bertha waving to him from the window with tears in her eyes, he came in for the counter-attack.

One after the other the protesting masses of good sense rolled up.

He picked his way out of the avenue with a reasoning gesticulation of the body; a chicken-like motion of sensible fastidious defence in front of buffonic violence. At the gate he exploded in harsh laughter, looking bravely and railingly out into the world through his glasses. Then he walked slowly away in his short jacket, his buttocks moving methodically just beneath its rim.

"Ha ha! Ha ha! Kreisleriana!" he shouted without his voice.

The indignant plebs of his glorious organism rioted around his mind.

"Ha ha! Ha ha! *Sacré farceur*, where are you leading us?" They were vociferous. "You have kept us fooling in this neighbourhood so long, and now you are pledging us to your idiotic fancy for ever. Ha ha! Ha ha!"

"Be reasonable! What are you doing, master of our destiny? We shall all be lost!"

A faction clamoured, "Anastasya!" Certain sense-sections attacked him in vulnerable spots with Anastasya's voluptuous banner unfurled and fragrant.

He buffeted his way along, as though spray were dashing in his face, watchful behind his glasses. He met his thoughts with a contemptuous stiff veteran smile. This capricious and dangerous master had an offensive stylistic coolness, similar to Wellington breakfasting at Salamanca while Marmont hurried exultingly into traps; although he resembled his great countryman in no other way.

Those thoughts that bellowed, "Anastasya!" however, worried him. He answered them.

"Anastasya! Anastasya!! I know all about that! What do you take me for? You will still have your Anastasya. I am not selling myself or you. A man such as I does not dispose of himself in a case like this. I am going to marry Bertha Lunken. Well? Shall I be any the less my own master for that reason? If I want to sleep with Anastasya, I shall do so. Why marry Bertha Lunken, and shoulder all that semi-contagious muck? Because it is only the points or movements in life that matter, and one of those points indicates that course, namely, to keep faith with another person: and secretly to show my contempt for the world by choosing the *premier venu* to be my body-servant and body-companion; my contempt for my body too."

He sought to overcome his reasons by appeals to their corporate vanity.

He had experienced rather a wrench as regards Anastasya. The swanky sex with which he had ornamented his future could not be dismissed so easily. He was astonished that it could be dismissed at all, and asked himself the reason. He sacrificed Anastasya with a comparatively light heart. It was chiefly his vanity that gave trouble.

He came back to his earlier conclusions. Such successful people as Anastasya and himself were by themselves. It was as impossible to combine or *wed* them as to compound the genius of two great artists. If you mixed together into one whole Gainsborough and Goya you would get *nothing*, for they would be mutually destructive. Beyond a certain point of perfection individual instinct was its own law. A subtle lyrical wail would gain nothing from living with a rough and powerful talent, or vice versa. Success is always personal. Co-operation, group-genius was, he was convinced, a slavish pretence and absurdity. Only when the group was so big that it became a person again, as with a nation, did you get mob-talent or popular art. This big, diffuse, vehement giant was the next best thing to the great artist; Patchin Tcherana coming just below.

He saw this quite clearly. He and Anastasya were a superfluity, and destructive conflict. It was like a mother being given a child to bear the same size already as herself. Anastasya was in every way too big; she was too big physically. But did not sex change the whole question, when it was a *woman*? He did not agree to this. Woman and the sexual sphere seemed to him to be an average from which *everything* came: from it everything rose, or attempted to rise. There was no mysterious opposition extending up into Heaven, and dividing Heavenly Beings into Gods and Goddesses. There was only one God, and he was a man. A woman was a lower form of life. Everything was female to begin with. A jellyish diffuseness spread itself and gaped on the beds and in the *bas-fonds* of everything. Above a certain level of life sex disappeared, just as in highly organized sensualism sex vanishes. And, on the other hand, *everything* beneath that line was female. Bard, Simpson, Mackenzie, Townsend, Annandale—he enumerated acquaintances evidently below the absolute line, and who displayed a lack of energy, permanently mesmeric state, and almost purely emotional reactions. He knew that everything on the superior side of that line was not purged of jellyish attributes; also that Anastasya's flaccid and fundamental charms were formidable, although the line had been crossed by her. One thing was impressive, however. The loss of Anastasya did not worry him, except magnified through the legal acquisition of Bertha. What did he *want*? Well, he did not want Anastasya *as much as he should*. He was incorrigible, he concluded. He regarded the Anastasya evening as a sort of personal defeat even. The call of duty was nevertheless very strong. He *ought* to love Anastasya; and his present intentions as regards his despicable fiancée were a disgraceful betrayal, etc. etc. The mutterings of reason continued.

That evening he met Anastasya. The moment he saw her he realized the abysses of indignity and poorness he was flinging himself into with Bertha Lunken. A sudden humbleness entered him and put him out of conceit with his judgment, formed away from bright objects like Anastasya. The selfishness that caused his sentimentality when alone with Bertha was dissipated or not used in presence of more or less successful objects and people. None of his ego was required by his new woman. She possessed plenty of her own. This, he realized later, was the cause of his lack of attachment. He needed an empty vessel to flood with his vitality, and not an equal and foreign vitality to exist side by side with coldly. He had taken into sex the *procédés* and selfish arrangements of life in general. He had humanized sex too much. He frequently admitted this, but with his defence lost sight of the flagrancy of the permanent fact.

He felt in Anastasya for the first time now an element of protection and safety. She was a touchwood and harbour from his perplexed interior life. She had a sort of ovation from him. All his obstinacy in favour of his fiancée had vanished. With Anastasya's appearance an entirely different world was revealed that demanded completely new arguments.

They went to the same restaurant as the night before. He talked quietly, until they had drunk too much, and Bertha was not mentioned.

"And what of Bertha?" she asked finally.

"Never mind about Bertha."

"Is she extinct?"

"No. She threatens an entirely new sort of eruption."

"Oh. In what way new—?"

"It doesn't matter. It won't come our way."

"Are you going there to-morrow?"

"I suppose I must. But I shall not make many more visits of—"

"What's that?"

"I shall give up going, I say." He shifted restlessly in his chair.

After breakfast next morning they parted, Tarr going back to work. Butcher, whom he had not seen for some days, came in. He agreed to go down into town and have lunch with him. Tarr put on a clean shirt. Talking to Butcher while he was changing, he stood behind his bedroom door. Men of ambitious physique, like himself, he had always noticed, were inclined to puff themselves out or let their arms hang in a position favourable to their muscles while changing before another man. To avoid this embarrassment or absurdity, he made a point of never exhibiting himself unclothed.

His conversation with Butcher did not fall on matters in hand. As with Anastasya, he was unusually reticent. He had turned over a new leaf. He became rather alarmed at this himself when he realized it. After lunch he left Butcher and went to the Mairie of the Quartier du Paradis and made inquiries about civil marriages. He did it like a sleep-walker.

He was particularly amiable with Bertha that day, and told her of his activities at the Mairie and made an appointment with her there for the next day.

Daily, then, he proceeded with his marriage arrangements in the afternoons, saw Bertha regularly, but without modifying the changed "correctness" of his attitude. The evenings he spent with Anastasya.

By the time the marriage preliminaries had been gone through, and Bertha and he could finally be united, his relations with Anastasya had become as close as formerly his friendship with Bertha had been. With the exception of the time from three in the afternoon to seven in the evening that he took off every day to see his fiancée, he was with her.

On September 29. three weeks after Bertha had told him that she was pregnant, he married her—in the time between three in the afternoon and seven in the evening set aside for her. Anastasya knew nothing about these things. Neither Bertha nor she were seeing their German women friends for the moment.

After the marriage at the Mairie Bertha and Tarr walked back to the Luxembourg Gardens and sat down. She had not during the three intervening weeks mentioned Anastasya. It was no time for generosity; she had done too much of that. Fräulein Vasek was the last person for whom she felt inclined to revive chivalry. She let Tarr marry her out of pity, and never referred to his confidence about his other love.

They sat for some time without speaking, as though they had quarrelled. She said, then:

"I am afraid, Sorbert, I have been selfish—"

"You—selfish? How's that? Don't talk nonsense." He had turned at once to her with a hurried fondness genuinely assumed.

She looked at him with her wistful, democratic face, full of effort and sentiment.

"You are very unhappy, Sorbert—"

He laughed convincingly.

"No, I'm all right. Don't worry about me. I'm a little meditative. That is only natural on such a solemn occasion. I was thinking, Bertha, we must set up house somewhere, and announce our marriage. We must do this for appearance' sake. You will soon be incapacitated—"

"Oh, I shan't be just yet."

"In any case, we have gone through this form because—We must make this move efficacious. What are your ideas as to an establishment? Let us take a flat together somewhere round here. The Rue Servandoni is a nice street. Do you know it?"

"No." She put her head on one side and puckered up her forehead.

"Near the Luxembourg Museum."

They discussed a possible domicile.

He got up.

"It's rather chilly. Let's get back."

They walked for some time without speaking. So much unsaid had to be got rid of, without necessarily being said. Bertha did not know at all where she was. Their "establishment," as discussed by Tarr, appeared very unreal, and also, what there was of it, disagreeable. She wondered what he was going to do with her.

"You remember what I said to you some weeks ago—about Anastasya Vasek. I am afraid there has been no change in that. You do not mind that?"

"No, Sorbert. You are perfectly free."

"I am afraid I shall seem unkind. This is not a nice marriage for you. Perhaps I was wrong to suggest it?"

"How, wrong? I have not been complaining."

They arrived at the iron gate.

"Well, I'd better not come up now. I will come along to-morrow—at the usual time."

"Good-bye, Sorbert. *A demain!*"

"*A demain!*"

CHAPTER VI

Anastasya and he were dining that night in Montmartre as usual. His piece of news hovered over their conversation like a bird hesitating as to the right spot at which to establish its nest.

"I saw Bertha to-day," he said, forcing the opening at last.

"You still see her then."

"Yes. I married her this afternoon."

"You *what*? What do you mean?"

"What I say, my dear. I married her."

"You mean you—?" She put an imaginary ring on her finger.

"Yes. I married her at the Mairie."

Anastasya looked blankly into him, as though he contained cheerless stretches where no living thing could grow.

"You mean to say you've done that!"

"Yes; I have."

"Why?"

Tarr stopped a moment.

"Well, the alleged reason was that she is enceinte."

"But—whose is the child?"

"Kreisler's, she says."

The statement, she saw, was genuine. He was telling her what he had been doing. They both immediately retired into themselves, she to distance and stow away their former dialogue and consider the meaning of this new fact; he to wait, his hand near his mouth holding a pipe, until she should have collected herself. But he began speaking first:

"Things are exactly the same as before. I was bound to do that. I had allowed her to consider herself engaged a year ago, and had to keep to that. I have merely gone back a year into the past and fulfilled a pledge, and now return to you. All is in perfect order."

"All is *not* in perfect order. It is Kreisler's child to begin with, you say—"

"Yes, but it would be very mean to use that fact to justify one in escaping from an obligation."

"That is sentimentality."

"Sentimentality! Sentimentality! Cannot *we*, you and I, afford to give Bertha *that*? Sentimentality! What an absurd word that is with its fierce use in our poor modern hands! What does it mean? Has life become such an affair of economic calculation that men are too timid to allow themselves any complicated pleasures? Where there is abundance you can afford waste. Sentimentality is a cry on a level with the Simple Life! The ideal of perfect success is an ideal belonging to the same sort of individual as the inventor of Equal Rights of Man and Perfectibility. Sentimentality is a *privilege*. It is a luxury that the crowd does not feel itself equal to, once it begins to think about it. Besides, it is different in different hands."

"That may be true as regards sentimentality in general. But in this case you have been guilty of a popular softness—"

"No. Listen. I will explain something to you You said a moment ago that it was *Kreisler's* child. Well, that is my security! That *enables* me to commit this folly, without too great danger. It is an earnest of the altruistic origin of the action not being forgotten!"

"But *that*—to return to *your* words—is surely a very mean calculation?"

"Therefore it takes the softness out of the generous action it is allied to—"

"No. It takes its *raison d'être* away altogether. It leaves it merely a stupid and unnecessary fact. It cancels the generosity, but leaves the fact—your marriage."

"But the *fact itself* is altered by that!"

"In what way? You are now married to Bertha—"

"Yes, but what does that mean? I married Bertha this afternoon, and here I am punctually and as usual with you this evening—"

"But the fact of your having married Bertha this afternoon will prevent your making any one else your wife in the future. Supposing I had a child by *you*—not by Kreisler—it would be impossible to legitimatize him. The thing is of no importance in itself. But you have given Kreisler's child what you should have kept for your own! What's the good of giving your sex over into the hands of a swanky expert, as you describe it, if you continue to act on your own initiative? I throw up my job. *Garçon, l'addition!*"

But a move to the café opposite satisfied her as a demonstration. Tarr was sure of her, and remained passive. She extorted a promise from him: to conduct no more obscure diplomacies in the future.

Bertha and Tarr took a flat in the Boulevard Port Royal, not far from the Jardin des Plantes. They gave a party to which Fräulein Lipmann and a good many other people came. He maintained the rule of four to seven, roughly, for Bertha, with the utmost punctiliousness. Anastasya and Bertha did not meet.

Bertha's child came, and absorbed her energies for upwards of a year. It bore some resemblance to Tarr. Tarr's afternoon visits became less frequent. He lived now publicly with his illicit and splendid bride.

Two years after the birth of the child, Bertha divorced Tarr. She then married an eye-doctor, and lived with a brooding severity in his company and that of her only child.

Tarr and Anastasya did not marry. They had no children. Tarr, however, had three children by a lady of the name of Rose Fawcett, who consoled him eventually for the splendours of his "perfect woman." But yet beyond the dim though solid figure of Rose Fawcett, another rises. This one represents the swing-back of the pendulum once more to the swagger side. The cheerless and stodgy absurdity of Rose Fawcett required the painted, fine and inquiring face of Prism Dirkes.

EPILOGUE

The artists of this country make the following plain and pressing appeal to their fellow-citizens. I have heard them in the places where they meet.

(1) That in these tragic days when the forces of the nation, of intellect, of character, are being tested, they should grant more freedom to the artists and thinkers to develop their visions and ideas. That they should make an effort of sympathy. That the maudlin and the self-defensive Grin should be dropped.

(2) That the Englishman should become ashamed of his Grin as he is at present ashamed of solemnity. That he should cease to be ashamed of his "feelings": then he would automatically become less proud of his Grin.

(3) That he should remember that seriousness and unsentimentality are quite compatible. Whereas a Grin usually accompanies loose emotionality.

(4) That in "facing the facts of existence" as he is at present compelled to do, he should allow artists to economize time in not having to circumvent and get round those facts, but to use them simply and directly.

(5) That he should restrain his vanity, and not always imagine that his leg is being pulled. A symbolism is of the nature of all human effort. There is no necessity to be literal to be in earnest. Humour, even, may be a symbol. The recognizing of a few simple facts of that sort would help much.

In these onslaughts on Humour I am not suggesting that anybody should laugh less over his beer or wine or forgo the consolation of the ridiculous. There are circumstances when it is a blessing. But the *worship of the ridiculous* is the thing that should be forgone. The worship (or craze, we call it) of Charlie Chaplin is a mad substitution of a chaotic tickling for all the other more organically important ticklings of life.

Nor do I mean here that you or I, if we are above suspicion in the matter of those other fundamentals, should not allow ourselves the little scurvy totem of Charlie on the mantlepiece. It is not a grinning face we object to but a face that is mean when it is serious and that takes to its grin as a duck takes to water. We must stop grinning. You will say that I do not practise what I preach. I do: for if you look closely at my grin you will perceive that it is a very logical and deliberate grimace.

P. Wyndham Lewis

1915